"Ripe with SUSPENSE, INTRIGUE, and RIVETING ACTION, Nathan Goodman's beautifully written novel preys upon our worst fears: Terrorism in our own backyard. LIKE JOHN GRISHAM'S *THE FIRM*, *The Fourteenth Protocol* introduces characters on the climb in over their head, a plot that keeps you guessing, and an ending that will leave you hungry for more."

—Michael Lucker, Screenwriter to Paramount, Disney, DreamWorks, Fox, Universal

"CONSPIRACY WRAPPED BY SUSPENSE and tied in knots. If you read one thriller this year, this should be it."

—Kevin McLaughlin, Special Agent, DEA

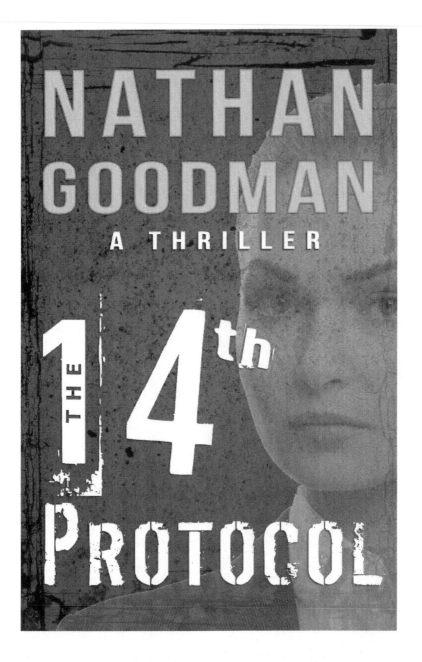

NATHAN
GOODMAN
A THRILLER

THE 1 4 th
PROTOCOL

NATHAN A. GOODMAN

THOUGHT REACH PRESS

THOUGHT REACH PRESS, a publishing division of Thought Reach, LLC. Atlanta, Georgia, United States of America

ISBN: 978-0-9905738-0-7

First Thought Reach Press printing August 2014

Presidential speech adapted from President Barack Obama's speech on May 1, 2011.

For information regarding special discounts for bulk purchases, or permission to reproduce any content other than mentioned above, contact the publisher at support@thoughtreach.com.

Cover illustrations by Le Femme Couture Agency

Printed in the USA

To my wife, without whom I would be a lost soul, spinning about the universe, flailing for a purpose.

To my daughter Jenna, the first person to read and edit the finished work. And to my daughter Meg, whose creative artwork inspired me to create something of my own making.

This novel is dedicated to the men and women who have lost their lives in the defense of freedom. Their burden has lifted. And to those whose shoulders are still heavy—God be with you all.

For somewhere within all of our souls lies the demon, and the demon is hungry.

1

May 1, 2011

"One minute," yelled the commander over the thumping helicopter rotor blades as they thrashed through the night air.

The SEAL team operators flipped down night-vision goggles, popped safety catches on their weapons, and flashed thumbs-up to one another. Fifty feet from the ground, a metallic cracking sound burst from the helicopter's tail section, reminiscent of an aging piano cord giving up its long fight. The pilot wrenched the stick in a violent attempt to prevent the craft from rolling sideways as the tail swung in a wild circle. The helicopter impacted the top of a twelve-foot cement wall surrounding the compound. Navy SEALs spilled on top of one another as the craft teetered onto its side and slid to a stop. Unfazed, the operators burst from the damaged craft and ran towards the first of several doors they would breach.

The president made the announcement on a Sunday evening. "Today, at my direction, the United States launched a targeted operation against a compound in Abbottabad, Pakistan. A small team of Americans carried out the operation with extraordinary courage and capability. No Americans were harmed. They took care to avoid civilian casualties. After a firefight, they killed Osama bin Laden and took custody of his body. We give thanks to the countless intelligence and counterterrorism professionals who've worked tirelessly to achieve this outcome. The American people do not see their work, nor know their names. But tonight, they feel the result of their pursuit of justice."

2
Present Day

It was a cool, springtime day in Atlanta under a crisp blue sky. Cade Williams' windows sat half-open on his aging Honda/Toyota wannabe four-door. The car wasn't going to attract any women, but it was paid for and had plenty of life left in it. He pulled out of his apartment, which was a pre-fab'd clone of every other apartment complex in the city. The grounds were so covered with pansies, it looked as if the owners had purchased a lifetime supply of the flower.

"Those are probably why my rent is so high," he said to no one in particular. But being young and single in Atlanta meant you lived in the Buckhead area because that's where the women were. Not that Cade knew any of them.

It was only a mile up Lenox Road to Peachtree Street and then to the office. Cade turned up the radio to hear the news as he limped through Peachtree Street traffic. Atlanta's awful traffic was another reason he lived inside the perimeter. A tiny smile curled up the left side of his mouth. He had to admit, the rent was too high, but living inside the perimeter—or ITP, as they called it—had its perks. There was no reason to pay attention to the traffic report when you lived a mile from your office.

"Another explosion last night, this one at a Little League baseball field in Tucson, Arizona. Four are confirmed dead, one of them a child. Reports are still coming in from the scene. This makes the eleventh bombing in eleven months. The bomb appears to have detonated as the players were coming off the field. Fourteen are known to be hospitalized, two in critical condition. Tucson Sheriff's Department spokesperson, Amy Rumbaugh. 'We're still assessing the situation. The FBI is on the scene with sheriff's deputies. But it looks to me like another homemade device. We're going to do everything in our power to find who is responsible.'"

Cade's stomach tightened. *Little League baseball fields?* he thought. He'd played Little League ball at Murphey Candler Park in Atlanta when he was a kid. That seemed like a long time ago. He wasn't exactly skilled at much of anything baseball-related back then, and as such, his backside became expert at cleaning the bench seats in the dugout. *Man, it's so hard to picture sitting there on the bench and having a freaking bomb go off,* thought Cade.

Baseball was truly an American sport and was always played on great spring days like these. *Nice weather, maybe a little hot, but my God, who the hell would set off a bomb? What are they trying to do, take away our ability to relax anywhere?* Eleven small terrorist attacks. These weren't the big ones like the Trade Centers or anything, but still. Kids. *Kids.*

Cade hit a red light in front of Lenox Mall, cruised farther down Peachtree, and turned into the office, a towering monstrosity that loomed over its neighbors. The black glass didn't reveal much about the building's hidden superstructure and thus looked like any other building. But underneath that layer of reflective mirror was a hardened shell designed to withstand tornados and even mild earthquakes. No, this was no ordinary building. It was a place designed to hide its secrets, and hide them well. In fact, Cade had slept here on more than one occasion as predicted tornados skirted the city. And Atlanta had its share of tornados.

"That building is the safest place in the city if one were ever to come through," Cade had told his father. All of the glass on the exterior of the first eight floors was bulletproof. Not that the company expected an actual zombie apocalypse or anything. But bulletproof glass was an excellent way to shield the computer data center and its customers' corporate secrets as they flowed across the servers.

Cade was an e-mail operations admin for a true Wall Street darling. Thoughtstorm, Inc. exploded onto the stock market four years prior. He loved his job running the highly technical e-mail servers, but it wasn't something he'd ever tell a girl. Being a geek just didn't pay when it came to women.

Thoughtstorm was the largest e-mail service provider in North America. Billions of corporate e-mails flowed across eighteen floors of rack after rack of servers. Telling anyone he worked in the e-mail service provider business, Cade would often see a glaze form over their eyes, but there was a lot of cool stuff hidden inside the racks of metal boxes covered in blinky lights. With all the corporate secrets flowing through, it was no wonder security was so ridiculous.

Cruising down Peachtree, Cade turned towards the parking deck. The morning sun reflected off the building and nearly blinded him. As he pulled up to the security gate, Cade leaned out the window, holding his ID badge for a guard known only as "Chuck," who scanned it.

"Hey, Chuck," said Cade, looking for any response. For four years Cade had been trying to get Chuck to say anything. Cade had been through a phase when he even tried treating Chuck like one of those London Royal Guards who won't smile, no matter what you do. But he got bored with that as well. Chuck pointed to the finger scanner. Cade reached out his hand and put his pinky finger onto the scanner. He would try a different finger each day of the week, hoping that the scan would fail, and Chuck wouldn't let him pass. Going through this check at the front gate each morning was almost stupid. Chuck knew good and well that he worked here and had access to go to the parking lot. But, the company did love its petty policies.

Chuck motioned Cade forward and raised the gate. Cade stopped at his usual parking spot, way up on the eighth floor of the deck. He went through the glass doors and scanned his card at the elevator. The lobby was another story. It always took a few minutes to get through. Cade put his whole hand on the scanner this time and keyed his security code onto the pad. The keypad itself was quite a piece of work. It wasn't just a normal pad with ten numbers on it. This keypad was digital. The ten numbers, instead of being placed in numeric order, would randomly move around the pad each time it was accessed. This made it harder for someone to peer over your shoulder and steal your code.

A security guard behind a reinforced cement wall watched through four inches of bulletproof glass. Cade walked through the eight-foot-tall revolving turnstiles and put his hand on the cold, case-hardened door. He looked over his shoulder, waiting for the guard to buzz him in. Finally, Cade was "free" to go to the elevator. In the elevator, Cade had one more round of fussing through the same revolving keypad to get the elevator to grant him access to the sixteenth floor. This part of the job made Cade laugh—a Central Intelligence Agency security system and a Mayberry paycheck.

Cade reached his cube, not far from the server racks. The cube farm was separated from the servers by a long glass wall. This wall, however, was not meant to stop an armor-piercing round; instead, it was simply designed to keep the fifty-nine-degree air temperature of the server room separated from the employees who preferred to work without freezing their asses off.

Cade's cube was a sight to behold, a true thing of beauty. He was easily the only guy in the building with a velvet Elvis tapestry hanging in his cube. Artwork of this quality was usually only found at the corner gas station, the local bowling alley, or hanging in a place of respect, right above the fireplace in some redneck's single-wide trailer. But Cade, who was partial to being partial, admitted he was a bit eclectic. He had acquired the tapestry from an old friend who swiped it from a Dairy Queen late one night. None of his coworkers seemed to mind the bright yellow mustard stain on Elvis's white leather pant leg.

Cade flipped open his laptop, which was secured to the desk by means of the obligatory cable lock. With all this tight security, Cade thought it amusing that a person without a key could easily open the lock with no more than an empty toilet paper roll, or anything else that would fit in the key slot, for that matter.

To say Thoughtstorm was paranoid wouldn't quite sum it up. The paranoia level was palpable, something that could be seen and touched. Once, Cade had seen an employee, who he suspected worked upstairs on the seventeenth floor, be taken into the security office. Word was they had strip-searched him. Needless to say, that guy's keycard was deactivated that day. But no one seemed to know what he had done in the first place to get fired, much less strip-searched. Cade knew, although he couldn't prove it, that there were cameras watching all of them. It was really just a sneaking suspicion. So one day, Cade decided to place a little piece of masking tape over the camera built into his laptop. He always hated those things. You never knew if the camera was turned on or off. The thought that the Thoughtstorm security team was watching, all the time, sat on his stomach like a pint of rotten moonshine. He had affixed the tape to the camera fairly well, and sure enough, the next morning the tape was gone. *No way that just fell off, no way.* That was a while back. He hadn't tried it again, figuring if they were going to watch, he might as well not fight the system. Besides, the job actually did pay well, and Cade pretty much got his run of the place. His immediate supervisor didn't even work in Atlanta, so no one hovered over him, micromanaging his every project. The freedom was excellent.

"Dude," came the lispy voice from the other side of Cade's cube wall.

"Hey, man."

"Did you see that instant messenger was down again?" Whitmore was Cade's cube-neighbor. At five feet nothing, Whitmore could almost stand up and walk under his cube. He was an effeminate guy to say the least, but could be trusted with anything.

"No. Hey, give me a chance to boot up will you? And by the way, what time do you get in here anyway? It's like you never leave. Is that the same shirt you had on yesterday?"

"Oh, go screw yourself."

"Well, you know you and I can't function without instant messenger. I mean, we work four feet apart. God forbid we'd have to speak to one another instead of using IM."

"No way I'm talking to you, man." Whitmore couldn't contain the sarcasm that came so naturally. He was a real piece of work, as they say. He never seemed to be seen outside of the office. A hermit, but an office hermit; the kind of guy every company secretly loves to hire. Tireless, smart, never whines. The true team player. "Never fear. I'll figure a way to fix that IM before the day is out."

Standing up and leaning over the cube wall, Cade said, "So how exactly does an art director fix the instant messenger software, anyway?"

"Not your problem, my man. Not your problem."

Cade sat down, spun his chair into position, and started in on the day. His job was to project manage all upkeep and maintenance of the servers on the sixteenth floor. Eleven hundred and fifty-six servers, to be exact. The floor space rivaled that of a Wal-Mart.

"That's a lot of black boxes with blinky lights on them," Cade would say as he entered the server room each day. No matter who was walking by as he said it, they'd always give him a look as if to say, *What a nimrod.* That was the fun of it. Know your shit inside and out, and you can act like an idiot. And Cade did know his stuff. At twenty-eight, he was by far the youngest admin in the company. He graduated just ahead of schedule from Georgia Tech and had gone straight into the work of managing e-mail servers. He didn't care so much about the business of e-mail itself; it was just a gig he fell into while co-oping towards the end of undergrad. And why not? Thoughtstorm was growing like crazy despite a million know-it-alls predicting the end of e-mail due to the rise of social media. If e-mail was dying, all these blinky lights wouldn't be going bonkers all day long firing out millions of e-mails.

Even though Cade had been at Thoughtstorm six years, there was always one thing that bothered him. There was something wrong with the seventeenth floor. That floor was packed to the gills with servers as well. But you never seemed to meet anyone that worked on that floor. Not at lunchtime, the company Christmas party, on the elevator, nowhere. Hell, occasionally you'd meet someone from the company that you didn't know at Good Old Days, the hole-in-the-wall bar across the street. But, even then, they never worked on seventeen.

The Buckhead area was the epicenter of nightlife in Atlanta. And after all, even server geeks go out once in a while. Thoughtstorm employees packed the place after work on Fridays because you could just walk across the street. Well, that and the fact that if you got there before six p.m., the pitchers were half price. The place was hopping.

But no one from the seventeenth floor, never. The more Cade thought about it, the more he realized how odd this was. He worked one floor below, yet never met anyone from there. Stranger still, there had to be a group of server dudes up there just like him, all operating black, blinky boxes, yet you never saw them. *What the hell is that all about?* thought Cade. *Do they have their own sneaky elevator or something?* At any rate, it wasn't a mystery Cade was going to solve today. Not before he waded through all the e-mails in his inbox anyway. Cade had to admit, he might get paid a lot to control servers that sent massive amounts of e-mail, but he hated an inbox full of the damn things.

Cade culled his inbox. Not that any of these were spam, mind you. The company ensured spam didn't make it past the front door. No, most of the stuff that he deleted was typical corporate hoo-ha. Training opportunities, the hours the building would be open during the MLK holiday, updates to the employee privacy policy, and when the refrigerators would be cleaned out. Unfortunately though, Cade's inbox was always full of e-mails that were action items. There was always something to do.

Cade was supposed to make it out onto the server room floor by nine thirty each morning to make his rounds. It was not a bad idea actually. Sometimes being up close and personal to the machines gave you a better sense of what was going on with them and what they were thinking. However, he could just as easily monitor them from his desk on three wide-screen monitors. Cade opened his server monitoring software and gave a quick look across all his monitors to make sure he didn't see anything with the color red. Red was the color of bad. Red meant his phone was about to ring as some server box entered a problem state such as an overload. His grandma would have called it a "conniption." No red meant no server conniptions today. The servers were grouped together in what Thoughtstorm called "pods." The pods all had boring names like "ACA" or "DRT" to identify them during times of trouble. Most pods played host to over fifty customers at a time. But one, pod GSV, held just a single customer. GSV stood for Government Services and was located on the seventeenth floor.

Although it had taken a long time to build up the trust required, Cade could see the health of all servers in the building. The GSV pod was showing yellow. Cade noticed the pod appeared to be pushing out a huge volume of e-mails at the moment. The yellow would soon die down and turn soft green once the sending job was done. *Why in the hell does a government agency need to send that much e-mail?* thought Cade.

Most of the time, Cade had access to all data on the servers, which meant he could also see things like the list of e-mail recipients and even the content of e-mails they were sending. Not that the content was all that interesting. Most of the time, it was just a company sending out a boring e-mail newsletter to its customers.

But there was one exception. The GSV pod was blocked. Cade could only see the server health screens for that pod. *What the hell is on that pod that makes it so special? And just how trusted does a guy have to be before they'll open up that access? What do they think I'm going to do, steal the data?* Cade mused. He'd never done anything like that in his life. And after all, if that server cluster ever had any real difficulty and started to redline, crap out, get flummoxed, or choke whilst uttering gurgling noises, somebody would be calling on good old Cade to look into the problem. But without access to the whole thing, that would be impossible. *Not my problem,* he thought. And even if they ever did call him to help out with that pod, he'd have to get some new permissions on his keycard. His keycard wouldn't let him on the seventeenth floor, much less out into the server room. The likelihood was that that pod was locked off behind some metal mesh cages anyway and security officers would hover nearby.

The yellow slowly changed back to green on pod GSV, and all was once again well with the world. Cade spent a bunch of time in a planning meeting that day. Thoughtstorm was expanding the available server rack space at the headquarters building but was also opening up a new data center in Germany. Too many of Thoughtstorm's

European customers had been complaining that sending their e-mail data to the United States violated European Union privacy regulations.

Cade grabbed a Caffè Americano coffee in the cafeteria downstairs, which was a lot easier than exiting the building and fighting through all that security again. Back at his desk, he rubbed tired eyes and put his hand on his mouse. The three computer monitors glowed to life. Cade was surprised to find pod GSV in the yellow once again. This time it was closer towards redline than it had been in the morning. He focused on the screen and looked at the server readings. Something was definitely wrong. *How much e-mail volume are they sending up there? My God,* he thought. Normally, if a customer sends this much e-mail, the company adds more servers onto the pod, thereby spreading out the load. But that hadn't been done in this case.

He was just about to go back to his own work, figuring someone on seventeen who actually has ACCESS will handle it, when the iPhone buzzed in his pocket. The ringtone that accompanied the phone's vibration was only used when a server text alert was sent. That didn't happen often, but when it did, it meant that you drop whatever crap you were working on. This was the not-so-fun part of Cade's job—even if he was at home, sleeping like a big baby, having been rejected by another girl on a Saturday night, he had to get up and come to the office.

He looked at his pocket as if there might be a tarantula in there. *An alert? For a yellow server?* he thought. He already knew what the alert was about but had never been alerted to trouble on that pod before. Hell, he had never been alerted to trouble on the seventeenth floor before. When he read the text, his shoulders slumped and his eyes shut. He hated this. The text said "Alert: EMERGENCY CODE RED. Server cluster GSV. 13:23 HRS EST." Cade had but a single pet peeve. It was use of the word "emergency" in a business setting. Cade's father narrowly survived Vietnam and knew the true meaning of the word. He never allowed anyone in the house to so much as utter it unless someone was bleeding. *We send e-mails, for God's sake,* thought Cade. *There are no emergencies in e-mail. No one is bleeding.*

Cade's dad had been a right-seat pilot in a Navy EA-6B Prowler, a kind of jamming plane used to screw up the enemy's radar. His dad was the technical type and not a warrior so sitting right-seat in a "box of electronics with wings" had suited him just fine. But it was one dark-skied night in January 1971, where Cade's dad learned firsthand what the word "emergency" was really used for. A SAM missile had zipped off the jungle floor five thousand feet below and snaked across the sky when it clipped the portside engine. Cade's dad had a hard time telling that story. He would avert his eyes as he recalled his best friend, Dan Tarlton, yelling into the mic, "Mayday, mayday, mayday, this is Voodoo Zero One Niner declaring an emergency . . ." The story always stopped right there. His father just couldn't relive it. It was like pouring salt on a raw wound. There were four men in the plane on that night in January. Three of them lived long enough to see their parachutes deploy, but Cade's father, Cal Williams, was the only one to sneak out of the jungle alive.

3

"You can't see America from the interstate," Alyssa McTee's mom would always say. From the time Alyssa left Atlanta, she glued herself to the rural roads and vowed to never use the highway. She pushed the thick-rimmed glasses back up the bridge of her nose and touched the play button on her phone tucked inside the docking station in the VW Beetle. Another Indigo Girls song harmonized across the car speakers as her fingers tapped in rhythm. She shifted in her seat to adjust the frumpy dress. Most girls her age were wearing tight-fitting skirts, but Alyssa never seemed to show any interest. Not that she had anything to hide in those loose-fitting dresses. Actually, she was quite trim. Although, according to her, no one would notice it. Lifeless hair drifted across her forehead. She tucked it back behind her ear and glanced in the rearview mirror only to see an image of her mom staring back at her. Having reached her early twenties, Alyssa now knew she really did look like her mother at this age. In fact, Alyssa had looked like her mom at all ages. The likeness was in the blue eyes and straight hair. There was a photo from 1969 of her mom, dressed in true Woodstock attire at the age of six. The long straight hair, little leather bandana, and bell-bottom jeans truly captured the era. The resemblance was striking.

Alyssa needed this vacation. Work had been pressure-filled the past few months, and she needed to get out of there and go see something—something different. And she needed to be alone for a while too.

Never one to speak up at meetings, she more or less followed the crowd, except in the way she dressed. Her normal attire hid her figure and probably hadn't exactly helped in the guy department. Still, this trip had been good for her wandering spirit—a spirit inside her that she attributed to her mom. Sitting in that cubicle at work didn't exactly capture the essence of a free spirit on the open road. Her mom never said so directly, but Alyssa knew that deep inside her mother, there was something wanting to come out. Her mom had somehow lost herself along the way through life. Alyssa was determined that wasn't going to happen to her. She wasn't going to look back and wish she had done something really great with her life. *Regrets are the food of conformers*, she thought, and she didn't like regrets.

Wandering the rural roads through the southeast had been her outlet. Her obsession for funky coffee shops had inadvertently created an odyssey of sorts. Alyssa's first idea was to drive—simply drive. Go out and see something of the country. Wind her way into small towns, find the town square, eat at a little corner diner, see if there were actually any waitresses named Flo, and maybe make just one friend along the way.

Then the trip kind of took on a life of its own. She had stopped in what she thought was the coolest little mom-and-pop coffeehouse she'd ever seen. It was a little place not far from Helen, Georgia, on her way out of the state. It was called simply Sweetwater Coffeehouse, and sweet it was. Soft velour couches, rustic planks on the floor, and an aroma, something reminiscent of hickory-smoked barbeque folded into roasted coffee. Apparently the guy in the shop next door made the pottery mugs himself. Real local charm with not even a hint of tourist-ish-ness. And better still, not a hint of corporate. Alyssa had done something there she normally wouldn't. She had ordered a scone.

"What the hell is a scone anyway?" she asked the barista. This pastry looked nothing like the scone-things she'd seen at the big chain coffee shops in town. No, this was homemade, fluffy deliciousness.

Alyssa looked around at the place as if to check if anyone was watching her. She was on her own. For the *first time* in her life, she was on her own. It made her feel so at peace, so in charge of herself. A candle lit inside her, and the delicate smoke that wafted off of it was pride.

It occurred to her that she hadn't even thought of work since she left her apartment near Little Five Points in Atlanta. In that coffeehouse, a few things changed for Alyssa. She couldn't quite put her finger on it, but something settled inside her. She felt like she knew who she was. She thought about that picture of her mom. Her mom would be so proud of her right now. She was on an odyssey. Her mom would have never had the nerve to do this, not after she got married anyway.

Alyssa knew this would be a trip she'd never forget. She'd go out and find the country. Literally find the people of the country. Find her roots. And maybe find just a little bit of herself that she thought was lost. Somewhere in the untapped subculture hidden within the coffeehouses of this country, she'd make peace with herself.

And she would discover more than that along the way. One thing struck her as funny. Unlike all the coffeehouses she had been to in Atlanta, the baristas in this one, near North Georgia's Sautee Valley, didn't have even a single body piercing or visible tattoo.

"I guess it's hard to find true grunge in the North Georgia mountains," she said.

Alyssa took the last sip of coffee goodness. She glanced over at the stone fireplace. *Man, it would be so nice to curl up here on this couch on a freezing day in front of the fire.* She took one last glance around, swearing to memorize the scene. A small poster clung to the old stone mantel. There was something so relaxed about its design and the way the fonts and colors drew your attention.

> Tammy Lynn's Bluegrass Pickin' Party and Hog Roast
> — Pineville, Kentucky.
> If you're looking for authentic Kentucky flavor and tradition, head to the mountains at the height of bluegrass season and enjoy America's finest bluegrass festival and hog roast!

Alyssa stared at the poster a minute. This was America. If you wanted to meet the people, you had to be where they worked and lived.

Maybe it was the caffeine talking, but she stood up with a new resoluteness. She was sick of being scared, sick of being shy, and sick and tired of being sick and tired. She wasn't going to live the same demure, quiet, proper existence she had always known.

Alyssa walked out the swinging wooden door and got into her car. When she put the key in the door, she realized it—she hadn't locked the car door when she pulled up to this place. To Alyssa, not locking the car door was akin to walking into a coffeehouse and ordering some fluffy, fat-laden coffee flavored with pumpkin-mango-spice, crème-hazelnut, froth-de-blah-blah. You just didn't do it. She smiled. Not locking the car door was a strange experience for her. Never did she remember not locking a car door in Atlanta. The Little Five Points area where she lived was like a haven for car-pilfering thugs who mixed in with the peace-loving, hippie crowd. Nonetheless, she hadn't realized when she pulled up to this little place, way out here in the North Georgia mountains, that a comfort level like that would drape across her. It felt like a warm blanket soaked with safety, confidence.

She backed out and glanced down at the map on her smartphone. Thinking better of it, she put the map down. It's not an adventure with too much of a plan. *No plans, no agenda, no schedule. Just discovery*, she thought. *That bluegrass festival might be nice though.* About the only thing she knew was that she'd weave her way north, glued to the back roads.

So she headed up the road into whatever it would bring. The world lay at her feet, and she wanted to drink it in. She pushed her way north through tiny Georgia towns with names like Cornelia, Walhalla, Pickens, Travelers Rest, and Landrum, slowly drinking in the smell of pine trees and simple quiet of life outside the city. As long as she was far away from the interstate, she was happy. After all, interstates were for suckers, for conformers.

4

Cade snapped out of his fixation about the use of the word *emergency* and picked up the phone. What did they want him to do about some server going haywire on the seventeenth floor? He'd never been called to go to seventeen, ever.

"Cade Williams," he said into the phone.

"Williams? This is Johnston. I have a real situation here. Drop what you're doing and get up here."

"Yes, sir. Ah, sir?"

"Don't worry, I'll meet you at the elevator on sixteen, and I'll bring you up. Time to earn your pay, boy."

Cade hadn't even gone to the bathroom yet. Well, this was shaping up to be a fun day. And by "fun" he meant "giant pain in the ass."

"They better have coffee on seventeen," Cade said as he stood up.

"SEVENTEEN?!" came the retort from Whitmore. "Come on, man. You and I both know there is no seventeenth floor. It doesn't exist. It's like a ghost or something."

"Well, time to find out. Do you think they have cream and sugar, or do you think I should bring my own? And maybe I should bring one of those little wooden stirrer things?" The sarcasm hung thick.

"Oh. My. God," said Whitmore. "Mr. Big Shot. 'Just git yer ass up there, mister!'" Cade thought it was hilarious when Whitmore imitated the accent of Rupert Johnston. True southern redneck-speak combined with a lisp. Both of them knew Cade going up to seventeen was a big deal. No one on his floor had ever been asked up there.

"Maybe I'll be named CEO by the end of the day," said Cade, breathing a little uneasy. *I need to calm down. Man, it's not as if Elvis is up there or something.*

By the time Cade walked the fifty feet from his desk into the lobby, Rupert Johnston was standing there, peering down at him. Rupert Johnston was every bit of six feet five inches tall, at least 220 pounds, and not exactly what you would call "portly" either. He was old to be sure, but it was like seeing a man made out of sinew and covered in striated leather. Cade had never met him in person and had never wanted to. His heavy-rimmed glasses and furrowed brow did not exactly invite conversation. *Old guys like this look at me like I'm such a wuss*, thought Cade, his eyes looking anywhere but into Johnston's, where they would meet utter defeat.

There was a story going around the office about Rupert Johnston. Cade never knew what to believe, but the story was that Johnston had snuck out of his mother's farmhouse at the age of fifteen, hiked into town, and gone to the recruiting station. Vietnam was heating up in 1965, and Johnston was going to "git him some." *Some what?* Cade wondered. Apparently he either fooled or scared the physician at the recruiting post enough to make him believe he was seventeen. His mother had no idea what had happened to him. To her, Rupert had just up and disappeared off the face of the earth. She even reported him as missing to the county sheriff. The poor old lady probably had a hell of a time raising that pain in the ass anyway.

At any rate, at the time there were no computer systems that would alert police as to Johnston's whereabouts. So no one knew where he was. His mom looked everywhere. By the time anyone thought to check with the armed services, Johnston had finished Marine Corp basic training at Paris Island and was on a troop transport, somewhere out in the Pacific Ocean. He was not likely to be plucked off of the thing and brought home "because he didn't have his momma's permission."

Johnston stared at Cade for a moment, looking him up and down, and then just walked into the elevator. Cade followed as Johnston pressed the button for seventeen and turned to the digital touch screen panel to input his clearance code. Cade didn't even glance in that direction. *Can you imagine getting caught looking over Johnston's shoulder?* Cade shuddered at the thought. If Johnston suspected you of trying to spy his elevator clearance code, he'd probably give you a pounding to the top of your head, sending you through the elevator floor, or perhaps a spinning crane kick to the jaw. It wasn't as if Cade wanted to sneak onto a restricted floor anyway. He didn't like this asshole Johnston, but he liked keeping his job.

The elevator opened, and to Cade's surprise, the lobby of the seventeenth floor looked identical to the rest of the floors. Somehow he had envisioned armed Navy SEALs standing post, perhaps dressed in body amour and standing behind bulletproof glass. *Kind of a letdown actually*, he mused.

They walked out, and Johnston swiped his keycard against the outer door. The door chirped in response, and they walked in. Johnston's legs were as long as tent poles; Cade found it hard to keep pace. Johnston suddenly stopped and spun around, his finger in Cade's face.

"Now, look, what you see up here stays up here. You got me?"

"Yes, sir," was all Cade could muster.

The racks of servers looked the same as on all the other floors. Then again, Cade hadn't exactly expected an interior designer to come up with new and ergonomic designs for racks of black metal boxes with blinky lights on them. Several people Cade had never seen were milling around the server floor, some with iPads in hand. *Man, they do a lot of monitoring up here. Or maybe that's just because of the trouble they're having at the moment. Hell, we don't have iPads,* Cade thought. As they walked towards the glass entry door to the server room, Cade noticed something odd. Down one of the rows of server racks were several men in business suits. That alone was out of place. None of the executive "suits" ever came down to the server floors. Why would they? Those guys stayed up on the executive floors with their espresso machines. Hell, it wouldn't matter if the entire building had a sudden power spike that caused the servers to go haywire. The execs couldn't do anything about it anyway.

The absence of "suits" on server floors made Cade feel just a bit inferior. It was as if he'd detect a slight condescending look when the suits were seen with server guys. The suits looked at them as if they were "just the technical staff," something easily replaced by calling Linda in human resources and saying, "Hey, go hire me a couple of new server geeks, okay?" It pissed Cade off.

In this case, it looked like that group of suits was not happy. They were having what Cade's mom would have sarcastically called "a discussion." Cade only had a few "discussions" with his parents growing up. You know, the kind of discussion that ends with your mom saying, "Well, we'll just wait until your father gets home." Hearing that was never a good sign. Cade's dad was not a violent man, but his disappointment would be evident. That was worse than getting smacked in the rear with a belt a couple of times. Cade always hated the idea of his dad being disappointed in him.

As they got to the server floor, Cade couldn't help wonder why they needed him up here. *I mean, it's not as if this floor is short-staffed or something. Look around. Plenty of non-suit-clad geeks to go around. Not like I know any of these guys, but you can't tell me one of them couldn't handle a simple code yellow on a blinky server box,* he thought.

Cade heard voices just over the sound of the server fans. Not just voices, but unhappy voices. An argument was in full swing. As they walked past one server row after another, the argument escalated. When they turned down the row where the suits were arguing, Cade could hear what was being said.

"This isn't about Tucson, goddammit!" Anger frothed from the voice.

Another replied, "What the hell do you think we're doing here! This ain't the boy scouts!"

"Ah hem." Johnston cleared his throat to interrupt the argument. The suits looked up, and the argument ended abruptly. *Whatever was being said was not supposed to be said in front of someone who doesn't work up here, that's for sure,* thought Cade. Something about the word Tucson stuck with him. The suits looked at him and one in particular; a kind of William-Macy-from-the-movie-*Fargo*-looking guy, stared at him through black-rimmed glasses. He struck Cade as kind of familiar-looking, but then again, Cade had seen that movie five hundred times or so. *I bet people tell him he looks like a buzz-cut William Macy all the time. And then he slits their throats.* The thought wasn't as funny as he initially thought.

Cade made eye contact for a second then looked down at his John Belushi black canvas high tops. He glanced at the server rack on his left, then back at his shoes with a certain unnerving feeling in his gut.

In an abrupt introduction of sorts, Johnston pointed with his thumb and blurted, "Cade Williams, works on sixteen. He's the resource we need to analyze this."

William Macy turned his attention to some papers in his hand.

"No non-authorized personnel, goddammit."

Heat wafted from underneath Cade's T-shirt and rose past his face. He was uncomfortable to say the least. William Macy looked a little like he'd stepped out of a piece of news footage, circa 1955, where you'd see clips of old civil rights marches. The footage was always in black and white. And there was always some pinhead being interviewed and saying something about how "The white race was dominant." Cade didn't like him immediately.

"Now hold on, I thought you said the clearance was there," said Johnston, pointing his finger at William Macy. Johnston wasn't backing down, and it was hard to tell who was in charge. Whoever these guys were, they didn't look like they would take crap off anyone. And they didn't look like the typical executives at Thoughtstorm.

"You know what I meant," retorted William Macy, still not fully exposing his face. The only thing about him that didn't look like business was the way his glasses perched halfway down his nose. *It's hard to look like a tough guy when you've got those sissy-looking glasses hanging off your face,* Cade thought, wishing he could say that out loud.

"We only meant the clearance was okay if we were in a no-options scenario," said Macy as he put both hands on his hips, pulling back his jacket in the process. Cade's eyes flashed as he noticed something attached to Macy's right hip, and it darn sure wasn't a cell phone case. For the first time, Cade's uncomfortable feeling transformed into fear. *What the hell was that, a holster?* Cade looked back at his black canvas high tops. If it was a holster, Cade's next question was, what the hell would some pinhead be concealing a gun up here for? He hoped no one noticed his reaction to the gun, but just for good measure, he glanced to the servers to his right and pretended to be interested.

"Let me spell this out for you so you don't miss nothin'," said Johnston. "Based on the patterns we're seein', we've got about twenty-five minutes until the intermittent failures synchronize with one another. At that point, we have a total system collapse, and your e-mail stops going out. Is that plain enough for you?"

Cade couldn't believe what he just heard. *System collapse? My God, what the hell is going on up here?* The only time he'd ever seen a system collapse was when it was done on purpose. The year he started working at Thoughtstorm, Cade watched with a group of e-mail system admins as the chief technology officer entered the control room and announced he was going to perform the "mother of all system tests." In the e-mail world, e-mail servers were supposed to never go down. Otherwise, you'd have lots of pissed off customers. Every piece of equipment is supposed to have a redundant backup, a second e-mail server paired with the first. During normal operation, the pair would work together as if they were one. In the event that one of them failed, which was certainly possible, the other would take up the slack. The customer would not know the difference because they wouldn't even be aware of the outage.

This was also how software upgrades on the e-mail servers were possible. One of the pair would be shut down and upgraded while the other took the full load. Then the process would be repeated on the other server. On the rare occasions when a server actually did fail, an alert would be sent to the admins on duty who could literally swap out the downed server for another waiting in reserve.

The chief technology officer, Tim Wright, was never satisfied with that though. He kept asking the question, "Well, suppose we have an entire facility that goes down all at once? What's going to take over the slack in that case?" The company had several server farms across the globe. Eventually, Wright convinced the execs to fund the development of a system that would allow one server farm to back up another. So if the facility in Atlanta went down, the one in Reno would instantly pick up all the slack. That was the theory anyway.

Well, on this particular day, Wright announced that "Today was D-day." He was going to take the entire Atlanta facility offline. This was, in fact, the mother of all system tests. To do a live shutdown on real equipment that was sending out real e-mail for real customers took balls. So Wright tripped the system. People who had spent their entire careers dreading just such an event held their breath as one was performed right in front of their eyes. All the servers in the entire Atlanta facility went dark. On the phone with Reno, Wright listened intently. You could tell the guy was about to pee himself. The Reno center was talking nonstop, giving updates. Within a few seconds, the Reno facility picked up all the slack of the e-mail sending. It had worked, and it had worked perfectly. Wright made his career that day; the guy was like a legend.

William Macy looked at Johnston above the stupid glasses hanging from his nose. There was a protracted silence that felt like it went on for at least a minute. He nodded his consent, which apparently meant Cade was cleared to be on the elusive seventeenth floor.

"It's about damn time," said Johnston, motioning to Cade. "Williams, get your ass over here."

Cade wasn't used to being called by his last name, but he wasn't about to tell Johnston that. Johnston was walking at high speed back to the work station that contained all the monitors displaying server status.

"Look," continued Johnston, "don't pay attention to them assholes. They don't add up to a pile of dried grits." Cade wasn't so sure about that. "Take a look at these logs. The e-mail being sent across these servers can't be stopped, understand me? We gotta figure out what in the Sam Hill is the matter. For some reason, we're seeing a power spike every thirty-nine seconds. It's sending the server past its max load, and it's really starting to piss me off."

Johnston's description of the problem was bizarre. Cade had never seen something like this. His head swirled with questions. What would make the server load spike like that? Why was it happening every thirty-nine seconds? Who were the guys in suits, and why was one of them carrying a gun?

"Every thirty-nine seconds exactly?" Cade said.

Johnston just looked at him. "Did I stutter, boy?" Johnston gave Cade a look that reminded him of tenth grade at Chamblee High School when Mr. Butler, the vice principal, had seen Cade shove an envelope into the slot of a locker and then run off like a ten-year-old girl hyped up on sugar. Butler couldn't decide if he wanted to laugh or resume his disciplinarian role to make Cade explain what was in that envelope. Cade was just dropping a note into a girl's locker to tell her he liked her.

"Sorry, dumb question," he said. "Um, sir, has this pod ever shown this type of activity? I mean, what in the world are we sending in this e-mail job?"

"We're seein' this type of activity repeat itself durin' e-mail jobs about every two weeks. It cycles higher each time. And this time, it looks like it's going to finally blow that pod apart like my daddy's grain silo," said Johnston, evading the question.

"Sir, I've never seen a pattern like this. Are you sure you want me up here? I mean, surely there's somebody more experienced who can . . ."

Johnston cut him off. "You are who I need right now. Sit down, take a look. Be thorough. That pod can't go down, son. It can't." Somewhere deep inside his southern accent was a sense of urgency far more extreme than when a normal customer's e-mail job was having trouble. No, this was something different.

"But, sir, the redundant server will kick in if this box blows past max load. The e-mail job won't skip a beat."

"There is no redundant backup."

Cade looked up at him. "That's not possible, sir; Wright said every server would have a redundant . . ." But Johnston's face made it clear there was no redundant server. It was as if he was saying you're not in Kansas anymore, Toto. This was not the sixteenth floor, this was someplace different, and Cade had no idea why.

The suits turned in the opposite direction, and the argument heated. This time, over the drone of the servers, Cade couldn't hear a word of it.

5

It was midafternoon and across town, Cade's father, Cal Williams, was pulling out of Dobbins Air Force Base in Marietta. The retired Navy pilot had a lot of friends still in active service at NAS Atlanta, the naval air station, which was located smack-dab in the middle of Dobbins. Since the base was primarily for reservists, much of it only came to life on the weekends. But, with all the activity in Iraq, Afghanistan, and North Korea, there weren't many pilots left on maneuvers inside US airspace.

Cal always found an excuse to make his way over to the naval air station. He may have been retired, but he liked staying in touch with the guys. Cade had heard him say on more than one occasion that the only time he really felt alive was when he was being flung off the deck of a carrier and headed into harm's way. Strange to hear that from the same man who had also told Cade how glad he was to have never killed a man, not directly anyway.

Cal's job as an Electronic Countermeasures Officer, known as ECMOs, was to run the electronic gear that jammed enemy radar and produced false radar trails, making the enemy think there were US planes in a spot where they weren't.

Cal always had the radio in his SUV tuned to WBS, so he could hear the news.

"... more reports coming in to the news desk now. The death toll in that Tucson bombing has risen again. Skyrocketed, in fact..." There was a short period of silence. It was as if the newscaster, Mike Slayden, had dropped his script or something.

"Ah, helloooooo," said Cal towards the radio with a little smile, wondering why Slayden had stopped mid-sentence while on the air.

There was a shuffling, echoey noise. Slayden was speaking but was turned away from the microphone.

"... what do you mean? But... but he was fine, I just talked to him thirty minutes ago," Slayden continued. Cal's expression turned serious. Something was dreadfully wrong. He'd never heard anything like this out of WBS radio before. Mike Slayden was a consummate professional and had been on the air there as long as Cal could remember.

"Mike, we're on the air," boomed a voice from the background.

A sound reminiscent of an office chair overturning, rushed footsteps, then Slayden's voice trailed off as it moved farther out of range of the microphone.

"He can't be! He can't be! It was just a flesh wound. I talked to Stephen not thirty minutes ago! The shrapnel passed right through. They gave him twelve stitches and released him. The only thing he said was bothering him was the ringing in his ears from the blast . . ."

The voice was gone. More shuffling sounds were audible, then dead air space.

After a protracted silence, a voice came on the radio and said, "Folks, if you can bear with us for a minute here, ah, we've had some events here, right now we're going to go to a station break. You're listening to Newstalk 780, WBS Radio."

A commercial began playing, and Cal sat baffled. He reached Cobb Parkway and turned left. Atlanta traffic was a royal pain in the ass most of the time but was light at this time of day. Cal continued north and passed the Big Chicken, a 1950s-style Kentucky Fried Chicken restaurant built into the shape of an enormous chicken—a true Atlanta landmark. The Big Chicken always caused Cal to grin when he drove past the thing. It was the most well-known landmark in this part of the city—in this part of the state, for that matter.

A few minutes later, the commercials ended, and Cal turned up the volume.

"WBS. News, weather, traffic. Always on at 780AM. John Carden here, sitting in for Mike Slayden. The death toll at that deadly bombing in Tucson, Arizona, has risen from the earlier confirmed number of four, to twenty-nine."

Cal's eyes darted to the car stereo, his mouth hanging open.

"Earlier reports indicated four had died in the initial blast at a Little League baseball park in the Sabino Canyon area, a suburb of Tucson, Arizona. Another twenty-five were treated and released with minor injuries. Now, emergency officials at the Tucson Sheriff's Department are confirming that every one of the twenty-five minor injuries have resulted in fatality. No explanation for the sudden spike in loss of life has been given at this time. We'll have more on this developing story as it unfolds. Now, in other news . . ."

Cal turned the volume down, a sinking feeling in the pit of his stomach. He didn't know anyone from Tucson, but Mike Slayden sure must have. He couldn't imagine a Little League baseball field being the scene of such a tragedy. Cal thought back to those days when Cade was a Little Leaguer. Cal had been an assistant coach for the first half of one season when his unit had been abruptly deployed. He missed the rest of the season. Cal remembered how upset Cade had been at his leaving. That was 1994. Cade was just six years old at the time.

The first George Bush was in office, and Cal's unit was deployed to enforce the no-fly zone over Iraq. Serving your country was very important to Cal, but serving his son . . . well, that was a big deal too. Early on, Cal knew much of his son's life would be spent without his dad around. It wasn't exactly what Cal had intended. In fact, he never thought he'd qualify for jets in the first place.

But, he'd wanted to fly for as long as he could remember. And it's not as if he was even married at the time, much less married with kids. One thing led to another, and the next thing he knew, he had qualified for a jet. He never told any of his Navy friends, but the truth of the matter was he struggled terribly in those early days of flight school. After he made it past the first few rounds of cuts, he knew most of these jobs with small jets involved killing people. Actually being the guy who was given the order to put his finger on a firing device and deploy a deadly weapon was something he wanted to avoid. Cal knew he'd do it. He knew if ordered he'd pull the trigger, but that he'd have hell to pay later. His conscience was different than the typical fighter jock. Those guys are warriors. They may not walk across a battlefield wearing armor, but they are warriors in their souls. Cal wanted to have a clear conscience later in life and to find a seat flying into a warzone where you didn't have to pull the trigger was a dream come true.

6

ade wasn't exactly solving the server problem. Having Rupert Johnston, a man the size of a modern-day gorilla, standing over him wasn't helping matters. He tried to concentrate on the endless sea of code spilling across the server log files that were displayed on his monitors. Whatever was causing the servers to yellow line wasn't going to be easy to find. In fact, it was a giant pain in the ass.

"Dammit!" yelled Johnston, looking over his shoulder. "There goes another one. What the hell is going on with my damn servers, son?!"

The iPhone in Cade's pocket vibrated, then rang. The ringtone was reserved for Cade's dad, and Cade scrambled to shut it up.

"Crap, ah, sir, give me a minute, I don't know. I just need some more time." Johnston pulled out an actual calculator. One of those ancient HP financial calculators you still see bankers use. *Why anyone would carry a calculator is beyond me,* thought Cade. Johnston banged away at the thing like a mad scientist.

"We're down to fourteen minutes. Shit-fire! This thing is cyclin' faster than we thought. That server is going to crash." A red strobe light mounted on the ceiling started pulsing and reflecting off Cade's monitors.

"That's the warning," yelled Johnston, "we just hit redline."

"Fourteen minutes? I thought we had twenty-five . . . ."

"Hush, boy, concentrate. Look at them log files. Tell me what cha see." Cade noticed for the first time that Johnston seemed to revert back to his stronger southern drawl when his blood pressure got up. But this time he sounded more like a football coach revving up his players for the big game. Cade drew a deep breath and exhaled like he was trying to rid his lungs of a toxin. The pulsing red light bounced off his monitors.

This server was cycling on a predictable, timed pattern. The processor was now hitting 89 percent capacity, which was definitely in redline. If the pattern didn't stop—and quick—the box was going to sputter to a halt.

Cade couldn't help wondering why there were no redundant servers up here. The pressure was intensifying to stop the server from crashing. *But we're still just talking about e-mail. I mean, no one dies right? It's just e-mails going out. What's the big deal?* But just then a piercing alarm sounded at the other end of the server floor. The noise was deafening.

"Oh shit!" yelled Johnston, running towards the lame server rack. People flooded onto the server floor from all directions, and out of the corner of his eye, Cade saw the suits rush back through the door at the far side. *They're running, actually running,* thought Cade. The William-Macy-looking one slid to a stop, his leather-soled Johnston & Murphys having no traction on the slick floor. Cade shook his head at all the commotion. People were panicked. Johnston looked frantically back over his shoulder in Cade's direction; the men surrounded the ill server. Johnston tried to hide it, but his face betrayed an underlying terror. At that moment, Cade knew something was dreadfully, dreadfully wrong. This wasn't just some e-mail marketing campaign that announced a 30-percent-off sale at Penney's; this was something far different. Whatever it was, it was serious, and Cade was petrified.

7

Cal Williams didn't qualify for a pilot slot on a fighter; instead he qualified for a role that suited him much better. He could use his technical skills to run radar-jamming equipment and protect other American pilots. And he got to be in the front of everything. Every mini-war that flared up, his unit would be deployed. Since there aren't many radar jammers, Cal would get frequent deployment orders, and he and his crew would saddle up and fly out to the soon-to-be warzone. They'd fly for up to eighteen hours, refueling in midair to get to the carrier that might be stationed in the Persian Gulf or off the Gulf of Tonkin. From that point on, he had a great job. The best part was that it was rare for anyone to shoot at you in one of these things. Most of the time, the enemy had no idea you were there because Cal would so badly screw up their radar screens; the enemy wouldn't know where to tell his pilots to go.

Cal realized early that his son was paying the price for his success. A son growing up with an absentee father doesn't get off easy. Through different deployments, Cal would return to Dobbins Air Force Base to a local high school band playing a welcome-home greeting. But as he would get off the transport plane and jog across the tarmac towards his wife and child, little Cade would stop. Just stop dead in his tracks and not come any closer to his father.

There he would be, nine years old, then ten, then twelve. And with each homecoming, it got a little worse. Cade was mad at his father, no question. Mad at him for not being there. Over the next couple of days, Cade would come around, but Cal noticed harsh temper tantrums from Cade during those early years. Like he was lashing back at a father he didn't understand.

Cal would respond by over-responding. He would immerse himself into activities with Cade, trying to rebuild the damaged relationship. Cade was a good kid, but he needed something, and that something was his dad. The pattern repeated itself with each deployment. There was Bosnia in 1994, Somalia in 1995, Haiti, also in '95, back to Bosnia in '96, Sierra Leone in 1997 . . . the list went on. Many of these deployments were talked about infrequently on the news. Some of them weren't talked about at all. A lot of the time it involved flying cover for evacuations of American citizens from places that no one really ever heard of. And to make matters worse, Cal often couldn't talk about where he had been or why he had to be gone. He'd do his best to make it up to Cade, but Cade would have none of it.

Now that Cal was retired from the service, he had done a pretty good job of reconnecting with Cade. But he carried a guilt complex with him. It was like boarding a commercial flight and having an extra carry-on bag that wouldn't quite fit into the overhead compartment. But, unfortunately, this was not a bag he could check.

Cal picked up his cellphone and, even though he was driving, flipped it open and hit *2 to speed-dial Cade. Holding the phone to his ear, he thought about how Cade always razzed him about still having a flip phone, especially since he came out of such a high-tech background. After the second ring, Cal knew he wasn't going to get Cade to answer. Cade never let his phone ring more than once before answering if he wasn't busy. After the fourth ring, Cal hung up. Things were still uncomfortable between father and son.

Cal continued up Cobb Parkway, turned left on Roswell Street, and headed towards Cool Beans, a favorite local coffee shop where grunge was the norm.

He may have been way older than the kids in here, but that's what made it what it was. It was a place he could relax. Before any doctor's appointment, like the one he had today, he would come here, take a cup of coffee onto the back patio, and read his paper or just people watch. Cool Beans had a coffee roaster machine that sat just inside the shop. The aroma of freshly roasted coffee only added to the smooth bitterness that was unique to the bean. Cal sat under the shade trees, leaned back in his chair, and closed his eyes. As the door swung open and closed, the aroma wafted out onto the patio. It was intoxicating. *Just take that in. Man, kids today don't pay enough attention to the little pleasures,* he thought. His mortality had been on his mind a lot lately. *Hell, I never paid enough attention. Just to sit back, relax, close your eyes, and take it all in.* The sounds, the smells. In his mind's eye, he drifted. This particular aroma took him back to a godsend of a place in Kandahar they nicknamed "the Starbucks of Afghanistan." Being in such an unfamiliar place was always unsettling. So whether in Kandahar or Kabul, Cal would go down to a local coffee joint, assuming they had one, and in a country where nothing looked, tasted, or smelled like home, he'd get to sip something familiar. The coffee was great. In

Kabul, there was this little place called Chaila. Just walking in felt like you were stepping off the surface of the moon and into a café like the one his dad had taken him to in the 1950s. The place had a brick oven, and the pizza that came out of it had Uncle Sam written all over it.

Cal hung out at the coffee shop for a little while, wanting to stay longer, but that damn doctor's appointment was calling his name. He glanced at a young couple leaning across their table and kissing. They looked to be in their young twenties—a nose ring here, a tattoo there; they melded into the atmosphere of the place well. "I don't think I knew a single girl with a tattoo when I was that age," he mumbled to himself, taking the last sip. He pulled out a set of old aviator sunglasses from his top pocket and slipped them onto his nose, then walked off the patio, down the couple of steps, and out to the car.

This next part was not something he wanted to face. Out loud he said, "They flung you off the deck of a carrier in the middle of a typhoon, and you're scared to go hear the news from some stupid doctor?" The small lump in his throat turned a little bigger.

8

"Three minutes!" came a booming voice from the speaker system overhead. The loud alarm switched to a higher frequency pulse, piercing Cade's ears. It was like being on a nuclear submarine that had just pitched into darkness, alarm blaring, strobe lights pulsing.

Cade turned back to the monitors with his heart pounding to each pulse of light. The only thing notable in the log files was that whenever the server usage spiked, it wasn't recovering. It was as if a new load was put on it, and it didn't know how to relax itself. He scrambled across the logs, looking for anything. Then his eye caught a series of error codes. Finally, here was something, here was the real problem.

"Mr. Johnston!" yelled Cade, his voice cracking at first. "You need to see this."

Johnston came running, followed by the suits. They all clamored around the cubicle.

"What cha got, boy?"

"Sir, look at this. Each cycle of excessive server usage is preceded by this block of code that's getting executed on the server. I don't know what that code block is, but that's it. That's what's causing your problem. We just need to shut that code off."

"Do it, boy, now."

But no sooner had Cade reached for his mouse than a sharp hand crashed on his shoulder. It felt like cold-fingered steel, and it meant business. It was William Macy, the one he'd seen carrying a weapon.

"Don't touch that code," said the fingers. Johnston turned to the man and started to speak, but Macy's hand rose to cut him off.

"Don't touch that code." The vise grip crunched harder into the shoulder.

Johnston stammered, "It's gonna do an auto shutdown. It will cause a cascading failure . . ."

"Ten seconds!" the overhead speaker blurted.

But Cade saw the look on Macy's face; it was resolute. Changing his mind would be like putting chunks of granite into a blender and expecting them to be pulverized into sand. Cade curled in pain under the vise grip. No expression.

"Mr. Johnston, I'm getting the impression he doesn't want us to touch the code." The attempt at levity in a very uncomfortable spot went nowhere.

"Seven seconds! Six, five, four . . ." screamed the overhead voice across the speakers. Cade didn't know what to expect. Whatever it was, he just wanted it to end. A second or two passed, but the countdown went silent.

"Clear!" said the booming voice with the excitement of a ten-year-old on a roller coaster. "We're clear. Job completed! The e-mail job finished! We're clear."

The vise grip, however, didn't budge. Cade was still turned, staring at the man, his shoulder throbbing. Whatever it was, it was over now, and the piercing alarm and strobe lights stopped. The overhead lighting flickered back to life. The man stared at Johnston and Johnston stared back. It was an old-school matchup that Cade didn't want to be in the middle of. Moments later, Johnston's eyes darted down for a split second. He had conceded and knew he had to bite his tongue.

Cade winced from the pain.

"Ah, sir . . ."

Macy's head snapped down, glaring at Cade; his eyes were angry. He released his hand and stepped into Johnston's face. His stare was cold and unsympathetic. Johnston looked away. He was a man who had never lost at anything, and he didn't know how to act. Macy walked away with a saunter. In his mind, he had reached into the mouth of death and had kicked its ass, again.

Cade looked at Johnston, but nothing was said. Cade stood up, slid his chair back, and walked toward the corridor and the elevators. When he turned and looked back, Johnston was already gone.

9

The smell of the previous night's spilled ale wafted out of Porter Bar in Atlanta's Little Five Points area and covered the sidewalk with its staleness. To say the closing crew hadn't done the best job mopping up the previous night's froth was an understatement. Porter Bar was famous for seriously dark beer. Their trademarked overfilled steins wreaked havoc on the floor's aging wooden planks. Customers didn't seem to mind though. In Little Five Points, the head on beer was considered a food group.

A bright reflection cascaded through the windows and onto the deep wooden tones of the bar. The bar was adorned with a smattering of half-empty beer mugs, steins, and porter glasses, the odd paper napkin, and a few plates left behind from the lunch crowd. Old-world woodwork dripped from the walls, heavy with ringed stains of cigarette smoke. The place was a virtual time capsule, as if someone in Ireland had long ago slid the narrow pub into a huge box, put it on a container ship, and floated it across the pond to Atlanta, leaving all the tables and chairs in place.

The bell over the door clinked as Waseem's clean-shaven face leaned into the pub. New, cheap clothes draped his narrow shoulders, but it was hard to look into his coal-black eyes and make any assumptions. They betrayed nothing other than cold. Still, seeing the dark-skinned Middle Easterner walk into a place like this was reminiscent of a pigeon landing on second base at a major league baseball game—everyone stared. He was clearly out of place compared to the funky, pale-skinned, tattooed, and body-pierced crowd so at home in Little Five Points.

On weekends, Porter Bar was so filled with an array of tattoos and body piercings that token yuppies who strayed past the door would not stay for long. A clique of truly unique souls defined Little Five Points like no other place in Atlanta. It was like a tiny slice of San Francisco's Castro district, somehow nestled in the south.

Bastian Mokolo sat at the bar wearing thick-rimmed shades. He peered at Waseem through the reflection of a large mirror emblazoned

NATHAN GOODMAN □ 39

with the words "Lagunitas Maximus," and studied Waseem's body language. The skin on the beard area was pale in contrast to the rest of the dark features, apparently unfamiliar with the recently applied razor. To Bastian, it was a sign that Waseem was new. The new ones often wanted to keep their thick facial hair, but once they arrived in the United States, they stood out like a man in a four-buttoned suit in the middle of a livestock auction—shaving was just a matter of time.

At two p.m. on a Monday, the establishment was down to four patrons. The usual lunch crowd had left, having to return to their day jobs. Waseem paused near the entrance and leaned his shoulder against the doorframe. His emotionless face scanned the barstools and locked on Bastian who didn't return the glance but instead studied the half inch of foam still left in his glass. Waseem walked over to him but Bastian didn't acknowledge his presence. Instead, he held the glass up in the reflecting light, taking more notice of the translucence of the dark beer than Waseem.

Bastian said, "A damn food group, mon. Dey joke 'bout de head on beer being a food group. Like you cood slice eet and poot eet on bread," his Jamaican accent as thick as the head on the beer.

Waseem pulled out the barstool, looking Bastian up and down. Bastian took another sip, paying no mind.

"Your ass ain' gonna seet itself, mon. You got to guide eet down."

As Waseem eased onto the stool, he gazed at Bastian out of the corner of his eye and then began the first scripted code phrase. "Mon looks in de abyss."

Waseem drew a haggard breath. "There's nothing staring back at him."

"At dat mowment, mon finds his charactar."

"And character is what keeps him out of the abyss." The passcode exchange between the two confirmed their identities to one another.

The Jamaican peered over his left shoulder at two patrons seated across the long room, cigarette smoke rising from their ashtray. They paid him no attention.

"I am toold you wanna speak wit me," said Bastian.

"You don't look like the type of person I'd want to talk to," said Waseem, turning his head toward the man.

Bastian's head snapped, eye to eye with Waseem, dreadlocks bouncing.

"Don' hand me dat double-talk crap!" he said.

Both glared at each other, sizing the other up. Suddenly, Bastian grabbed Waseem's drab green military jacket by the lapel and dragged him down the hall, knocking over a chair at a nearby table. A man, whose back was to them, spun around, startled. Once in the men's room, Bastian pushed the light-framed Waseem against the cold surface of the tile wall.

"YOU called me, mon," barked Bastian. "I don' wanna hear none of dat sheet bout you don' truss me. In fact, why don' you tell me who de hell YOU are." His anger was visceral. "What de hell you got unda here, mon?" he asked, searching Waseem's coat and clothes. "You de heet, mon! You got on a wire?"

Bastian's hand vanished into his Rasta hippie-top shirt producing a switchblade, which flicked open with a metallic crack. He held it against Waseem's already raw throat.

"Tell me who de hell you is, mon," said Bastian, easing pressure off Waseem's throat, allowing him to cough.

"You know who the hell I am," said Waseem. "My brother Kasra knows you. He told you I was coming. He told you what I looked like. And he told you to relax, you fucking pig! Now take that damn blade off of my throat!" Waseem's nostrils flared, eying Bastian hard. They stared at each other. Finally, Bastian backed off and slid the blade out of sight.

Waseem exhaled and said, "Let's go for a walk, I don't like talking inside a closed space like this."

The two meandered back past the bar, and a few glances followed them outside. They crossed McLendon Avenue, cut down a side street, and walked behind a couple of theatre buildings. Having reached the baseball fields, Bastian headed through the dugout and onto the field towards the pitcher's mound.

He looked in all directions. Just as he suspected, the area was deserted. The lone exception was a female seated in the far distance who shifted her wavy hair in the breeze. As Bastian looked away, she removed the bag from across her shoulder and placed it on the ground where she had spread out a small blanket. The thermos and Tupperware added to the appearance of just a woman on a short lunch break. She removed a particularly expensive laser microphone built for eavesdropping from the bag and extended the small, attached tripod. Her camera had a large lens, but at two hundred yards, she would draw no attention from the men.

10

Cal took his time as he made his way to Kennestone Hospital. There wasn't much traffic, and he liked driving the back roads in Marietta where the town square was a throwback to another era. It had been burned to the ground during the Civil War, with the exception of the corner hotel. The hotel owner had acted as a spy for the Union. General Sherman spared the hotel from the fires. But, after he left, the townspeople burned that one down themselves. The Marietta Square boasted a large green space in the center, which made for a great little park. The surrounding buildings were mostly filled with small businesses, a sign of a good economy. Nothing on the square stood taller than two stories, and history was evident with mismatched brick adjoining one building to the next. The sides of buildings still evidenced old hand-painted advertisements for RC Cola, something of a sacrilege this close to Atlanta where Coca-Cola is consumed as if it were a life-sustaining sustenance.

Cal came to the square more often than he cared to admit. He hadn't spent much time around the square until these doctor visits started becoming a thing of regularity. The Strand Theatre had stood proudly on the corner since the 1930s. Apparently, the first flicker show ever played here was a Fred Astaire and Ginger Rogers musical. Cal parked on the street in front of the theatre and sat with his hands on the steering wheel. He thought back thirty years to when he had taken a cute girl named Susan Felker on their first date. The theatre hadn't changed a bit. It had been remodeled, perhaps, but in the true spirit of the history of the place, it looked the same.

Cal opened the car door and walked to the heavy glass doors. The door handles dripped with ornate brass. Cal knew without looking that they were the same door handles he had pulled open for Susan on that night. For just a moment, he smelled the perfume she wore. To his surprise, the door was unlocked. He walked inside, taking in the vivid red carpet, the heavy columns in the lobby, and the sight of that same glass concession counter being stocked with candy for tonight's show.

"Help you?" came a voice from behind the counter.

The young man was dressed in candy-striper red and white, complete with bow tie and hat. It was all circa 1960. He paused a moment and blinked his eyes because standing behind the counter was actually a young man dressed in jeans and a T-shirt. Cal's daydream of that night long ago had ended.

He snapped back into reality and said, "No. Sorry, mind if I take a look inside?"

The man glanced at him as if to find a reason to say no, but couldn't. "Help yourself," said the man, too busy to worry about it, and too polite to say no.

Cal pushed his way through the double doors into the theatre. A grand sight it was, and bigger than he remembered. The Strand had seating for at least a thousand if you included the grand balcony above. The seats were more modern now, but the charm of the place oozed from the velvet red walls. Down the center and to his right were the seats they sat in that night. That was when Cal had become intoxicated with feelings for Susan. He was a goner from then on.

His head drooped as he considered everything that had happened since that night so many years ago. His sobbing was low, quiet, personal. There were so many memories, so many joys, and so many mistakes. Not realizing he had been standing there several minutes, a soft hand touched his shoulder.

"Sir, is everything all right?" It was the young man.

"What, huh?" Cal's embarrassment was not necessary as the young man's voice was soft and carried an understanding that said "whatever is going on, this person needs to be here at this moment."

"Ah, ahem, no, I'm fine. Really, I appreciate it. Just wanted to take a look at the place, you know, for old time's sake."

"Yes, sir, it's fine. Sir, you don't need to leave or anything. Just take your time."

But the moment had broken. Cal knew what he had to do.

He looked at the young man through tear-filled eyes, "Thank you, son," and then headed out to what he knew would be bad news.

11

The office of Dr. Thomas Inman had become a familiar place for Cal in recent months. The name Inman was well known throughout Atlanta and smelled of old southern money. Inman Park was the most well-known representation of the name, but the family had become very wealthy decades earlier through various business interests and was known for generosity. The more prominent universities in the area were prime benefactors of family money, including Cal's alma mater, Georgia Tech. Without Inman money, the school may have never been founded.

Tom Inman, MD, carried nothing in his walk of the pretense of old family money. He grew up in a wealthy family to be sure, but his father, having seen disastrous results of raising children in that type of environment, resolved things would be different. They moved into a nice, upper-middle-class neighborhood and more or less hid their wealth. No, they wanted their kids to be shielded from all of that.

Tom went to public school, and earned his way into Stanford University the hard way. Since he was footing his own bill, and in order to afford the exorbitant costs of medical school, he decided to let Uncle Sam pay the tuition for him. Tom signed a commission in the US Navy, promising to serve five years after med school. So, like Cal, Tom had served onboard a ship. And unknown to either of them at the time, they had served onboard that same ship in the Persian Gulf. They never met during that six-month deployment because, frankly, Cal was never sick. Not until now anyway.

Cal walked into the waiting room, glanced at the receptionist, and had a seat. He didn't bother giving his name; she knew it. A short while later he was ushered down the hall and into Tom's personal office. Today wasn't a day for an exam—the exams were through. Today was the day Cal would learn what he feared would be his final diagnosis. The cancer was probably everywhere by now, and there was nothing Tom or anyone else was going to be able to do about it. Up until now, Cal hadn't wanted to tell Cade. There was no sense in worrying him. But now, it looked like he'd have to break his silence.

"Hello, Cal," came Tom's familiar voice.

After discovering their overlapping tour of duty, and having spent so much time together, the two had become fast friends.

"Hey, Tom."

"That's Dr. Inman to you, scumbag," Tom joked.

"Tom, I know we've got serious business to discuss."

Tom had hoped to get in some small talk first. He hated this part. During his residency he had trained himself to emotionally detach from his patients. As an oncologist, he'd had to tell his share of patients the bad news. But it was different with them. Cal was a friend, he was dying, and there wasn't a damn thing he could do about it.

12

Cade walked to the elevator and hit the button. "What the hell was that all about?" he said aloud. His breathing was irregular and his palms sweaty. The elevator door opened, and he stepped in, standing there for a moment, staring at the buttons. *Something is very, very wrong up here,* his eyes fixed on the button numbered sixteen. The doors closed, but he just stood, motionless. Finally, he raised his hand but stopped it just shy of pressing the button. His hand was shaking. He had to get outside for a bit and go cool off.

Working at Thoughtstorm isn't supposed to be this stressful. He hit the button for the lobby and, instead of heading to the cafeteria where he might normally grab a coffee, he went straight out the front doors and onto Peachtree Street.

Outside, the spring breeze hit him. Peachtree Street was busy at lunch time. Hell, it was busy most of the time. He shook his head, still baffled over what he'd just experienced. *What was going on up there? Why had there been so much pressure over that e-mail job? What was in that e-mail anyway?* He had to find out. Although, Cade wasn't sure he really wanted to know. Whatever was going on, it was way more than the normal fire drill where some e-mail marketer was having a hissy fit about his e-mail not executing at the scheduled time.

Cade crossed Peachtree and walked a few blocks down Buckhead Avenue to Fado, a familiar Irish pub that had been on this corner for as long as he could remember. The pub food could be described as "not bad," but the beer was cold and creamy. It was early yet, but Cade didn't care. He needed to cool off and think things through. The lunch crowd was yet to arrive, and most booths were empty. He loved coming here after work to hang out with the guys from the office. It's not that the wait staff knew him, but still, he'd been here enough for the place to hold a lot of memories.

He put his hands in his hair and leaned his elbows on the table, something his mother would have never approved. Cade's mom had been a stable rock for most of his early life. Up until high school, he'd had an otherwise normal childhood. Things went bad that year with

Mom. It was as if she had reached the end of her allotted stability and then just stopped caring. Trying to raise a child for all those years with an absentee husband had taken its toll. She blamed Cal for leaving her alone as he went on all those long deployments. It wasn't easy being a Navy wife. Cal seemed to not recognize how much pain his absences were causing. After a while, it was like she just zoned out. The day after Cade went away to school, she moved out of the house and left Cade's dad. The divorce was filed, and Cal was left in a pool of misery, not that he didn't see it coming or deserve it.

Cal's long absences took their toll on Cade as well. When he was younger, Cade saw how sad his mom was, and it made him angry. Those same feelings continued into adulthood and would flare when the stress level was high. Cade took a deep breath, held it, and exhaled in one long, slow motion. The wait staff, busy filling ketchup bottles and salt shakers, hadn't noticed him entering.

He was really confused from the morning's events. One thing was certain, he had to know what was going on. He had to find out who those guys were. Then something occurred to him—he now had the security access. If he snooped around the network from his laptop, he may be able to hide his tracks. As an administrator, he could even hide his activities from the log files. He would log in and look at the e-mail content of the job that had caused such uproar. Maybe there was something he missed. The thought scared him a little bit. He'd always had access to see whatever was heading out across the company servers, but that was always done in service to the customer, never in prying. There was a lot of data customers considered very private—most importantly, extensive customer e-mail lists: a virtual treasure trove of e-mail addresses. People paid a lot of money for lists like that. Cade never dared pry into a customer's e-mails or data. He wondered if he'd have the guts to do it.

His iPhone buzzed and startled him back into reality. He fished out the phone and looked at the screen. It was his dad. He and his dad hadn't spoken in many months. The anger buried deep within would probably poison their relationship for the rest of their lives. He let the phone ring a couple of times, just staring at it. Then, inexplicably, he decided to answer the call.

"Hello?" Cade knew who it was but didn't want to admit it.

"Cade? It's your dad."

Silence hung in the air like a thick morning fog. Cade looked down and picked at the crack in the heavy wooden table.

"Cade, ah . . . listen, I'm sorry to bother you at work. I know I'm not someone you want to talk to. It's just that, that . . . look, I want to talk. I need to talk to you. Can we do that?"

Cade hesitated. "What do you want to talk about?"

"Not now, not over the phone. Cade, I need to see you."

Something in the way the voice trailed off made Cade realize whatever it was, it was important. The last time they talked, Cade ended up yelling at him for never being around when Mom needed him. The truth was Cade's mom had an affair the summer of his tenth grade year. It wasn't until Cade was older that he realized his mom was just a flesh and blood woman and was so very alone. His anger, once directed at his mother, had been redirected at his dad who put service to his country above service to his family, year after year after year. It was like she was getting back at Cal for all the hurt inside her. The affair was very short lived, but it festered and continued to cling to life inside Cade's gut.

Finally, Cade said, "Is it that important to you?"

"Yes, son. Yes, it's that important. How about I come over your way Friday after you're off work?"

"I can't do it on Friday," said Cade. "I'm headed up to see Kyle's graduation."

"Kyle? You mean that friend of yours in college? Graduation? I thought he graduated a few years before you did?"

"He did, yeah, from undergrad. He's graduating from Quantico this weekend," said Cade.

"Quantico? You mean the FBI academy? Wow. He's in the FBI? That's great. Man, I bet his parents are so proud of him . . ." Cal stopped, realizing how that must have sounded. "I mean, Cade, listen, I didn't mean that what he is doing is any more important than what you do. Look, I'm amazed at what you do. Hell, I don't even understand it."

But it was too late. Cade's eyes rolled. His dad had always wanted him to apply to the Naval Academy or at least go through ROTC and then do something big, something important. But the interest was never there. Cade had seen enough "service" in his childhood to last a lifetime.

"I'm not back until late Sunday night. Call me next week." Cade hung up the phone, shook his head, and raised a hand to flag down a waitress. He needed a beer. The four waitresses, however, appeared to be engrossed with topping off a tray full of salt shakers. The radio was on, and they were listening to a news report, which was out of Cade's earshot.

". . . appears that the final death toll in that tragic blast at the Morris K. Udall Little League Park in the Sabino Canyon area of Tucson is now listed at thirty-one. We've confirmed further that the original report of four dead and twenty-seven injured was accurate. The initial blast killed four, and many of the wounded were treated and released with minor injuries from shrapnel. Reports are coming in that many of the wounded, previously discharged from treatment, have died in their homes of causes unknown. A medical mystery unfolding now . . . wait, hold on, okay, I'm getting word now that we're going live to a press conference at the Tucson Medical Center, where the largest number of victims was originally transported; the news conference is already in progress."

"Let me introduce Dr. Charles Ramirez of the Tucson Medical Center as well as Special Agent in Charge Stephen Bolz of the FBI's counterterrorism task force."

Dr. Ramirez began, "Let me just say that in thirty-five years of practicing medicine, I've never seen anything like this. Our heartfelt sorrow is extended to each and every family member of the thirty-one lost souls." The doctor's voice shook as he cleared his throat. "Of the thirty-one people that were injured in the blast, seventeen were brought here, eleven of them children. Four were pronounced dead upon arrival." The doctor spoke mechanically now, devoid of emotion. "One was admitted in critical condition. His condition was later upgraded to stable. Approximately two-and-one-half hours later, his condition deteriorated, and he went into cardiac arrest. We were unable to resuscitate him." There was silence; the doctor was struggling to maintain his composure. "Our triage staff responded swiftly to all injuries. The rest of the injuries were non-life threatening. The remaining eleven victims were treated for minor lacerations and contusions. All were later released." The silence began again, this one protracted. Through the radio, sounds of snapping camera lenses were audible. The doctor mustered enough courage to continue. "Then, beginning at approximately 1:15 p.m., emergency calls began pouring into the 911 service and into our hospital. Our service was once again flooded with patients. As they arrived by ambulance, all eleven of the originally discharged patients were declared dead upon arrival. At this time, the cause of death is unknown. We'll have to wait for the coroner's report, but in my estimation, there must have been some kind of toxin involved in that explosion."

Reporters all spoke at once, clamoring to ask a question, but then Agent Bolz interrupted. "Let me assure you that all available resources are being employed by the FBI, other federal agencies, and with cooperation from the Tucson Sheriff's Department. Forensic evidence is being gathered as we speak. We'll let you know more as we find out." He quickly left.

The radio newscast switched from the news conference in Phoenix, back to the WBS anchors in Atlanta. "Well, that's what we know from the scene in Arizona. To recap, of the thirty-one known dead, seventeen were rushed to the Tucson Medical Center. Of those, eleven were treated and released, but later died of unknown causes. There was possibly a toxin of some type used in the explosive device. We'll stay on top of this story and bring you the news as it happens. For now, in for Mike Slayden, I'm John Carden, reporting live. You're listening to Newstalk 780, WBS."

13

After eating what turned out to be a quiet lunch, Cade headed back out Fado's heavy oak doors and onto the street. He felt more at ease now that he'd had a break. The cobalt blue sky was bright and clear as he walked down the hill towards the office. Behind him, a man also exited Fado, crossed to the opposite side of the street and walked in the same direction as Cade. A slight gust of wind flapped his un-tucked shirt tails. The man put his right hand to his ear. "Secure channel," he said softly.

"Channel secure," came a crisp reply into his earpiece.

"Subject en route."

"Roger, subject en route. Distance?"

"Distance, three hundred meters." The blowing breeze caused a slight rustling sound across the mic. "Be in view in zero-two minutes."

"Roger that, zero-two minutes."

Cade waited a moment for a MARTA bus to clear and then crossed Peachtree Road towards his office. Behind him shone the black mirrored glass of the sprawling Atlanta Financial Center building. In a vacant office on the sixth floor, a tripod-mounted camera with a high-powered lens recorded with intent.

Once inside the building, Cade rode up to the sixteenth floor and sat down in his cube. Whitmore stood up and walked around. If he ever wanted to talk to Cade, Whitmore walked all the way around the cube; standing up to talk over the cube wall was pointless, as his height created only a view of the top of Cade's head that way.

"Where'd you go for lunch? I was going to see if you wanted to grab something at Fado."

"Aw man, sorry," said Cade. "That's where I went. Sorry, I just needed to get out of here and take a breather."

Whitmore didn't hide his disappointment very well.

"Oh no, that's cool. We'll do it again soon." He paused and said, "Hey, what was the big hubbub with them calling you upstairs? Everything cool?"

"Oh, yeah. Yeah, no big deal. Some guy who normally works up there was out today or something. They just had a server that needed a little medi-Cade," Cade said, trying to cover up what had happened.

"Medi-Cade?"

"You caught that? See what I did there? My name is Cade . . ."

"Cade, dude, now that's just gay," joked Whitmore.

"Gay? You're gay."

"Yes, I'm gay. We all know I'm gay. But damn, I'm not that gay."

Cade looked at him then laughed. For the first time that day he felt good.

Whitmore's demeanor shifted. "Hey, can you believe it about those kids? Thirty-one people, man, unbelievable."

Cade replied, "Wait, what? What thirty-one people? You mean the Tucson thing? They said there were four."

"Dude, no. It's unreal—every single one of the survivors are now dead. It's like the bomb fragments were poisoned or something. No one knows."

Cade flopped back in his chair and stared at the ceiling. "Thirty-one? Holy crap." Cade wanted to search the news on his browser but thought better of it, knowing the company logged website visits. Then, another thought crossed his mind. He remembered the incident when he placed masking tape over the lens of the laptop webcam, and it was gone the next day. *Did that have anything to do with those guys on seventeen?* Cade's mind raced. Maybe he wasn't being so paranoid after all. Maybe there was something to it. He glanced at the little lens of the webcam. *What if they're watching me right now?* he wondered. The thought gave him the willies.

Down here, it seemed like a typical day. People in a conference room, others moving in that direction. Others on the phone, several banging away at their keyboards. But Cade didn't feel comfortable anymore.

The desk phone rang again. "202 area code? Who the hell is calling me from New York?"

"No, nimrod. 202 is DC," replied an amused Whitmore.

The phone rang again. "DC? Who do I know . . . holy crap!" Cade answered the call, "Cade Williams."

"Hey, man!"

"Kyle! Hell yeah. I knew it must be you," he said, glancing back at Whitmore who smirked at him. "Man, how's it going?!" Cade said as he walked toward the break room.

"God, it's almost over! I'm stoked, but damn I'm tired," said Kyle.

Kyle MacKerron had taken Cade under his wing in college. Cade had been just a green freshman pledging the fraternity when Kyle was a senior. Cade always looked up to him like the big brother he never had.

Cade cut in with his trademark sarcasm, "So you're telling me you're about ready to graduate? Those suckers in the FBI want to give you a badge and a gun!" Cade knew the FBI had literally recruited Kyle. They were after him. Kyle's subtle southern drawl was pure coastal Georgia, but bespoke nothing of what talents lay underneath. Kyle possessed everything the bureau was looking for—a graduate degree in forensic accounting, fluency in Farsi, a private pilot's license, and letters of commendation for distinguished service in the Gulf War.

Kyle jabbed back, "Hey, when you get up here on Friday, I'll let you hold it."

"Hey, man, I don't even want to speculate on what 'it' you're talking about."

"The gun, nimbleweed, the gun. If you promise not to shoot your toe off, I'll let you hold the handgun. Just don't tell anybody. I don't want to get kicked out of here because of some pencil-neck."

"Yeah, yeah," said Cade. "I'm taking Friday off and driving up. What happens when I get to the gate and some military dude asks me what the hell I'm doing on his base?"

"Don't worry about it. You're officially on the invite list. They'll have your name at the guard gate. But whatever you do, don't forget your driver's license. You'll never get in here without that."

"Hey, now don't forget, you promised me you'd take me on the Jodie Foster tour. I expect to see anywhere they filmed *The Silence of the Lambs*," said Cade.

"Yeah, yeah. I've got your lamb right here. Just have the Marine guard point you over to the dorms. I'm in the middle building, on the fourth floor. Room 463."

Thursday came quickly, and once home, Cade realized how much crap he had yet to pack for the weekend. The plan was to leave early to avoid the traffic and to get a start on the ten-and-a-half-hour drive. Not that he minded it—the drive would give him some time to decompress and see a bit of the country he hadn't seen. The last time he'd been in DC was in the seventh grade. All the school safety patrols from the county piled onto a train, with a mass of parent-chaperones in tow, and struck out to see the capital. That was four years before the 9/11 attacks. Now security was tighter. *I bet they don't show up at the*

White House with a ton of kids and ask to see the President anymore. He laughed. He was really looking forward to seeing Kyle.

Kyle had been like a guide his freshman year, steering him through all the boneheaded mistakes he was walking into. Cade thought back about going to Kyle's home in Savannah that first year. They had some good times. Kyle, though, was a bit of a dichotomy. He could just about party anybody under the table, yet there was a serious side to him. Even being just a college kid, anywhere he was, Kyle always studied the situation. He had a sixth sense. He'd walk into a room, stop, turn around, and pull Cade out. It was like Kyle could smell trouble before it happened. His sense of smell for trouble didn't cause him to avoid it himself though. If ever there was a drunken asshole at one of the frat parties, Kyle would position himself close enough to pound the guy if needed. And pound he did. Cade saw him tangle with a belligerent redneck at a sorority social one time. It was like watching a cat with fists made of bricks. His quickness was amazing. Kyle was everything Cade was not. That's why one of them was in the FBI and the other was working a server room. The truth though was that Kyle was very proud of Cade. Cade had been just a scared little kid that first day of freshman year, and today he had made something of himself.

14

C ade was pretty pleased with himself for getting out of town so early that Friday morning. He woke up much earlier than his alarm, probably due to the anticipation, and spent no time stuck in traffic. He didn't really mind the driving. The truth was, he was really excited to be seeing Kyle. He and "Cool Mac" had become even better friends after undergrad. In the past year though, they didn't get much time together, and Cade hoped this would be one last weekend of fun before Kyle headed out to his duty station. Kyle had been assigned to the San Diego field office—a prime assignment, to say the least. Lots of new agents instead find themselves assigned to Detroit or Jersey City or some place that looked like a desert wasteland near the border with Mexico.

No, Kyle had really lucked out. *Come to think of it,* thought Cade, *I doubt he lucked out. I bet he won that placement like he's won out so many other things in his life.* Kyle was the kind of guy that always had a plan. Even back in school, Kyle mapped out his future. He knew where he wanted to go from the time he was a teenager. Cade, on the other hand, more or less bumbled his way into wherever he ended up. Not that he was complaining. It was a good thing he'd never wanted to be a doctor or an FBI agent or anything like that, because that takes years of planning and Kyle was just that type of planner.

Cade crossed into Virginia, glanced down at the GPS to see how far away his exit would be. Kyle was busy today, his last day of training before graduation, so Cade easily had time to check into his hotel in the Aquia Harbor area, not far from the Marine base at Quantico.

The phone's generic ringtone went off, and he glanced down at the incoming number; it was not a number he recognized. "A 678 exchange? But that's the same exchange as the office. Crap, what the hell do they want? I'm on vacation."

"Hello, this is Cade."

"Williams? Rupert Johnston."

The car swerved. "Ah, yes, sir, Mr. Johnston." Cade had no idea what this was about. His mind scrambled back to the screaming sirens and popping strobe lights. Yes, he was sure he had booked today on his calendar as being out of office.

"Williams, look, know you're out today but wanted to let you know of a change that hits you on Mundee mornin'." Johnston's accent came through clearer than ever. Perhaps it surfaced when his guard was down, or perhaps in talking to Cade, he had no one to impress. "See, you'll be workin' up here on seventeen from now on. Just didn' wan' you comin' to the wrong floor come Mundee."

Cade was shocked. "Ah, well, okay . . . ah, sir? Um, what, I mean, ah, how did this come up? I didn't know I'd be transferred anywhere."

"Well, don't worry about it, son. We need someone up here with skills like you got, and since you already been up here and know the lay o' the land and all. Well, we figured you would be the best. Congratulations, this is a step up," finished Johnston.

Cade was trying to wrap his head around this. "Oh, ah, thank you, sir. Um, sir? Are you sure I'm the right guy—I mean man—for the job? I mean, um, I was a little uncomfortable up there, what with all the sirens and flashing lights and stuff."

"Oh them? Oh don' worry yourself too much about them. We hardly ever have nothin' like that happen. And don' worry about those assholes none neither. They's a bunch a blowhards. You just git on up here come Mundee, and we'll be just fine."

Johnston hung up. Cade lowered the phone to his side and stared straight ahead, his face vacant. It was a moment before he realized he hadn't even hung up the call. He shook his head. "Great, I move from the Disney World of server farms over to a nuclear submarine at DEFCON 4. Wonderful."

He drew in some deep breaths to try to relax. He wasn't supposed to have to do deep breathing exercises or yoga or anything on vacation. Vacations were supposed to induce the relaxation without all the effort. A short time later, he pulled off the little back road of Highway 1 and followed the signs for Quantico Marine Corps Base. He was a little hungry and checked his phone, looking for a restaurant that had customer reviews that were slightly above death sentences. He followed the map up to a little house-looking place called Bella Café. There were several cars in the parking lot, which stood right next to a tacky place that sold outdoor pools. Inside though, the restaurant was lively. A guy playing guitar sat in the far corner and faded photos of customers littered the wood plank walls. Cade needed to wake up after all that driving. Mixed into the middle of the chalkboard menu full of gyro sandwiches, burgers, and chicken wraps, Cade's eye stopped. Lobster Bisque.

"Well, there it is. The reviews raved about the Lobster Bisque. How good could lobster bisque be in a place like this?" he laughed. "Ah, yes, ma'am, I'll have a cup of the bisque, and a large coffee please." She tilted her head at him for just a second, thinking it to be an odd combination of bisque and beverage.

"I've been on the road," he said, "just need a little caffeine." She smiled and disappeared into the back. Cade stood for a minute waiting to pay. The guy on the guitar wasn't half bad. The soft sounds were familiar, but he couldn't quite place it. He shut his eyes and tried to concentrate.

The Indigo Girls. Cade sometimes caught hell from his guy friends over how much he loved their music, but he always made it to their outdoor shows when they were in Atlanta. Sometimes it was at Chastain Park and other times at the Atlanta Botanical Gardens. It was always a good time though.

"Never heard a guy sing this song before," said a soft voice as a hand touched his shoulder. He was startled out of his fog as he looked down at the cute girl in glasses whose hand was withdrawing now. Her face was vaguely familiar, but he couldn't place her. She smiled and his mind raced, trying to place her before the embarrassment set in that he didn't know her name.

She grinned. "You always talk to yourself?"

"What? Oh, that . . ."

"Don't you work at Thoughtstorm?" she said. "You look so familiar." Relief washed over him. She didn't know his name either.

"Yeah. Yeah, hey, ah, I'm Cade, Cade Williams."

"I'm Alyssa, Alyssa McTee. I work down on six."

"Wow, how cool. What are you doing all the way up here?"

"Oh, I'm taking some time off." Alyssa beamed. It was like she was looking at an old friend she hadn't seen in a long time.

"You have family up here? I mean, you're on vacation. You didn't want to head down to the beach or something? Oh, sorry, I didn't mean this wouldn't be a good place to vacation or anything . . ." Cade backtracked.

"Oh no, no, it's okay. No, I'm not exactly vacationing here. I'm cruising all over the place. I'm just out seeing the country. I move from place to place each day." Alyssa oozed a newly found confidence. "The truth is, I took a leave of absence from work."

"Really? A leave of absence? And you're cruising around and just seeing the sights? And you're alone?" Cade secretly prayed that she was alone. "Hey, you want to join me?" he said as the bisque and coffee were handed through the window. "I was going to hang out for a little while with two things that go great together, bisque and coffee." He hoped his attempt at humor would come out sounding funnier than it was. He really sucked at talking to girls.

"Oh, no. I wouldn't want to join you," she said with a straight face.

Cade was a little taken aback. She looked at him, trying to stifle an outburst of laughter. "Why don't you join me instead," she said, pointing to her table, grinning ear to ear. Alyssa was rather pleased with herself next to Cade who looked like a lost pup.

"Oh," he laughed, "yeah, good one. Sure, I'll join you." Cade slid into the sturdy oak chair. His sleeve stuck to the stapled vinyl tablecloth that had played host to thousands of locals over the years.

Alyssa slid her wax-paper-lined plastic basket aside. "So how about you? What are you doing up here? You're not down at the beach or something?" she said, mocking through a toothy smile. "Is that where all the cool people go?"

"Okay, all right, I'm sorry. I didn't mean to insult you. No, I'm not at the beach or something either. I'm just off for a long weekend. A friend of mine is graduating from the FBI Academy up here. It was something I couldn't miss."

"Very cool," said Alyssa, looking genuinely impressed. "Man, I bet he's excited. Or, well, or she's excited. Which is it?"

"No, it's a he. He and I went to undergrad together. He's a great guy." Cade glanced out the window but saw nothing. "It's kind of funny thinking about it actually. I mean, he and I were in this fraternity together. He was kind of like a big brother to me. We had some fun times. And to think about him in the FBI . . ." There was something about Alyssa that was disarming. Cade was carrying on a perfectly normal conversation. And she was a girl. He wasn't stuttering and hadn't even knocked his drink over or anything. It was like she was just one of the guys. Not that she looked like a guy. No, she was pretty, and Cade knew it. But still, something about the way she carried herself. It made him feel like he'd known her for years.

The two talked and talked. The conversation went from Cade's time in college with Kyle to Alyssa talking about all the places she had been on this trip, the things she'd seen, the people she'd met.

"Okay," she said, "tell me the funniest story about you and Kyle in college." She nearly burst a blood vessel laughing at him, knowing she was putting him on the spot.

Cade laughed at her and thought about it for a second. He closed his eyes and then started laughing himself.

"Well, okay. I had this roommate that loved to play practical jokes on me. He was pretty good at it, I have to admit. So anyway, he'd brought these old inversion boots to school." Her head cocked to the side in confusion.

"Oh, you know, those kind of boots that lock around your ankle, and you use them to hang upside down from a bar or something," said Cade. "People use them to do hard-core sit-ups or to help stretch out their back and stuff like that."

Alyssa's giggle was infectious.

"Anyway," he smirked back at her, "so he brings these inversion boots to school so he could do sit-ups. See, the closets in the dorm just had a curtain across them, and the curtain rods were these heavy steel bars. So Jim, my roommate, hung upside down from his closet curtain rod bar thing and did all these sit-ups. So then, he convinces me to do a few sets." Cade paused, trying not to laugh as he told the story. "Anyway, I'm hanging there like an idiot doing these sit-ups. And the whole time, Jim is yelling, 'Come on, man, you can do it. Oh come on, is that all you got, you can do better than that!' and I'm doing all these sit-ups and it's starting to get impossible to do any more and I'm starting to laugh because Jim is yelling at me to keep going, and I can't even lift my own body weight up to reach the bar anymore."

Alyssa wiped tears from her eyes as she laughed.

"I mean, I can't even lift myself to get my feet off of the bar at this point. So Jim starts yelling, 'Is that it? Is that all you got? Come on, you can't even get yourself off of there?'" Cade stopped for a second. "So I'm laughing, I can't raise myself up, and Jim just walks out of the room."

"He walked out and left you there? Hanging upside down," she said, fingers to her eyes and laughing.

"Yeah, so then, a minute later, the door swings open and in walks Kyle with this straight face. He walks over to me and leans down and says, 'Ah, what seems to be the problem?' and I'm hanging there upside down and laughing and I can't get myself up. So then, from behind his back, Kyle pulls out this can of shaving cream. And sure enough, he starts hosing me down with the thing. By the time it was over, Kyle had emptied the shaving cream can all over me and was walking up and down the halls getting guys to come out and take a look."

Alyssa's deep laughter rocked her body, but not a sound escaped. "Oh my God. Guys are so mean to each other," she said. The two sat for a minute and let the laughter subside.

"And that was Kyle," Cade said, shaking his head back and forth.

Alyssa felt for the first time in her life that she was her own person. The two were confiding in each other like old friends, yet they were nearly total strangers. An hour later, Cade noticed that the sun was dropping on the horizon. "Oh man, what time is it?" he said, still laughing.

"Why, you have an important date?" she jabbed.

"No. Not exactly. Not with a girl anyway. I've got to go over and meet Kyle. Um, I was thinking . . ." Cade's confidence faded for a millisecond, then he got up the nerve and said, "Can I call you? I mean, I was thinking we could go do something." He tried to avoid the word *date*; it sounded so serious, like it was a commitment on her part or something.

"You mean we'd go out somewhere and have coffee and bisque?" Alyssa said, enjoying Cade's squirming.

"Yeah, coffee and bisque . . . when will you be back in town?"

"Yes, I'd love to. I have to be honest though, I don't know yet when I'll be back." She wasn't ready to stop torturing him yet. Her grin, however, betrayed her. She pulled out her phone, and the two exchanged numbers.

Cade left the place with a feeling that hadn't been with him in a long, long time. He had talked to Alyssa for over an hour. Both of them worked at the same office, yet not one word was spoken about work. Neither of them knew what the other even did for a living. The lighter-than-air feeling didn't stay with him long though as the thought of working up on seventeen soured his stomach. He shook his head. Still, as bad as that sounded, he could put up with anything if he could look forward to a date with Alyssa. Even if he didn't call it a date.

15

The entrance to the FBI Academy wasn't as daunting looking as he imagined. Still, there were lots of reinforced concrete barricades, and the Marine guards at the gate didn't help to diffuse the ominousness of the place. Automatic weapons clung to the soldiers' chests. Cade pulled up to the guard station and lowered the window.

"Yes, sir, how can I help you?"

Cade held out his driver's license. "My name's Cade Williams. I'm here for graduation at the Academy. I should be on the list." The guard glanced across the interior of the car, then at the driver's license. He handed the license to another guard who disappeared into the guard shack.

"Would you mind popping the trunk please, sir?" It was more of a command than a question. Once in the trunk, the guard waved a digital device around while another guard searched the underside of the car with a long mirrored pole. The guard came out of the guard house and handed Cade back his license.

"You're all clear, sir. If you proceed to the left up through the quad, sir, and follow the signs to the dormitories, you'll find the parking area."

Cade pulled away and called Kyle.

"Hey, man! I'm pulling away from the front gate."

"You're here? I'm just about back at the dorm now. I'll see you out front. You know where to go?"

Their reunion was prototypically male. The big high five and a quick hug as both men slapped each other on the back. They hadn't seen each other in months.

"Damn, man. You look lean!" said Cade. "Lean" was guy code for "muscular."

"Well, they run us pretty hard up here. I'm just glad it's over. Come on inside, I'll show you what your government dollars are paying for."

"They run you hard? Oh come on, what the hell is this?" said Cade, pounding Kyle on the bicep.

"Oh," said Kyle, "that's man, that's what that is."

They went up to the fourth floor and down the long corridor to Kyle's room. The dorms were a little more like hotel rooms than the dormitories he had pictured. The rooms were small, and there was no kitchen, but the carpeting and furniture had a distinctive Comfort Suites feel to it.

"Hey, nice hotel, man. You gonna take this furniture with you when you leave tomorrow?"

"Yeah, they'd love that. A trainee makes it into the FBI, all the way through training, then steals seventy-five dollars' worth of government furniture thereby creating the shortest FBI career in history."

"All right, so show me the campus. I want to see anywhere Jodie Foster ever walked. I want the behind-the-scenes tour, where only people with top secret security clearances can see, I want . . ."

"You want a good swift kick in the pants is what you want," said Kyle. "Come on, let's go have a look. I wouldn't want to deprive anyone of their Jodie Foster worshiping."

The campus wasn't all that different from a typical college campus. Several buildings scattered about, shaded by pine trees. There was a lot of open space and greenery, islands of pine straw, but overall, the place was immaculate. Not a fleck of paper or a cigarette butt anywhere.

"This place is clean enough to be a dang military base," said Cade.

"It is a military base, you nimrod."

"Yeah, yeah, I know. So where's the jogging trail through the woods where young agent trainee Starling flipped over that ropes course thing?"

"You are so sad. It's up here," said Kyle heading into the woods to the running trail where he had spent so much time. "Cade, now just so you understand a few things, Jodie Foster isn't actually in the FBI. You understand that, right? And you also understand that just because you're infatuated with her, doesn't mean she feels the same way. And you get the fact that she's gay, right? I mean, not that there's anything wrong with that."

"Oh shut up, she might like me. If she ever met me. And the whole 'gay' thing. I don't know about that. I think she's still making up her mind. Give her a chance, you'll see. She'll come around."

The two came across the wooded hilltop to the ropes course. Kyle said, "Okay, so there it is, the ropes course. Give me your phone; I'll video you flipping over that thing."

The short amount of daylight gave them just enough time to see a few sights and catch up with each other. Cade told Kyle about meeting a great new girl, but he didn't talk about what was really bothering him—the whole scene that unfolded this week at work, the panic, the firearm, none of it. It was like Cade didn't want to spoil a good time with his sob story. He decided not to mention it. They walked through several enclosed bridges that ran between buildings, what the bureau called "the habitrail" and saw Hogan's Alley, a small makeshift town where trainees practiced car chases and arrest procedures.

In a large open breezeway room there were couches scattered about. A number of photos and award plaques hung on the wall, and Kyle stopped at one in particular. It was a plaque that listed agents who had been killed while serving their country. He looked at it. Nothing was said. Nothing needed to be said. The two men knew what Kyle being in the FBI could mean, but they didn't want to acknowledge it. Kyle looked at Cade and said, "Man, we've known each other a long time. We've had a lot of good times together. I've known you since you were just a little punk. But we've also been though our share of stuff together." *Stuff* was the operative guy term for tough times. "So what is it you're not telling me?"

Cade looked a little surprised; his glance down at the floor didn't help much. "It's that obvious?"

"Sit down, tell me what's going on," Kyle's duty as a big brother was not over.

"Something happened at work . . ."

The two sat for several minutes as Cade retold the story. When he got to the part about the guys in suits, Kyle stopped him.

"Wait, these guys are dressed in business suits, up on a server floor? You're sure the guy had a weapon on his belt?"

"Yeah, well, pretty sure, yeah. I mean, you can't make this stuff up. I have no idea who these guys are," he said, thinking about what he was going to say next. Cade looked at his friend. "Kyle, there's something else. When I first walked onto the server floor, those guys were arguing, and I distinctly heard them mention a word that scared the shit out of me. It was the word 'Tucson.' They were arguing about Tucson. I know it sounds crazy, but they were arguing about it on the morning of the bombing at that Little League field."

Kyle's stern look would serve him well in the FBI. "Tucson? We've been studying the bombings. At first they didn't share all the info with us, but in the last couple of weeks, our security clearances came through, and they told us everything. I can't talk about much of it."

Cade slumped back on the couch. He could tell there was a lot more Kyle knew about the Tucson bombings that he wanted to say.

"I don't know what to make of it," said Kyle. "You work for an e-mail service provider. There should never be a time when sirens sound and men concealing firearms pour onto the server room floor. But based on how you describe those guys, it would seem like government men of some type. Nothing else makes sense. I have no idea which agency it would be, but I don't like the sound of it. And you say that on another occasion you put masking tape across the camera lens on the webcam on your laptop," Kyle spoke as if assembling a puzzle, "and the next day, the tape was gone? The two might not be connected, but it certainly sounds like someone in that company is watching you, or maybe watching everybody, I don't know." After a few moments of protracted silence, Kyle said, "I know you, Cade, I know you. You don't look good. Tell me what you're thinking." Kyle's newly acquired interview techniques had gone into full swing.

Cade glanced down again and leaned his elbows on his knees.

"What if my company is doing something wrong? I mean really wrong. What if they're involved in something really illegal, and I get caught up in the middle of it?"

"You think there's some connection between these guys and the bombing in Tucson? Cade, look at me"—he was serious now—"I don't know what the hell is going on at your office, but one thing they've taught us here is to go with our instincts. I don't care how farfetched it sounds. If your gut tells you something is wrong, don't ignore it. You're going to have to find out though. Before you get caught in the middle of something bad, you're going to have to find out."

Cade stared straight ahead, like he was looking right through the wall to the other side. "Yeah, I know. I know."

16

In the morning sun, nothing seemed as bleak as it had the previous night talking with Kyle. Good old Cool Mac. With Kyle busying for the morning's graduation ceremony, Cade drove back by the Bella Café only to find they weren't open for breakfast. He grabbed a bite to eat at a little place at the corner of Potomac and Broadway and then headed over to the FBI auditorium. Parking was tight, but once inside the auditorium, Cade had no trouble finding a seat. The auditorium held exactly one thousand and one people. Apparently, J. Edgar Hoover had specified when it was built that it was to accommodate "over one thousand people."

Cade sat as close to the front as he could get. Not only did he want to see Kyle walk across the stage to receive his badge and credentials, but the stage of the auditorium itself had also been graced by Jodie Foster.

Graduating from undergrad was a great thing, but this was on a whole different scale. It was a huge accomplishment. Less than 1 percent of applicants are accepted into the FBI. And some of those don't make it through training. He was really excited for Kyle. Cade glanced around at all the families finding their way to seats. For the first time it occurred to him that he was the only person here who came to see Kyle. Kyle's mom had passed during childbirth. Kyle's dad had been a firefighter. Being a single parent working as a firefighter had not been easy for John MacKerron. The work schedule was brutal. He'd work a twenty-four-hour shift and then have the next two to three days off. That meant Kyle's aunt had to step up to be mom-for-a-day, as she called it.

Kyle was shuffled between houses just like some of his friends whose parents were divorced. One day, Cade happened to be in Kyle's dorm room when someone knocked on the door. He remembered it like it was yesterday. A knock on the door was somewhat strange in the dorm because no one ever knocked. Kyle yelled, "Come in," but the knock repeated itself. Kyle yelled again, but there was no response. He then got up and opened the door. A campus police officer was standing there, his drill-sergeant-style hat in his hands. The guy was so tall it looked like he'd hit his head on the top of the doorframe if he tried to walk in. "Are you Kyle MacKerron?" Kyle stood there, not knowing if he was in trouble or if it were something much worse.

"Yes, sir."

The officer tilted his head down slightly, stepped in, and closed the door behind him. "Son, you might want to sit down." But Kyle's feet were glued to the floor. "Son, I'm sorry to report that there's been an accident. It's your father. He's been killed, apparently in the line of duty. I'm sorry . . ."

Even Cade couldn't remember what else was said after that. The officer was speaking, but the words coming out of his mouth were not audible, as though they'd been eaten in midair. For the first time, for the only time, Cade watched his friend crumple to the ground and cry.

The funeral was unlike anything Cade had ever witnessed. Six or seven hundred firefighters from communities all over the state—and even a few from the other side of the country—attended. Firefighters in full dress uniform lined the route all the way from the church to the cemetery. Apparently, Mr. MacKerron had become trapped inside a collapsing warehouse fire. The roof above him caved in, and he had suffered a few broken ribs. His partner was knocked to the ground, unconscious. In what must have been excruciating pain, MacKerron wedged the heavy timber off of his partner, axed his way through the exterior wall of the building, and pushed his partner out into the arms of other firefighters. Then, the interior of the building collapsed. Kyle's dad was gone, but not before saving one last life.

It wasn't long before the auditorium was almost full. The graduating class of agent trainees all walked in together. Seventeen men and three women all in their Sunday best occupied the front two rows. The place was a collection of dark navy business suits. The stage itself wasn't dissimilar to so many others. Huge, long drapes hung across, and a lectern stood front and center with the FBI emblem blazing in front. There were four empty chairs that stood just off to the right. A few minutes later, a man with wiry salt-and-pepper hair in a navy business suit walked out.

"Folks, thanks for being here today. At the FBI, we are a big family, and we're glad to see you all, our extended family, here. Today marks a very important moment, the graduation of twenty outstanding agent trainees. These young men and women will go out into the world and make this country a better place. We owe them a debt of gratitude." He began clapping, which cascaded throughout the auditorium. "So before we get started, let me make an announcement. As I look around, I see several families with young children, so I do need to go over the rules of what to do if your child has an outburst. This is the Federal Bureau of Investigation. This is a very solemn occasion, and we have rules here. Under the guidance of Stephen Latent, the director of the FBI, the rules regarding crying children are as follows." He removed a piece of paper from his coat pocket, unfolded it, and began to read, "If you have a crying child, please, please, please, whatever you do . . . do not move from your seat." He paused for effect and looked up over his glasses. "You are not allowed to remove crying children!" The grin on his face was contagious and elicited laughter. "Folks, the director has four young boys of his own—he understands family, and he understands what an important occasion this is for you. He also knows many of you have travelled long distances to be here, so if your child cries, don't worry about it. We don't want you to miss this. This is something you'll never forget."

The tone for the ceremony had been set. Yes, this might be a solemn occasion, but they were going to have some fun with it too. Director Latent walked out, and after talking about the training and how proud they were of these graduates, the names began to be read. Each trainee walked singly to the stage where the director awarded them their badge and credentials. This was followed by a brief photo opportunity on the stage with the director, the trainee, and family. When Kyle's name was called, Cade knew Kyle would be thinking about his father, wishing he was there.

After the ceremony, Cade walked up to Kyle and shook his hand, a firm, vise-like grip, and looking directly into his eyes said, "Kyle, your dad would be really proud of you right now." Kyle smiled as he fought hard against his emotions.

"Thanks, man. Thanks for being here."

Back at the dorms, the last of Kyle's bags were thrown into his over-packed car. Kyle's new duty station in San Diego would put him to work in the bank robbery division just five days from today.

"Come on, I've got one more thing to do before I leave this place," said Kyle.

They walked across campus to a building they had not toured the previous day. Past a small gift shop where trainees and a few guests were buying FBI paraphernalia, they descended a wide set of stairs underneath a sign that read "Armory." They were going to check out Kyle's firearm for the very last time. Cade hadn't even thought about it. But this whole time, Kyle had been just a trainee. Trainees used firearms daily here, but they were not permitted to carry them. It wasn't until they had been awarded their FBI credentials that they became federal agents. It was only now that they were authorized to carry their weapons.

"Oh, by the way," said Kyle, "Jodie Foster walked through the middle of that room in the movie." Cade looked across the hall into the large room. It was full of what appeared to be DEA agent-trainees. They were dressed in black fatigues, distinguishing them from the gray sweats worn by FBI trainees. The trainees stood at long tables, cleaning their firearms before checking them back in to the armory. Chatter pervaded the room.

"Hey, wait a minute," said Cade. "In the movie, she walked right through this room like she had come from some other hallway or something. There's nothing over there but a solid wall. They faked it."

Cade stood off to the side of the hallway while Kyle stood in line with a few other new agents at the armory window. Watching them closely, he noticed something about the stone-cold look in their faces. They were about to walk out of there as real federal agents. From this moment forward, if anything happened right in front of them, they were expected to react. Hell, Kyle could be driving to his duty station at the San Diego field office and step into the middle of a robbery in a McDonald's. He would have to react; he was responsible now. This was for real, and these guys knew it.

17

Jana Baker had been on the FBI's counterterrorism squad for just a few months. The truth was, she was a rookie, fresh out of Quantico. Atlanta was a prized assignment to new trainees, and she was excited beyond words to be there. The city was vibrant, clean, and a hell of a lot more affordable than other places. There were no easy assignments in the FBI, but some duty stations were worse than others. Detroit was dreaded. And even New York City, which carried so much appeal, was so expensive that agents routinely lived ninety minutes away. No, Atlanta was a prize. It beat the hell out of Brownsville, Texas, that's for sure.

A multi-year stack of transfer requests hung over the Atlanta field office. But this particular field office was short on young female agents. Some surveillance roles desperately needed a female to play the part. As an agent on the counterterrorism squad, she spent much of her time assigned to track suspected terrorists, or those that might sponsor them. Although the bureau would never have said it publicly, they not only needed a female, they needed a young, attractive female to fit into some undercover assignments.

Jana hadn't thought of this type of work while in college, but she inadvertently created the perfect background for just such a career. Her major in accounting gave her a decided advantage over other applicants. She spoke fluent Spanish after years of high school and college classes. And she was a marathon runner; the bureau loved athletic applicants. After all, this was the FBI, not some charm school.

Even though she never considered a career in federal law enforcement, the truth was, she was exhilarated by it. Counterterrorism was the pinnacle unit within the bureau, and she wasn't about to screw it up. Just after she arrived in Atlanta, the office had received a call from a Homeland Security agent who interviewed a Saudi Arabian citizen named Waseem Jarrah as he entered the country in New York. He wasn't on a watch list, but the agent didn't like some of the answers to questions he provided. There was nothing illegal about his entry, and they had no choice but to release him from the customs holding area at La Guardia. The agent called the FBI because of what he called "a hunch." The bureau had made a few mistakes of late in not following up on potential terror leads and so had tightened its stance on suspicious persons.

New agents typically work with a senior trainer, but Jana was ready to be out on her own, particularly where surveillance was concerned. Waseem Jarrah was her first solo assignment. She was the one to field the call from Homeland Security, and since this suspect was a "no-priority," her shift supervisor gave her the green light. After all, he figured this would be a good case for a rookie to start on. He told her he wanted solid background work. Where did Jarrah come from? What was his real name? Who were his associates? Where was he going? Who was he meeting with? Arriving from Saudi Arabia on an Air Emirates flight didn't exactly win him points with Homeland Security. It would be Jana's job to fill in the blanks.

The high sun created a glare across the closely mowed grass of the baseball field. She watched the men as they stood on the pitcher's mound facing each other. Baker looked for anything to exchange hands and needed to find out who this Jamaican-looking male was, his neck draped in long dreadlocks. As she slipped the small earphones over her head, she looked more like she was listening to music than working a terrorist suspect. Aiming the laser mic, she strained to hear the conversation through her headphones. The light breeze caused some distortion, but she double checked and found the mic was working properly. She didn't want to return to the office and have nothing to show for it. The camera shutter discharged once, twice, then several times in rapid succession. The two men paid her no attention. She was too far away. The breeze eased, and the conversation became clear in the headset.

". . . and der ain' gonna be no more o' dis bullshit, mon. You got me?" said the tall Rastafarian.

"No bullshit?" replied Waseem Jarrah. "What the hell are you talking about? Your money is being used for exactly what we said it would be. You wanted people to die? People are dying. You wanted people to panic; people are panicking. The eleventh strike of our jihad happened yesterday morning. Perhaps you've heard about it?" Waseem said, his impatience beginning to boil. The Tucson bombing had been splashed across every news outlet in the country. "And something else. I told you we exemplify precision. No one can hit like this. Eleven events in eleven months. Precision. And did you notice the timing of the events? They are cycling down," needled Waseem. "Each occurring one day sooner than the last. These pigs will panic once they figure that out."

Jana's heart leapt into her throat. She could barely believe what she was hearing.

"Oh. So de timin' of de bombin's goin' to put de fear o' God in dem, heh?" replied Bastian, pounding a finger into Waseem's chest.

"Back off me, motherfucker. Not only does each bombing happen one day closer than the last, they happen one hour, one minute, and one second earlier than the last. Just watch and see. The media will get hold of that piece of information, and it will spread like a wave of panic across this armpit of a country. You just wait. They'll have a countdown to the next bombing. Everyone will know exactly when it will happen, but no one will know where. The pigs will be so scared, they won't even leave their houses. Commerce will stop, and commerce is what moves the beast."

But the Jamaican, Bastian, was not impressed. "I was lookin' far a little bigger bang for de buck, mon." His anger was apparent. "Your timin' of little bombs, heh? We be up to one million dollars US. Dat's a lot of green. Could buy me a lot o' ganja for dat mon," he said. "I tol' your man dat I was lookin' for revenge in a beeg way."

In the excitement, Agent Baker strained to hear over her heavy breathing. "Holy Christ!" she said out loud, quickly stopping herself, afraid her excitement would be on the recording. It was like adrenaline mixed with crack cocaine and sex all wrapped up into one euphoria. She almost didn't know what to do.

"And where de hell is Rashid, anyway?" continued Bastian.

"Rashid"—Waseem yawned—"ah, yes, Rashid." Waseem squinted across into right field. "Well, Rashid is the reason you are talking to me right now, isn't it?"

"Tell me what I don't know, mon," said Bastian. "Where de hell is he? I tol' him de bank was gonna run dry unless he put me onto the sons o' bitches what could make a decision. I suppose dat's you? Are you Meestah Beeg Shot? I was sick a talkin' to a message delivery ser-veece. But de fact is, I don' truss you, mon. You don' look like you know your ass from a hole in de wall."

Waseem's glare pierced. "Rashid will not be joining us." The words ricocheted out of his mouth like spitfire. "As these pagan-worshiping Christians would say, Rashid received his 'calling.' We invited him to go to a little town in the southwest. A little place called Tucson. He performed admirably. However, his usefulness is now scattered across a Little League ball field, not unlike this one."

Jana's camera clicked repeatedly as she struggled against shaking hands.

Bastian's only response was a glare. His earlier contact, Rashid, was dead. He knew he was now dealing with what he was looking for: a decision maker. Having slowly given chunks of money to the terrorist organization, he had worked his way up to the level of the real players, the ones who controlled the smaller terror cells that had spread across the United States like a cancer seeding itself in an unknowing body—quiet, patient, then deadly.

18

Cade got into work early on Monday. As much as he dreaded it, he knew today was D-Day. It was time to start working on the seventeenth floor, what he had not-so-affectionately began to call "Red October," named after the famed Russian submarine movie. He grabbed a cardboard box from the copy room and emptied his desk contents, not that there was that much to grab.

Whitmore walked over but stopped short. "What the . . . ? What are you doing? Wait a minute, there's no way they fired you! Well, you can just kiss my gay white ass if they think they can fire you! You know, I'm so sick of this crap!"

Cade held up his hands, already laughing. Just like old Whitmore to get all spun up about something that he didn't yet understand.

"No, no. Dude, relax. I'm not fired." Cade's scrunched face foretold that whatever he was about to say, he wasn't happy about. "I've been moved upstairs. I've got to go work on DEFCON 4 up on seventeen. I guess you can tell I'm thrilled about it."

"Seventeen? What the hell do they want with you up there?" The heavy emphasis made it sound like Cade was not "upper-floor" material. "I mean, not that you're not good enough or something. You know, I mean I'm sure they think you're good at your job and all, I just meant . . ."

"Whitmore, Whitmore, Whitmore. Slow down there, Mr. McBacktracker. I'm sure they think I'm okay at my job. No, that's not it. I just got called up there last week, and they were in a big mess. But honestly, I don't know why they want me. I didn't fix anything. It was like, I found out what was going wrong, but before I could do anything about it, the e-mail send job was over anyway, and they sent me out."

Whitmore said, "So what was the big deal they couldn't fix themselves? What, was it some big important e-mail or something?"

Cade didn't want to say too much, but he also hated being evasive. "Oh, I don't know. I'm sure it was some critical e-mail job that alerted customers to the 5 percent off sale at Penney's or something. I never even saw the e-mail content. I don't know what happened. Whoever normally worked up there wasn't around, so they came and grabbed me. Now that I think about it, I wonder what happened to the other guy."

"Well, if you find a big box up there full of body parts, let me know; I'll help you move it," said Whitmore grinning.

"Hey, maybe we can get together for lunch. I don't know about today, but maybe tomorrow if things settle down."

In the elevator, Cade wondered if his keycard would give him access to that floor. He swiped it, and to his surprise, the button for seventeen lit up, and the doors closed. *Hmm. Must have gotten me cleared onto the floor.* Cade's keycard unlocked the door from the hallway as well. He went ahead and set his box on an empty cube, looking around for Mr. Johnston.

An icy voice walked up behind him—"Hey, Radio Shack, over this way"—and continued on, never glancing at Cade. It was the William-Macy-looking guy. A slight thump of irritation registered in Cade's gut. He didn't like this guy, nor did he like being called "Radio Shack," like he was just some tech nerd who had forgotten to wear his pocket protector today. Cade followed but had to catch up because William Macy was walking so fast. They walked out onto the server floor and back towards the same desk he'd been seated at last week during the Red October battle-stations alert. Fortunately, this morning, the lighting was much better, and no red strobes pulsed overhead.

Macy didn't slow his stride but instead walked right by the desk and tapped it. He disappeared down the server rows and was gone.

Cade stopped at the desk, box still in hand and mumbled, "What an asshole."

"I heard that," bellowed Macy's voice from somewhere down the server rows.

"Good God," said Cade very softly. "The guy can hear better than Jesus."

He unloaded the box and placed his coffee thermos on the desk along with his jar of pens and a few notepads. He hesitated to lay out his Snoopy mouse pad, but then thought, *Screw them, Snoopy stays.* His headphones went into the top drawer, but he wasn't too sure what the policy would be up here about listening to music while you worked. *Perhaps instead of listening to music, we have to listen to old speeches of Der Fuehrer.*

Rupert Johnston walked in, leaned over Cade's desk, and said, "Gimme ten, then come into my office."

Johnston's office was brighter than the rest of the dark interior space; the morning light poured in with a soft hue. Cade stood at the door, not sure if it was okay to just walk in or if there would be some Doberman that would pounce. Johnston was busy banging away on his laptop, using the hunt-and-peck method of typing. Long pointer fingers flew in angry succession across the keys as if they were trying to poke someone's eye out. Cade gazed out the window and noticed a blurry Stone Mountain off in the distance. He squinted into the blur, but it seemed like everything out of Johnston's windows was hazy and hard to focus on.

Johnston stopped typing and extended his hand towards a chair. Cade spoke first. "Sir, are the windows dirty or something? Everything looks so blurry, like there's something on the window."

Johnston blurted out, "Countermeasure film. Blocks eavesdroppers and other such assholes from pointin' a laser mic at the winder and listen'n' in to what we're sayin'."

Cade stared at him like his head had just spun around 360 degrees.

Johnston glared back. "Look, son, it's like this. Up here on seventeen, this is what we call the federal zone. We have customers that are either govermints, like state, ceety, or even the fed'ral govermint, or, they's big cumpnees like banks and such that want their data protected real special-like. You understan', son?"

"Yes, sir." Cade was tiring of the apprehension that weighed upon his chest over the last three days. He couldn't hold it in any longer. "Sir, what I don't understand is, well . . . sir, what happened when I was up here last week? What was all of that?" There it was. He said it. It was out on the table now.

It was clear as Johnston shifted in his seat and cleared his throat that he was uncomfortable being cornered. *Guess somebody would rather I hadn't asked.*

"Son, sometimes, it's jest better ta know when it's time to ask questions and when ya should jest git on with her and git her done." He wasn't angry as Cade had expected. The tone was more fatherly than anything else. Cade had a strong feeling that there was more Johnston wanted to say, but he wasn't going to.

Cade had pressed enough for one day and let the subject die. But he wanted to leave the room on a good footing with his new boss, asshole or not. There was a picture frame with Johnston holding a heavily antlered deer head. He was just about to comment on it when the set of framed diplomas beside it made him do a double take. He read and reread the text on each. The one on the left read

Massachusetts Institute of Technology—the one on the right, Harvard University.

"Sir, you went to MIT and got an MBA at Harvard?" The diplomas were as clear as day. Cade couldn't believe what he was seeing.

Johnston glanced out the corner of his eye and let out a long sigh. "Yes, dammit. I went to MIT and Harvard. Me an' my southern drawl went up to fancy-pants Harvard and showed them northern boys what a bunch of sissies they was. Jes cause a man's got a drawl don' make him a fool. Folks up there could hardly understan' what I was sayin'." He almost smiled.

When Cade sat down at his desk, he thought about the last thing Kyle told him over their weekend together—*you've got to find out what was going on during that e-mail job*. He shuddered at the thought of being caught prying into anything he wasn't supposed to. But under the pretense of being the new server guy, and since server guys were troubleshooters and always had to know what was going on during a problem, he took it as his ticket to start snooping.

19

C
ade was curious to see what network access he'd been given in his new role. He logged into the administrative console and started by doing his normal duties. He checked server status, looked for any alerts that had been posted, and generally made sure things on the server floor were running on par. An hour later, however, he could wait no longer. He accessed the server log files, searching for the e-mail job that seemed to nearly cause the company to explode. Scanning through hundreds of lines of code, he began to see the code pattern he'd noticed earlier. There was a spike of server activity that occurred on a repeated, timed basis. It was the strangest thing he'd ever seen. Digging further, he noticed that during each interval, the server was calling for a set of code to execute. Cade looked up and down, but the code it was calling was nowhere to be found.

"What in the hell are they calling?" he said. Then, he spotted it. It was a code snippet sending calls to an outside server. That was highly unusual. The servers never communicated outside of the Thoughtstorm building. That was a breach of security protocols.

This code then received something in return, and that something was getting inserted into the body of the e-mails. But what? This was completely outside the scope of what an e-mail server was designed to do. No wonder the server nearly blew up. What kind of assholes try to execute code then inject it into an e-mail right before it sends? He'd have to find out what was being injected into the body of those e-mails. But he also knew that the first thing Kyle would ask was where they were calling the code from. Cade heard footsteps and looked over his shoulder. He closed out of his computer screens and pretended to be reviewing server status. Someone was coming.

20

Baker sat motionless, her mouth hanging open, almost not wanting to believe what she had just heard. It would have been like staring at the series of numbers on a winning lottery ticket, reading them over and over. The men were wrapping up their conversation and would soon split up. She had to act. The question was, which one should she follow? The initial assignment was to follow Waseem Jarrah, but that was before the quiet game of intramural flag football turned into the Super Bowl. They would both be considered targets of the highest priority.

Her hand dashed into the bag to grab her phone. "This would be so much quicker with a radio." But she knew that typical one-man stakeout assignments had no need for instant communications.

On the other end of the line, a male voice answered, "FBI, Agent Clemente."

Jana blurted out, "Clemente, this is Agent Baker."

"Give me the SAC."

"Baker, the Special Agent in Charge is on a call with Washington right now . . ."

"Clemente, this is priority level 4! I don't care who he's talking to! Yank him out of there right now!"

"Good Christ, Baker, hold the line."

A few moments later, SAC David Stark came on the line. "Priority level 4, my ass. What the hell is it, Baker? You better not have gotten me off that call to discuss knitting patterns."

"Sir, I just recorded a convo with Waseem Jarrah, the target level six you assigned me to. Jarrah and another man just discussed the funding of the terror cell that's apparently responsible for the string of bombings. They just talked about Tucson! The targets are at my twelve o'clock right now!"

"Jesus Christ," said Stark. "Okay, calm down, Baker. You're sure of what you heard?"

"That's an affirmative, sir. Sir, they're about to split up. Who do I follow? Oh, shit, they're separating!"

"All right, all right. So you're on top of Jarrah's current whereabouts? You know where he's living, his daily habits, affirm?" replied Stark.

"Yes, sir, I've been on him several days." Jana was out of breath, still holding the camera's zoom lens in focus, shutter banging away.

"Follow the second target. We need full cover on him. We at least know where Jarrah lives. We can find him again. What's your location? I'm sending a flash team to you right now."

Stark began yelling over his shoulder, "Clemente! Get your ass in here! Put Blue Team on a code 4 right now! Get them moving, we'll send them a target package en route."

"Baker, give me your twenty."

He scribbled the address of the ball field on a pad as fast as he could.

"All right, Baker, stay with target number two. Turn on the ping. And, Baker, don't lose him." His voice echoed in a firm directive, but Jana could hear the faint sound of hope. *Jesus Christ*, she thought, *if I'm right, this will be the FBI's highest priority, and the Atlanta field office will be right in the center of it.*

Jana forced the laser mic and camera back into the bag and flipped to the app on her phone that the bureau referred to as simply "the ping." Once activated, all agents deployed to the scene would be able to track her exact location.

Without looking too suspicious, she grabbed the blanket, not bothering to brush off the clippings of dead grass, and draped it across her shoulder bag. She slid her sunglasses on and watched as the Jamaican exited the first base side of the field. Bastian Mokolo was covering a lot of ground, and within moments, he would disappear into the shuffling streets of Little Five Points and be gone. She ducked behind a row of trees, hoping they would keep her just out of sight, and began to sprint. Her mind raced; her adrenaline surged. But Bastian dropped out of view.

21

Cade tried to ignore the approaching footsteps, not wanting to look suspicious. It was William Macy and his intimidating glare. Cade knew he was about to receive a speech.

"Williams, you have one job here. And that's to make sure my servers stay up. I want you monitoring things closely. This is the federal zone, and what we do here is important. Oh, and one other thing. Today at three p.m. I've got an e-mail job going out. It's top priority. It's to receive priority bandwidth across the system, you understand me?"

"Yes, sir. Ah, sir, I just, ah, I don't know, well"—Cade stumbled to find the words—"I don't know what to call you, sir."

William Macy's perfect Windsor knot looked like it would choke him.

"I'm no one." He began to walk off. "I'm a ghost, that's all you need to know."

After Macy left, and Cade was certain he was out of earshot, he again muttered, "What an asshole." Cade's phone vibrated in his pocket. It was his father.

"Hey, Dad," said Cade in a voice devoid of enthusiasm.

"Cade! Hey, glad to catch you. So, how are things going at work?"

Cade looked around to make sure no one was listening. The floor was deserted. It was like he no longer had coworkers, just the sound of server fans running in the background. "Well, Dad, it's going okay, I guess."

"Hey, you don't sound so good. Is anything wrong?" Cal winced, wondering if it was just his phone call that was upsetting Cade.

"Well, no, not really. Things here have changed. I've moved upstairs."

"Isn't that a promotion? That sounds great," said Cal.

"Yeah. Kind of. I'm not so sure it's a promotion I want though. Kind of hard to talk about right now."

"Cade, listen. I know you're busy. I need to see you. There's . . . there's some things we need to talk about." There was silence on the phone. "And it can't wait. Can I meet you for lunch?" Cade thought for a moment. "Sure, Dad." He didn't want to see his dad, but he had run out of excuses.

An hour later, Cade crossed Peachtree in between red lights. It was another busy Monday in Buckhead. On the other side of the six-lane thoroughfare, Cade slowed his pace and glanced at the tall buildings to his left and at all the people. They were moving from place to place, just like any normal day, busying themselves with their various concerns. But Cade didn't feel normal. There was a sick feeling in his gut. He was concerned something was dangerously wrong at work and that something was wrong with his dad.

Cal Williams walked through the heavy wooden front doors of Fado and found Cade waiting in a booth. A waitress breezed by, heading for another table carrying a platter of four Guinness, their thick creamy heads holding firm. The heavy oak table was still wet from being wiped down after the last customer. Cal slid across the slick, fake-leather booth seat and smiled at his only son. The silence was awkward, and they both knew it.

"Cade, I'm really glad to see you. Listen, I know you don't want to be here, and I know we haven't gotten on in the best way in recent years."

Cade didn't speak; he just looked his father in the eye. That was one thing his father had instilled upon him—you look a man in the eyes.

"I want you to know I love you."

The same sinking feeling that Cade had when his father was about to be deployed rushed back. "Dad, you don't have to say that. I know that." Cade had not wanted to toss an "I love you" back.

Cal's mouth hung open like words were trying to come out, but no breath would move them. His eyes darted back and forth; he was fidgety, strangely fidgety. Just before he spoke, Cade blurted, "Are you drinking again?"

There it was. It was out like an eleven-hundred-pound elephant no one wanted to talk about.

Cal's eyes snapped to Cade's, full of regret. They misted over, but he held his emotions in check. Then Cal uttered, "No, son, no. I'm not drinking again. I lost everything dear to me doing that . . ."

Cade lashed out, "Except your goddamn flying."

Cal almost allowed irritation to gush out of him, but stopped himself, knowing Cade was right. He had lost his wife and the love of his son over his constant deployments and drinking, but he had not lost his military pilot's wings.

"Son, you're right. You're right about everything. I lost your mom, I lost you . . . I guess I ran away from you two. Ran away and just jumped into a plane and never came back. I know these are just words to you, but I'm sorry. I mean that, I'm sorry." This time, Cal's voice cracked.

In his lifetime, Cade had never seen his father cry.

"Is that what you came here to tell me? Well, you've said it."

A waitress stopped dead in her tracks. She could see this was no time to suggest an appetizer of jalapeño cheese poppers. As she retreated, Cal looked at Cade.

"No, son, that's not what I came here to say." Silence was as thick as the head on a Guinness. "Cade, I have cancer."

22

Jana broke into a sprint, rounded a corner, and accidentally smashed into a teenager, knocking him to the ground. She stumbled but didn't fall. "Sorry!" She charged across the intersection, knowing that if she didn't get a clear line of sight, the Jamaican subject would be lost forever. Baker cleared the next block and ducked behind the corner of a building, panting like the bulls of Pamplona. Jana was in excellent shape, but the enormous anxiety took its toll as adrenaline surged throughout her body. She glanced around the corner and saw nothing. He was nowhere. People milled about, walking in and out of shops and sitting at outdoor cafes where the bright sun melted into them. The Jamaican's clothing and hair made it easy for him to disappear into the sea of body piercings and dreadlocks.

Up at the next block, she looked across the street into the reflection in the store windows. A man with dreadlocks was moving down the sidewalk. The reflection was blurry. Was it him? She rounded the corner but kept her glance downward, not wanting him to turn and see her. As she closed in, it was still too hard to tell. The hair . . . his body size . . . the shirt! *Shit, that's him!* She wasn't sure if she was breathing so hard due to the sprinting or due to the adrenaline. The Jamaican was on a cellphone as he crossed the street and disappeared over the hill just outside an outdoor patio full of people at a Mexican restaurant.

Baker had to close ground. She burst forward, knowing the hill would shield her from his vision. Losing sight of him again wasn't an option. She glanced behind her, hoping to see a bureau car or van approaching.

"Where the hell are those guys?" As she rounded the top of the sidewalk, a sizzling hot plate was being delivered to a table next to the sidewalk. Steam rose from the metal as it scorched the razor-thin fajita meat. The Jamaican was gone. It was like he had vanished. A white work van with a ladder on its roof drove down the street.

"Where the hell did he go?" Baker looked left and right, focusing on anything she could see. Then she turned to a man sitting alone at the sidewalk table, his eyes wide at the sizzling fajitas he was about to lay into.

"Excuse me, did you see a big black guy with dreadlocks just come by here?"

"You mean a Jamaican-looking guy?" he said, rather interested in her athletic, trim build.

"Yes!" She paused, trying to not sound as excited as a nine-year-old schoolgirl at a sleepover. "Yes, did you see where he went?" She reached in her jeans pocket to pull out her credentials wallet. "He, ah, he dropped his wallet, and I want to give it back to him."

"Oh, bummer, the dude got in a van right there, man," he said, still chewing the fajitas. Baker's eyes shot down the street. "Say, you wouldn't want a bite to eat or anything, would you? You know, I mean, I got all this food and stuff and, you know, maybe you want to eat."

Baker spun around in a frantic search; that van could be blocks away by now. She needed a car, and she needed one right this second. She looked back at the man, his tie-dyed shirt muted against the backdrop of steam rising from the plate of searing food.

"FBI. I need your car. I need your car right now," she demanded, speaking through clenched teeth, credentials in front of her.

"Holy crap, man, you mean like FBI, FBI? No way." He gazed at the identity card and badge; it was the only thing that could draw his attention away from staring at her body.

Jana pocketed the credentials. "Your car," she said with her hand extended. "Where's your car? Right now, goddammit," she repeated, grabbing his shoulder. "Give me your keys. Which one is it?"

His mouth hung open, still full of food. "Right there, man," he said, pointing to a black Volkswagen Beetle. He fished the keys from his pocket, dropped them on the ground, then hit his head on the table bending over to pick them up.

"Ow! Shit, man," he said with one hand on his head and one handing over the keys. Jana snatched them and bolted for the car.

"A Beetle, that figures," she said, revving the engine. She threw the car in gear and tore off, her right hand knocking down the little plastic flower affixed to the dash.

The man stood up, his napkin dropping to the ground as he watched his baby disappear.

Jana gunned the accelerator in a frantic dash to catch the van, only guessing where it might have headed. She flew down Euclid Avenue past Hurt Street and blew a red light at fifty miles per hour. *They can give me a ticket if I don't die.* She flew past the last stretch of Inman Park, her head wrenching in all directions as she scanned for the white van. The light at Randolph Street was red, and she slammed on the brakes, skidding to a halt.

A blur of white crossed her vision and then disappeared. She threw the steering wheel to the right and blasted out into traffic. A Honda Accord locked its brakes, and a minivan screeched to the left to avoid crashing into the Honda. Baker's foot jammed the accelerator to the floor. It was the van. She had to close the huge gap between them. The Beetle just wasn't quick enough.

"Damn hippie car!" she screamed as the engine whined in complaint.

The gap was closing, and Jana started to catch her breath. She glanced in the rearview mirror, desperate to see the arrival of her backup, but knew it was a lot to ask for field agents to close in on her tracking device so quickly.

The van headed over Freedom Parkway and continued up Randolph. She was now close enough to the van to maintain a safe distance without being detected. As they neared Ponce de Leon Avenue, the van slowed and jerked to the right.

Baker rounded the corner and took note of a sign that said "Ponce City Market." The Beetle moved slowly as she watched the van turn into the construction entrance of Atlanta's sprawling City Hall East building complex, a massive six-story brick building built decades earlier and formerly housing much of the Atlanta city government. The building had fallen into disrepair in recent years and was being redeveloped. The van crunched slowly across the gravel parking area, past a huge pile of broken concrete at least thirty feet high, and came to a stop at the edge of the building.

Baker froze. *What the hell do I do now?* She had to get her car out of sight. Ponce de Leon was bustling with six lanes of traffic. All she could do was pull the car up on the sidewalk, just out of the van's view. But just as she popped the driver's door open, she jerked it back as a car in the right lane careened past, nearly tearing it off. Once the lane was clear, she jumped out of the car and ran up to the corner of the building, being sure to stay out of the van's field of view. She pushed open a rusted metal door into the cavernous brick monstrosity. The door scraped against the buildup of grit on the cement floor.

Inside, there was a broken window and a set of stairs. This was obviously an exit stairwell. A breeze blew across the jagged edges of broken glass. More glass crunched under her feet as she peered out the window. The crunching of glass echoed in the vacant cement stairwell. Jana felt so alone; the sheer weight of the endeavor hung on her shoulders. She pulled the camera out of her shoulder bag, squatted down, and peered through the viewfinder as the camera shook in her grip. She could see the Jamaican now; he was close to the edge of the building, talking to someone just out of view.

It would be mission-critical to photograph whomever he was talking to. *Is this his contact? If I move closer I might be seen.* Her stomach filled with butterflies and began to cramp—the adrenaline was getting the best of the rookie. Her heart surged in stroke to the firing of the camera shutter. She wanted to throw up, yet she couldn't move without that photo. It was not only a career-making surveillance she was on, it might mean saving countless American lives. Heat rose over her neck and face as she glanced down, dizzy under the pressure. She gagged, then darted behind the terminating stairwell and vomited. She had never in her life been so scared, so jacked, so overwhelmed with responsibility, yet so exhilarated. She hit her head on the cement staircase as she stood up but determined herself to get that goddamn photo. One thought etched itself into her mind, *I'm not going to miss this. Not on my watch. Not on my watch.*

Back at the window, the Jamaican disappeared from sight.

"Shit," she said as she muscled out past the scraping door. She glanced around the corner of the building, but they were nowhere to be seen. It was time to make a move, "Right now, right damn now," she said, as she started a brisk walk out into the open. She was totally exposed, but if she didn't get into a different position, she'd lose the only chance to see the Jamaican's contact. She walked straight ahead, keeping her face forward, not daring to turn towards the building. Long hair obscured her face, but a strong gust blew it over her shoulder, kicking up some cement dust. At the street corner, she was hidden from view. She peered between bending branches and tree bows full of new growth with leaves painted a vibrant, springtime green.

Through all the brush, and barely visible, was the Jamaican and another man. The camera lens revealed little, her view obstructed by the leaves. Jana felt so conspicuous to the cars on the street that she crouched down behind a clump of Bradford Pear trees and again worked the lens. The shutter fired and captured the Jamaican, but the other man was in the shadows, the lens only recording a black blob. Contrasted against dark shadows was brilliant sunlight reflecting off the Jamaican's brow as the two men talked. Wind gusts kicked up more dust from the cement pile. The camera couldn't pick up the dark figure but she kept snapping away. Maybe they could enhance the photos back at the field office.

"Come on, dammit, I need more light," she said. "Show me your face." Seconds later the shadowy figure's hands emerged, one holding a pack of cigarettes. *Holy crap, the cigarette lighter!* Knowing the cigarette lighter would momentarily illuminate his face, she wrenched the F-stop on the camera into position. The instant the flame ignited, the shutter blazed in automatic fashion, capturing every millisecond. Jana had no idea if she had gotten anything, but something in her peripheral vision caught her eye. It was a tow truck, and it was backing up to the VW Beetle.

"Oh. My. God," was the only thing she could come out with.

Her first thought was to the poor guy who owned the car. But then she realized if one of these subjects got into a vehicle, she was screwed. She'd have no way to pursue. Her eyes darted between the subjects and back to the VW.

I ought to go throttle that damn tow truck driver, she thought, but stopped herself and instead shot photos of the license plate on the VW and the tow truck, knowing she'd need that information later. Then Jana realized she didn't have the license plate of the suspect's van. *You stupid rookie,* she thought, grateful her supervisor wasn't there to see that one. Several photos later, close-ups of the van's plate were captured.

The tow truck was moments away from leaving with the VW when the Jamaican eased back into the white van's sliding door. *Oh my God. Oh my fucking God. How the hell do I tail him now?*

The phone buzzed in her pocket and caused her to jump.

"Baker," she answered.

"This is Agent Murphy, HRT right behind you," said a thick male voice over the phone.

Baker turned around. On the street behind her was a gray, unmarked work van with several agents inside, all of them members of the FBI's elite Hostage Rescue Team. They were dressed in workman clothes, and looked at her through tinted windows. Jana was both shocked and relieved.

"Don't move," she said. "Stay right there. You pull any farther forward, you'll be exposed. Subject vehicle is the white van pulling out."

"Roger that," said Murphy.

"Wait," said Jana into the phone, "there's a second subject still on site."

"What? Oh shit," said Murphy. He paused, thinking on his feet, "all right, you stay on the second subject; we've got orders to follow your Jamaican. He's the known entity. We don't know who the other subject is."

"Stay on him? What the hell does that mean? I've got no vehicle!" blurted Baker as the FBI van pulled out onto Ponce de Leon to trail the Jamaican.

"No vehicle? We tracked you here—how the hell did you get here?"

"Check the top of the hill, to your twelve o'clock. See the black VW Beetle?"

Murphy peered up Ponce de Leon through long binoculars.

"You mean the one that's pushing that tow truck up the hill?" Murphy smiled, knowing Baker wouldn't find that funny.

Baker knew this was a boys' club, and she'd have to roll with the punches if she wanted to be one of the guys.

She smiled and into the phone said, "Anyone in HRT ever had their ass kicked by a 118-pound girl?" Jana could see the other agents in the back of the van lean back laughing as their vehicle sped off in stealthy pursuit.

"Don't worry," replied Murphy. "Should be another Bue-car coming up right behind us. We'll radio and give them the sitrep. This is good work, Baker. Really good work."

Jana smiled as a feeling of relief washed over her shaking body. At least one subject was being covered.

Focusing back on the second subject, she strained through the camera lens but could no longer see him. A vehicle she assumed to be his car was still there, however. Jana looked around for a better place to continue her surveillance. Diagonal across the busy intersection of Ponce and Glen Iris Drive sat a little restaurant called Eats. It had a perfect vantage point if she could somehow find privacy there. She glanced back and forth before crossing six lanes of traffic and entered through the reflective glass door. Inside were a handful of customers seated throughout the sparsely filled room. This location was not going to work. She couldn't have a restaurant full of patrons staring at her as she pointed high-powered photography equipment at the building across the street. There would be no way of knowing if someone inside would alert her subject. The adrenaline coursing through her system overtook her, and she felt as though she might explode. Before it was too late, she pushed through into the ladies' room. It was filthy and smelled of stale urine.

"What a lovely spot," she said. The excitement and emotion poured out. Although she didn't need to vomit again, tears burst forth as her erratic breathing accelerated. Jana struggled to get a hold of herself. *No agent would lose it right now. No agent! I'm not a fucking little girl anymore. This is real, this is now, and this is me. Now quit your whining.* She exhaled hard several times, calming herself down. *The other agents can never see me like this, ever.*

Jana collected her bag, determined to not screw up, and shook the nerves out of her system. Back out in the front, a loud car horn blared as she pushed her way through the front door and into the bright sunlight. The smell of black exhaust was thick. Still, there was no activity in the gravel parking lot across the street; the vehicle was still there. How would she explain it if she had lost the new subject? "Ah, sorry, I thought I was going to hurl" wouldn't sound too convincing.

Around the side of Eats was a dumpster. It reeked of month-old beer and rotting food, yet would provide an unbelievable view of the gravel lot across the street.

"Well, you wanted to be in the FBI," she said, her determination resolute. Behind the building she found the parking lot deserted. Jana jumped through the heavy metal sliding door and into the dumpster. The putrid smell and stagnant air struggled to move in and out of her lungs. She gagged as the taste of vomit lingered in her mouth. Trudging forward over the refuse, Jana slid the other door ajar and looked through the camera lens. Her phone rang again. "Baker," she said, coughing.

"Baker, this is Agent Stark; I see your twenty still at the corner of Ponce and Glen Iris. We're two clicks out and coming your way. What's the sitrep?"

Jana's eyes widened. Stark was the special agent in charge of the Atlanta field office. Normally the SAC wouldn't be in the field. It was a signal of how big a deal this really was.

"Yes, sir, status is nominal. I'm positioned across from subject number two. He's inside the building; his vehicle is a black Ford sedan . . . oh shit, he's coming out; he's getting in the vehicle. I say again, subject two is leaving the scene! I have no vehicle. I have no way to pursue."

"What? You don't have a . . . shit, speed up, we've got to be there right now!" Stark said to the agent driving the car.

"No, wait," Jana said. "He stopped the car. He's backing up. He's pulling back into the lot."

"All right, Baker, we're moving your way heavy. Be there in zero-three mics. What's he doing now?" Jana could hear the siren and a thunderous car engine over the phone.

"He's out of the car. Headed back in the building. I think the engine is still running," Jana said as her breath quickened. The smell of rotting food dissipated as adrenaline again surged into her veins.

"Baker! Listen to me. Get out of your position. Move as fast as you can to the subject's vehicle. We can't lose him. We can't! You've got to plant your tracking device on that vehicle," demanded Stark.

"You want me to just go up there and casually drop a tracker into his car? But he'll see me . . . we need a warrant, don't we?" Jana stammered.

"Dammit, Baker! Fuck the warrant. Get that tracker onto his car or we'll lose him. Do it now!" Stark was screaming.

There was no way Stark and the other agents would be on the scene before the subject left. Jana had to act. She flung open the sliding door of the dumpster, tripped as she leapt onto the sidewalk, and gouged her knee on the unforgiving pavement in the process. She jumped to her feet, leaving a bloody knee print behind, and sprinted across the street as a car on Ponce de Leon locked its brakes to avoid hitting her. Her feet pounded the pavement; her hair flew back as she charged across onto the gravel lot. She was fully exposed; if the subject came outside now, the surveillance would be blown. She quieted her feet running forward, gravel crunching more quietly now. The tracking device was already in hand. Fifty feet, thirty feet, fifteen feet, *almost there, almost there* . . . Suddenly, the swinging metal door of the building banged open against the brick facade. Jana ducked behind the car. Out walked the subject; he was fifteen feet away from her, and she had to act fast. She had no way to know if he would walk around the cars' front or rear. The sound of footsteps switched from cement to gravel.

She had to chance it and ducked behind the rear side of the car. She reached under the rear metal bumper of the Ford, fishing in terror for a place to stow the tracking device. Even though the device wasn't meant to be placed on a vehicle, it was designed to be carried by a person, she stuffed the tracker inside the bumper, praying it wouldn't fall out. The footsteps drew near as the subject rounded the front side of the car and headed straight for the driver's door. She couldn't decide where to look—forward at him, because he may see her, or towards the building, fearing someone would be standing there. She wanted to just disappear, if only for a few seconds. The footsteps stopped. The only sound was that of car tires whining their way up Ponce de Leon. The man wasn't moving. She held her breath and didn't dare look up. *What the hell is he doing?* It felt like time froze; Jana froze; everything went into slow motion. Finally, the car door opened, and he got in. The car pulled away as Jana huddled motionless, terrified he might see her in the rearview mirror. The car pulled onto Ponce and disappeared beyond sight of the building.

Jana looked to her right to see if anyone was in the doorway. It was empty. *Thank God,* she thought. She wanted nothing more than to get away from this place.

This time, the rush of adrenaline felt different. She didn't want to vomit, she didn't want to flee, and she wasn't shaking. She exhaled, and it felt good. The adrenaline was a high, and it was an exhilaration on a whole new level. That was better than sex, well, maybe not all sex, but pretty darn good just the same.

Back behind the cover of Bradford Pear trees, she pulled out her phone again and realized she had never hung it up—it had been on the whole time. She had been so focused on getting the tracker in place, she'd forgotten about Stark and the other agents rushing to the scene.

She held the phone to her ear where Stark was speed talking. "Baker? Baker? Dammit, I can't tell what's going on . . . Baker?"

"Yes, sir, I'm here."

"Baker? Jesus Christ, are you all right? What's the situation?" said Stark.

"We're good, sir. The tracker is in place. We're good," she said.

"Holy shit! You did it? I mean, you did it. Excellent work, Baker. I could hear footsteps. What happened?"

The car pulled up, and Stark put the phone down and motioned Jana to the back seat.

"I did what you told me to do," she said as she got in. "I hauled ass across the street and stuck the tracker up under his bumper," said Jana.

"Wow. I didn't think you'd do it. Man, that was ballsy. Okay, we've been in comm with HRT. They're tailing your Jamaican. Were those footsteps I heard from the second subject?"

"Yes, sir, I had to crouch behind the car to avoid being seen," Jana said. She thought her voice cracked, but no one seemed to notice. "He stood there a minute and then got in his car with me right behind it. I was afraid he'd see me once he pulled away."

"Great work, Baker. Hey, your leg's bleeding, are you okay? That's a pretty bad cut. You need medical?" Jana stared out the window, ignoring the question. Stark continued, "The HRT guys said something about a tow truck?"

"Yeah, some asshole towed away the car I commandeered. But . . . those HRT guys are pussies, anyway," she said, smiling.

Laughter erupted in the car. The male agents were impressed. Agent Baker was going to fit right in.

23

gent Stark fixated on the iPad's map application as he watched two dots move across the screen on a detailed street view of Atlanta. The dot representing subject two's vehicle trailed a faint white line as it traversed the map. Speaking to the driver, Stark said, "All right, keep your distance. With this tracker in place, there's no need to get too close and blow our surveillance."

Baker spoke up, "Sir, I had no time to get that tracker into place sufficiently. It's stuck inside the rear bumper. It's not like it's got a magnet or anything on it."

The other agents looked at each other.

"It would sure suck if it fell out and we lost him," said Stark, still fixated on the map. "This guy's all over the place. Charlie, take a look at this, he starts out heading east on Ponce, turns south, darts into a neighborhood, weaves his way around it, then comes right back out. Now he's heading back west again."

Charlie, another agent in the vehicle, replied, "Sounds like he's trying to make sure no one is following him. It would be impossible to tail right behind him and not give yourself away as he weaves all over those neighborhoods. Damn good thing we have that tracker." He looked over at Jana, his eyebrows raised in a slight nod of approval.

The agents followed the tracker's signal for half an hour as the car took turn after turn.

"All right, looks like we're headed into Buckhead. He's heading up Lenox Road towards the mall," said Stark, looking into the distance ahead of them. "He's turning south on Peachtree."

The agents pulled into the mall parking lot. "Don't go in the parking garage, we might lose the signal," said Stark to the steely eyed driver. "He's slowing down. He's not half a mile from us. Okay, looks like he's turned right down there."

Jana said, "He must be turning into one of those tall buildings. There's no through street right there."

She was right. On the map, Stark could see the blip on the map pull in between two buildings, and then the signal went dead.

"Shit. It's gone. The signal's gone," said Stark, tapping the iPad.

"Probably went into a below-ground parking deck," said Charlie. "Don't worry; the range on that tracker is excellent. And we should have a few weeks of battery life left. All right, let's see what that building is. Okay, I have it. It's that tall one down there. You know, the newer one they built last year? It's the one that went up right next to Cheesecake Factory where an old 1970s bank building used to stand. Some software company was in that old bank building . . ."

Stark interrupted, "Charlie, Jesus. Enough with the history of Atlanta development. What's the building that's there now?"

"Oh, sorry. Thoughtstorm, it's a company called Thoughtstorm. Anybody know what that is? I'll pull the building schematics. We need to get down there, get into the underground parking area, and find that car. We're going to need to affix a more permanent tracker." Charlie was an expert in the technology of tracking and surveillance. His nickname around the office was "Hound," a reference to his ability to track a suspect across any surface. Jana didn't know if it was true or not, but rumor around the office was that he once apprehended a wounded suspect after tracking him across half a mile of cement. The specks of blood were said to be so faint on the darkened surface that Charlie crawled on his hands and knees to locate them.

Stark turned around. "All right, we need to get on foot. Baker, what's the subject's description?"

Jana's stomach dropped. She wanted so badly to impress these guys, but the truth was, she had no idea what he looked like. She looked Stark in the eye and said, "Sir, I didn't get a good look at him. He was in the shadows. I could barely see him." She was making no excuses, and she wasn't backing down.

"But he walked within nine feet of you," he said.

Jana needed something professional to say. "I wasn't going to compromise my mission by giving away my location, sir."

Stark looked at her, started to say something, but stopped.

"Ten-four. How about photography—you said he was in the shadows? Did you get him on camera? Maybe we can enhance the digital images."

"I snapped several shots of him while he was in the shadows talking with the Jamaican. I don't know if the photos will show anything. It was dark where he was standing, but I got a few of him when he lit a cigarette. There may have been enough light then. It all happened so fast."

"Roger that. Go ahead and wirelessly upload those photos to HQ right now. I'll set a priority status on them."

The Thoughtstorm building loomed in the sky, towering over the surrounding buildings, like a Goliath to their David. Its shadow darkened Peachtree Road.

"Pull in across the street, into the Atlanta Financial Center building. Take the first entrance," said Agent in Charge Stark. "Let's park and walk across." He turned to the driver. "Joe, I want you to stay in the vehicle; we may need to get moving quickly."

"I've got an idea," said Charlie. "These buildings are connected to the MARTA train below through a tunnel that runs under Peachtree Road. Why don't two of us take the tunnel. It connects with that monstrosity across the street. Then we can come up into the building as though we just got off the train. It won't look as obvious as three of us walking straight across the street and into the front door."

"Good plan," said Stark. "Set your comm to channel six one five. You two head down to the garage levels. Find that vehicle, but look sharp. We don't know what we're walking into. I'll get a surveillance team heated up. We're going to have to build a camp right here and watch this place. You two act like you're dating. You know, hold hands or something." Stark took a good look at the two agents. Charlie, the tough and chiseled type, had too much gray hair for someone Jana's age. "Well, eighty-six that idea. Charlie, you're too, well, too . . . too old, and frankly, she's out of your league." Stark realized his lack of political correctness too late. "Baker, sorry. Listen, look sharp for this guy. Finding that car is critical, but we need the suspect identified."

The pair worked their way through the long, wide tunnel underneath Peachtree Street that connected the train platform to both the Atlanta Financial Center and the Thoughtstorm buildings. Once inside, they took the elevator down to parking level B. Charlie removed his iPad from its case, hoping to find a signal from the tracking device. But there was nothing. Two floors below however, on level D, the iPad blipped a small alert sound. "This is it," Charlie whispered from underneath a burly mustache, "your car is on this floor. Should be down that way a bit." A sound echoed from the floor above as a car moved up the ramp, its tires squeaking across the painted surface.

"We have a problem," said Jana.

"Holy shit," replied Charlie, surveying all the cars on level D. Every car was exactly the same. All of them were identical, black, four-door

Ford sedans. "I've never seen so many Crown Vics in my life," said Charlie. "Looks like a Ford parade down here."

"Who in the hell is stupid enough to have a fleet of Crown Vics besides the government?" said Jana. "And how are we going to find a dark Ford sedan in a sea of dark Ford sedans?"

"This tracking signal isn't going to get us that close," said Charlie. "We'll never know which car it is. But, we're going to have to find it, somehow."

The two were walking down the long rows when they heard the loud screeching of tires.

"Move it!" said Charlie, grabbing Jana's arm and yanking her behind a car. The vehicle rolled past. "Whew," said Charlie, "that was close."

As he stood up, Jana grabbed his hand. "Charlie," she whispered, "this is it. This is the car. This is it!"

"What are you talking about? There's a hundred cars in here. How could you possibly know that? The tracker isn't that accurate."

"Because this is my blood," she said, pointing at the bumper. Jana positioned her skinned knee against the darkly smeared blood stain. It was a perfect match.

Charlie looked at the blood then glanced at Jana, his head shaking back and forth. "Well good God. They're never going to believe this one." He pulled a radio from underneath his gray canvas jacket. "Stark, this is point, over."

"Go ahead, point."

"The eagle has landed, over," said Charlie, grinning. Bureau agents had a long running joke of always using code-speak. The team hadn't planned any code be given, but Stark knew what he meant.

"It's landed, has it? You've been looking for thirty seconds, and large birds of prey are landing? Can't wait to hear this one."

24

Within hours, three sets of surveillance teams took up position. One was assigned to the Jamaican. Another was situated outside the walk-up apartment of Waseem Jarrah, the suspected terrorist. And a third camped across Peachtree Street from the Thoughtstorm building. All three subjects were somehow interconnected, and pressure mounted on Agent in Charge David Stark and his team to find out everything.

Stark placed a flash message to Washington, signaling he was sitting on a case of epic proportions. The safety of the American people was highly compromised, and national security might be at stake. Washington responded and responded with vigor. One hundred and seventy-five agents were flown to Atlanta over the next eighteen hours. This was to become the single highest priority for the FBI as the bureau now faced off with a terror cell that had slipped into the country and apparently pulled off eleven bombings. Up until now, nothing was known about who was behind the spate of attacks. These weren't the large-scale attacks of 9/11 which took years of planning, a huge, unencumbered budget, and dozens of jihadists. In recent years, with all the work of the FBI, CIA, NSA, US military forces, and intelligence services all over the world, most organized terror groups had splintered. It was much harder for them to obtain large-scale financing without attracting attention. Now the jihadists regrouped under a new plan: to bring the US economy to a crawl through the use of small-scale terror attacks. These attacks were easier to pull off and required far fewer resources and manpower. And yet, since the American media swarmed on any terror attack, every man, woman, and child in the country would be made aware. And if Americans were afraid to leave their own homes, the repercussions to the economy would be catastrophic.

The effectiveness of these attacks could further be magnified if the terrorists followed a predictable pattern. After that precise pattern and timing became common knowledge, the media would propagate a nationwide countdown to the next attack. People would be terrified as the countdown neared. Not only would they be afraid to leave their homes, they would have no idea where the next strike would occur. And, since each attack occurred sooner than the last, the anxiety of the collective consciousness would intensify. Since May, there had been one bombing each month. The body count was piling up. People were afraid, angry, and they wanted action. The attacks hit different targets in different cities of different sizes. Some were in major metropolitan areas like Chicago, where a bomb detonated in a crowded shopping mall. Then there was the smaller town of Sheboygan, Wisconsin, where a bomb ripped apart a city bus. Bombs had detonated in each corner of the country. And each time, although the bombs were small-scale, they targeted the highest number of people possible.

Americans began to feel they were not safe anywhere. Subway trains, ball games, hospitals, schools, restaurants, theatres, and airports had all been targets. And the epicenter of the entire case seemed to hinge on Atlanta. The FBI hadn't had a single break in the case until now. They'd exhausted every avenue of investigation, but each bomb had been different from the last. The explosive materials were different, the casings were different, the targets were different, the time of day was different. Nothing seemed to match. And this last bombing in Tucson was different as well. The explosive was laced with toxic residue, which meant anyone with even a superficial wound was dead within hours. The use of toxic residue was highly advanced and required significant training to implement.

At the highest levels of government, concern was immense. The president ordered a full-court press. The CIA began leaning on its sources in the Middle East for information about Waseem Jarrah, and information flowed in. The two other subjects, however, were drawing a blank. No one had any information about the Jamaican. The bureau didn't even know his name at this point. Making matters worse, the FBI could not identify the subject in the photos taken by Agent Jana Baker. His face was visible in the enhanced photographs, but facial recognition software had failed to come up with a match. He was the proverbial riddle, wrapped in a mystery, inside an enigma.

The president was already being briefed daily by the FBI on the bombing investigation. But with each event, his mood darkened. He was determined that no bomb would go off on his watch ever again. To that end, under an executive order, the president directed the NSA to do something illegal—they were to spy on an American company. Not since the days of FBI director J. Edgar Hoover had a government agency been authorized to use this level of investigation on American citizens. Every Thoughtstorm employee would be scrutinized. Every home phone, business phone, cell phone, or VOIP phone was wiretapped. Every social media account like Twitter, Facebook, Pinterest, and more were tracked. All e-mail addresses, both work and personal, were hacked. Every one of the over three thousand employees in Thoughtstorm's Atlanta office was under the microscope. In the name of terror, everything in their lives became known to the government.

25

A crowd gathered in the dusty little field just north of Shelby, Montana. The Lake Shel-Oole campground was a small, flat place whose only notable feature was the distinct absence of grass—or anything green, for that matter. The grayish soil was beaten and barren. Old wooden fence posts leaned in different directions lining Highway 15, each held upright by the light tension of wires adjoining them. Across the road from the entrance to the tiny park was what appeared to be a Gomer Pyle-style barracks building. It looked like a giant barrel, about forty feet long, that had been cut in half and laid on its side. It had been there since the 1960s, but the shoddy tin structure held its shape well. For snow country like this, a half-barrel-shaped building was ideal in the heavy winters. Several farm trucks were parked nearby with nothing under their wheels but the burnt earth, trampled under years of wear. A few small buildings stood adjacent to the old Highway 15 and 67 North sign markers.

The sky was big, and the flat landscape rolled, bleeding into the distance. A sparse, yellow light leaked out from the last few street lamps that terminated this far north of town. The street lights were dimmed by the burnt glow of the setting sun, having just dipped below the horizon, like the melting of an ice cream cone. The evening was crisp, and the last vestiges of daylight were giving up their fight and yielding to a darkening eastern horizon. The mild breeze too gave up its efforts and became quiet.

But the campground was anything but vacant on this particular evening. Dozens and dozens of cars and trucks parked neatly along the small roadway. The event was known as the largest annual bonfire in Montana; its golden orange light brightly illuminated the crowd of smiling faces.

Toole County Sheriff's Deputy Brian Norton was working traffic at the entrance to the park. He turned his cruiser's strobe lights off and walked over to the activity where the smell of home-cooked food and laughter hung in stark contrast to the night air. The steady stream of traffic coming to the cookout had slowed, and Deputy Norton was joined by several other sheriff's deputies.

"Hey, what gives?" said Norton. "I thought the old lady put you guys on town patrol tonight."

"Well, she did, but then she told us to come on up and join you. She didn't want you eating all the food," laughed Deputy Tom Watkins.

Most everyone in town was already there. It was Shelby Township's annual "Welcoming of Spring" cookout. Having been cooped up in their homes for much of the winter, third- and fourth-generation Shelbians gathered each year to mark the beginning of the growing season. But mainly they were here to just have a good time. Men gathered in large groups around the fire, backing away as the bonfire grew hotter and hotter. Women busied themselves around folding tables, stretching blue and red plaid tablecloths of shimmering plastic across each one, alternating the colors. Others arranged the abundance of covered dishes, sorting where each should be placed, and even fussing over whose homemade pie would get front billing on the dessert tables.

At the far left of the long span of tables, mountains of barbequed beef brisket lay nestled in large, disposable aluminum trays. An entire cow had been dedicated by the county for the event. The middle tables were weighed down under all manner of glass dishes filled with coleslaw, barbeque beans, corn, green beans, and snap peas. Half of one of the tables was covered in store-bought bread, stacked five loaves high.

Four boys, all wearing worn jeans, blue jean jackets, and baseball caps that advertised farm equipment of one type or another, spread out on opposing sides of the great fire. A football flew between them high across the top of the bonfire, the flames licking the old, cracked leather before being caught by a boy on the other side. They dared each other to catch the hot ball, each believing the other would chicken out.

"Johnnie is a chicken, bok, bok, bok, bok," said Tommy Randall.

"Am not! You just throw that ball, and don't let it get stuck in the fire, neither!" belted Johnnie.

A mother arranging loaves of bread yelled, "Now, you boys stop that throwing. Someone's gonna get hurt."

"Aw, let 'em be, Delores. They aren't hurtin' anyone," said a man from beneath the brim of his worn John Deere baseball cap.

The town mayor, Harry Bonderman, was dressed in his best baby blue leisure suit, his wide smile illuminated in the firelight. He shed the baseball cap that had been perched on his head, revealing his bright, shiny baldness that he attempted to disguise under a bad comb-over. His temples were dented from the constant presence of the hat, which he now crunched in his hands. A grin painted a childlike expression on his face as he took the bullhorn. The sound of the piercing loudspeaker squawked, and everyone covered their ears, wincing.

"Folks, can I have your attention? Sorry about that, folks. Everyone gather round. We're going to bless the food."

"You boys git over here and quit that throwin'," said the same father who had earlier told the boys to continue. "And take off them hats."

About a quarter of a mile away, at the corner of Deer Lodge Avenue and Silver Bow Street, stood the Toole County Sheriff's Department. Sheriff Doris Thompkins was the only person in the one-story tan building. The sheriff's office looked small next to its large radio tower silhouetted against sparse, jagged clouds now disappearing into the darkening sky. For a town as small as Shelby, Sheriff Thompkins was pleased with the support she received from the county. She grinned to no one in particular, thinking back to earlier in the day when she'd given the deputies a tongue lashing about maintaining their town patrol shifts tonight, even during the annual feast. Then, not two hours later, she'd capitulated and sent them to the bonfire. They all wanted to be there. In fact, she wanted to be there. But, being the sheriff had its responsibilities, and someone needed to man the fort.

Stepping outside through the glass double doors of the front entrance, the crisp night air worked its way into her lungs. On the top step of the portico, she peered to the north, the glow of the flickering bonfire visible on the horizon. She thought for a moment about all the families that would be there and about her six young deputies who would surely give her grief tomorrow morning about first playing tough, then letting them go to the gathering at the last minute. In the distance, she could hear low, audible voices and laugher and the mayor's voice on that old bullhorn of his. Although his words were not clear, she assumed he was saying a prayer before the big feast. *Well, maybe my boys will bring me a plate, but perhaps that's too much to ask. They are boys after all.*

After a few moments of praying, the mayor's voice quieted. Doris could almost hear a collective "Amen," and all the voices went quiet.

Then, out of the bleak silence, an enormous white-hot flash of light erupted, engulfing most of the night sky. Doris's mouth dropped as her eyes squinted into the shattering pulse of light. Half a second later, the concussive blast slammed into her body, followed by an eruption of noise whose volume was so much louder than anything in her experience, it was almost beyond comprehension. The shockwave rocked her backwards, slamming her shoulder blades into the glass doors, which shattered behind her as the ground rattled underneath. Her drill-instructor-style hat flipped to the ground as all manner of debris and shrapnel rained down, pelting the building, slamming into the cement walkway, and crashing into the metallic roof of the building across the way. Doris's pupils, still dilated from the bright flash, were shocked once more as a piece of sizzling metal sliced through the air with a whirring sound and tore the flesh from her cheekbone to her ear. The scar it would leave on her face would become symbolic of the one that later etched itself onto her soul. Doris collapsed at the base of the glass doors in a crumpled ball, then rolled down the three stairs, spilling onto the lush grass lawn, now strewn with raining debris.

The realization of what had happened was yet to be comprehended. The sheriff struggled to her feet, wobbling as she rose, her arms and hands held out to catch herself if she fell. She could hear nothing over the cacophonous ringing in her ears. She looked around with hazy eyes as confusion painted itself across a deepening look of horror. She first began walking, then running towards the scene. It didn't occur to her to get in her patrol car; she simply ran towards the danger.

The once enormous bonfire was reduced to shards of little glowing embers, the logs splintered across great distances. The once happy flames had been extinguished by the blast, which consumed all nearby oxygen. Debris was everywhere. Doris tripped over something and collapsed in a heap on the pavement. Glancing under her feet, it looked like the remnants of a car bumper. Under wobbling knees she rose with her left hand bleeding from the fresh scrape. The acrid smell of burnt hair layered the area like a fog, and Doris's stomach soured. Stumbling forward, terrified of what she might find, Doris again began to run. The ringing in her ears was deafening.

She screamed out, "Boys, boys," after her young deputies. Even if they had been able to respond, she wouldn't know. What her ears would not reveal were the low, muffled cries coming from the few that had survived the enormous blast. In the coming minutes, the cries would silence, and nothing would move.

The landscape had transformed. No longer were buildings standing nearby. Everything had been leveled. Even the fence and lamp posts were nowhere to be found. It wasn't possible to distinguish the once modest entrance to the camp. Doris gazed at the scattered debris— shattered wood, glowing embers, twisted metal, food items, car parts, and broken glass. There were other things strewn in the debris as well. These were the things Doris would never speak of. To her it looked as though human blood and pieces of flesh had fallen from the sky and covered the ground like raindrops.

She sank to her knees. Her weeping was that of someone whose soul had been irreparably torn. With hands on her lap, she raised her eyes to the sky and found the only normalcy in the hellish scene. Quietly shimmering above, in the same place they had been a few minutes earlier, were the stars and a silvery glow from the rising moon. Nothing in them decried the abomination that surrounded her. Doris would never be able to verbalize what she had seen that night. It was a burden she would carry with her to her grave.

26

After lunch with his dad, Cade's mind went blurry. His head hurt, and he was racked with guilt. The weight of his dad's cancer pushed on his chest like a three-hundred-pound barbell. On top of his dad's health, this seventeenth floor crap was mind numbing. Rupert Johnston was taking his orders from William Macy, and Macy's temper was combustible. Never a smile, never a nod hello, and then, out of nowhere, Macy would explode in anger. Whatever was driving him was driving him hard, and Cade couldn't get out of the way.

Cade would watch the two men in meetings from behind glass walls. He couldn't hear what was being said, but every meeting ended the same way—yelling. Johnston's anger was visceral. It looked like he would burst a blood vessel in his forehead during the shouting matches. Then he would storm out and slam the door to his office. Tensions weren't just high, they were out of control.

Cade no longer worked a normal schedule. His days were dragging later and later than the last. And tonight, he hadn't left the office until eight thirty p.m. Down in the garage he climbed into his car a whipped man. It was close to nine when he got home, flopped down on the couch, and turned on the news.

"We're going live now to Montana, the apparent scene of another bombing. We're moments away . . . yes, we're going live to the scene outside of the township of Shelby, Montana, to a news conference with Montana Attorney General John Farr."

Silence folded over the scene and then was interrupted by the sound of camera shutters firing away.

"Folks, if you can settle down please, we can begin." The Attorney General paused again. "I have the unfortunate responsibility to pass along the news that approximately ninety minutes ago, Montana joined the sad list of places to suffer what appears to be a terrorist attack. I've just toured the area behind me . . . the devastation . . . it's hard to put into words." Farr struggled but won the battle over his emotions.

"Here in the town of Shelby, this annual event represents the largest bonfire in the state of Montana. Most of Shelby's town residents normally attend."

A flurry of hurried reporters' voices tried to speak over one another. The reporters began shouting. The tallest voice overshadowed the rest. "Do we know how many casualties?"

"The number of casualties is unknown at this time. We anticipate that over one hundred people would have been in attendance here." The words rolled off his tongue like thunder.

"And how many wounded? What hospital were the wounded taken to?" continued the reporter.

Farr stared at his feet as though the answer might be written in shoe polish on his Florsheims.

Seated in the shadows of the bright camera lights, Sheriff Doris Thompkins struggled to her feet and put her hand on the Attorney General's shoulder. Gauze bandages stained in dark dried blood clung to her face and hand. The Attorney General stepped aside with an expression that decried a mixture of reverence and relief. Sheriff Thompkins' blank pallor gazed forward into the sea of reporters and bright lights. She made eye contact with nothing. The hand dangling at her side trembled. In a low voice devoid of emotion, she said, "There were no survivors."

A hush fell over the group of reporters. None knew how to react. No one wanted to be the one to ask the next question.

After a moment, one reporter stood up with a sullen face and asked, "Are you sure it was a terrorist attack? Could the explosion have been caused by a gas main, or a grain silo, anything?"

Attorney General Farr put his arms around Doris's shoulders and helped her back to her seat.

"Let me turn that question over to the FBI."

"My name is Special Agent Stephen Bolz. I lead the task force investigating the spate of terrorist incidents that have occurred in this country over the past eleven months. Although this explosion is an early stage investigation, we're treating it as a crime scene. Let me be perfectly clear. There is no other working explanation outside of a deliberate attack. The geographic area has no city services, no gas lines, no sewer lines; there are no grain silos, no factories, no fuel dumps. The sheer size of the blast zone indicates that this was no accident. Whatever caused this explosion was manmade and deliberate."

There was a man standing behind Bolz wearing a distinctive blue FBI windbreaker. Cade leaned forward on the couch and squinted at the television. Cade looked harder at the man. "Holy crap," he said, "that's Kyle."

Bolz continued, "We'll bring you more information as we have it." The press conference ended in abrupt silence.

Cade dialed Kyle without hesitation.

"Agent MacKerron," answered Kyle.

"Cool Mac, dude! Holy crap, I just saw you on WBS News. Are you okay? I thought you were working bank robbery. What are you doing at a bombing in Montana?"

"Cade, I can't talk about it right now. But yeah, I've been transferred. And, Cade, you're not going to believe why."

"Why? What do you mean? Kyle . . ."

"Can't talk now. I'll see you tomorrow."

"You'll see me tomorrow? Kyle, what does that mean?" But the phone was dead. Confused and exhausted, he turned off the TV and shuffled into the double bed still covered by the comforter he'd had since tenth grade. As his head hit the pillow, sounds from a thumping bass guitar droned in the background. The neighbors were having another party. *Well, it is Tuesday, after all. Why wait till Friday?*

27

The next day at lunchtime, Cade was still tired. He needed to get out, at least for a short time. At the stroke of noon, he was out the front doors and onto Peachtree Street, walking towards the mall.

Across the street a man stood reading his paper, his reflection silhouetted against the black glass of the sprawling Atlanta Financial Center building. The man turned and walked in the same direction, parallel, but well behind Cade. In his left hand he keyed the small radio transmitter. "Secure channel," he said in a low voice.

"Channel secure," came the crisp reply.

"Subject heading north on foot."

"Roger that, subject heading north. Keep your distance. Don't make contact," said the voice.

At the corner, Cade waited a moment as a MARTA bus cleared before crossing Peachtree Street.

"Copy that, no contact . . . hold one. New course, subject crossing Peachtree. Could be headed to Lenox Mall." A car's horn blared on the busy Buckhead thoroughfare.

"Roger that, assets are en route. ETA two minutes."

"Copy, assets ETA two minutes."

Cade walked through the main entrance of the mall and worked his way all the way to the back of the enormous facility and into the bustling food court. Descending the escalator, bright springtime light glowed through skylights down onto the marble floor below. A sea of people moved about as if woven into a tapestry of humanity, each disorganized thread with its own purpose. Restaurant tables spread across the wide indoor area as aromas competed, each trying to outdo the other. Cade walked past several restaurants where employees stood in front, holding plates of food, little toothpicks pointing straight to the day-lit ceiling.

"Sample, sir? Sample?"

Cade put up his hand. But as he came to the last restaurant on the right, he slowed. The line was long, as usual. His favorite place boasted sizzling teriyaki chicken that when cooked, steamed as though angry at the piping hot skillet they sat on. The staff struggled to keep pace with demand. Another mountain of fresh marinated chicken was brought out from the back and dumped unceremoniously on the scorching surface. Patrons moved down the line, their plates steaming with fresh white rice, grilled vegetables, and dark, rich teriyaki chicken. Cade already knew he would eat here and started to walk past a pretty Asian sample-giver when she stepped into his path, blocking his way.

"Sample, sir?" she said, holding a skewered piece of dripping chicken.

"Oh, no thank you," said Cade.

"Have a sample. Meet Cool Mac in the employee stairwell, directly behind you. Don't ask questions. Meet Cool Mac in the employee stairwell directly behind you." She pushed the toothpick into his hand and turned towards another customer.

Cade stared. *Cool Mac? What the hell?*

"Sample, ma'am? Yes, ma'am, teriyaki chicken, just $6.99. Sir, a sample for you? Teriyaki chicken." The sample-giver backed up, paying Cade no more attention. "Sample, sir, teriyaki chicken . . ." Cade glanced across the rows of tables behind him and saw the stairwell door. *Cool Mac is here? Kyle?*

Cade walked towards the stairwell door but felt stupid, like he was being watched and this was all just a prank. It felt like something out of the movies. Still, no one outside of Kyle's closest friends ever used the nickname Cool Mac. He pushed open the door into the echoing stairwell. The door closed behind him with a heavy metallic thud, the sounds of the busy food court muffled behind him. A janitor whose gray uniform was stained with yellow mustard trotted down the stairs, taking them two at a time.

"Cool Mac, top floor. On the right is a door marked 'Employees Only.'" The man turned his back to the door and pushed it open. Cade's confused eyes followed him as he disappeared into the food court.

Cade's feet shuffled their way up the steps as echoes reverberated off beige cinder block walls. The casual-soled shoes thudded against the steel steps. He was nervous but really a little bit more bewildered than anything. On the third flight of stairs, Cade stared at a set of doors marked "Employees Only."

Now what? thought Cade. *I suppose there's a secret knock?* He started to put his hand on the knob but then withdrew it. It was as though he

thought the handle might be red-hot. To his surprise, the door handle
turned, and he pushed it open.

28

"**H**ey, man," said a jubilant Kyle MacKerron. "Cool Mac!" Cade laughed. "What the hell are you doing to me, man? You've gone all 007 on me." There were three other people in the room seated at a heavy steel table. Each stood up as Cade entered—two men and one very attractive female. Cade's eyes stopped on her. He tried not to stare, but he couldn't help it. Otherwise it looked like a business suit convention in the small, cement room.

"Hey, sorry, man. It couldn't be avoided," said Kyle. "Don't worry; we're going to explain everything. This is Special Agent Stephen Bolz out of our San Diego office. He's in charge of . . . ah, well, he's in charge of what we're going to explain to you. This is Special Agent David Stark, the agent in charge of the FBI's Atlanta field office."

Cade shook hands with the men. "And this is Special Agent Jana Baker. Agent Baker is working with us on this case. Come over here. Let's sit down for a minute."

"We don't have much time," said Jana, sitting on the edge of the table. "We don't want him to be gone too long."

"Much time?" said Cade. "What, am I going to be late to pick up my date for the prom or something? Kyle, what's going on? What is all this? What are you doing in Atlanta?"

Kyle looked at Cade then back over to Agent Bolz with a question in his eye. Bolz nodded, signaling his approval.

"Have a seat," said Kyle. "Cade, we're here because of you."

Cade looked at each person around the table in turn.

"What? You're here for me? This isn't about that time in Statesboro that I stole that state trooper's hat is it? I can explain . . ."

"Cade. There's a problem. A real problem. And no, it's not about that time you stole that state trooper's hat." Kyle looked down at the table. "I'll just say it. We think there's a problem with your employer."

"My employer? Well sure there's a problem. There's a bunch of assholes working there." Cade laughed, but no one else did. "What kind of a problem?"

"You've seen the news over the last several months. About all the bombings?" Kyle looked sideways at Cade.

"The bombings? Yeah. What about the bombings? What's that got to do with Thoughtstorm?" Cade was on the edge of his seat, his shoulders tensing.

"Cade, what we're about to tell you is classified," said Kyle. "I'm not joking about that. It's classified. We had to get clearance from the director to brief you on this."

"Brief me on what?"

"We've traced an individual we believe to be involved in the bombings to your office. In fact, we've been investigating your company, Thoughtstorm, and we believe there's something very wrong there."

Cade looked like a kid who'd just dropped the gum out of his new package of baseball cards and couldn't find it.

"What? Wait, I'm lost. You're saying somebody at Thoughtstorm is behind the bombings? We send e-mail. Are you out of your mind? What's this got to do with me? I mean, other than the fact that I apparently work for The Firm."

Jana let out a tiny giggle then cleared her throat, trying to maintain a professional appearance. She glanced at the other agents and took over the conversation.

"Mr. Williams," she began.

"Cade. Call me Cade."

"Cade, a few days ago, I recorded a conversation between a known terrorist and an unknown individual of Jamaican descent."

Cade stared at her. He was disoriented with the entire conversation, but her attractiveness was disarming. He struggled not to look at her body.

"I'd like to show you some photos," she said.

She began reaching for the photos when Agent Bolz interrupted. "Mr. Williams, we believe there is an advanced terror cell operating within the contiguous borders of the United States."

Cade stared at his chiseled jaw and perfect hair. It was like looking at a mannequin.

"We believe they are highly sophisticated and are responsible for all of the bombings," said Agent Bolz. "We further believe that the terrorists are using a very advanced, encrypted form of electronic communication to coordinate their activities."

"Why are you telling me this? I'm not getting it," said Cade.

Bolz didn't skip a beat. "You work at a firm that offers very advanced, encrypted forms of electronic communication." He let that sink in for a moment, studying Cade's reaction. "You work for a company that is supplying communications technology and infrastructure to terrorists."

Cade's blank look decried nothing of the upheaval dancing in his gut.

"I work . . . I work for . . . you're saying I work . . ." Cade's face flushed, and his breathing went erratic. He didn't know how to react.

Agent Jana Baker pulled out a manila envelope and withdrew an eight by ten, black and white photo. She placed the photo in front of Cade.

"Have you ever seen this man?" she said. "His name is Waseem Jarrah. He's a known terrorist from Syria."

Cade looked at the photo but couldn't focus. He was no longer aware of Jana's attractiveness. He felt sick. He simply shook his head from side to side.

She held out another photo.

"How about this man? Have you ever seen this man?" The photo was of the Jamaican.

Cade again shook his head in the negative.

"Almost done. Cade, look closely, have you ever seen this man?"

The third black and white photo was a little dark, but clearly distinguishable was a man in a business suit, white shirt, and a distinctive buzz cut. Cade's face dropped.

"Oh shit," said Cade. A wave of heat wafted out from under his collar and up across his jaw. It was William Macy.

Jana looked at Bolz whose gaze had never left Cade's face. Bolz was fishing for any hidden meaning in Cade's expressions, reading him like a book. Bolz jumped up, his chair slinging backwards across the floor and slamming into the cinder block wall. "How do you know this man?" Bolz yelled as he pounded the table.

Rattled, Cade stammered, "He, he, he works at Thoughtstorm. He's on the same floor as me. He seems to run things up there. This is William Macy. Well, that's just what I call him because he looks so much like the actor William Macy." Cade looked down, his eyes tracing the table. "I don't even know his real name."

"Bullshit!" fired Bolz. "That's not good enough. Who—is—he!"

Cade felt he was under attack. "I said I don't know."

Kyle jumped up to intervene, putting his hands on Bolz's shoulders.

"Okay, okay. Let's all calm down here. Agent Bolz, I've made it clear that Cade would never be tied up in anything like this. He's not the enemy. We need his help to fight the enemy." The words rolled off his tongue like a John F. Kennedy sound bite.

"Oh yeah?" said Bolz, looking squarely at Kyle. "Are you willing to bet your career on that, rookie?"

Kyle looked down at Cade who had turned white as a ghost.

"Career, my ass," said Kyle. "I'd bet my life on it."

Bolz paced to the edge of the room, his hands rubbing the back of his stiff neck. "All right, all right." He turned back and looked at Cade. "I'm sorry. I had to check. I had to see your reaction. Let's start with what you do know. When did you first see this man?"

"It was a couple of weeks ago. I've always worked on the sixteenth floor, but I was called up to the seventeenth that day. I'd never been up there before. The floor was always *restricted*." The word tasted of venom.

"Why did they call you up there?" probed Bolz.

"Thoughtstorm provides large-scale e-mail marketing software. We send huge e-mail jobs for customers. Anyway, there was some big situation up there. Something wrong with one of the servers." Cade looked down with confusion on his face. "I don't know why they needed me. I never knew what happened to whoever else used to work up there."

"And that's when you first saw him, this person you call William Macy?" quizzed Jana.

Cade looked at her blue eyes. "Yeah, I saw him pretty much right away. He was on the server floor, standing way down one of the rows of servers, arguing with some other business-suit-wearing pinheads." Cade glanced at Bolz and Kyle, dressed in their dark blue business suits. "Sorry, when I see a guy in a business suit, I call him a pinhead. No offense."

For the first time, Bolz smiled. "Could you hear what they were arguing about?"

"A little bit. There was something really wrong with a big e-mail job they were sending. The server was going haywire. These guys were arguing. They were freaking out about the e-mail job. It was failing. I'd never seen anyone react like that in my life. Why freak out about an e-mail job? I mean, it's not life and death." Cade closed his eyes and thought back to that moment when he first walked onto the server floor on seventeen. "But, when they were arguing, I could swear I heard him say something about Tucson." Cade stopped. Everyone stared at him. *Tucson.* He had said Tucson.

"Wait, wait, wait just a minute," Cade said, in complete denial of what he was thinking. "You don't mean to tell me this William Macy asshole has something to do with the bombing in Tucson? That that e-mail job had something to do with the bombing in Tucson? But what about . . . I mean, it can't be . . . what about all those other bombings . . . you're saying . . ." Denial morphed into terror as color again drained from Cade's face.

"Cade, calm down, calm down," repeated Kyle.

Jana leaned down. Her blonde hair was in a long pony tail which then dripped off her shoulder. In the smoothest voice Cade had ever heard, she said, "Cade, look at me. Look at me." His breathing was irregular and his skin clammy. But staring into her eyes was the only thing that kept him from passing out. "Calm. Just calm down. Take a deep breath with me." Her eyes were a serene blue with little flecks of green around the edges. Together the colors reminded him of the clear blue-green waters off of Rosemary Beach. He'd never seen anything so beautiful. His breathing became more regulated and with less gasping. "Now, Cade. Just think for a minute. What were they sending out? What was in the e-mail? Did you see it? Did you see who they were sending it to? Take your time. Just tell us what you saw."

Cade breathed in deep and exhaled, still staring into Jana's eyes.

Agent Stark looked at Bolz who looked at Kyle. The three men were thinking the same thing—Agent Baker's presence was unmistakably a good thing. This wasn't just an attractive female; she was really good at this. Cade was the most important witness in this entire investigation, and she had a calming effect on him. They had to have his help. Without him, they were sunk. Everything was riding on this one man. Having Kyle, who knew Cade well, was very helpful, but Jana Baker provided the fountain of calm that Cade needed. Jana had only been an agent for a few months, but she was operating on her own plane. Her skill leading this witness down the path she wanted him to go was something normally not seen until an agent had been in the bureau ten or fifteen years.

Cade said, "Yeah, I saw the e-mail. It was just a regular marketing e-mail. Nothing unusual. Just something with some weekly newsletter content and a sidebar that promoted their product."

"Cade, why was this e-mail job such a big deal? You say the job was failing. What do you mean?" questioned Jana.

"When I got up there, they were freaking out that the e-mail server was about to crash. I didn't see what the big deal was. If it crashed, all that would happen is that un-e-mailed items would get sent right after the server rebooted. But it was like they thought the world would end if anything interrupted that job. And there was something else strange. All of our servers have redundant backups, so normally, if a job fails, the paired server picks up the slack and keeps on sending. For some reason, there are no backup servers on the seventeenth floor."

Jana started to ask about the lack of redundant servers, but stopped. "So you have no idea why they thought this e-mail job was so important that it couldn't possibly be interrupted?" said Jana.

"No, none," said Cade, "and when I say they were freaking out, I mean this was like DEFCON 5 or something. Sirens were sounding, strobe lights were, well, strobing. Did you ever see *Alien*? I mean, this was all Sigourney Weaver, the spaceship's going to blow kind of stuff. People were screaming. I thought I was onboard a nuclear submarine."

Jana stood up, her perfect eyebrows the picture of concentration.

"So we have what appears to be a normal marketing e-mail, a non-normal situation where a server might crash, and a really non-normal reaction to the potential of the server crashing."

"Right," said Cade.

Bolz wanted to interrupt and inject his own questions, but he bit his tongue. He could see Jana at work, and it was an awesome thing to behold. *Twenty-eight years old, two months in the field, and she's better at leading a witness than me*, thought Bolz.

Kyle stood at the edge of the room, watching, learning everything he could.

"And you've been permanently moved up to seventeen?" said Jana.

"Yeah, thrill of my life." Cade was not serious. He shook his head side to side. "Since I work there now, they've been having me look at what was going wrong, and look at ways to prevent it."

"You mean, look at what was going wrong with the server job? Did you find out what was going wrong?" Jana had no idea why it might matter what was going wrong on some server, but she wasn't going to lie awake at night wishing she had asked.

Cade looked over at Kyle and Bolz. "Well, yes and no. I mean, not to be a smartass or anything. It's just that, I found something weird. There was something weird in that server job."

"What do you mean?"

"Normally, when a mass e-mail is sending, everything the e-mail needs is given to the server ahead of time. You know, things like the e-mail content, the list of who's going to receive it. Then there's the personalization stuff . . ."

Jana interrupted, "Personalization stuff? Is that a technical term?"

Cade paused, not sure if she was flirting with him. Either way, he was all too glad to keep talking. It gave him more time to stare at her. "Yeah, highly technical," he joked. "No, it's just things like 'Dear Firstname' and all that. Whatever information the marketer sets up in the e-mail to be personalized to the recipient is sent to the server ahead of time." He looked at the four of them, noting they were not following. "My point is that in this e-mail job, the server wasn't given all that stuff ahead of time; instead, it was also calling outside for some data that it didn't have. And I mean outside of the firewall. It was doing this intermittently during the e-mail job. Every time it would call outside for whatever it was looking for, the server load would skyrocket. The box was redlining. It was about to blow. Whatever it was calling for was draining the system, and badly." Cade looked at them again, and they seemed to be tracking.

"Calling outside the firewall? You mean it was calling outside of the building? What was it calling for?" said Jana.

"I don't know," replied Cade, "but the important question might not be *what* was it calling, but instead, *where* was it calling?"

"Where was it calling?" repeated Jana.

"I did a little snooping," said Cade. "Our server was calling outside our building. That's something that's never done. And I mean never. But that's not the problem; well, okay, that *is* the reason the server is failing, but that's not what concerns me. It was calling to an IP address . . . that's like an address out on the Internet . . . this IP address is, well, it's like it's not there. Like a ghost."

"What does that mean, a ghost?" said Jana.

"I was hoping you could tell me," said Cade, with nervous laughter. "Okay, an IP address is like the street address on a house. You can hide the name of who lives there, but the street address itself is public information. I've never even heard of the concept of a ghost IP address. I can't even look up this IP. It's like it doesn't exist."

"And that's not normal?" said Jana.

"There *are* no IP addresses that aren't visible. It's impossible," Cade said. "Look, all I know is that our server is calling outside our building to a ghost server. And the process of calling for whatever data it's looking for is killing the server."

Jana sat down across from Cade. She stretched her hands out and put them on top of his. She looked him in the eye.

"Cade, we need your help." Cade was melting on the inside but tried not to show it. "There's a direct connection between your company, that e-mail job, that asshole in the picture, and the bombings. Right now, as of this moment, you're on the front line. You *are* the front line. You're the only one with access. You are our best hope."

Cade pulled away from her grip, and a shiver went up his spine. He was scared out of his mind. He was in danger, and he knew it. But looking into her eyes, those soft blue eyes, and listening to her words, there was no way in hell he was going to chicken out. A speech like that would have even made Dr. Martin Luther King proud.

"Yeah . . . I know . . . I know." Cade put his hands on his face then exhaled. "Shit, you're going to ask me to gather info, aren't you?" He turned and looked at Kyle. "I'm working in a pit of terrorists, right?" No one said a word. They didn't have to. Cade knew the answer before he asked the question.

Agent Bolz looked at Cade. "I've got to call the director right after this. Cade, what can I tell him? Can I tell him you're in?"

"The director of the FBI knows who I am?" said Cade.

Bolz wasn't even going to wait for an answer. He opened the door, turned back, and said, "The director will be briefing the president in a few hours. Agent MacKerron, Agent Baker, pay close attention. Special Agent in Charge Stark will brief Mr. Williams on what happens next. I want you two to learn everything you can about how to handle the situation. Mr. Williams' safety is our top priority." He let the door close behind him.

With everyone quiet, Cade looked at the three remaining agents. "So it's not exactly like I have a choice, do I? All right. Shit. All right. I'm in."

Jana's lips curled upward. But, her look didn't say "I got you"—instead it said, "Damn, he's got guts." Cade read her, but wasn't sure if he should be proud of himself, mad at himself for risking his life just to impress a girl, scared shitless, or all three.

Agent Stark leaned forward and walked to the table.

"Mr. Williams, I need to brief you now. You've just become the most important material witness in the United States. I'm not bullshitting you about that. People's lives depend on you, son." The gravity of what Stark was saying started to sink in. "Time is short. We've got sixteen days left before the next bombing."

Cade cut him off. "What do you mean, sixteen days? How do you know when the next bombing will be?" Cade looked around and realized he was the only person in the room who seemed to be confused.

Agent Stark said, "We have reason to believe the next one will happen in sixteen days. We've got to find out what's going on, fast. And we've got to prevent the next bombing. You're our only hope."

Kyle spoke up, "Cade, no one knows we have an idea when the next bombing will be. It's imperative that we not give that information away. We don't want the terrorists to know we've discovered anything. And we don't want the American public to be in a panic. We have no idea *where* the next bomb will go off."

"We need you to go back to work. Act like nothing is different," said Stark.

"Nothing is different, my ass!" snapped Cade. "I'm surrounded by a bunch of terrorists! They'll probably find out I'm spying on them and smash my fingers to bits with a hammer. My body will wind up in a fucking dumpster somewhere, and you act like nothing is different!"

Jana jumped up and put her hands on his shoulders. "We need you, Cade." Her soft voice sounded like two silk sheets rubbing together. "Yes, things are very different now. I'm afraid this is the new normal. But your role here is life and death. We need you to gather information. This information could prevent the next bombing. We need to see the e-mail content, we need to see who the e-mail was sent to, we need to know exactly what is causing the server problem, and where the server is calling to. We need it, Cade. Without you, people are going to die."

29

Across town, FBI agents and surveillance specialists were tracking every move of known terrorist Waseem Jarrah and the Jamaican whose name turned out to be Bastian Mokolo. Data was pouring into the command center on the tenth floor of Century Center, the building housing the Atlanta field office. Strangely, Waseem Jarrah had been easier to investigate. US intelligence sources from overseas already had a thick dossier on him.

The Jamaican, Bastian Mokolo, was proving to be a different story. The only US records that could be found of him were a state-issued driver's license and an apartment lease contract. No trace of him, however, could be found in Jamaica or the surrounding islands. There were no birth certificates, tax records, drivers' licenses, voter registrations, or cell phone records—not even a library card. And stranger still, NCIC, the National Crime Information Center federal database, drew a complete blank. It was like he existed in the flesh but not in the system.

On the first night, agents attempted to enter Mokolo's vehicle under cover of darkness. After witnessing the lengths that Mokolo went in order to avoid surveillance, paranoia ran high, and agents used extreme caution to avoid leaving any trace of their presence. At a minimum, their hope was to extract fingerprints. However, prior to even opening the driver's side door, they became alarmed. They noticed a tiny piece of lint that was placed into the door jamb at the very bottom of the door. If the door was opened, the lint would fall, a signal to Mokolo that someone had entered the vehicle. This upped the game. Agents knew without doubt they were dealing with a very sophisticated subject who would take any precaution to avoid detection. An inspection of the passenger's side door revealed no such countermeasures. However, once inside the car, agents found it devoid of fingerprints anywhere. Whoever Bastian Mokolo was remained a mystery. At this point, the only thing known about him was that he was a total professional.

Tailing Mokolo as he drove through town proved difficult as well. He would duck into side streets and neighborhoods, weave his way around, then pop out on another street. This was an effective method for finding out if someone was tailing you. On the third night, agents slipped the smallest, most advanced tracking device available onto the underside of the car. Its state-of-the-art digital circuitry enabled them to control when the device would ping its location. That meant if Mokolo electronically swept the vehicle for bugs, the tracking device would be dormant, and nearly impossible to locate. It might be their only way to keep up with him.

Another problem was that Mokolo seemed to switch cellphones daily. It was a trick taken from the playbook of Osama bin Laden, who never spoke on the same cellphone twice. Since they couldn't tap his phone line, the only way to listen to cellphone conversations was to be within line-of-sight when he placed a call. Surveillance agents used laser microphones and electronic eavesdropping equipment to focus and catch bits and pieces of his cryptic conversations.

What the bureau knew at this point was that they had isolated two controlling individuals involved in the spate of deadly bombings. What they didn't have—and what they desperately needed—was the rest of the terror cell's members. Even if the FBI swept in and arrested Bastian Mokolo and Waseem Jarrah, other members of the terror cell might carry out attacks preplanned in the event the cell was compromised. No, they couldn't arrest anyone without more information, and the clock was ticking.

Cade was briefed on all necessary precautions. His fraternity brother, Kyle, was a source of comfort. Cade knew he could call Kyle at any time. But Cade was more than just a bit smitten with Jana Baker. Being around her was distracting—downright intoxicating. He had to concentrate whenever she spoke, otherwise, he found he wasn't hearing anything she said.

Cade knew the bureau would be listening to any cell conversations he'd have. But he also knew his cellphone was not being tracked or tapped by anyone else. The bureau was confident of that. Big Brother was listening, but terrorists were not. *How comforting,* thought Cade. Kyle assigned electronic specialists from the Atlanta field office to sweep Cade's car and apartment for any bugs or tracking devices. His car would be checked daily; well, it would be checked nightly, anyway. The bureau wanted to keep as low a profile as possible, not being seen by anyone as it worked to protect Cade.

Both Jana and Kyle would be present on most days. Instead of trying to sneak around, they'd hide in plain sight. After all, they were both about the same age as Cade, and it wouldn't look out of the ordinary. They would appear to just be friends.

Cade tried to relax on the couch in his apartment, but on top of the stress of trying to gather information right out from under the noses of terrorists, Cade was also very distracted by the situation with his father. He'd started to realize the cancer might be worse than his dad was letting on. It was a familiar theme. When he was growing up, his father would be deployed on short notice, and he'd always say something to make sure his wife and child weren't worried about him. Flying a plane off the deck of a Navy carrier was never safe, particularly in hostile regions of the world. But talking to him on the phone in those days, you'd never know. Cal would speak in a calm, soft tone and assure them that all was well. Sometimes though, the news media would report a US military strike in a far-flung corner of the globe. The target was destroyed, yet in the process, ground-to-air missiles had been fired on US warplanes. Cade would glance at his mom to gauge her reaction. She was prone to crumbling under the stress of it all. She withdrew into depression. It was as if she retreated into a dark cave and couldn't find her way out. Cade hated his father for that.

Now, though, Cade was mad at himself for spending the last fifteen or more years of his life carrying anger. It was always there, deep in the pit of his stomach. He tried to bury it deep down, but a burden like that comes with a price—and that price must be paid.

Cade looked down at his cellphone. He wanted to call his dad but thought about the fact that someone would be listening. He decided he might as well get used to it. He'd been worried about being monitored at work for months, and now the feeling would just transfer to his personal life as well.

The phone rang on the other end. But instead of his father answering, a sweet southern female voice answered, "Mr. Williams' cell phone. Hello, this is Lou Anne speakin'."

Cade paused, not knowing what to say. "Ah, yeah. This is Cade, Mr. Williams' son. Is he around?" Cade felt stupid.

"Oh yes, honey. He's here. Can you hold on just a minute, he's puttin' himself back together."

Cade shifted in his chair. He'd interrupted his dad with some girl. It was as awkward as it gets.

"Oh, ah, well, that's okay. If he's busy, I can call back later."

The silky voice laughed. "Oh no, honey, it's no trouble. We were just finishing his X-ray."

"His X-ray? Where is he?"

"Now don't you worry your purty little head about it now. He's down here in the ER at Crawford Long. But we're gonna take good care of 'im. Don't you worry. Here he is, hun."

The emergency room?

"Hey, Cade," said Cal with a raspy tone in his voice.

"Dad. What's going on? Why are you in the ER? Are you okay?"

"Well, as good as can be expected, son. I'm not feeling the greatest. It's like I've got no energy. I just can't seem to catch my breath. Look, I'll be okay. I don't want you worrying about me."

But Cade was moving towards his car. He may be forever mad at his dad, but if this cancer thing was serious, and apparently it was, he wasn't going to chicken out of reconciling now.

Twenty minutes later, Cade walked into Crawford Long, a sprawling hospital complex in midtown Atlanta. The massive ceiling at the entrance was filled with light. Marble adorned everything. Cade double stepped across the floor, while a marble waterfall cascaded down the wall from high above. The reception nurse escorted Cade back into the emergency room and into the side room where Cal lay in a bed, several beeping devices hooked up to him.

"Cade! I didn't want to bother you with this. You didn't need to come down here. I'm sure it's nothing. I'm just getting old."

"Come on, Dad, you can't catch your breath. What's up with that? Besides, I didn't want you to be down here alone." The fact that Cal had left his family alone on so many occasions hung in the air like thick molasses. After an awkward pause, Cade said, "How come you're at Crawford Long? I thought you had a doctor friend out at Kennestone."

Cal looked at his lap. "That's where I told them to take me, but ambulances have to take you to the nearest hospital, which is here." Cade's insides buckled. *You had to take an ambulance?*

The two talked in awkward fits and starts, mostly about mundane things. Then Cal asked how things were going at work. Cade had shut his father out for so long. Now he wanted to break down the dam and tell him everything about what was really happening at his office. But he couldn't.

A rap on the door's glass window startled them. They both looked up as a nurse that had to be Lou Anne breezed through the door; her red hair was pulled back tightly in a bun. She was a bold, smiling presence in the room. Behind her was a clean-cut man in dress slacks, a crisp white dress shirt, and a tie. Cade thought it odd that the man wore no lab coat and carried no clipboard.

"Now, y'all, I want to introduce somebody," said Lou Anne. "This is Eddie. Eddie visits us every day, making his rounds. He's a chaplain here at the hospital, and he's one of my favorites!" Her smile was as big as her stark white teeth. Lou Anne scooted back out the door with the energy of someone twenty years younger.

Eddie laughed. "Don't you just love her? Hi, I'm Eddie Jenkins."

Cade and Cal introduced themselves.

"Like Lou Anne said, I'm a chaplain here. I make rounds in the ER every day. I was passing through and wanted to pop in and say hello. I'm sorry you're not feeling well, Mr. Williams. Is there anything I can get you while you wait? A magazine? A tall Scotch? Lou Anne's phone number?" Eddie was a confident guy, and his magnetism broke the tension. They both liked him immediately. There was peace and warmth spilling off of him that said "everything's going to be all right." And he was one of those rare people who seemed to have arrived at a higher plane of knowledge; he knew what to worry about and what to ignore. After telling a few stories to help pass the time, he stood up to leave.

"Oh, here's my card," said Eddie. "If you need to talk about anything, just let me know. They pay me the big bucks for that, you know." He grinned and was gone.

After a few moments of silence, Cal looked up.

"Son, I can tell something's eating at you. You've got that look in your eye just like when you were a kid. It's true; you used to look just like that. You'd have gotten a bad grade or something and had to have your test paper signed and didn't want to bring it up. I know that look. What's troubling you, son? Is it me?" Cal knew far more about his cancer than he was letting on, and he didn't want to have any regrets.

Cade picked at a tear in the fake leather seat on his chair and wished he could disappear.

"Dad, you ever get into a situation that you just can't get out of?"

"There's a way out of anything, son. I've been in more than a scrape or two in my time. Cade, you've got a whole life ahead of you. Is it your job? Don't bog down if your job is the wrong place for you to be. Go out and find what makes your insides want to *sing*." The word was emphasized like the last word of a sermon. Chaplain Eddie had gotten to him. "For some people, that's flying a plane at Mach two with their hair on fire, headed into harm's way. For others, it's a woman. You just have to find out what it is for you."

"I know what you're going to say," replied Cade.

"I'll say it anyway. Don't do anything you're going to regret for the rest of your life." It was a mantra Cade had heard a thousand times growing up. "You've grown up a lot," said Cal. "You've grown up without me being there for you. I regret that. I regret that more than anything I've ever done. And now I have to live with it. Do you know what it means now, son? To not do anything that you're going to regret?"

Cade looked over at his father. That was the deepest apology he had ever envisioned. His dad's eyes streamed tears, but his voice was granite.

"Yeah, Dad."

Through the door's window, Lou Anne waved, inviting Cade out. He left the room with lines etched across his forehead.

Lou Anne took his hand and patted it, walking him forward.

"Now, hun, listen. There's somethin' I want to show you." Lou Anne was quieter than before. Her voice was soft and sweet like honey. Cade knew that whatever she wanted to show him, it was something he didn't want to see. She led him around the large circular desk of the nurses' station and over to a large computer monitor. The nurse seated in front of the monitor saw them coming, stood, and then walked off. Lou Anne didn't say a word. On the screen of the oversized monitor was the image of a chest X-ray. The lungs on the X-ray were striated with bright white steaks, scarring their way across the fragile organs. There was no need for a physician to interpret the X-ray for Cade. Any layman could see that his dad's lungs were racked with cancer. The streaks looked like sharpened fingers, each thirsting to grow farther and faster than the others. Cade stared at the screen.

The large room, normally bustling with activity, had gone silent. There was no activity. Nurses stared at the ground, doctors across the room looked down, technicians stood still. Everyone who worked in that ER had been informed of what was happening. A family member was being told that their loved one's medical condition was terminal, and there was nothing anyone could do about it.

Lou Anne gripped Cade's hand, pulling it against herself, her lower lip quivering. A small tear pooled in Cade's eye. Lou Anne was a genteel southern lady and no longer bothered to fight back her emotions. She had one unwritten rule—no one was allowed to cry alone in her presence.

Soft footsteps approached Cade followed by a firm, comforting hand on his shoulder. It was Chaplain Eddie. Eddie stood. There was nothing to be said. It wasn't his words that were needed; it was his compassion, his comfort, his presence. It was no fluke that Eddie happened to be passing through the ER earlier that day. After the X-ray had been taken, Lou Anne called him. He was called, and he came. He answered the call, like he always did, with warmth that penetrated everything he touched. By visiting Cal's triage room before the X-ray was disclosed, he was able to offer the type of comfort a stranger can't.

Cade's knees shook beneath him. He looked at the X-ray but no longer really saw it. He put his arms around Lou Anne on one side and Eddie on the other.

And they all stood, and they all knew.

30

The morning's threat assessment was delivered to the president by the director of the FBI. This happened six days a week, and sometimes on Sunday. Today's assessment was grim. Another bombing was anticipated in four days. The countdown was on, the clock ticking. Under the enormous burden of an impending attack, the president signed Executive Order number 4636, something he had never done before. The weight of his office bore down on him with unforgiving relentlessness. EO 4636 was a directive that authorized the bureau to take whatever means necessary to stop the threat. In short, the executive order secretly authorized any level of force required, including assassination.

FBI Director Stephen Latent had never received such an order. But he understood the president's decision. The citizens of the United States knew another bombing could happen at any time. They were not only scared, they were in grave danger, and they knew it. Danger was imminent, but it was fear that ruled the day.

The country's reaction to the bombings was divided. People in small towns seemed more determined to go about their daily lives, refusing to let terror best them. Yet those in major cities avoided leaving their homes. Gripped with fear, they avoided events like baseball games, soccer matches, outdoor concerts, and graduation ceremonies. Restaurants in most major cities were vacant. Grocery store shelves emptied as families stocked up on food. Many flights were cancelled due to the number of open seats. School attendance began to falter. Fear impacted the US economy, though not badly yet. Worse, fear was impacting the American way of life, and that was exactly what the terrorists wanted.

Agent Philip Murphy, commander of the Hostage Rescue Team based out of the Atlanta field office, took the news of the executive order without visible reaction. His insides, however, reminded him of being in middle school and forgetting that a term paper was due. He'd killed people before, during the first and second Gulf Wars, but it was not something he relished. In fact, it made him sick. But he would do what he was told in order to secure a nation. HRT had been involved during the surveillance of Bastian Mokolo. If Mokolo was financing terrorists, the threat was extremely high, and the Hostage Rescue Team needed to be close by at all times.

Members from other HRT units had been temporarily assigned to the case; all were men Murphy either trained with or had served with in various warzones. Although Cade didn't know it, a few HRT members were near him through all hours of the day.

Today, like any day, when Mokolo went on the move, dozens of vehicles moved with him. Two vehicles followed, never tailing too closely. Several others fanned out in all directions ahead of him, watching the map as the tracking device pinged its way around the city. Guessing where his car was headed was one thing, but being there in case he stopped early was another. As a precaution, every vehicle was equipped with advanced photographic and recording instrumentation. Everyone focused on one goal, to try to record anything he said.

On this particular day, two blips appeared on the tracking map in Agent Murphy's vehicle; the first was the signal from Bastian Mokolo's car, the second emanated from the vehicle used by William Macy. Even though tracking down his true identity had been a top priority, no one knew his real name yet.

The blips were converging. Murphy's heart raced as he wondered if the two would come face to face, just like that first day when Agent Jana Baker's frantic surveillance pursuit blew the case wide open. Bureau cars of all descriptions swarmed around the two blips, which were headed down Piedmont Road. Coming from different directions, the two turned into the main entrance of the Atlanta Botanical Gardens, a sprawling and heavily wooded park near midtown Atlanta. Murphy barked orders into the radio. All vehicles were to surround the park, and one plainclothes agent from each vehicle was to get inside at all costs. "And, people," he said, "stay out of sight, be inconspicuous. We can't risk blowing this surveillance." If the two subjects were face to face, their conversation had to be recorded.

Murphy jacked his vehicle onto the curb, got out, and leapt the eight-foot fence in one gazelle-like motion. He too was dressed in civilian clothes, and to his benefit, as long as no one saw him leap the fence, the appearance of a man with a large camera strapped around his neck was not the least bit unusual in the gardens. He looked like any other visitor.

And there they were, Mokolo and Macy, separately strolling on the brick pathway that worked its way through the manicured forest of heavy pine and oak trees.

Murphy whispered into his microphone, "All units, all units, subjects spotted en route to the canopy walk. In position in zero-two mics. Keep your distance, I've got the point."

He moved up the path until reaching the base of the stunning canopy walk bridge, a 600-foot span of bridge that snaked its way back and forth just under the tree tops. He crouched behind a huge bronze plaque dedicated to the bridge mounted onto heavy granite as Mokolo and Macy entered the bridge from opposite sides.

From his hidden vantage point, Murphy pointed the TC-150 recording device at the two subjects as they walked up the bridge moving towards each. To Murphy, it appeared that the two strolled through the park as if they hadn't a care in the world. When the laser microphone picked up its first sounds, his mood darkened.

"So, you be pleased with de work, eh, mon?" The thick Jamaican accent stuck to his tongue like honey to a brown bear's jaw.

Murphy's eyes widened, but it was what was said next that stopped his heart.

"You can drop that bullshit Jamaican accent, asshole," said Macy.

"All right, all right. Whatever," said Mokolo. The accent had vanished. "Damn, you're a pain in the ass sometimes." All Mokolo's mannerisms changed. He stood more upright and with less shuffle in his walk. It was like watching a chrysalis morph into a butterfly in a matter of seconds. His voice now contained hints of Brooklyn.

Murphy sat, stunned. *What the hell's going on? This guy's not Jamaican?*

"Yeah," replied Macy, "why don't you go screw yourself?" The statement was toxic.

"And who the fuck do you think you are? I'm delivering exactly what I was tasked to deliver," said Mokolo. "You now know more about this terror cell than you've ever known about any in the past."

Macy yelled back, "And how many people!" He stopped, looked in each direction, then lowered his voice, not wanting to attract attention. "We started this thing in order to climb the ropes within the terror cell. These events are supposed to be small, goddammit. There's too much breakage. Three hundred and seven in that event in Montana? These events are supposed to generate closer to twenty. What in the flying fuck is going on?"

"Why don't you lick my balls," retorted Mokolo. "You give me a load of cash to 'invest' with these assholes; what do you expect, that they're going to let me place an order for a certain body count? In fact, now that we're talking about balls, it's *my* balls on the line here. Those pricks get wind that I'm working against them and not for them, the next time you see me my body will be scattered into tiny parts, like so many of da leaves fallin' off da tree, mon."

Murphy concentrated, his hand crushed against his earpiece. The conversation was baffling. It sounded like the terrorists were trying to scam the terrorists.

"What's the next target?" said Macy, having calmed down.

"As usual, I don't know. I never know. In fact, I don't want to know. These are Americans we're talking about here."

"No shit! Just shut up and do your job," said Macy. "This will pay off in the end. There's no way to accomplish this without breakage. I know that. But that Montana thing . . . we go from a few dozen per incident to 307. Jesus Christ. You can bet the bureau is going to throw every asset they have at this." Macy jammed a sharp finger in Mokolo's chest. "You keep your head down. No mistakes. We're getting close, and the stakes are getting higher."

31

Jana heard the radio traffic regarding the surveillance of Bastian Mokolo and William Macy. She pulled into the parking lot of the Atlanta field office at Century Center just as a spring rain shower finished washing a thick layer of pollen from her car. She dodged the few remaining rain drops, and darted across the parking lot towards the sleek rectangular building. Pollen pooled into bright yellow streams as it washed off the pavement and found its way into drainage grates.

On the tenth floor, she walked through the lobby to the heavy, steel-reinforced door that led into the FBI office. She pressed her cheekbone against the retinal scanner, the door opened, and she walked in. In the conference room, agents were gathering. Ever since the Montana bombing, the Atlanta office had been swarmed with agents from all over the United States. Kyle MacKerron was already inside, as was Agent in Charge David Stark. It was standing room only, although an empty chair was at the head of the table.

Jana did a double take as FBI Director Stephen Latent walked in and took the open seat. She was shocked. But then again, this was the bureau's top priority. She'd only met him once; he had been the commencement speaker at her graduation from the FBI Academy at Quantico. Other than that, the only time she'd laid eyes on him was on CNN.

"All right, everyone, settle down. Quiet, people," said the director. Among the agents, he was well-liked and considered a fair guy, but he didn't look to be in the mood for any games. "There's something I want everyone to hear. It's a recording between two of our prime suspects. This was recorded an hour ago at the Atlanta Botanical Gardens." The room went silent. He motioned to Agent Stark who hit the play button on his laptop, and the conversation unfolded.

After the recording ended, confusion spilled into a sea of confused looks.

One agent piped up, "Sir, I don't follow. I thought these were the terrorists? I don't understand what they're discussing. What does the

Jamaican, or whatever his nationality really is, mean by 'if they find out I'm working against them and not for them'?"

"We have no idea yet," said the director. "Like I said, this was recorded an hour ago. Anyone care to advance a theory?"

Muffled conversations began, but no one wanted to sound stupid in front of the director. Jana looked across the room. She wasn't bold by nature, but from the first day she walked onto the Marine base at Quantico, she was determined to make her mark in this man's world. Keeping her mouth shut was not going to accomplish that goal. The room was full of senior agents whose collective testosterone level rivaled that of a division-one collegiate football team. It was time to make a move.

"They sound like undercovers," she said.

It was as if someone had yanked the needle off of an old record player, scraping the vinyl in the process. Heads turned to see who was talking, some craning upwards or sideways. "They sound like spooks to me, sir."

Conversations erupted across the room as heads shook back and forth. The reaction told Jana she may have, in fact, made a fool of herself. But she wasn't backing down.

The director looked at her, wanting to hear more. "Go on," he said.

"Mokolo, the Jamaican, sounds like he's working undercover. Macy appears to be his sponsor, or boss. We've traced over a million dollars flowing into sealed bank accounts in Zurich and the Cayman Islands, right? We know the money is real." Jana stood and walked towards the front of the room. She could feel male eyes move up and down her trim body, and that pissed her off. She was a special agent, and it wasn't her job to be eye candy. It was her job to catch terrorists, then kick their collective asses. She ignored the stares. Muffled conversations again murmured across the room; it was obvious many senior agents were scoffing at her theory. Her anger got the best of her.

"Excuse me"—her voice boomed—"we have one day before the next bomb goes off at some Girl Scout event or high school lacrosse match or yachting competition or wherever. Is there something you'd rather be discussing right now?"

The gauntlet had been thrown, and the room went silent. The director grinned.

"Listen to what they're saying. They're talking about climbing the ladder of a terror cell." She turned to the director. "It sounds like the same tactic the DEA employs to climb the ladder of a drug ring. They start by making buys from street-level dealers, then work their way up to larger and larger parts of the organization. Then they bust the entire ring wide open."

The director respected boldness, but boldness was not enough. He challenged Jana to defend her theory.

"Your theory is that some government agency is funding a terror cell, in order to bust the cell wide open?"

The door to the conference room burst open, and a technician charged in. "Sir! Oh . . . shit. I'm sorry to interrupt. Director, the results are back . . . on the fingerprints you wanted? We've got both of them, the one we were finally able to pull from the Jamaican's car, and the other from the subject known as William Macy. But, you're not going to like it."

"No match?" questioned the director.

"Not exactly, sir. We've got a hit on both all right. It's just that the NCIC computer blocks access to their identities."

Latent jumped up, rocking his chair backwards and nearly toppling it. "What the hell does that mean?"

"None of us have ever seen anything like this, sir," said the technician. "We don't know what it means. When we ran the fingerprints on both, we got this NCIC error code. I printed it so you could see what it says."

The paper simply read,

Classified: 14.6 EO
Access level C12 required.

The director's face went pale. Latent fumbled behind himself, struggling for his chair. He flopped down in heap. No one said a word. The troops under his command during the first Gulf War would have said he had *the thousand-yard stare*—the glassy look of exhaustion, depression, and defeat, only worse. The paper began to quiver in his hand.

He looked up at Jana and realized her theory now had sudden validity. The technician left as Latent cast his gaze down at the table.

"Fourteen," he said. "Four-fucking-teen. It can't be. It just can't be."

From across the room, Agent in Charge David Stark was almost afraid to ask. "What's fourteen, sir? What's 14.6?"

The air stagnated. Director Latent replied like a man speaking from within an abyss. "14.6 EO," he said, emphasizing the *E* and *O* like they were somehow burning his throat. "After the 9/11 attacks, the president authorized a series of secret, classified directives designed to protect the sovereignty of the United States. There are fifteen protocols in total. Number fourteen, or the Fourteenth Protocol, corresponds to actions relegated to Central Intelligence." He leaned his head into his hands. "These fingerprints belong to Company men. These prints belong to CIA operatives. It means our government is funding terrorists. It means our government is funding the slaughter of innocent Americans under the guise of breaking a terror cell." A muffled hush filtered across the room. "I think Agent Baker is right. Like she said, they sound like spooks. Maybe the CIA *is* trying to break apart a large terror cell by starting at the ground-level, and working their way up." He looked up at Jana. "Like the way the DEA busts a street-level dealer first, then works their way up the organization." His nod of approval at the young agent resonated in all corners of the room.

Jana turned to face him. "What's the plan, sir?"

Director Latent snapped back, "Priorities. First, we find out where in the flying fuck that next bomb is going to go off. Stark, how many hours do we have left?"

"Twenty-one hours, thirty-eight minutes."

"This—is—our—mission. Find that goddamn bomb and find it now. We'll figure out how to deal with the CIA separately. I don't care if I have to kick the president's ass right in the oval office. No one breathes a word of this. The CIA can't know we're onto them. If I find out any one of you talked, they'll be peeling your facial skin off my knuckles, understood?"

A collective "yes, sir" echoed across the room, and people scattered into the hallway.

Kyle and Jana exchanged worried glances. Kyle spoke first.

"We've got to get Cade to find that information. I don't care if he's got to steal it right out from under their noses. We have to know what's in that next mass e-mail. We have to know who it's being sent to. And we've got to figure out whatever that encryption process is. That mass e-mail system has got to be the way they are communicating to the terror cell. Everything points to Thoughtstorm."

"Remember how Cade said that the servers were calling outside the Thoughtstorm building to an IP address that was untraceable?" said Jana.

"Yeah?"

"Makes sense, doesn't it? It's untraceable because it's owned by the goddamned CIA," said Jana. "They're spoofing it so its origin can't be traced."

"All right, let's get Stark onboard with this," said Kyle. "We're going to need some heavy hitters to figure this technical crap out. Maybe he can get the NSA to trace that IP address and crack whatever encryption is being applied to those e-mails. If we can learn what's in those e-mails, we might be able to get to the bomber before it's too late."

"Kyle, Cade said there are hundreds of thousands of e-mail addresses that receive those e-mails. I mean, there's no way all those people are involved; it would have to be just a small group from within the larger set. How are we going to know which e-mail addresses we're looking for?"

Kyle thought about the question. "Remember what Cade said? He said during the e-mail job, the server would be fine, and then it would ramp up and almost crash, and that it was doing this intermittently during the e-mail send?"

"Yeah?"

"It sounds like every time the server goes haywire, that's when it's calling outside of Thoughtstorm to get that encryption code to execute. If we can identify which e-mail addresses are being treated with that encryption, we'll have our list."

The two raced down to find Stark talking with Director Latent. They barged in and laid out their expanded theory.

32

"The NSA will never be able to crack a CIA-level encryption algorithm in a matter of hours. And besides—" said Stark. But the director cut him off.

"Wait a minute. Even if the NSA can't crack the code in time, based on what Agent MacKerron here is saying, we still might be able to find out which e-mail addresses belong to terrorists. Don't you get it? Maybe from there we can track down where those people open their e-mails. I'm going to get on the horn to the NSA myself and keep it quiet. I've got a contact over there that I trust. I don't want the CIA to get wind of this from anyone, including the NSA. And get a tech team in here right now. I want this whole office swept for bugs. This CIA thing is giving me the willies."

Stark left the room in a hurry, and Director Latent turned back to Jana and Kyle.

"Sir, you've got a contact at NSA?" said Jana. "Are you sure you can trust him? I mean, what if . . ."

Latent held up his hand. "Don't worry, Baker. Uncle Bill and I go way back. All the way to Georgetown. I'd trust him with my life. In fact," Latent started to laugh, "if anyone ever finds out how many times he held my head over the toilet . . . You two, get back to your witness. Tonight is the night. I don't care if we don't have a warrant. We need his help to get in that building and get the data. I'm putting special ops on standby. You'll have an HRT assault team with you tonight. Pay attention to what they say. Learn from them. You're both going in that building. It's time to earn your pay."

Jana and Kyle looked at one another; the gravity of the situation pulled against them like the tow of a tsunami. They were down the elevator and out the building two minutes later. The springtime air was heavy with steam as they ran across the wet, pollen-washed parking lot. They drove straight to Cade's apartment. Kyle never felt so exhilarated in his life.

33

It was after seven p.m. when Cade got home. He looked exhausted. Kyle was in the arm chair in the main room of the apartment, but for once, Cade wasn't happy to see him.

"Aw man, I was afraid you'd be here," said Cade.

"Well kiss my ass. Who was it that was there to take care of you after you hurled at that homecoming party?" Kyle jabbed, grinning.

"Yeah, yeah. I know you'd do anything for me. You'd bail me out of jail, you'd kill for me, all that fraternity crap, blah, blah, blah," said Cade.

Cade walked into the kitchen and put down his laptop bag, still not seeing Jana sitting across the room.

"I don't have anything new yet. They're watching me like a hawk. My computer is being monitored. I can see the network sniffer on it. If I download any data, they'd know."

"Oh really? Can't get the data, huh? Well what if I told you I could get you a date with Jana? I bet you'd suddenly find a way to get the data then, wouldn't you?" Kyle ribbed, never letting on that Jana was sitting right there. "Admit it, you love her, don't you? Come on, admit it."

"How do you . . . aw man, don't tell her, all right? I mean, shit, a girl like that? I'd never get a date with her. She's way out of my league. Look, don't tell her. And I'm not in love with her. I'm just . . . obsessed. You happy now?"

Kyle's attempt to hold his laughter broke. "Okay, I won't say a word. Honest." Laughter burst out of both Kyle and Jana. Cade poked his head around the wall and saw Jana sitting there, gripping her mouth with both hands to stifle herself.

Cade had to laugh at himself. There was nothing left to do; it was too late—he'd already made a fool of himself. "Okay, okay, now I feel like an ass. Are you both happy?" Laughter erupted in the small apartment.

"Cade, all right, all right. I'm sorry, I didn't mean to laugh," said Jana. "Let's put the whole thing behind us, okay? But listen, in all seriousness, we need to talk. We brought food. We'll talk while we eat. We've got a lot to do tonight."

Cade's face was still flushed. "We do?" He looked at the two of them. "What do we have to do tonight?" Cade held both hands up as if to surrender. "Wait, wait, don't tell me. Good God, whatever it is, I don't think I want to know."

Kyle and Jana laughed at him, hoping to ease the tension as Cade turned back towards Kyle.

"Cool Mac, okay, there's something that's been eating at me. It's something I didn't notice at first, and now I can't stop thinking about it. The other night . . . that night I saw you on TV at the news conference. I called your cell, and you were on the scene of the Montana bombing, right?"

"Yeah?" said Kyle.

"I don't understand. The bombing happened, what, like an hour beforehand?"

"And?"

"Dude. You live in San Diego. How is it that you were on the scene of a bombing that's fifteen hundred miles away in less than an hour? And thinking about it, you must have been there much sooner, because your boss knew all the details of what happened, right?"

Kyle paused. "Shit, I knew this would come up . . . I tell you what, let's take a breather. Let's eat first, then we'll talk."

Jana and Kyle didn't say anything work related until after all the reheated pizza was cleared from the coffee table. They wanted Cade to relax and decompress. What they were about to tell him was going to wig him out. And if the truth be told, both Kyle and Jana were a bit wigged out themselves.

Jana began, "Cade, what we're going to tell you is going to be a shock."

Cade looked at her. She was the sultriest thing he'd ever seen. Whatever she had to tell him, he was going to listen because listening meant he got to look at her without her thinking he was gawking, which he was.

"There's no easy way to say this, so I'm just going to say it. You work at spook central."

Cade smiled, glancing back and forth at the two of them. "What? What do you mean? What, like Ghostbusters or something? There are ghosts in my office?"

Jana looked to Kyle. "No. Not those kinds of spooks."

Cade's eyes squinted in confusion.

"Spooks. Wait, you mean spies? Those kind of spooks? What are you talking about?" But before Jana could respond, realization took hold of Cade. *Spies. They're spies. That's what all the secrecy is about. That's what the DEFCON 4 fire drills are about. That's what Rupert Johnston meant when he talked about the seventeenth floor having a special coating on the glass to thwart laser mics from being able to eavesdrop.*

"I, I, I . . . they're spies? Like, real spies?!" Cade was beginning to panic.

"Calm down," said Jana, sitting on the couch next to him. "But yes, we mean spies . . . Cade, your coworkers are employed by the CIA."

Cade broke free from the trance of Jana's deep blue eyes and stood up, knocking hard into the glass top of the coffee table. It slid down to the carpeted floor with a thud.

"Whaaat in the blue FUCK are you talking about?! How could they be CIA?! There's just . . . there's no way . . ."

Kyle jumped up and put his hands on Cade's shoulders. "Look at me. Look at me! There's nothing we can do about it, Cade. It is what it is. You remember that time in the frat when that dumbass Matt Lumson threw that beer bottle way up in the air? And it landed on Dr. Lick's car? The president of the damn university? We were screwed, right? The whole frat was put on probation, and we just had to suck on it. It was what it was. There was no way out. It's like that, man. It is what it is. And now, we have to deal with it. Now, we make our move."

Jana interrupted. "Kyle. Hold on. Don't go there yet. Before we tell him our plans, he has to know why. He has to know what's at stake."

Jana had a structured way of thinking. A way of compartmentalizing and speed-thinking three sentences ahead of whomever she was talking to.

"What do you mean? What's at stake?" said Cade.

Kyle exhaled. "Sit down, man. Let's talk about this thing."

Cade's eyes locked on Kyle as he found his seat on the couch again, his left arm feeling behind him like a blind man. He collapsed into the couch, terrified of what they might say next.

Kyle laid out their theory. Thoughtstorm was the nerve center of a communications system for a CIA-sponsored terror cell that was spread out across the United States. After it was over, Cade looked like he was going to be sick.

"You think Thoughtstorm is run by the CIA? You think the CIA is funding terrorists? Funding terrorists so that they can work their way higher and higher up within the terrorist organization until they can bust the whole thing wide open? Are you out of your fucking minds?" Kyle and Jana said nothing.

Cade's breathing became erratic. "But in the process, people and kids and moms and shit are dying? Are you kidding me?"

Jana put her hand onto Cade's shoulder and slid closer to him. "Okay, okay. Let's lean back. Breathe, Cade, breathe. Relax. Long breaths, in and out. That's better. It's a lot to take in, I know. But we're pretty damn sure we're right. We lifted a fingerprint from the one you call William Macy." Agent Baker paused, looking up at Kyle. She knew that by revealing these things she may be breaching national security. But too much was riding on Cade Williams. The clock was ticking, and people were going to die, again.

"I'm not supposed to tell you things like this, Cade," said Jana. "I could get into trouble. A lot of trouble. But my father drilled one thing into my head that I carry with me every day. He told me to never ever do anything I'm going to regret for the rest of my life."

Cade looked at her, stunned. He'd heard the exact same phrase from his dad so many times growing up he'd wanted to puke. But now he was starting to understand what his father meant.

"I might get in trouble now, but I'd never be able to live with myself if there was some way for me to stop these assholes from killing again," she said. "And frankly, I couldn't give a fuck. I'm not going to sit here and watch it happen. I'm going to stop it, and stop it hard."

"So what about this fingerprint?" Cade regained some of his composure, and his breathing normalized.

"William Macy's fingerprint was found in the NCIC database. But access to the identity was blocked by something called the Fourteenth Protocol. When Director Latent saw that, I swear, he turned white as a ghost."

Kyle spoke up, "None of us even knew what the Fourteenth Protocol was. Latent was the only one in the whole office. That's how classified it is."

Then Jana said, "As the stories around the office go, when Latent was a field agent, he was tougher than nails. They said he'd kick your ass if you tried to get in front of him when it was time to breach a door as a raid was about to happen. He doesn't back down for anything. But, man, this thing scared the shit out of him."

Cade was ready to learn more and sat up a little. "All right, so what is this protocol thing?"

"It's apparently one of fifteen executive protocols created after 9/11. I don't know what the rest of them mean, but the fourteenth corresponds to the CIA. It means William Macy, or whatever his real name is, is a Company man. He works for the Central Intelligence Agency."

"That's not all that you have to tell me, is it?"

Kyle looked at him out of the side of his eye. "No. No, it's not."

"All right, so what else do you have to tell me? What is it you've been working up to?"

Kyle walked across the room and stood with his back to Cade, staring at a span of wall where a framed picture would normally hang.

"Montana. You asked me how it was I got from San Diego to Shelby, Montana, in under an hour." Kyle thought back to that night, to the horrible things he'd seen, sights that would haunt him for the rest of his life.

"I didn't get from San Diego to Shelby in an hour. I was in a Gulfstream jet an hour before the bomb went off. We were flying around the center of the country, just waiting for it to happen."

"You were just waiting for it to happen?"

"Remember, Cade, these attacks are timed," said Kyle. "The bombing in Montana occurred eighteen days after the one in Tucson. We know when they're going to go off, but we don't know where." Kyle was still staring straight ahead. "We were airborne ahead of the attack so we could respond as quickly as possible. When we got onto the scene of that bombing . . . I just . . . I can't explain how bad it was. It was like being on the surface of the moon. Everything was gray, except for the splattering of red—everything. The dirt, the road, the buildings that were still standing; human remains were everywhere."

Kyle turned back around to look at Cade, but Cade looked away.

"No, no. I don't want to hear this, I can't hear this," said Cade.

"I have to tell you. You have to know. Otherwise, you won't understand . . . you won't understand what we have to do."

Cade looked up. Jana held her hands over her mouth. She couldn't imagine the horror of the things Kyle had seen. She now knew that this job, and the things she would see and hear, would mark her for the rest of her life.

Kyle continued, "Like I was saying, there were tiny body parts everywhere, just little fragments. There was one though, one that brought me to my knees. It was a hand. It was a tiny, tiny hand. The child must have only been about a year old. And there at my feet, I looked down. Other than the dirt, it was this perfect little hand. I just fell to my knees and lost it. I wretched like I've never wretched in my life. I lost it big time."

Cade shook his head and placed his hands over his ears.

Kyle grabbed him, hard. "Cade, Cade! Goddammit! Listen to me. Listen! That little hand—it wasn't just some piece of crime scene evidence. It was a tiny life. A real person. Some kid who never got a chance. I had to fingerprint it. I think Supervisory Special Agent Bolz wanted me to have that experience, to be emotionally tied to the investigation. When we matched the prints with the birth records at the local hospital, it led us to..." Kyle stopped and collected his thoughts. "There's a set of grandparents who live just south of Shelby who will never see their daughter or little grandchild again. I had to tell them that the only thing we could find of their granddaughter was a . . . a . . ." He stopped, unable to finish his sentence. "Cade, we are three of the only people in the country who can stop it before it happens again. Everyone else is out there, afraid to leave their homes. People are in hiding. They're taking away our way of life, our whole economy . . ." Kyle was walking the room, his arms flailing as he made his point. "This is not America anymore; they've taken that away from us. Goddammit! I need your help. We need your help." Kyle looked despondent. "The whole damn country needs your help."

After a long silence, Cade capitulated. "All right, Kyle, all right. Fuck it. I've known you forever. Whatever it is, I'm in. What is it we have to do?"

Jana looked to Kyle who had just received a call on his cell. By the look on his face, it was the call they'd been waiting for from HRT. Kyle's thumbs-up told Jana they had the green light.

Jana said, "You've done everything you could to try to get us the data we need. But, it hasn't worked. We're going. Tonight."

"Going where?" said Cade. "My office?" Jana looked at him with no acknowledgement. Cade's expression went from confusion to resignation. "Oh shit, I knew you were going to say that. Son of a bitch."

"Yes, we're going in," said Jana, "and we're going to steal whatever in the hell we need to solve this. And we need you. We need you to get us in there. We've got to try to get in undetected. If the Company finds out, the game is up. We'll never find out who all the members of the terror cell are."

"The company? You mean Thoughtstorm, right?"

"No, when we say Company, we mean CIA," said Jana. "We'll be after several things. We need the entire list of e-mail addresses that are a part of that campaign. We need that damn encryption code; without it, we can't crack it, which means we are blind to what the cell members are being told. And we need to see when that e-mail list is going to be sent another e-mail."

"Not that I'm arguing, but why tonight?" said Cade.

"There'll be another bombing tomorrow morning." Jana's face told Cade she was as serious as a heart attack. "Yes, tomorrow morning. Like Kyle said earlier, these assholes are following a pre-timed countdown to each attack. That's why we have to go tonight. We have less than ten hours until the next bomb goes off. We've got to try to at least find the location of the next attack so we can stop it. The tricky part is, even if we could stop it, we'll have to do it in such a way as to not let the terror cell know we've broken their code."

Cade thought about that for a moment. "So why can't you go in and arrest that William Macy jackass? And Rupert Johnston for that matter, he's got to be in on it too. And what about that Jamaican you talked about?"

"Even if we did, we don't have enough evidence to charge them. Yeah, we've got our hands on some seriously incriminating-sounding conversations, but the director already talked to the US Attorney who made it clear that we don't have jack-shit—we'd never get a conviction. Not to mention the fact that we'd still be no closer to locating the other members of the cell. We're afraid that if we tipped our hand too early, that the cell would continue its mission."

Kyle interrupted Jana as his call finished. "We've learned from experience," said Kyle, "some of these terror cells have a final set of instructions that they are to carry out in the event it looks like the cell is compromised. No, we've got to be able to nail all of them at once."

Cade could feel the pressure mounting. There would be no turning back.

Kyle continued, "And in this case, we've got a terror cell that's on a countdown. Not just a countdown to tomorrow's attack, but to a final countdown. Each attack is coming earlier and earlier than the last. They're counting down to something. I'd hate to think that they have something bigger up their sleeve. If they get wind we're onto them, they might just execute whatever that bigger something is."

Jana said, "Okay, Cade, what's the move? How do we get in there and get what we need?"

Cade looked at her, shaking his head back and forth. "I knew you were going to ask me that. Damn. All right. The only way we're going to get the data we need is to get into Rupert Johnston's computer. And

NATHAN GOODMAN □ 143

no, there's no way to hack into it from the outside. Computer systems on the seventeenth floor are totally closed loop. They're isolated from any outside access. We're going to have to get his laptop in our hands, somehow."

"It will be in his office? Will it be a password to log in?" said Jana.

"No, his uses a biometric log-in; he finger-swipes across a sensor. Basically, I'm saying we need him to log in to the laptop for us." Cade laughed, but no one else did.

Then Kyle said, "We can do it. Really, we can do it." He looked over at Jana. "We've got Johnston's fingerprints too. We can have a gel copy of his print made and have it delivered over to us within the hour. You'll apply it to your right index finger and swipe the laptop."

Cade said, "Wait a minute, why are you looking at her? You don't mean to say she's going to log on to Johnston's laptop do you? She can't be on the seventeenth floor—only I can go. No one is allowed up there."

But Kyle was confident. "Cade, security is lax during the late night."

"How the hell do you know that?"

Kyle smirked. "We've got more surveillance on that place than we do on the Syrian embassy. We've been tracking each Thoughtstorm security employee. We know when each one comes and goes. The nighttime hours are a little more lax. And let's not forget one other important thing. It's only the seventeenth floor that's crawling with Virginia farm boys . . . sorry, CIA boys. The rest of the employees are not CIA. The seventeenth floor has its own security contingent. Late at night, there will be fewer Company men on duty up there. The other security personnel you'll see work for Thoughtstorm, not the CIA."

Cade said, "But how am I going to get anyone in there besides myself?"

"The two of you will go into the office together," said Kyle. "If anyone is watching, you'll play it like you just wanted to show your girlfriend how cool the place where you work is."

"My girlfriend?" Cade looked at Jana, unsure if he should laugh because of how out of his league she was, or cry, because of how much time he'd like to spend staring into her eyes.

Jana's smile was demure. "Yes, Cade, your girlfriend."

"Now listen," said Kyle. "There's a decent chance that you will be spotted."

"And?"

"And you better look convincing as a couple."

Jana's grin betrayed her hidden schoolgirl. The truth was, she never really had been in a long-term relationship. It's not that she wasn't interested; instead it was that she'd been so engaged with academics, athletics, or her career. Nowadays, most men she met were either intimidated by her striking looks or by the fact that she could throw them to the ground and slap handcuffs on them faster than they could ask her on a second date.

"What he means is that you and I are going to have to practice looking natural together," said Jana. "Practice getting to know one another. You know, physical touch?" She laughed at Cade whose face was flushed. "We have to look like we're romantically involved, like on a second or third date. I mean, think about it, if you and I were on our third date, and having a great time together, wouldn't you want to show me how cool your job is?"

"Even if it would put a girl to sleep?" replied Cade. "No, no. Look, I get it. I know, yeah, we have to look convincing. And we're going in later tonight, right? So . . . what, we're supposed to start practicing right now?"

Kyle slapped Cade on the back. "Get in there, big man. Show her what you're worth. I mean, who is she anyway, right? She's just another girl, right? Just like back in the frat."

"Cool Mac," said Cade, "back in the frat, if you recall, I didn't exactly have a girl under each arm, remember? That was you, you nimrod."

Kyle laughed. "Yeah, yeah. But that was then. Now, you're a rock star. And remember, all of this is in service to your country, okay? So get in there and give-us-a-kiss." His voice decried a mix of English accent mottled in southern drawl. "Oh, but don't get too handsy. She might snap your wrist off or something."

Jana landed a playful smack on Kyle's shoulder.

"Ow!" he said, only half kidding.

The three had needed the release of tension.

Jana's smile, however, vacated her face. She looked directly at Cade, placed both hands flat on his chest, and telegraphed her next move with a sultry grin. She kissed Cade. It was an acting job to be sure, but not one she minded. It had been a long time since she'd kissed a man.

Cade wasn't backing down in front of Cool Mac who had been a fraternity legend with women. The two showed no signs of breaking off their embrace.

NATHAN GOODMAN ▪ 145

Kyle, feeling completely awkward, laid into the two of them. "Oh my. Oh my goodness. Why I've never . . . oh, oh, I'm starting to blush. Gee, Cade, let her breathe, man. You know, I think the Brits call that snogging . . ."

Jana pulled away, placing a single finger on Cade's lips as if to say *I'm not done with you*. She pinched Kyle's ear in a firm grip, pulled until his head arced downwards, and walked him straight out the front door.

Closing it behind her, she said, "Aaahhh, that's better. Now, where were we?"

34

"He's really nervous," said Jana, standing out on the balcony.

"I know. I think he'll be fine," replied Kyle.

"That's easier said than done," said Jana. "He's got to come off looking completely at home when we go in there. I mean, if we are stopped by a guard, he's going to have to up his game."

"Listen, he hasn't really had a girlfriend before. So you just keep locking lips with him. I think his confidence will be fine," Kyle said with a playful grin on his face.

Jana laughed and smacked him across the shoulder. "Oh stop it. He's cute, and he's so innocent. What worries me though is the possibility of us running into a Virginia farm boy or two up on seventeen."

"Listen, we've got HRT deployed 360 degrees around the facility. They've got every manner of listening device trained on that building. And, they are ready to rock."

"Meaning?"

"Meaning they're in full body armor. Remember something, these guys don't do pinpricks. If they detect danger, they're going in, and going in hard. Flash bangs, stun grenades, pack-charges to breach doors, the whole thing."

"Jesus. They anticipate that much trouble?" said Jana.

"No, they don't. It will be fine. We do have a blind spot though."

"Oh great, what's the problem?"

"We can't send you in there wearing a wire," said Kyle. "They might sweep you for a transmitter. If you get seen, it's got to come off like you and Cade are on a date. We can't let them know the bureau is on to them. It's a Friday night. Nightlife in Buckhead is in full swing. It should look fine. But . . ."

Jana interrupted. "But what?"

"But," Kyle's pure Savannah accent stretched the word into two syllables, "we can't laser mic seventeen. We have agents stationed on all sides with laser mics so we can hear what's going on everywhere else inside the building. But seventeen is an issue. It's the only place we'll be deaf to what's going on inside."

"Dammit! That's the only floor we really need ears in place. What if they grab us? Why can't we laser mic seventeen?"

"Virginia farm boys don't play games," said Kyle. "They've skinned the building's outer windows on seventeen. The skin is a copper shielding designed to block surveillance and trap any sounds, especially from laser mics. We can't even see in there, much less hear. Just stay focused. Don't lose sight of the prize. You know as well as I do, at around 8:45 a.m. Eastern tomorrow, another attack is going down. We have to get our hands on that data. Without it, we're blind. Everything is riding on this. Everything."

Jana responded, "Oh, is that all? Well, at least there's no pressure."

"You can do this." Kyle looked out at the skyline, deep in thought. "Latent called earlier," he said. He turned to look Jana in the eye. "After you've gotten the data and you're on the outside, you two will be picked up by a van, a minivan."

"What are you talking about? Who'll be inside the minivan? Bob Marley?"

"Not exactly," said Kyle. "This guy is a little more hardcore than Bob Marley. This is the guy Latent mentioned to us earlier, Uncle Bill."

"Ah, so let me get this straight," replied Jana, "Director Latent wants me to do like this high-level espionage stuff. Go into a secure building that's run by the most sophisticated spy agency in the world, steal some of their secret data, then come outside and hand the data to some guy in a minivan named Uncle Bill?"

Kyle laughed. "Yup, pretty much. But seriously, Latent said this guy was his roommate at Georgetown. He's NSA, and he's the best there is. If anyone can decrypt that data, it's him. And something else, no one else knows Uncle Bill is here in Atlanta right now. Not even the NSA. Latent is growing paranoid. He doesn't know who to trust anymore."

Jana thought about that a long moment. "Let me ask you this. I thought the NSA couldn't operate within the borders of the United States. Doesn't this sort of violate that wee little principle?"

"Latent says he's going to do whatever it takes to stop these attacks. He says the gloves come off," said Kyle.

"What do you think he means by that?" said Jana.

"It means he doesn't care what we have to do, even if we have to break the law. He will stop this terror cell, no matter what. His job be damned."

Jana looked rattled. "He said that? Exactly? Breaking the law?"

"He can't say what he knows he can't say. No, he didn't say that directly. But that's exactly what he means. 'The gloves come off' means break, steal, kill. Anything and everything. He knows there will be a heavy price to pay in the end, but he's willing to pay it. I'm willing to pay it too. I can't look into the eyes of another mother whose child's blood is smeared across the soles of my shoes and explain to her why I failed. I can't—I can't."

Cade walked out the sliding glass door and onto the back patio to find Kyle and Jana looking at one another in an abrupt silence. Kyle cleared his throat.

Cade said, "Did I interrupt something? Cool Mac, how much time do we have?"

"No worries, Romeo," teased Kyle. "No, seriously, we're going to be fine. We've got about thirty minutes before we leave. Then, it's go-time. Oh, and both of you listen up. HRT is giving you twenty-five minutes to get in and out of there."

"What?" said Cade. "Why the timeline?"

Kyle replied, "Remember, once you're inside we won't have any communication with you. You can't carry anything electronic since it appears they track and monitor all of that. If you had any type of device on you, it might trigger an alarm somewhere. That means we can't put a wire on you. It's just too risky. The same is true for your cell phones. Go ahead and hand them to me and I'll put them in my pack until you're out of there. We won't have comm with you. Other than listening in to what we can hear on the other floors, there's no way we'll know what's going on once you enter the building. You've got to get in, grab that data, and get out without Virginia farm boys being any the wiser."

"Oh, you're full of good news," said Cade. "Shit. Twenty-five minutes should be plenty, but damn. Look, I've been thinking. The thing is, we can't just sneak in there and download data off of Rupert Johnston's laptop. It will be too obvious. The breach will be detected in the morning. They'd see what data was breached, and they'd put two and two together. They'd know the FBI or someone was onto them."

A vein in Kyle's forehead throbbed. "But if they find out we're onto them, the terror cell might not get further instructions from all those e-mails going out. The break in communication could signal them to carry out their final, pre-planned objective, whatever that is." He looked at Jana with immediate concern. "So what the hell do we do? Goddammit, why didn't I think of that? We've got to get this data without being caught."

Cade put his hand on Kyle's shoulder and joked, "You didn't think of it because you never studied. And because you were so busy with women chasing you, you never had time to . . . well, never had time to think."

"All right, genius, what do we do?"

For the first time in the investigation, Cade looked confident, almost as if he was now in his element.

"We're going to plant a virus on Johnston's computer," said Cade.

Kyle and Jana's eyes squinted, but Cade continued.

"We'll download the data first, plant a computer virus on his laptop, then get the hell out of there—simple. Why are you looking at me like that? Don't you get it?"

"No," said Kyle.

Cade laughed then glanced at Jana. "He never studied. Look, by planting the virus, it will screw the entire computer up. They won't even be able to tell anything was downloaded. Just in case, we'll download his entire hard drive. That way, even if they are suspicious, they won't be able to know someone accessed his system with a specific agenda to download specific data. The assholes won't know what we were after since we'll download everything."

Jana put her hand on Cade's chest, which sent goose bumps down his spine. "That's brilliant, Cade, brilliant."

Cade turned three shades of red and averted his eyes, obviously proud of himself.

"I'll get it ready." He started to walk away, but turned back. "Hey, shouldn't Jana and I be seen in Buckhead first? You know, seen on a security camera or something, like we're on a date? They might think to check that kind of thing out . . . assuming we get caught, that is. I mean, if we get caught, couldn't the CIA access whatever security cameras they wanted? Wouldn't they want to check out our story?"

Cool Mac and Jana looked at each other. Each knew Cade had unearthed another critical point that they had missed.

"Son of a bitch," said Jana.

35

The MARTA rail system ran underneath Peachtree Street. In a difficult feat of engineering, this portion of rail line was tunneled after construction of the Atlanta Financial Center complex. Twenty-five years earlier, Atlanta's then mayor argued that the city should fund the extension of the MARTA rail into Buckhead prior to the construction of the huge glass, marble, and steel buildings. But unchecked corruption that plagued Atlanta's city government at the time prevented the approval.

Straight across Peachtree Street's six lanes from the Financial Center was Thoughtstorm's corporate headquarters. The towering building's shadow darkened a wide swath of Buckhead, Atlanta's premier business district. The Buckhead area was also well-known for courting the nightlife crowd. Upscale bars and dance clubs abounded in the '80s and '90s, but many of the clubs had been swallowed by real estate deals promising to usher in an era of businesses and expensive restaurants. Still, a few clubs survived.

Jana plopped in the passenger seat of the car.

"Okay, Cade, we're on our big date now. Where to, you big lug?"

She had grown fond of teasing him. And, if the truth be known, she was enjoying being with him—there was something about his innocence. She began to realize it was a waste of time to search for a great-looking guy when instead she should look for someone who made her happy.

"Well," he said, "there's always Lulu's Bait Shack." And off they went on their first "date" to a place known more for its red-punch alcoholic drinks served in a fish bowl than anything else. Turning onto Pharr Road, Lulu's was just a couple of blocks down on the left. The location was perfect. They would go in and mill around, being sure to be caught on a few surveillance cameras. Then it was just a few blocks' walk to Thoughtstorm and up onto its ominous seventeenth floor.

The streets were crowded as they walked towards Lulu's. Just outside the door, they both turned and looked high over their shoulders at the hulking building silhouetted against the dark night sky.

Dimly lit clouds rolled behind the building and continued on their northeast path, unconcerned about the trouble brewing below. Yet inside that building was a world of conflicting forces. Most of the functions of the e-mail service provider company were geared towards selling e-mail software and services to many of America's largest corporations. The seventeenth floor, however, housed the CIA, the very heart of what terrorists around the world called The Beast. As far as the FBI could tell, the seventeenth floor was pure Central Intelligence Agency. It also appeared that the terror cell was still unaware the CIA was secretly behind their funding—funding that Stephen Latent thought of as an abomination against the American people.

Cade shuddered to think of the task in front of them. Standing in front of one of the old hangouts of his drinking days, he never imagined life could get so complicated, so serious. By instinct, Jana took his hand as they stood at the entrance waiting to be carded by the bouncer. Cade was drunk with the smell of her hair. It was like an intoxicating infusion of fresh jasmine vine splashed with salty beach air. He was quite taken with her, and she knew it. He just didn't want to make a fool of himself. They descended the handful of stairs that went down to the club and went inside.

36

Thirty minutes later, the couple left the club and walked down Peachtree. If ever Cade felt like he was being watched, now was that time. Six sets of FBI snipers were deployed on rooftops, each sniper with a complimenting spotter, an agent trained to assist with visualization of targets and communications with other agents. Binoculars focused down from different angles. Lots of encrypted radio chatter was ongoing as groups of agents communicated back and forth. But to Cade and Jana, there was only the whooshing sound of a passing bus, a car horn in the distance, and the dull hum of music permeating from nightclubs in the neighboring blocks.

There were four additional HRT teams deployed at three hundred and sixty-five degrees around the building. Each team pointed a laser mic at various floors, listening for anything unusual. The agents of the Hostage Rescue Team were keyed up. In their vernacular, cocked, locked, and ready to rock. These guys lived for this stuff. To an HRT member, this is what it was all about; this is where they earn their pay. For some HRT agents, this was their first live deployment, although every one of them came out of a military background and had extensive experience in live firefights in the Gulf War.

Jana continued to hold Cade's hand and led him down the wide stairwell off Peachtree Street to the MARTA tunnel below. The tunnel crossed underneath the road to the train platform on the other side. It was somewhat deserted at this time of night, with the exception of a few people waiting on trains, and one Kyle MacKerron, seated on a marble bench at the far end adjacent to the north-bound train line. Kyle wore an Atlanta Braves ball cap and carried a messenger bag over his shoulder. Inside that bag, there was certainly no laptop computer or notepad. Instead, Kyle's MP5 subcompact machine gun lay quiet, hoping beyond hope not to be needed. One of his best friends was walking into harm's way, along with a fellow agent. The tough part was Kyle couldn't do anything about it. It wasn't like they could avoid this situation. No, the danger was there, and it was something that had to be done. Cade and Jana would have to face it alone.

Kyle watched them from the corner of his eye as he listened to his earpiece, awaiting the go-code from HRT that the two were cleared to enter the building. Once they entered, the twenty-five-minute countdown would begin, and there would be no turning back. HRT watched for the building's guards to change shifts.

Since Kyle was from Savannah and sported a southern drawl, the HRT guys honed in on him like a bug to a windshield; to them he seemed to be tough as nails, and they liked him from their first meeting. To lighten the tension of such an intense operation, HRT loved to invent amusing radio codenames for each other. Kyle would be identified as Savannah across any radio chatter. And it seemed only fitting to use call sign Paula Deen, in reference to the famous Savannah chef, to identify Agent in Charge Murphy. Although he too was tough as nails, he had a well-known passion for cooking—something his men kidded him about. He was on the twelfth floor of the Atlanta Financial Center and would be personally overseeing all ground operations.

Then came a crackle in the encrypted radio signal as Kyle's earpiece barked to life. "Savannah, cheese grits are ready for the oven," chirped the radio. "Savannah, cheese grits are ready for the oven." It was Kyle's signal to give the green light to Cade and Agent Baker to make their entrance.

Jana and Cade busied themselves looking at the rail line map. Kyle removed his baseball cap and ran his fingers through his hair—the signal to enter the building. Without glancing in their direction, he tapped his watch, a reminder that the twenty-five-minute countdown had started. Should they fail to exit the building in twenty-five minutes, the Hostage Rescue Team would breach the structure with what they called *extreme prejudice*. They turned and walked through the double sliding doors. To Kyle, the two looked perfectly natural and relaxed, but his insides were eating him alive.

High atop the Atlanta Financial Center, an HRT sniper and his spotter focused. One watched through polished Steiner optics, the other through the Leupold scope of the sniper rifle chambered in .270 Weatherby Magnum.

Cade and Jana disappeared from sight and moved farther down the long, underground hallway, which led from the station platform to the Thoughtstorm building. Since both buildings literally straddled the train line, these entrances became a mainstay for employees to commute to work using the MARTA rail. The HRT team thought it advisable for Cade and Jana to use this entrance so as to avoid the main entrance off of Peachtree Street. Entering down here, they'd be able to access the elevator up to seventeen without having to walk past building security.

The white hallway stood in stark contrast from the dingy train platform. Its fluorescent lights glowed brilliantly through the translucent laminate material clinging to the ceiling and walls. Cade had never used the tunnel at night, and he squinted against the light. He felt so exposed, like he was walking into the mouth of an alligator. Tiny hairs on the back of his neck stood tall.

Kyle keyed the tiny transmitter in his left hand and whispered into the mic. "Paula Deen, this is Savannah. The cheese grits are in the oven. Paula D, the cheese grits are in the oven."

Cade swiped his keycard across the security bar, and they entered the elevator. It was the same elevator he had stepped into so many times before, but this time it felt like stepping into a honed glass coffin. His stomach had that feeling of having just dropped down the screaming hill of a roller coaster; only this time, the feeling wouldn't go away.

There was no turning back. He turned to look at Jana then began to reach for the button labeled 17 when her hand interrupted his. She darted her eyes upwards towards the small security camera peering at them from the corner. Knowing they may be watched, she wanted to make this look real. The appearance of being young and in love would work in their favor if they were caught, and it wouldn't hurt if they seemed a bit drunk either. She feigned losing her balance to carry off the appearance of being a bit tipsy. But if she told herself the truth, the lines between working this undercover role versus falling for Cade were blurring. She leveled sultry eyes, put her hand on his chin, and kissed him. After a moment, she pressed the button herself, but since it was a secure floor, the elevator door didn't move. Cade swiped his keycard, tapped his security code into the digital keypad, and the elevator was cleared. They were headed into uncertainty.

37

Jana kissed him again as they embraced for the camera. For Cade, the problem was deeper. He was falling hard; he couldn't help it. And riding up this elevator-to-terror at the same time he was kissing the most beautiful girl in the world represented a paradox he couldn't quite comprehend. He was dizzy. The elevator ride seemed to go on and on in an endless rise. Cade was falling in love with this girl whether she was acting for the cameras or not. When this whole damnable terrorism case was over, he was going to crash, and crash hard.

The elevator rose and a faint chime announced each floor.

Ground, One, Two, Three, Four . . .

Kyle assured him the guards would be changing shifts right at this moment. If the timing was perfect, they would get to seventeen without being seen. Cade's chest heaved, a sure sign of nerves that had been fraying for days.

Outside, HRT operators pressed headsets tightly against their ears. There were no fewer than twelve pairs of eyes. Each agent pair had a laser mic mounted on a heavy tripod pointed at the Thoughtstorm building. They listened with intent for any sounds inside the building that could signal trouble.

Agent in Charge Murphy, the senior-most agent on the Hostage Rescue Team, whose earlier recording of Bastian Mokolo and William Macy had played so prominently in the case, broke into the silent radio.

"All eyes, all eyes, this is Paula Deen. You are code yellow. I repeat, you are code yellow. Do not fire unless fired upon. Do not fire unless fired upon, over."

Each operator in the HRT team knew what that meant. Unless the yellow code status elevated, permission was required in order to discharge their weapons. One thing working in their favor was that the mirrored glass of the building was now completely translucent. The darkness outside the building and the brightness inside caused a reversal of the mirrored shine. They may not have direct communication with Agent Baker and Cade Williams, but on the first sixteen floors, they were able to see inside several interior spaces.

An HRT pair stationed across from the southwest corner of the building had their laser microphone pointed at the uppermost floor. The building's blueprints had revealed that to be the location of the elevator winch, and thus, the most likely place to detect elevator movement. The agent's eyes were closed as he focused on the diminutive sounds emanating from his headset. He heard the distinctive sound of an elevator winch kick into motion and keyed his headset.

"Paula D, this is nine. Paula D, this is nine. The grits are rising in the oven. We confirm vertical movement. I say again, the grits are rising, over."

Inside the elevator, the security camera mounted in a corner near the ceiling leered at them. Jana was unsure if the elevators were also bugged for sound, and she too felt very exposed.

Five, Six, Seven . . . chimed the elevator.

She whispered in Cade's ear.

"Relax, Cade. Whatever happens, it'll be fine." She smiled at him. "Remember, we've got heavy backup outside. There are more guns trained on this place than protecting the White House."

Eight, Nine, Ten . . . the elevator rose.

Cade drew in a deep breath, closed his eyes, and held it.

Eleven, Twelve, Thirteen . . .

His ears began to pop against the elevation. He exhaled hard, blowing out as many jitters as he could.

Fourteen, Fifteen, Sixteen . . .

Jana squeezed his hand.

Seventeen. Cade stopped breathing.

Kyle crushed his hand against his radio earpiece. HRT operator nine said in a whisper, "Paula D, this is nine. The grits are scattered, smothered, and covered. Repeat, the grits are scattered, smothered, and covered." Kyle shook his head. *Jesus, these HRT guys must all be from the south. Only a southerner would be familiar enough with the Waffle House diner to understand grits humor.* He smiled and began to appreciate the need to relieve a little tension.

The elevator doors slid open into a vacuum of bleak silence. At the far end of the sterile hallway, the guard desk stood vacant as an empty chair swiveled, letting out a slight squeaking sound. The shift change was happening; the guard had just stepped out.

Cade whispered, "I'm not sure having more guns pointed at this place than protecting the White House makes me feel any better right now." To Cade, the tension was as thick as trying to breathe through a mouth full of peanut butter. They walked across the white tiled floor as the heels of their shoes echoed onto their own straining eardrums. Cade swiped his keycard against the thick metal security door leading onto the server floor. A digital beep was chased by the sound of the door's steel throw-bolt sliding clear. Cade pushed his way through the door and was suddenly terrified that he would see William Macy standing with folded arms on the other side.

Silence. Cade's eyes darted from left to right praying no one would be there. The server floor was empty except for the hum of spinning hard drives and glowing light. Cade had never seen it so quiet. He felt very vulnerable as the pair walked in, Jana pulling him along.

"Jesus, it's freezing in here," she whispered.

"Yeah, they keep it at fifty-nine degrees to keep the servers happy. Most days I don't bother putting my lunch in the fridge."

They walked over to Cade's desk. "Well, this is me. But over there is where we need to go. That's Johnston's office. Pray to God he left his laptop in there. Otherwise, we're hosed."

"Remind me to get you a picture frame or something for your desk. Man, you guys have no sense of decoration," said Jana, still clinging his arm.

Across the radio outside, "All eyes, all eyes. This is Paula D. Any audible signs from the oven? Repeat, any audible signs from the oven? Over."

There was no reply. The skin coating the exterior of the seventeenth floor not only blocked laser mics but also reduced visibility to near zero. It was like looking into the translucent smoke of a forest fire and trying to see what was behind it. As far as knowing what was going on inside, HRT was dead in the water.

In the command center, Agent Murphy leaned over. "Christ, this blindness is like waiting for Apollo 11 to clear the far side of the goddamned moon."

Cade and Jana approached Rupert Johnston's office. Cade sighed in relief, halfway expecting the man to be sitting right there with a "what in the Sam Hill are you doin'" look on his face. The office was empty. On the dark mahogany desk, underneath a stack of loose papers, the black laptop sat sleeping, its lid closed. Cade darted behind the desk, opened the laptop, and held down the power button.

"That smell," said Jana. "It's . . . it's . . . bourbon or something. Damn, where's that coming from?" Glancing in the oblong trash can under the desk, Jana had her answer. She reached in and pulled out the empty bottle of Jim Beam. The lid was on, but a drop of the Kentucky whiskey made an escape attempt down the side of the bottle.

"That's weird," said Cade. "I've never seen Johnston drink. Then again, I've never seen him out of the office either."

"Cade, the smell is strong in here. I don't see any spills anywhere. It's like the smell is fresh."

"Well, let's just get this over with," said Cade.

Just as little LED lights blinked to life on the laptop, the login screen appeared. Jana pulled out a lipstick, pulled off the top, and removed the gel copy of Johnston's fingerprint. She slipped it on her index finger and swiped it over the laptop's scanner. A message appeared on the monitor indicating the print had been authenticated. But then another login screen appeared—this one required a password.

"Shit," said Cade. "Fingerprint *and* password authentication."

"What do we do now?"

"I can get through it, but it'll take a minute."

Cade inserted a thumb drive. Jana focused on the monitor, but became distracted by the array of loose papers fanned across the desk.

"Man, look at all this stuff," she said. "It's all handwritten. Who handwrites anything anymore?"

"Jana, even south Georgia boys know how to write. Check out his diplomas on the wall."

Running her hands through the papers, she said, "And look how old some of this is. These on the bottom of the stack look like they're fifty years old. They're all yellowed." Jana fingered her way through the stack, up to the top. "And these on the top are much more recent. They're all dated. It starts back in . . . 1965."

Without glancing over, Cade said, "Ah, kind of busy over here trying to steal the secret files, remember?"

"There's different handwriting on some of the older ones," she said. "Wow, looks like these were love letters from his service in Vietnam. He must have had a girl back home. I feel like I'm invading something private here."

"What? Private? Oh, yeah, I think he started out as a private during the war."

"Oh, you aren't listening to me." Jana read on. Private or not, she was captivated. It was like peering into a little piece of history you weren't supposed to see. Some of the passages revealed two young kids in love, separated by a god-awful war. A smile spread across her mouth, but as she flipped farther in the stack, her smile disappeared.

"Cade?"

"Yeah?"

"Look at these. Some of them have perfect watermarks on them. Someone's tears fell on these letters. This one is still damp."

Cade looked up, but only for a moment. "Well, they couldn't be Johnston's tears, I can tell you that. I don't think he has tears. And if he did, he'd probably kick his own ass just for crying."

The screen on the laptop went blue, and a message read "Boot from external drive?" Cade clicked yes.

"What's it doing?" said Jana.

"We don't have Johnston's password, so I loaded an NT boot registry app onto the thumb drive. The laptop is booting from there."

Jana shook her head at the technobabble. The farther she thumbed forward through the papers, the more recent the dates on the papers became. Jana skimmed faster and faster through the stack and started to realize this was more than a collection of love letters.

"Cade, it's like the rest of this is a journal or something. This part starts about a year ago . . . it's like he's recording all his work."

"His work? What work?"

"His work here. Here at Thoughtstorm," she said. "Holy shit, he's documenting his work here. My God, look at this! Dates and times of e-mail campaigns, names of recipient lists . . . this part talks about some kind of . . . encryption . . . wait, look at this! CIA! Oh my God. He's recording conversations he had with the CIA. Jesus Christ, Cade, this is evidence. This is like, this is like . . . finding the damned Rosetta stone. This is the key to everything we need to tie this all together."

For once, Cade looked up at the papers. His mind was trying to concentrate on two things at once, and it wasn't working.

Jana dug her fingernails into his arm, "Where's the copy machine? I've got to copy this right now."

"Ouch. My, we are old-school, aren't we? There is no copy machine. Server dudes don't copy anything. Here, take out your phone. Use the camera and take pictures of all this stuff. I've got to crack into this damn laptop. Those papers might be the Rosetta stone, but it won't help us much without the actual data."

"Kyle has our phones." Jana's eyes ran across the page at the very top of the stack, the most recent writings. She turned her back to the desk and leaned against it.

"This, this . . . was written today," she said. "He's talking about . . . about . . . it's like he's conflicted. He's talking about blowing the lid on the whole thing, the whole cover-up. But wait . . . look at that. He sounds desperate to blow the whole thing wide open, but he knows he can't. It doesn't say why."

She lowered the stack and said, "He knows he can't? What does he know that we don't know? What's the laptop doing now? You said something about we didn't have his password. That thumb drive thing, it's going to crack his password?"

"No, not exactly. It's going to bypass his password and allow me to set a new one. In the morning, when Johnston logs in, he'll be asked to reset his password. We have to reset our passwords monthly anyway. There's a chance he won't suspect a thing."

Just then, a towering, hoarse voice exploded from the doorway. "Won't suspect a thing!"

Jana and Cade froze in terror, wide-eyed at the oversized man blocking their only exit. It was Rupert Johnston.

"What in the Sam Hill are you doin' at my computer, Williams?! And who in the hell is this?!"

Thoughts raced through Jana's head. *Should I draw my weapon? Should we just take the laptop and run for it?* Then, a horrifying thought popped into her head from all those months of training at Quantico. Her instructors practically beat it into her head. *"If you ever use your weapon, one shot, one kill."* The voices echoed like the beating of a drum.

"Uh, ah, um . . . yeah, ah, Mr. Johnston . . .," babbled Cade, "no, ah, well, see we were just in here and . . ."

Johnston was furious, yet his eyes were swollen and brimming with tears.

He yelled, "I said, what in the Sam Hill are you doin' on my computer!"

Then his eyes locked on the papers Jana was holding. "Them's, them's personal!" He lunged forward; his left hand grabbed her neck and wedged her against the wall. The papers splayed out onto the floor.

"Mr. Johnston! No!" yelled Cade, jumping up, his hands on Johnston's crushing, steely forearm.

But as quickly as the rage started, it stopped. Johnston released his grip on Jana's neck and looked at his left hand as though it were a beast beyond his control. Jana coughed violently.

He reeked of bourbon. "I, I . . . I don't even know who I is anymore," said Johnston still gazing at his hand. He stumbled backwards and fell into a heap on the ground, his salt and pepper hair jarring in the process.

Jana's initial shock faded as she regained her composure and cleared her throat. Without anyone noticing, she slipped her firearm back into its holster. She had nearly pulled the trigger at point-blank range. She shook herself off and stood tall. It was like looking at a cross between a petite young woman and someone who'd just faced down insensate evil. The terrified young girl crumpled into ashes and the agent emerged. Jana had crossed over.

"They got their claws into me. I can't even r'cognize muh-self anymore," said Johnston, still staring off into oblivion.

Cade was petrified.

"Rupert?" The softness in her voice was like a fork cutting into Boston Crème Pie. She knelt down and put her hand on his shoulder. "Rupert," she whispered, "it's over now. It's all over. You don't have to be a part of this anymore."

As though he didn't even hear her, he said, "She thought I was dead, ya see."

Jana and Cade looked at each other, bewildered. Johnston seemed to be in his own world where alcohol wedged itself between past and present.

"Darlene . . . Darlene was, Darlene was a waitin' on me."

Jana placed a finger against her pursed lips, signaling Cade to stay quiet. She circled around Johnston's side, knelt down, and glided her hands across his broad shoulders.

Rupert's glazed eyes registered her presence but looked more like he was watching a movie.

"She's a waitin'. You'll see. She's just 'roun' the bend up here. When this here bus stops, you'll see. She'll be a standin' right there at the station."

Leaning behind him, Cade half-mouthed, "What the hell is he talking about?" but Jana held up her hand.

"Tell me about Darlene, Rupert," said Jana.

"See, there was a mistake, see," his speech slurred. "I had done lost a set of dog tags durin' a firefight, and see, sumhow somebuddy foun' them dog tags and thought I was dead, an', an', an', they sent a chaplain to tell Darlene, an', an', an' she thought I was dead. Truth be tolt, I thot I was dead a time er two muhself. And whut, with Jimmy Joe dyin' right in front a me and that, that dollar bill a his." He was still in his own world but focused on Jana now. "Jimmy Joe had this dollar bill in his pockit," his inflection flared, "and when that grenade went off, well, Jimmy Joe was . . . was . . . all a mess." Rupert burst into tears and leaned into Jana's shoulder.

Words choked out of him. "He was all blowed up. He was all over me. And that dollar bill a his . . . it . . . it was stuck to my leg. Just stuck there like sumbuddy done painted it on me. It's stuck on me, an' I kent git it off."

Rupert began clawing at his left thigh at a dollar bill that existed only in his mind.

"It won't come offn' me! I kin never git it offn' me! Help me git it off!"

Jana reached out to steady his hand, but it was futile against his drunken strength.

Jana said, "Rupert! Rupert. Now you stop that. You just stop that." Her voice was strong and firm.

He looked up at her again as a slight glaze of terror melted from his eyes. Jana nodded to Cade and pointed to the laptop; she had Johnston distracted, and the twenty-five-minute timer was running.

"You remine me of my Darlene," said Johnston, the stony façade flaking away. "She was purty. I got a pitcher of us when I was jus' shippin' out. We was standin' there at the bus stop when I was leavin'. She looked jes like you." Rupert's eyes wandered far away, and he said, "That pitcher I got. It's like, like you kin jest see it. In our eyes, ya see. Like we was the only two people in the whole worl'. Two people who got the resta their lives in front of 'em." Heavy tears rolled off his face and landed on his lap.

Cade was making progress on the laptop. He looked at Jana and mouthed "almost there."

Jana looked back at Rupert and saw the shell of a man who looked like he had lost himself down a dark rabbit hole and found his way back up, but when he got there, the world had changed.

"Rupert, it's all over now," she said. "It's all going to be okay. Everything that's been going on here. You don't have to do it anymore. It's over now." She was stabbing in the dark, unsure of his reaction.

Tightened ropes that streaked Rupert's forehead loosened.

Jana continued, "I want you to come out with us now. It's time to walk away from all of this. It's time to tell the truth and just walk away." She stole a secretive glance at her watch.

Johnston leaned in toward Jana's ear. His whispering voice was almost childlike. "The doll'r bill, is it gone now?"

The dollar bill symbolized terror experienced in Vietnam. But now, it symbolized the terror of a CIA investigation that had gone wrong.

"It's gone now," she said. "And if you come out with us now, it will be gone forever."

The room went deathly quiet. Jana glanced at Cade, who flashed thumbs-up, nodded his head, then said, "It's done, I've got everything we need."

Jana said, "Rupert, I want you to stand up now. You come with us now."

A breeze of calm soberness drifted across Johnston as the tension in his shoulders eased.

"It ain't that simple no more. Nothin's that simple no more." He looked into Jana's eyes as if talking straight to her soul. "There ain't no way outta here for me. You don' understan'. If'n they find out, God knows what'll happen. I can't git out."

"Rupert, we can protect you. You'll be safe. Come out with us."

"It ain' my safety I'm talkin' 'bout. You don' understan'. If I stop— if they find out I'm tryin' to git out—they'll do somepin." He looked far off. "Somepin terrible. No, no. I can't go nowheres . . . I'm all used up."

Jana sat up in fear of the words coming out of Johnston's mouth and what they might mean. She was afraid to ask, but had to.

"Rupert? What do you mean something terrible?"

Rupert gazed at his own reflection in the darkened window. "I've never been so ashamed in all my life. It jes, it, it jes got away from me. I thought we was doin' somethin' good. But it jes . . . got away from me. And by then, it wus too late. Too late. I didn't know they was gonna do all that . . ."

"What is it they're going to do, Rupert?" But he wasn't really hearing her.

Johnston looked at Jana. "It's all in them papers, Darlene. Go on, you go on, Darlene. Y'all git outta here and take them papers with ya."

Cade was up and looking at his watch, mouthing, "It's time to go."

Jana pleaded, "Rupert, please. Please come with us. Do as Darlene says and come with me now."

Rupert watched tears drop onto his trousers. "Yer wrong, little lady. Dead wrong," he said. "It ain't gone. It ain't never gonna be gone. That doll'r bill, it's still stuck right there where it's always been. I kin only think of one way it's ever gonna be gone."

Cade entered the early stages of panic mode and moved behind Rupert, grabbing Jana by the arm. He pulled her up and noticed the pursing and quivering of her lips, her eyes tight and fighting back tears of their own. He looked at his watch again. Cade knew it was too late for Rupert; the two of them had to go—and go right now. Jana yanked against him as he tugged them out of the office. "No, wait. Look at his eyes," she whispered. "This is really wrong. He's going to do something crazy."

Rupert stood up and a mechanical blankness washed his face. It was as if all the emotion in the world had drained away. He bent down and reached underneath the desk. A tearing sound was audible as Rupert yanked open a Velcro strap, releasing a hidden handgun from its holster. Cade pulled against Jana. "Oh shit!"

But Jana yanked back again, ripping her arm free. "No, goddammit. He's not going to hurt us, he's going to hurt himself!" She screamed, "Rupert! No!"

But Rupert pushed past them like a robot, never feeling their weight. The large .45 caliber handgun pointed forward as he stormed past and headed for the door to the security desk.

38

"Goddamn Gooks is what they are," he said. "Got to go git me some Gooks."

"Rupert! No!" screamed Jana again. "Cade, we've got to get out of here! He's going to start shooting out there!" Tears were welling in her eyes. "Is there another exit? He's going to start shooting. We can't go that way! We've got to get down a stairwell!"

"It's over here! It's this way." Cade was still dazed but began running with Jana through the server racks toward the only other exit, a stairwell on the southeast corner of the building.

They ran through the maze of clustered servers and down the far wall to the corner of the building. They were now directly across the server floor from the door Rupert Johnston just kicked his way through. Cade yanked back on Jana just before she hit the door. "Wait! Wait! The alarm will go off! The door's got an alarm on it!"

Gunfire erupted from the far side of the floor. They could hear Rupert's muffled yelling, "You motherfuckin' Goooooooks!" Loud popping, muzzle blasts were answered by screams and more pops; CIA security personnel were returning fire.

Jana yelled, "I don't think they're going to notice the stupid door alarm," and kicked the door handle. The metal door burst open, slamming into the cement wall, and echoed as alarm sirens began wailing.

The pops of gunfire amplified in volume tenfold. The door where Rupert had disappeared now burst open. Rupert staggered and fell back into the server room. He regained his footing and fired again through the open doorway. Jana jammed her shoulder into Cade's midsection, literally tackling him through the door and into the stairwell. They hit the cement floor and landed with a painful thud. A sizzling sound ripped past Cade's left ear. The bullet passed in between them and slammed against the far wall of the stairwell, exploding. Tiny cement and lead shards pelted back at them. Jana recoiled from the sting in her flesh. She ignored it and yanked Cade off the floor,

"MOVEMOVEMOVE!" she yelled in one repeating sound, forcing them down the stairs and out of the line of fire.

Outside, on the roof of the W Hotel, the HRT agent recoiled as loud noises burst into his headset. "Paula D! Paula D! This is four! I've got an alarm sounding. Loud popping noises! I can't confirm but . . . oh hell no! Gunfire! I say again, I've got gunfire somewhere between sixteen and eighteen!"

Agent Murphy responded by yelling into the comm, "All cooks. All cooks. This is Paula D; you are code red! I say again, you are red and free. Breach the oven, I repeat, breach the oven!"

Even before the order to breach was given, Kyle MacKerron was in a full sprint from the train platform, knocking down two civilians in the process. He flung off his outer over shirt, exposing the telltale navy blue windbreaker embroidered with huge yellow letters, FBI. He bolted down the long, translucent corridor leading under the Thoughtstorm building and tore into the fanny pack tight against his waist, yanking out the MP5 submachine gun.

He ran. He ran straight into the face of danger. He'd trained for events like this, but this was the real thing. More senior federal agents use a phrase "meeting the dragon" to describe a time when faced with death; you'll either tear through your worst fears, or cower to save your own skin. The dragon is mean, he is cold, and he has no remorse. Kyle MacKerron sprinted towards his dragon, and prepared to kick its ass.

39

FBI Director Stephen Latent was four floors below ground level at FBI headquarters in Washington. The darkened war room looked like a control center; a myriad of massive computer monitors painted the wall where all eyes were locked. The secure satellite uplink to the scene in Atlanta provided instantaneous intel of what was happening at the Thoughtstorm building, the site of the biggest terrorism case since 9/11. Not a word was spoken. The concentration level was thick enough to taste.

As director of the FBI, Latent had full authority to control everything taking place. But he insisted from the first day he stepped into his post, he would never, ever play armchair quarterback with the Hostage Rescue Team. He would let the experts on the ground control what was happening.

A junior agent at the back of the room said the scene reminded him of a photo of Obama and Hillary Clinton watching the Bin Laden raid unfold in front of their eyes. Upon hearing Agent Murphy's command to breach the building, Latent stood straight up, his hands on his temples.

"Oh shit, oh shit," he said. The weight crushing his shoulders felt as heavy as the eighty-pound rucksack he'd once carried into war zones. He could hardly breathe, yet his exterior stayed glassy, solid. This was why active field agents loved him. They knew he'd do anything in the world to avoid handing another folded American flag to a new FBI widow.

Latent listened and watched the various camera angles. HRT members poured into the building. It was his worst nightmare. The bureau, under his authorization, was raiding a building controlled by the Central Intelligence Agency. Never in his wildest imagination would he have believed such a scenario could ever play itself out.

From three sides of the building, groups of six to ten agents ran full speed towards an entrance, detonated controlled charges of plastic explosives against the door, and raced inside. Glass and metal debris were everywhere.

Once inside, it was harder to determine what was happening. Each HRT operator had a miniature video transmitter affixed to their Kevlar helmet. But the cameras were bouncing in such a violent manner, interpreting the images on the video monitors was difficult to say the least.

Groups one and two stormed the southeast and northwest stairwells; the third split itself into two separate elevator banks. Agents clad in black fatigues, Kevlar helmets, and flak jackets flew up the stairwells without pausing. The teams in elevators purposely pressed the button for the eighteenth floor, but as the elevators crossed the restricted seventeenth floor, they jammed the elevator control panel, thwarting farther upward movement. They then breached the elevator doors on seventeen and tossed flash-bang grenades into the long, sterile hallway towards the guard desk. The flash-bangs erupted in blinding thunderclaps as agents poured out and ran into the torrent of thick gray smoke and into God knows what else.

Latent said, "Get me the president." His eyes never left the video monitors.

An agent next to him nodded and picked up a red phone.

"Director Latent for the president. This is a priority flash alert." The secret service agent that answered in the White House went silent, never having received such a call. He could be heard scrambling in the background. Latent took the phone and grimaced at what he'd have to say next. Worse still, he had as yet been unable to ascertain how much the president knew of the CIA's terrorist financing operation. He thought back to that moment in the Atlanta field office when he learned the fingerprints were protected under the Fourteenth Protocol. *Jesus Christ*, thought Latent. *The Fourteenth Protocol. The president has to know. None of the protocols established after 9/11 can be invoked without his direct signature.* Latent still just could not believe it.

In the first moments after the initial gunfire, while Latent stared at the monitors and briefed the president, Agent Kyle MacKerron crashed through a stairwell door and into the Thoughtstorm lobby ahead of HRT teams, finding nothing there. The immeasurable fear inside him was not registering. He raced through the open stairwell door on the southwest side of the building and leapt onto the stairs, his legs gorging on them like a bulldozer punching into an old house. On the ninth floor, his adrenaline peaked as he rounded the stairwell corner. A steel door burst open with five uniformed CIA security officers behind it. Kyle screamed out, "FBI! FBI! Show me your hands!" But the security officers recoiled backwards away from the open doorway and began firing wildly. Kyle rocked back and returned fire but continued screaming, "Federal agent! Drop your weapons!" The firefight intensified as the back of Kyle's neck and flak jacket were peppered with cement fragments as bullets bounced off the walls of the stairwell. The smell of gunpowder was acrid.

He could hear the CIA officers yelling at one another, "Do it! Do it now!" Kyle braced for whatever was coming. Whatever it was, he wasn't backing down. He leaned forward and squeezed off two rounds. There was no return fire. Instead, what came next was something Kyle never considered. Bouncing down the stairs in slow motion was an unmistakable small metal canister. *Tink, tink, tink* as it bounced off cinder block walls and across sheathed metal stairs. The threat registered immediately. It was a Willie Pete, a white phosphorous hand grenade. He'd only ever seen one once during training. He never thought he'd see another. And this one was bouncing right towards him. Without thinking, Kyle burst forward and snatched the Willie Pete out of the air as it bounced. He flung it back through the open ninth floor door and ran farther up the stairwell. He just cleared the next landing when the device exploded well inside the doorway. The screams from the CIA officers were horrifying.

Kyle keyed his mic, "Paula D, Paula D, this is Savannah. Live fire on nine. I say again, live fire on nine. Multiple casualties. Grenades! I say again, white phosphorous grenades. All teams, watch your ass. We've got bomb chuckers throwing Willie Petes."

40

Stephen Latent's right ear was occupied with the president of the United States who was barking in anger, when his left ear picked up flash traffic from an agent codenamed Savannah, who had just engaged and possibly killed several uniformed CIA officers. Latent pulled the red phone away from his ear. "Oh Christ," he said. It came out as a whisper.

He interrupted the president, "Mr. President, Mr. President! We've got live fire. CIA operatives are engaging our agents who are returning fire."

The president was furious. "How could this be happening?" he screamed. "What in the hell kind of FBI director are you?"

But Latent was having none of it and yelled back over the screaming president.

"Listen to me, you jackass! You authorized the Fourteenth Protocol? You authorized those assholes to conduct this operation? Against the people of the United States. What in the fuck were you thinking? You're in this up to your eyeballs, and I'm going to fry your ass for it!"

The president went silent as Latent slammed the red phone down.

Latent could hardly believe what had come out of his mouth. And he couldn't believe he just let slip that the FBI had been investigating the executive branch of the United States government for conspiracy. There would be hell to pay, and Latent didn't know how he would retain his position if the president moved to revoke his authority.

Kyle continued his charge up the stairwell. He was on twelve and wasn't stopping. His adrenaline raged, but he still couldn't catch his breath. It was slowing him down, and it pissed him off. He heard loud footsteps coming down the stairs. He froze, assumed a cover position, and locked his sights on the landing above. Maybe this pause would give him the moment he needed to catch his breath after all.

It sounded like two, maybe three people charging downwards. Kyle braced himself for an all-out firefight. One set of footsteps sounded loud and clacking, like the sound of hard leather soles. The other softer, more rubbery. What struck Kyle was that the sounds were different. CIA security officers wore identical, hard-soled boots. A handgun entered his field of vision, then Jana's face. She nearly shot him but saw the navy blue windbreaker just in time.

"Holy shit, Kyle!" she was gasping for air. "Oh my God, I nearly killed you."

"Same here. You guys all right? You hurt?" said Kyle, reaching toward the blood on Jana's face and blouse.

"We're okay," said Cade. "What about you? Are you hurt . . . wait, Cool Mac, what the fuck? Shit, you're bleeding. Wait, are you hit?" Cade lunged toward Kyle's left side. Frothy, bright red blood was all over the side and back of his FBI windbreaker. It was coming from just underneath his left arm.

"What? What are you talking about?" said Kyle.

Jana said, "Sit down. Let me look." But what she saw drained all the color out of her face. She went numb, then into immediate crisis mode, tearing Kyle's mic off his shoulder, "Paula D, Paula D, this is Baker." No one had bothered to give her a codename since her last name fit into the cooking theme anyway.

"Go ahead, Baker."

"Paula D, we're in the southwest stairwell, level twelve. Savannah is hit. I say again. Savannah is hit. Requesting immediate evac."

Kyle turned hard, struggling to see what they were talking about.

"I'm not hit, goddammit. Now let's get out of here. Did you get the data?"

"Roger that, Baker," came the radio reply. "Cooks on multiple floors are heavily engaged. Moving to you now. Use any and all force necessary to get out. You are free and clear."

Cade applied pressure to the wound that Kyle himself had yet to register.

"Free and clear, my ass," said Cade. "What does that mean?"

Kyle said, "It means shoot anything in your way and don't ask it questions." Kyle started to stand up but fell back down, dizzy.

Jana held down his shoulders. "Kyle, stop moving. You're hit. The blood is bright red and frothy. It's a lung shot. Now stay put until they get here."

Tink, tink, tink came another metallic sound of something bouncing down the stairs. Kyle rocketed up and screamed, "Everybody down!" He lunged forward, knocking Cade and Jana behind him. He chest-blocked the white phosphorous grenade then grabbed it and flung it straight down, in between the staircases. The sound of the explosion was cacophonous. The percussion and ringing in their ears was numbing. Thick, white smoke enshrouded the entire stairwell, and all of them began coughing. More screams from down the staircase were audible.

Gunfire erupted from above and then from below. Kyle called into his mic, "Paula D, Paula D, this is Savannah. Taking heavy fire! We're pinned down. Over."

Kyle couldn't hear the reply over the ringing in his ears. Jana fired her Sig Sauer nine millimeter up the staircase, causing scalding hot shell casings to rain down on Cade below. Kyle fired both up and down the stairwell as darker smoke from the gunpowder mixed with lighter. Visibility was near zero; they couldn't even see what they were shooting at.

More gunfire erupted from above. Had their ears not been already ringing, the sound would have been deafening. But this was different. An HRT team had entered the stairwell somewhere above and was engaging the CIA officers in a pitched gun battle. In all likelihood, the CIA had assumed the building was under attack and moved to defend it without even knowing they were shooting at FBI agents.

The smoke that obstructed their view also provided cover. They had to move, and Kyle knew the time was now. He jumped up and said, "Move! Move now! We're going." But as quickly as he was up, he collapsed on the landing in front of them.

"Kyle!" screamed Cade.

Kyle's injuries were far worse than he knew. He could barely inhale, his head was spinning, and all the energy in his body felt like it was draining out. He couldn't get up and began coughing up blood. The unfamiliar salty taste in his mouth shocked him.

"Take this," he said, as he handed the automatic weapon to Jana then pulled off the fanny pack, which contained extra clips of ammo. She started to refuse, but knew her duty had to supersede her emotions. She grabbed the MP5 assault rifle and pack then assumed a cover position below, aiming down the stairwell from where gunfire was still coming.

"Damn, I'm cold."

"Kyle, no!" pleaded Cade.

Kyle's eyes went slack then fixated on a spot just above Cade's shoulder. His eyes closed as he drifted in and out of consciousness.

"Cade, take this," he said, handing Cade a nine millimeter handgun.

"No. What? No, man. No," said Cade, incredulous to what he was seeing.

A tiny smile formed across Kyle's mouth. His hazy eyes locked and a certain peace began to glow in them. Then Kyle shook his head violently and snapped himself out of his daze. He grabbed Cade's shirt with both bloody hands.

Cade was shaking his head. "No. No. No, man. No. Don't you do it. Don't you leave me."

"Take it, damn you. Take the gun," said Kyle.

"Cool Mac! No, don't leave," said Cade. "I can't do this. I'm not a federal agent."

Kyle paused then blinked one time.

"You are today," he said. With that, his gaze floated away. The slight grin returned as dimness formed in his pupils. It was like watching the sun slowly disappear over the ocean's horizon as the burnt orange glow faded to darkness. And Cade knew. He just knew.

41

Jana's movement was mechanical as she pulled off Kyle's radio and earpiece. Then she ripped open his blood-soaked outer windbreaker, revealing the Kevlar vest underneath. She tore free each Velcro strap and wrestled the vest off of Kyle. She threw it over the top of Cade's head and attached it to him.

Cade yelled over the gunfire, "What are you doing? No, put this on you."

But Jana was having none of it.

"No. It's you we've got to get out of this building. You have the data, and you know how to interpret it. Now pick up that weapon. We're going, and we're not stopping for shit."

"But . . . I can't. Kyle . . ."

Jana knew time was short. The smoke screen that hung in the stairwell would soon dissipate and remove their only cover. She fired several rounds down into the stairwell. The battle raging a few floors above them intensified. Even over the gunfire, she could hear people yelling. She fired three more rounds, then turned on Cade and slapped him, hard.

"Listen to me, goddammit! Pick up that fucking weapon! I don't give a shit what you were ten minutes ago. Right now, you're a soldier, we're going down that stairwell, and you're going to shoot any damn thing that moves. Now stand up!"

Jana took his hands and oriented them correctly on the handgun.

"Hold tightly, point, then squeeze. Keep your eyes open. If anything happens to me, don't stop. Get out of the building. Find Uncle Bill. We've got to get the data to him." Then she yelled into the radio. "Paula D, Paula D, this is Baker. Agent down, agent down. Kilo Item Alpha, Kilo Item Alpha"—the signal for KIA, killed in action. The words bounced across her lips like the rhythm of a drum. "Any friendlies below level twelve better get the fuck out of the way, we're coming down hot."

Outside at the command post, a junior agent monitoring cameras and other equipment burst in on Supervisory Special Agent Murphy.

"Ah, sir, you might want to take a look at this."

"Not now, goddammit, not now," he said, then keyed his mic. "Roger that, Baker, all teams are converging on your twenty to draw fire away from you. No friendlies below you." Then, referring to Uncle Bill, he said, "We have verified, package pickup is on scene. I say again, package pickup is on scene. God speed."

The junior agent interrupted again, "Sir, I think you really need to see this."

Murphy wheeled around, "What in the hell is so damned important, son?" Disdain hung thick in his voice like frozen molasses. "I'm in the middle of a goddamned firefight at the moment."

"Sir, we've got incoming," said the junior agent.

Murphy squinted at him.

"Incoming." It was more of a statement than a question. "What in the Sam Hill are you talking about?" He walked over towards the laptop's screen muttering, "We ain't back in 'Nam, son." But there on the radar screen was a small, moving blip trailing across the digital outline of buildings. The blip disappeared only to reappear in a new location. "What the hell is that?"

"It's an *inbound*," said the junior agent. "And it's not one of ours. It's flying so low the radar is barely picking it up. But it's definitely heading this way."

"Wait, what the hell are you talking about?" said Murphy. "It's an inbound what?"

"It's air traffic, sir. Likely a chopper weaving its way in between the buildings to stay under the radar, but definitely coming in hot. It's headed right up our six."

"Air traffic?" said Murphy. "But . . . can you identify it?"

"No, its transponder is off, but based on its outline, attitude, speed, and the way it's weaving in between buildings, I'd say it's a helicopter gunship."

Murphy looked like he had seen a ghost.

"A gunship. Oh shit." Barking into the mic, he yelled, "All cooks, all cooks, this is Paula D. We've got company. We have inbound air traffic, definitely a hostile. All cooks on the outer perimeter prepare to repel. Traffic is inbound from the south. It's on the deck. If it stays on course, it will come right up our six on Peachtree Street."

Radio confirmation replies echoed back from all stations as sniper pairs turned their guns southward towards downtown Atlanta. Murphy pointed across the room at another agent. "Get me the tower at Dobbins Air Force Base, priority alert. Move, dammit!"

A few blocks north on Peachtree Street, an early model Honda Odyssey minivan sat idling. Inside the van was a lone driver whose hands rested across the "spare tire" he carried around his waist. He was in his fifties but looked a little older, with thinning, unkempt, salt-and-pepper hair. If the thick, graying beard had not obscured the outline of his entire mouth, one would have noticed bright orange crumbs left behind from a package of half-eaten peanut butter crackers still sitting on the seat.

If Stephen Latent had been standing on the sidewalk, he would have shaken his head and laughed, saying, "Same old Bill." Bill Tarleton had roomed with Latent during their last couple of years at Georgetown. Latent would say that Uncle Bill, as he had called him, was brilliant on a level he could never comprehend. Yet, Bill's free-thinking, unassuming air, and disheveled appearance made him look like more of an aging hippie than a senior leader in the National Security Agency's cryptography branch. When Bill was a junior analyst, he had written some code algorithms that even the senior-most code breakers in the agency had been unable to crack. It was brilliance like that that catapulted his career to higher and higher levels within the agency.

One thing was certain. Latent no longer knew whom to trust. But the one person he could always trust was Bill Tarleton. They had been together during the absolute best times in their lives. Back then, they were so full of energy, so full of ideals. The goals were clear, and both of them thrived at Georgetown. Now, things were so complicated you didn't even know who the enemy was.

There weren't many people who understood Bill in those days. He was a quiet guy. He'd never had an interest in the limelight that his stellar academic achievement afforded him. When graduation neared, Bill received offers from more top think tanks than anyone. Latent would find job offers lining the trash can underneath the desk in their tiny dorm room, still unopened. Latent secretly stashed all of them. There were offers from all over the world for ever-increasing sums of money. Yet, Uncle Bill was only interested in the arrival of one letter—one from the federal government.

When the envelope came, Bill stared at it for a long while. When at last he opened it, the expression on his face remained stoic. But then Latent saw something he'd never seen before. He saw Bill Tarleton crack a little smile. For the first time in three years, Bill Tarleton actually smiled. After that first smile, Bill stood up and walked out of the dorm without saying a word. He then proceeded towards another first; he got drunk. Blind, stinking drunk. Finally, it was Latent's turn to hold someone's head over the toilet.

And so it was. That one envelope. The only one Bill had opened. Although he wouldn't say, Latent knew that it was a job offer from the NSA. Bill never had an interest in money. He would serve his country and serve it in a way that would change the direction of code breaking in the United States for the decades that followed. Bill revolutionized cryptography, and tonight, he was the only person on the face of the earth that Stephen Latent could trust.

42

Shots came from above and below now, but most were fired wild. No one was able to see much in the dense smoke. Jana placed her hand on Cade's shoulder and yelled over the noise, "We can't stay here. Cade, we can't stay here. Listen to me. He's gone, Cade. There's nothing we can do for him now."

But Cade's face was hard and glazed—like just-fired pottery.

Jana grabbed his bloody shirt. "Cade!" she yelled. "Kyle would want us to get the hell out of here! Come on. We've got to go!"

Cade looked at her and nodded the nod of a defeated man.

"Stay right behind me!" Jana yelled. "Remember, you've got to get out and get the data to Uncle Bill. Don't stop for me. You've got to keep moving."

Jana jumped up and ran down the stairs, her feet devouring three and four steps at a time, firing the assault weapon. Shots were flying all around them as tiny shards of cement peppered their faces. Jana hugged the outer wall as she descended past an open stairwell door, firing several rounds into it as they ran. She tripped across something on the ground and barely caught herself. Cade was not so lucky. He tripped and flew forward, knocking Jana to the ground beneath him. She pushed him off just seconds before a dark shadow emerged from the smoke below.

A voice yelled, "Baker, no!" a millisecond before she pulled the trigger. It was an HRT agent whose squad jumped to assume cover positions above. The firefight from above intensified as HRT operators engaged with CIA officers attempting to descend the stairwell.

The gunfire was so loud and smoke so thick, no one heard or saw the white phosphorous grenade bounce down the stairs this time. When it detonated, the two agents up the stairwell and one crouched in front of Cade were killed, their bodies having acted as a shield. Jana yanked Cade off the ground, and they ran downwards once again, coughing violently against the acidic smoke.

Cade struggled to breathe and thought he would pass out, but kept to his feet. The farther down they went, the clearer the air became. At the bottom, they were both panting and out of breath.

Cade said, "Jesus, I can't breathe. I feel like a sledgehammer hit me in the back."

Jana spun him around and found what she'd expected, a bullet embedded in Cade's flak jacket. He'd been hit squarely in the back, but the vest had stopped the bullet.

"You're okay, that vest just saved your life." Jana barked into her mic, "Paula D, Paula D, this is Baker. We're coming out! I say again, we're coming out. Hold your fire, over."

"Roger that, Baker. All posts, all posts, this is Paula D. Hold your fire, hold your fire."

A few blocks away, Uncle Bill jammed his foot onto the accelerator and barreled towards the pickup point. Jana crashed through the stairwell door into the Thoughtstorm lobby and braced for whatever might be there. She turned and headed towards the side exit and then heard a shot. She wheeled around, weapon forward and fearing the worst. There Cade stood, the handgun Kyle had given him still pointing at the body of a CIA officer now quivering on the ground. A tiny swirl of smoke eased its way out of the barrel. Jana grabbed Cade around the collar and pulled, running to the exit door. Once outside, three HRT operators crouched against the shiny marble exterior as the white minivan sped towards them from the left and screeched to a halt. One of the agents yelled to her, "Come on! Let's move!" But it was impossible to hear his voice over the loudest sound Jana had ever heard.

Echoing between the buildings, the *whump, whump, whump* sound increased in volume tenfold as an Apache helicopter gunship rocketed around the buildings from the right. All hell broke loose. HRT agents from several directions opened fire on the gunship. Rounds were bouncing off its thick plate steel skin and bulletproof glass. The gunship's twin mounted cannons erupted, fire spewing from their barrels. Bullets chewed into the black pavement like a hammer tearing into a clay pot. Jana knocked Cade backwards into the building. Rounds ripped right up the sidewalk and tore into the building's core. There was an explosion. Jana looked out, frantically scanning for the minivan. When she spotted it, her stomach sank. The gas tank erupted into a ball of flame as the fifty caliber machine guns chewed the vehicle apart. Farther to her left, blood and body parts were strewn about. The HRT agents on the ground never stood a chance.

Agents atop the buildings illuminated huge spotlights to light up the Apache and zeroed their firepower on the more fragile tail section. The Apache roared forward just twelve feet off the street as it returned fire. To Jana, it seemed like it was moving in slow motion. That's when she saw him. Seated next to the pilot and leering straight at her was the cold face she had photographed that first day on the streets of Atlanta. It was William Macy.

As the chopper raged past, the spotlights and gunfire followed it. Jana grabbed Cade and ran out across the open street past scorching pieces of the destroyed minivan, then darted down a set of stairs to the MARTA train station below. Gunfire continued to rage on the street above. Jana and Cade jumped the turnstiles into the subway station and sprinted towards a train already in motion as it began to pull away. Jana ran alongside the train's last car and fired her weapon twice into the glass, shattering it. Before the train could pick up too much speed, they jumped in through the opening. *Thank God no one's on this car*, thought Jana. They collapsed, exhausted, and the train accelerated southward.

43

J ana's mind wrestled with what it had seen. She was barely able to register the face in the chopper. It was William Macy's face all right, and it was now frozen in her mind. She knew it was a face that would haunt her the rest of her days.

Sitting on the train, they looked like they hadn't slept in three days and had escaped a house fire. It was the point where mental exhaustion overtakes physical exhaustion. Cade sat in his flak jacket, and Kyle's fresh blood covered his hands where a handgun still dangled. Jana's face was bloody though most of it had dried. Neither had ever been in a similar situation to what they had just survived. Their emotions, held in check up to this point, bubbled near the surface. The brush with death crept up on them and tears began to roll off Cade's face onto the dingy, rubberized floor, splashing without a sound. He was not ashamed. Jana held it together for as long as she could, but losing Kyle who had been such a friend was overwhelming. The southbound train rolled forward, unaware of their anguish.

Jana did not know what to do or whom to turn to. They had to get the data into the right hands in time to prevent tomorrow morning's terrorist bomb plot. Many of the HRT agents were dead. The ones still alive were in a torrential firefight inside the bowels of the Thoughtstorm building. Uncle Bill's minivan had been blown apart by the chopper. He was the only one they could have trusted with the data. And now, he was gone.

Jana was afraid to use a radio or phone to call for help. What if the CIA was listening? How would she know if it was safe to disclose her location? What if they were somehow monitoring the FBI's secure lines? If she was caught, they'd recover the stolen data that came at such a heavy price. Her training kicked in, and she took a quick physical inventory of what they had in their possession. Inside Kyle's fanny pack were four fully loaded clips of ammunition for the MP5, and tucked into a side pocket were both of their cell phones. *My cell phone . . . wait . . . what if they're tracking my cell phone right now?*

"Cade, Cade. Our cell phones. They could be tracking our cell phones. Shit, we've got to get rid of our cell phones."

"Oh my God, you're right."

"We can toss them out the window we broke to get on this train," said Jana.

"Wait, not yet. Let's get off at the next stop. I've got a better idea."

Jana buried herself in thought. It was easier than facing the crushing loss of Kyle. Whatever happened, the CIA now knew their entire operation communicating with terrorists was compromised. There would be no more mass e-mails sent from Thoughtstorm containing what she assumed were instructions to terror members giving them their next assignments. And, since the e-mails would stop, the members of the terror cell would proceed to their final objectives. The only person that hinted at knowing those objectives was Rupert Johnston, and he was almost certainly dead. No, it was all too risky. She had to get Cade someplace safe so he could at least look at the data, and she needed somewhere where she could think. The train ambled south through the Atlanta city lights, swaying back and forth like the rocking of a baby's cradle.

44

During the day, Alyssa McTee drove her way west from the Maryland coast and headed into Virginia. She hugged the edge of the Marine base at Quantico and wove from one rural road to another. In the evening, after settling down at a quiet roadside motel, it became obvious to her that this was going to be one of those strange late nights where she just couldn't sleep. After an hour of trying, Alyssa climbed out of bed, got dressed, and went outside to stare up into the endless, yet brilliantly lit, night sky. There were more stars than anyone could possibly count, and Alyssa didn't bother trying.

About a hundred yards down the road, she could hear the low laughter of a few people gathered around a small country store she'd driven past. Back home in Atlanta, she wouldn't have thought of such a thing. But here in the Virginia countryside, she began the short walk without a second thought. The shop sat at the crossroad of Rural Routes 610 and 806. A dimly lit banner stretched across the faded gray building just above the porch that read "Elk Run Store." The handful of white plastic chairs nestled underneath the tin metal awning were occupied, with the exception of one. The empty chair looked inviting. Alyssa knew she was a stranger, and her clothes didn't exactly meld into the rural landscape that was otherwise skirted by hardwood trees and farms in all directions. But she had become comfortable with the idea of not fitting in. She walked onto the creaking porch across sagging planks. A man, who appeared to be the store clerk, wore a checkered button-down shirt that was missing one of the shiny studs on the right breast pocket. He looked at her as if to speak, but to Alyssa's surprise, he instead leaned closer to a dust-covered transistor radio to hear a news broadcast.

"You guys quiet down. I want ta hear this."

They all listened as the recorded newscast unfolded.

"And stand by for John Carden with a special report. This is John Carden in for Mike Slayden, WBS News interrupting our normal broadcast. An intense firefight is underway on the streets of Atlanta,

Georgia's Buckhead district. For more, we go live to the scene to news chopper two and Milt Franklin."

"That's right, John. The pitched gun battle is raging near the heart of Atlanta on Peachtree Street about a mile south of Lenox Mall. Early indications point to the FBI, but that's yet to be confirmed. We tried to overfly the scene a few moments ago and nearly had a midair collision with what appeared to be a military attack helicopter. From what we could see, debris is everywhere, and fires are burning in the street. At least one tall building is on fire. We're working to confirm which building that is. At this point, we've been ordered out of the airspace by federal authorities. We can see dozens of law enforcement vehicles surrounding the area and converging on the scene . . . wait, hold just a moment, John . . . hold on . . . my God! We were just overflown by two F-18 fighter jets, banking hard. They are flying extremely low. We were almost caught in their jet wash. The last time I saw fighter jets moving that aggressively above a major US city was on 9/11. We'll try to bring you more information as we get it. For now, live in Atlanta, Georgia, Milt Franklin, WBS News."

"My God," said the clerk. "What in hell's goin' on down there in Hotlanta? Good Lord."

"Makes ya glad to be from somewhere where nothin' like that ever happens, don't it, Miss?" said another man as his arm dangled over the shoulder of a woman whose front lip didn't quite cover her protruding teeth. "Where you from, Miss?"

Alyssa shrugged her shoulders. "Atlanta," she said as she cracked a little smile.

45

His name was Maqued, although no one would have known. Educated in the United Kingdom, Maqued had mastered the King's English. His accent was muted after years of practice—he wanted to be as inconspicuous as possible. Six months earlier, he had passed his commercial over-the-road driver's test. For a man of his distinct intelligence, truck driver's school was a mental drain. His classmates, pure Brooklyn and Jersey Shore, teased him about his UK terminology. He'd use phrases like "get into the queue," instead of "standing in line." And of particular amusement to his classmates was his use of the word lorry, which to a Brit meant a small truck.

It was only a few weeks after obtaining his commercial driver's license that he landed the job with the city of Stratford, Connecticut. His route as a city bus driver took him back and forth across the Housatonic River Bridge twenty-eight times per day. If he'd been asked to design a way to do surveillance on the bridge, this was it. Driving back and forth over the river, Maqued would glance down and to his north to study the target, an adjacent train trestle bridge just below the level of the highway bridge.

The struts supporting the train bridge were easily inventoried. The supporting steel trellis encased the bridge like a canopy bed, and added to the complexity of his task. On several occasions after the last run back to the depot, Maqued had quietly walked back to the bridge. On those cold, darkened evenings, no one noticed him slip down the river's embankment with a night vision camera in hand. The videos provided invaluable intel on what it would take to carry out his mission.

His preparations had gone on for months. There were to be three signals, and only three. The first call would signal him to physically prepare the target for destruction—a task that would take two or three days to complete. The second would come in exactly twenty-four hours before he was to actually carry out the final deed. And the third would give him only minutes to execute it. Although the first signal was painfully long in the coming, the call finally came.

That same night, Maqued began the nightly ritual of slipping down the embankment and climbing across the steel girders underneath the train trestle. At first, his backpack was heavy and bulging, but as he worked his way from one cold steel beam to the next, the load lightened as he secured the explosive packs into place. Each pack was concealed in a flat, wooden box that acted as a casement designed to camouflage the deadly intent of the Plastique. The boxes were painted a dull, grayish, rust tone, which blended perfectly into the aging steel structure. The casements also served to protect the delicate electronic circuitry of the receiver panels from corroding in the elements. Each plastic explosive brick was attached to a thin wireless receiver, which when activated would send a low voltage pulse into the waxy explosive block.

Maqued had never actually detonated any explosives. Instead, he had spent countless hours in the dorms back in London being taught how to assemble and detonate Plastique. Although he wished he had more direct experience in detonation, he well understood that the beast was always watching. One small step out of the ordinary, such as travel to a country on a watch list, and the FBI could red flag him. One mistaken word on a cell phone call might be intercepted by the NSA, who scanned the airwaves searching for any number of particular keywords. Those words when spoken across a digital channel triggered the NSA to automatically record the conversation for later analysis. Within a matter of hours, if someone in the terror cell misspoke, it could awaken the beast, and the beast was hungry. From that point forward, the label of "bomb chucker" would be assigned to Maqued and anyone in Maqued's known association—all his efforts would be in vain.

He had been very careful with his cell phone. It was a dreadfully older push-button Nokia model that was a throwback to the days before smartphones. Maqued used cash to prepay the monthly charges for the unregistered phone. There was no need to purchase any additional cell minutes because the phone remained dormant. Its only purpose had been to await the three coded signals.

Maqued had not known what day the second call would come, but when it did, it was at the exact time of day that had been preplanned. Since the phone had only rung once before, the ringtone startled him. 7:59 a.m., exactly. 7:59 a.m. Seven—fifty—nine. It was the exact time of day that American Airlines Flight 11, a Boeing 767 carrying eighty-one passengers and eleven crew, departed Logan International Airport in Boston in 2001. The plane plunged into one of the five sides of the beast itself, the western side of the Pentagon. 7:59 a.m.

Oh shit. The call. The *call.* Maqued was startled. He ripped the phone out of his pocket like it was on fire and burning his leg, his bus swerving in the process.

"Hello?" he said with all the fierceness of a mouse.

"Man looks in the abyss," replied a Middle Eastern voice, all depth, nerve, and gravel.

Maqued's throat tightened, and his breath vibrated out of his mouth. Out of the depths of his timidity, he said, "There's nothing staring back at him."

The voice came back solid, almost vehement.

"At that moment, man finds his character." The words were bitter like salt on vinegar.

Maqued reeled, his heart choking his vocal cords.

"And character . . . is what keeps him out of the abyss."

Maqued's eyes dilated, and he stared straight ahead, barely seeing the road. Without hanging up, he lowered the phone and rested it on his lap as if it were a dead fish.

46

Contrary to outside perceptions of what life was like in the Queens borough of New York, the neighborhood association was active, vibrant, and alive. It was common to see people jogging or walking their dogs. And cars drove slowly in fear a child on a bicycle might careen onto the road at any moment. The house sat at 217 175th Street, just a few blocks off the Union Turnpike near the corner of 76th Street. A quiet little Cape Cod whose dormers were never un-shaded. The yard was small but well-tended. Nothing drew attention to the unassuming structure which melded into the well-kept 1940s neighborhood. An effervescent red glowed through leaves of a maple in the front yard. Neither the front door nor the windowless garage door was ever left open. In fact, no one had ever seen either door open, not during daylight hours anyway.

Well-trimmed shrubs across the front sported what looked like little purple flower-skirts below. The blooms, nestled at the base of the bushes, appeared to await the homecoming of a mom, dad, or kids into the otherwise cheery brick home. The narrow walkway to the front door was sided by shrubs, and cement pineapples adorned the brick end posts to welcome visitors. Visitors, however, never came. Those that did arrived during the late night hours and were greeted only by a garage door that, when opened, looked more like a giant mouth. The door would open, and the vehicle would disappear behind it as if it had been swallowed by the night.

"Old Mrs. Neebody," who owned the home for longer than anyone could remember, had passed away during the previous fall, and neighbors knew nothing of the new owners. Nor was anyone aware that if a Geiger counter was placed anywhere inside the house, that its curious needle would bury itself to the right, indicating a heavy presence of radioactivity throughout the home, especially in the basement.

47

The train's next stop was the North Avenue station. Jana and Cade disembarked at the far end of the platform, as far away as possible from riders on other cars. They had to avoid being seen; the blood on their hands, faces, and clothes would cause quite a stir. Jana tried to obscure the submachine gun by pressing it lengthwise against her hip. Fortunately, at this time of night, there were only a handful of riders. The two slipped into the empty, stale smelling women's restroom. At the sinks, they scrubbed hard and fast, doing their best to clean themselves up. In broad daylight, this would have never worked, but under the cover of night, they had a good chance of not being noticed on the street.

The North Avenue station was nestled beneath the midtown business district. A few skyscrapers, restaurants, churches, and condos dotted this part of the city. Pushed by their real fear of being tracked, they darted out of the train station and onto the well-lit Atlanta streets above.

"So what's this big idea of yours?" said Jana.

"Just follow me. We'll get rid of these cell phones up here."

Jana trailed Cade, trying to keep up with his long stride as he headed up the hill. The Varsity restaurant had stood on this spot since the glory days of the 1950s when it opened. The Varsity had been built as the largest fast-food restaurant in the world and still maintained its drive-in parking spots where cars were once served by pretty girls on roller skates. In those days, The Varsity was the place for any self-respecting Georgia Tech student to be seen on a Friday night.

Cade stopped and surveyed the ten or so cars parked in the drive-in spaces. Then he spotted it. At the far end, an aging taxicab pulled in. The driver placed his order from the car window then walked into the restaurant, probably to use the head.

"Look at how old that cab is. It's perfect. That's it," said Cade, "we're going."

Jana still wasn't exactly sure what he was doing, but she handed him her cell phone. They walked past the row of cars and ducked behind the taxi's rusted rear side. Cade reached under the hollow metal bumper and tucked the cell phones inside. Jana realized now what he was doing. If the CIA were tracking the phones, they'd be led on a goose chase that could take them all over the city. It was perfect.

They walked back out onto North Avenue, and Jana said, "We've got to steal a car and get out of this area."

"You know how to steal a car? What, do they teach you how to hotwire cars at the FBI Academy?"

"Don't I wish," said Jana. "Where's the nearest restaurant with valet parking?"

A few minutes later, they were two blocks up. Station Number 11 was a restaurant that sat just adjacent to a sprawling condo building. It had been a fire station until about fifteen years ago when budget cuts plagued the city. The conversion to a restaurant and bar had been a hit with the locals, yet since crime was common in the midtown area, they'd elected for valet parking to help with security.

"Okay, we're here," said Cade. "Now what?"

"You wait here. I'll be back in a minute." Jana watched a few more cars stop in front of the valet station. As the valet drove the last car behind the building, she ran over to the key box, grabbed a set of keys, and ran back. As the valet ran back to the front, a young couple that looked like they were on a first date wandered outside of the restaurant and handed the valet their ticket.

Cade and Jana held hands and strolled towards the rear of the building as if they owned the place. The valet drove back past them, taking little notice. On the key chain, Jana pressed the key fob's unlock button, and a black Ford Explorer chirped, its parking lights blinking once. They were in and out in less than two minutes. They pulled out and headed south on Interstate 85, then exited quickly and took the back roads, holding to the speed limit. They were both still shell-shocked. A headache was brewing, and Jana squinted against the lights of oncoming cars. Exhaustion began to overtake them both. It wouldn't be long before they would need to find a place to pull off and conceal the car.

48

At this time of night, the Queens neighborhood was very quiet. The only sound that could be heard was a lone dog barking some blocks off in the distance. At 217 175th Street, two patient men in the basement entered their sixteenth hour of continuous work. Beads of sweat hung from their dark brows, and when it dripped, it nestled itself in thick, black beards. The temperature in the basement was a comfortable seventy-six, but the precision work was nerve-racking and required a steady hand. If they made a mistake now and accidentally detonated the device, it wouldn't be the worst thing. After all, the two of them would not survive very long anyway under radiation exposure of this magnitude. And, since the device was to be used against the beast, it would have served its purpose well having annihilated a dozen city blocks in the highly populated area of Queens, New York.

However, the pair would do everything in their power to bring the device to its fully active state. If successful in these final critical steps of assembly, the device would be transported to its true intended destination, thereby completing their final objective. *Allah's rewards will be grand*, thought one of them.

"Get me Senator Highton," said Latent into the phone. It was one thirty in the morning, and he was not in a good mood. "I know he's sleeping, goddammit! Wake him, and wake him right now."

A few moments later, the senator picked up the phone. "Latent— good Christ, man, do you know what time it is? You better damn well have a good reason for . . ."

"Senator, we have a Baker-Able scenario. I'm invoking Executive Order 2213."

The phone went silent as the seventy-three-year-old senator tried to process what he'd just heard.

"But, wait. You don't mean . . . ? Baker-Able? Holy shit. I'll assemble the committee and be down there in . . ."

But Latent interrupted him again. "No need, Senator. There are six agents standing outside your front door. Be dressed in five minutes. They'll take you to a secure location. All the other committee members are en route. And, senator, not a word of this to anyone."

Senator Leyland Highton was the chairman of the Senate Oversight Subcommittee, which held several special powers. One of the least known was a power that, until now, had never been invoked in the history of the United States. Executive Order 2213 had been enacted in 1865 under Abraham Lincoln. Lincoln was not in favor of the idea, but didn't exactly oppose it either. At the time of the Civil War, there was an enormous amount of espionage and deception on both sides. Fears of a presidential assassination were high. And if that happened, it might be possible for opposition forces to seat a new commander in chief that was sympathetic to the Confederacy. This caused deep-rooted fears of a new sitting president that might commit treason against the people of the United States.

Lourdes Bruhaus and Winthorp Algester were both congressmen at the time. Neither one had any love of slavery, but they had no love for the war either, nor were they alone. Fearing the country might slip into chaos if the war wasn't brought to a close, they went to work spreading their idea. They described a scenario in which a sitting president, who had more power than any single person in the country, might abuse his power. The Baker-Able scenario, as it became known, pointed out that Lincoln had gone against the will of the people and of Congress to enact the war in the first place. And, in their minds, this itself was an act of treason. The two congressmen were not able to gain popular support for an actual charge of treason against the president. However, their ideas resonated as they explained that there had to be a way to unseat a conspiratorial president. When the war finally ended, they quietly attached their amendment onto an existing ratification whose original purpose had been to return property rights to southern landowners. The mood in Congress was so positive right after the war, the bill was passed. Only a special Senate subcommittee could officially enact the measure against the president. It was time for Director Latent to sell his case.

49

In the shabby gray apartment that morning, Maqued glanced around. Dust caked the tops of the few creaky cabinets in the kitchen. The ancient linoleum was worn through in spots, exposing plywood hiding below. It was quiet, and only the hum of the murmuring refrigerator was audible. He placed the mat down at his feet facing east. His father gave him the mat when he was seven years old. Memories of his father only came in flashes, like the flickering of an old newsreel. Just spurts of a hint of a man—the feel of his rustling beard against Maqued's face, the faint little whistle his nose made when he breathed, the jingle of coins in his pocket, and the wafting smell of incense.

Maqued grinned at the thought of his father. It was 5:05 a.m. He dropped to his knees and went facedown, praying. He finished his morning prayers, and with one more glance around the Spartan dwelling with dirty curtains, he rose to his feet. Maqued knew Allah. Although Allah would be proud—and the rewards grand—Allah was unsympathetic. Maqued had no choice. He boarded his bus at 5:25 a.m. on perfect schedule. He made the first circle on his route, crossing the bridge for the first time that day. He glanced at his watch. *Tick, tick, tick.* The ticking came like echoing hammers pounding on forged bronze, and Maqued was afraid.

50

Waseem Jarrah's activities had been monitored closely, but nothing else in his behavior produced viable clues as to where the next bombing target would be. The next attack was only hours away. Agents from the bureau were frantic. No one was sleeping. Hundreds more agents from around the country had been reassigned to the case. They were pounding the pavement, looking for anything that might provide a clue. Since his appointment as director of the FBI, Stephen Latent was in the most precarious position he had ever conceived. Back in Washington, his daily security briefings with the president were set to resume. The president himself represented a conundrum of deadly proportions. How far up did this conspiracy go? If the president had invoked the Fourteenth Protocol, authorizing the CIA to conduct this operation, then he knew full well what was going on. Dozens, if not hundreds, of CIA operatives would be working the terrorism case in utter secrecy. In fact, if the president had authorized it, he could thwart Latent's attempts to stop the bombings in their tracks.

He stared at his own reflection in the framed mirror in his master bath. The mirror's twin hung empty over the sink next to him. He may as well have divorced his wife the day he took office. After a while of never being home for her, she thought of him more as a roommate that showed up late and was gone before she woke up in the morning. She had been a casualty of power, a casualty of the war on terror.

Dark circles outlined his upper cheekbones and he looked older. Out loud, but talking only to himself, he reassured himself, "This is not my agenda. I didn't sign up for this shit. This is not who we are. I don't care about anything else anymore. These bombings will stop, and no one will get in my way . . . not even the president."

The clock was ticking, and the only thing Latent could do was wait.

51

Twenty-four-year-old Mike McCutcheon arrived at the State Street train station with his web-purchased ticket in hand. It was the first Saturday after his second full week on the job at McFeny, Stein, and Lawson, a criminal defense practice on Fortieth Street in Manhattan. It had been Mike's dream to get this internship, and he knew that if he could prove himself to the three law partners, he could write his own ticket.

The burden of debt hanging over Mike's head from law school had brought him—for the third time in his young adult life—back home to New Haven to live with his parents. The commute from New Haven to Manhattan was over an hour and a half, and it was killing him. On weekdays, with a 6:23 a.m. departure, he would arrive in Manhattan at exactly 8:06. That left fifteen minutes to walk the two blocks from Grand Central down to Fortieth Street and the firm's office. He originally thought he'd work a few months, then find a roommate to share a dumpy apartment somewhere in the city. But this living at home crap was a real drag when it came to meeting girls. He needed to live in town now. He was saving money, but at around forty dollars per day, he was also spending a lot on his commute. It was a Saturday, and today, he would go into the city and begin looking at apartments.

Mike edged his way across the train platform, just one speck in the mosh pit of people climbing their way up the three steps and onto a rail car. He reveled at the number of people commuting on a Saturday morning; it was almost as full as a typical weekday. Many were tourists, but several appeared to be blue-collar workers headed to the job. Inside the train, if he could have seen the floor, he would have been revolted at the volume of filth that had accumulated after fifteen years of people slogging across it. But with riders shoulder to shoulder and face to back with each other as they looked for open seats, no one seemed to mind the stale smell of humanity clinging to the worn upholstery. He shuffled back to the first available seat, which happened to be on the right-hand side of the train. The seat next to him and the ones facing him were still empty, though not for long.

The overhead bins were filling fast as commuters snugged their bags into a tightly nestled jam. The various forms of leather and canvas bags melded together in a sort of temporary marriage. As the train filled, Mike noticed a family hustling their way onto the platform. The station platform was still soaked with the latest unmerciful rainfall that had deluged the New Haven area over the past four days. Combined with higher than average temperatures, the morning sun seared against the steel tracks and caused a steamy vapor to rise off of everything. It smelled like a wet Labrador on a hot summer day.

The State Street station was abutted by a little square of grass and trees called the Union Street Dog Park, a place not unfamiliar to mothers out for a morning walk, strollers leading the way. The park was small and covered with a small number of young trees. The few middle-aged oaks soaked up the remaining rays of sunlight that peeked through high clouds. There was no sign marking the park, only a single, dormant park bench facing the tracks, but everyone in the neighborhood knew it was there.

On this particular morning, a man sat on the bench with a cell phone in his hand. Had anyone noticed him, they would have said he was not nervous, jumpy, or displaying any outward show of emotion. Nothing about his appearance or demeanor would have telegraphed his intent.

The park's only other patron was an older gentleman walking his Corgi behind a tightly stretched leather leash. The spry little dog didn't appear to be aware of its small stature. Its narrow shoulders pinged up and down with each step in a sort of tiny-dog swagger.

The train smoothed itself into an ever-increasing pace as it began its morning leg. It ambled past the park, taking no notice of the crisp air, the rising sun, or the glimmer of light bouncing off the fresh oak leaves. On the park bench, the man glanced at the cell phone, and pressed the call button. Holding it to his ear, he heard the phone pick up. There was only silence. The man on the bench said in a stoic, almost hollow tone, "I am become Death."

The sole reply came, "The destroyer of worlds." The signal complete, the train was on its way . . . headed into certain catastrophe. The time was 7:59 a.m.

52

The small boy grinned ear to ear, proud to have won the race against his dad. They squeezed their way down the thin center aisle, holding onto seat backs against the train's rocking motion, and plopped into the empty seats—mom and child across from Mike and dad next to him.

Mike looked at the small boy still beaming over his victory and panting for breath. "Wow, just made it, huh? Did you race your dad?" said Mike.

"Yeah, and beat him too! I always beat him. Johnny says it's 'cause he lets me win, but it's a really 'cause I'm so fast," said the boy.

Mike leaned in, his brow raised in full attentiveness to the boy. "So, where are you going in such a hurry?"

"We're goin' to the Men-hatten. It's a big place with big buildings and stuff. S'pose to be an island, but Dad says we won't hardly know it."

Both parents looked relieved that their overly precocious child didn't seem to be disturbing Mike.

"Well, my name's Mike."

"I'm a Mike too! But Mom calls me Mikey. I'm six."

The train coaxed itself into motion and rocked back and forth as it pushed its way past the Union Street Dog Park and underneath an overhead roadway, shadows blinking throughout the car.

"Six! Wow," said Mike. "You're big for six. No wonder you beat your dad."

A voice came over the train's PA system, garbled and only half intelligible.

"This is the—stbound train. South—nd train. Next stop—anhattan—ext stop, Man—attan."

Picking up speed, the passengers settled into their ninety-minute commute with all the excitement of a summer siesta—newspapers and smartphones in hand, reading up on the morning's news, getting ahead on the usual slog of e-mail cramming their inboxes, and hoping the soaking rains had ended.

The train settled into its top speed of sixty-seven miles per hour. The multi-ton locomotive hurled itself down the decades old tracks, slicing the dense morning air, steel on steel. Vehicles on parallel roadways slogged through stop-and-go traffic, making their way southwest to the various New York boroughs. The train's slight rocking left and right elicited little response from sleeping passengers whose heads perched between the headrests and grimy outer windows.

As the train crossed over a bridge spanning the swollen West River, Big Mike looked down.

"Wow, hey, Mikey, look at all that water. That river is raging. I've never seen it like that."

"Why it's so much water, Big Mike?"

"It's just from all the rain we've been having. There was just so much of it, it's all rushing down that river. Hey, wouldn't it be fun to be on a river raft down there! It's like white water rafting!"

Somewhere deep down inside, Big Mike wondered if someday he'd be a dad. He wasn't ready for any of that now, but he had always known himself to be different from his friends. Scoring with girls and partying was all fun and good, but Mike wondered what the future would hold. This kid Mikey was cute. He was a bundle of energy, and his parents loved him; that much was obvious.

The train was eleven miles away from a span of track that stretched across the Housatonic River. The river waters were also raging in a torrent that had not been seen in decades. The wide river, which had snaked its way between the Upper Peninsula and the Long Island Sound for thousands of years, withstood countless seasonal floods. However, this spate of four days of torrential rains was different. One thing that concerned river authorities was the Millstone Nuclear Power Station that hugged its edge. The plant drew cooling capacity from the Housatonic's cool flowing waters, and authorities worried over the possibility of flooding at the plant.

The plant was massive. It spanned six football fields in length. Its twin nuclear cores were water cooled. The cooling towers themselves were over one hundred yards wide and so tall they cast a thick morning shadow across both the I-95 bridge and parallel train bridge.

During the plant's construction seventeen years prior, there had been a huge outpouring of protests. Environmentalists feared a potential catastrophe so close to such a densely populated section of the upper northeast. The facility even predated the construction of the highway. I-95 had not expanded this far north until five years after the facility first fired its reactors. When the eight-lane highway bridge and adjoining train track were under construction, no one envisioned any reason the facility's proximity to the planned bridges should be of concern. But that was before the word *jihad* had become a staple within the North American vernacular.

53

"Hey, Shakey, yous goin' to lunch today?"

"Paul, it's six thirty in the morning," he replied. Shakey's real name was Shakhar Kundi, but everyone at the plant called him Shakey. He was born in the United States, but grew up in Pakistan until it was time for his upper education. Shakey and his younger brother were raised in the Pashtun region in a mountainous area known as the Khojak Pass. His childhood taught him one thing: Westerners were not faithful to Allah. But it wasn't until he was twelve that his uncle brought him out of the mountains and into the sprawling city of Lahore near the Indian border. Being separated from his brother and father weighed heavily upon his mind, but both his father and uncle wanted him to concentrate on his education and mature in the ways of Islam. Shakey was an excellent student with a sharp mind. Both men knew he had a gift, and that gift must be fostered and developed.

Shakey's uncle was tough on him and demanded a rigorous study schedule including both schoolwork and study of the Koran. At the age of fourteen, teachers said he had a gift for engineering and that one day he should emigrate to the West where the best universities were located. Even though he spent most of his life in Pakistan as a Sunni Muslim, it wasn't until Shakey arrived at Rensselaer Polytechnic Institute in upstate New York that he experienced what Westerners call "true radicalization." Very few people at the university were Islamic, and only one, a university professor, was a true radical. His name was Waseem Jarrah.

Shakey graduated with a degree in nuclear engineering. The university was ranked in the top twenty in the United States in that discipline, and Shakey had taken to it well. Jarrah's insistence that he pursue a nuclear program had a strong influence on him. Waseem Jarrah returned to the Middle East sometime after Shakey's graduation, but he always stayed in touch, counseling Shakey on the finer points of his beliefs. Later, Jarrah would encourage Shakey to apply for work at a very particular nuclear facility. And although Shakey didn't know why, he knew there was a deeper purpose in Jarrah's request.

And so it came to be. Shakey applied for and was easily hired to the Millstone Nuclear Power Station on the Housatonic River near Stratford, Connecticut. Being a US citizen, no one questioned him about his nationality. Even when they ran a check on his background, nothing seemed out of order. Since he was accustomed to the northern winters, he did not mind the move, nor did he question Jarrah about it. There was one thing he was sure of though. One day, the phone would ring, and Jarrah would be on the other end. It would be then that Shakey would prove his worth in the service of Allah.

54

Jana was deep in the middle of a nightmare. In the dream, she was in the center of a stairwell, dangling hundreds of feet above the ground floor. She was flailing but couldn't pull herself up onto the side of the staircase. Just as she lost her grip, Kyle lunged forward and grabbed her, his vice-like strength nearly crushing her wrist. He was sprawled out across the stairs, reaching over the edge, yelling something to her. Jana could see his lips move, but there was no sound coming out. Then she could hear him, but only faintly. It sounded like he was yelling from inside of a large glass bottle. He was screaming to her, *Hang on, hang on. If you go, I go!* Then gunfire erupted, and Kyle was killed. His grip released. She fell and fell and fell . . . yelling back up the stairwell, *Noooooo! Kyle! Nooooo!* . . .

She startled herself awake only to hear Cade crying out the same words.

"No! No, Kyle! Nooooo . . . !"

She grabbed him by the shoulder and shook. "Cade, Cade. Wake up. You're having a dream. It's just a dream. Wake up."

Cade was covered in cold sweat. The temperature in the car was above eighty, and Jana struggled to orient herself. Then everything from their horrific night came rushing back: seeing Kyle die right in front of her, shooting their way out of the building, the terrifying face of William Macy leering at her as the military helicopter screamed past, stealing the Explorer, driving off, and then parking in this back alley. Everything in between was a blur. She wasn't even really sure where she was. The nightmare wasn't just a dream. It was real, and she was living it.

She had done a great job yesterday of holding it together and being the toughest agent she could. But now her throat tightened and that little frightened girl from her childhood burst forth. She wanted her mother to hold her. She wanted to ask her father what to do. She wanted her grandfather's reassuring hug. But then she realized something. The terrorists were not going to cry to their mothers; they were going to carry out their assignments. Jana wiped her eyes, checked herself in the mirror, and then started the Explorer's engine. It was 8:05 a.m.

Whatever happened, she was not going to bail out of this one. No regrets.

55

The firefight at the Thoughtstorm building had raged into the early morning hours, and every available agent had been deployed. In the end, over two hundred FBI agents had been involved in raiding the Thoughtstorm building. There were eleven agents who had died in the line of duty. Fourteen CIA officers were killed before the rest threw down their weapons.

The building sustained heavy damage. City building inspectors on the scene investigated the damage and called for structural engineers. Concern rose over the stability of the structure's southwest side, which had sustained a heavy blistering from automatic weapon fire coming from the Apache.

Much of the Buckhead area had been cordoned off. Cars, buses, trains, and even people on foot could not enter the area. Reporters screamed for answers. Local businesses demanded to know how they were going to get their people to work. Even the mayor's office was demanding to know the situation.

Finally, at 8:15 a.m., a press conference convened. The FBI spokesperson was brief and did not allow questions. In her statement, she indicated only that a terrorism investigation was ongoing and that a raid on the building last night had resulted in a prolonged firefight. When she revealed the number of agents lost, even the blood-sucking reporters went silent.

In the chaos of that previous night, one thing had slipped through the cracks. As all available agents were called to the scene, surveillance on one Waseem Jarrah had lapsed. It wasn't an oversight. The team whose priority had been to surveil one of the most dangerous terrorists in the world had simply responded to the call—the firefight took priority. Jarrah vanished. Not since the espionage case of Robert Hanssen in 2001 had the subject of such an important investigation slipped out of sight.

When Stephen Latent was told that terrorist Waseem Jarrah was nowhere to be found, he went apoplectic. The news just didn't get any worse than this. He hadn't slept in thirty-two hours, he had lost eleven dedicated members of the elite Hostage Rescue Team, another agent and the key material witness were missing, and now he didn't even have eyes on the key suspect. On top of that, his presentation to the Senate Oversight subcommittee regarding Executive Order 2213, the Baker-Able scenario, had not resulted in an indictment of the president.

56

He had sealed his fate. The third cell call had been the final signal. The train was on its way. Maqued's answer to the coded phone call was an affirmation of his readiness. They were the last words he would speak to any human that was not a part of the beast. It wouldn't be long before he met Allah. Without another thought, he thumbed the lever to slide down the drivers' window of the bus and hurled the still connected cell phone over the guard rail and into the Housatonic River below. No one on the bus noticed as it disappeared without a sound. They were too distracted, busying themselves with their various concerns. And although they couldn't have known, their bus driver would soon be held in highest honor amongst jihadists.

There were to be no other signals, no other communications. Maqued looked at his wristwatch—7:59 a.m. He had exactly forty-four minutes until he would complete his final objective. Every bomb pack would detonate on its supporting beam, and at the front and rear of the train bridge, a triple charge of explosives would slice the bridge like a surgeon's scalpel through an artery. 8:43 a.m. exactly. 8:43 a.m. The timing had to be perfect.

Traffic was moderate as the minutes ticked by—8:08 a.m. The bus would have time for four more passes back and forth across the bridge. In his preoccupation, Maqued looked at the old Timex watch so many times that twice he had to slam on the brakes to avoid a minor collision. On the fourth run across the bridge, it was 8:39 a.m. Three minutes left.

He pulled to the roadside pumping the brakes, feigning mechanical trouble. He brought the bus to a stop, turned towards the seven remaining passengers, and raised his hand as if to say just a minute, but didn't utter a word. Only one person was close enough to see his eyes. They were filled with chilling deadness. The only sign of life in them was a lone stream of tears that trailed down the left side of the clean-shaven, darkly tanned face. Old Mrs. Aubrey, as she was known by the children of her block, would later describe an intuition she felt. It was something in those eyes that decried the most pure sorrow she had ever seen. There was no regret, only sorrow. And she would use one word that she said was written on the bus driver's face. The word would be imprinted on her sharp mind for all the rest of her days. It was the word *intent*.

8:41 a.m.

The other riders on the bus were surprised to watch him simply shuffle down the embankment off the side of the bridge and disappear. Where was he going? If there was something wrong with the bus, what's he doing?

The Manhattan-bound train was a hundred yards away at the time, barreling forward at sixty-seven miles per hour.

"Okay, Mikey," said Big Mike, "here comes the next river. See it? Man, look at the water! Wow, it's moving so fast!" The nose of the train hurled forward and cut into the crosswind high above the river torrent.

8:43 a.m.

The shockwave from the detonation was so strong, people on the streets of Manhattan sixty miles away felt the vibration as it emanated through the leather soles of their Johnston and Murphy shoes, up through their ankle bones, and into their palms. Traffic-monitoring surveillance cameras gazed across the horrible scene. The bridge exploded one to two seconds ahead of the train, which was just entering the bridge. Eighty percent of the length of the bridge detonated simultaneously, collapsing the superstructure. The mass of hulking, rusted steel hurled into the unforgiving abyss below. The train engineer didn't even have time to register a problem, much less apply the braking system. The first car leapt into the abyss, disappearing into a smoky, watery oblivion. Train cars moving at sixty-seven miles per hour flung forward. It was like watching a snake strike a victim in slow motion. The hungry river swallowed the train cars in one large gulp.

The nuclear plant sustained only minor damage to non-critical components as the tail end of the train tore a section of roof off. Duty officers in the control room immediately scrammed the reactor, effectively putting the nuclear core into cold shutdown. Environmental lobbyists would hold this event in their front pockets for years to come, pulling it out when the time was right.

Four hundred and fifty-six human souls riding in twelve train cars, swallowed whole. Most were people on their way to work, trying to scratch out a living. But some were simply going to see the big fun buildings, run around Central Park throwing a Frisbee, and ride on what Mommy and Daddy called a double-decker bus.

8:43 a.m. Eight—forty—three.

57

BI Director Stephen Latent burst from the Oval Office door like he'd been vomited out. Just outside, the president's chief of staff stood stunned. He could hear yelling from the normally tranquil office as the door closed behind Latent.

"Four hundred and fifty-six people! Goddammit, Latent! What in the FUCK are you going to do about this! This is America, you sorry sack of shit!"

Latent closed the door behind him, thoughts still racing through his head. If the president had secretly authorized the CIA to use the Fourteenth Protocol, he damn sure wasn't acting like it. His reaction to the worst train disaster in US history revealed nothing of a man keeping a secret this big.

Latent, with years of interrogation experience, was looking for subtle signs of deception from the president. Anything that would indicate the presence of a lie—a slight darting of the eye, changes in position of his hands, the unconscious flicker of tiny facial muscles. But there had been nothing in the president's mannerisms.

Then again, Latent had watched this president during the election debates. His command of each and every technique to deliver the most effective speeches possible was uncanny. The perfect posture, the controlled yet direct use of hand motions, lightning quick glances at the teleprompter, perfect enunciation, and the way he shifted his head and eyes from one side of the audience to the other. He had been very well trained. If there was a person who had the training to deceive, it was the president. Latent left the West Wing confused but more determined than ever to uproot this terror cell and tear its roots out like so many handfuls of his thinning hair.

58

Dew was heavy on the grass, and sunlight glinted off the duck pond onto downtown buildings in the distance. Waseem Jarrah wore an Atlanta Braves ball cap over a freshly shaved head in an effort to reduce the chances of being identified. Having shaken the FBI from his trail the previous night, he now had three remaining objectives that he would tackle in a specific order. First, he wanted to extract one last round of money from Bastian Mokolo that he could use to make his escape. Second, he would ensure the terror cell's final and most important objective was put into motion. And third, he would simply disappear.

He walked into Piedmont Park underneath huge banners and into the throngs of humanity. The annual Dogwood Festival was filled with vendors selling everything from food to artwork, and with perfect spring weather, the crowds did not delay. He wove through the people over to a small replica of the Washington Monument that stood across the park. Three large plaques dedicated to Americans lost on 9/11 adorned the ground underneath. It was a fitting meeting spot.

Bastian Mokolo spoke in a voice reminiscent of the soft music of Bourbon Street. He leaned his Reggae net-covered head toward Jarrah.

"Dat train 'ting, mon. Dat was magic," his breath, was thick with the smell of cigarettes. "I won't bodder to ask how de hell you got de entayah train to disapeeah in dat rivah, mon. Dat was a ting of beauty."

"I told you we were professionals," said Jarrah, steeped in self-absorption.

The only person nearby was a man sprawled on a wooden park bench, some twenty yards away. Disheveled and unshaven, the thighs of his jeans were caked in dark dirt—one of Atlanta's homeless.

Jarrah continued, "The timing of that little event would make a Swiss watchmaker jealous. By the way, we believe our friends at the FBI are aware of our countdown."

Mokolo's head snapped violently towards Jarrah. "What de fuck you mean de FBI knows about de countdown? Dey bettah not know more dan dat!"

Jarrah stared into the bright morning reflection without flinching.

"They don't know shit," Jarrah said. "But they do know of the countdown." He looked over at Mokolo. "They have teams on the ground in less than an hour. No one could respond that quickly without knowing the timing."

"Wot you mean dey have teems on de groun'?"

"Within thirty minutes after one of our little 'events,' there are FBI boys swarming the scene. And not just the local agents that live nearby. It's the same crew of senior agents each time, the ones from Washington heading the investigation," said Jarrah.

The homeless man shifted on his bench; a crumpled paper bag choking an empty wine bottle fell to the ground.

Mokolo stopped dead in his tracks. The surprise of hearing that agents were on the scene so quickly tasted of innocence, like one who just realized this wasn't some farm team; they were now playing in the big leagues.

"They obviously are fully aware of the countdown," said Jarrah. "They put their team in the air just ahead of the next event. Then the team races out to the scene." Jarrah gazed through half-squinted eyes, black like lumps of coal. "You know what this means, of course," he said.

"Wot?" said Mokolo, trying to recover his composure.

"It means the stakes are higher now. The risk is higher." Jarrah turned and poked a sharp finger into Mokolo's chest. "And with higher risk, comes higher price."

"Hiyah price my ass, mon!" yelled Mokolo.

But Jarrah was unfazed. He continued his casual stroll past the park bench and towards the lake.

The homeless man grumbled something under his breath.

Jarrah continued, "Oh, you'll pay the new price, my friend. You'll pay it. The new price is two million *per event.*"

"Who de fock you tink you ah, mon? I'm de one payin' de bills here. I pay de bill, I make de decisions."

Mokolo directed his hands to his hips, exposing a handgun asleep in his waistline. Jarrah glanced at it and smiled.

"Threatening me is not a good idea, my friend," said Jarrah. "You have any idea how easy it would be to kill you? You think killing someone like you is going to cause me to lose sleep? Here, let me help you out. You see over there just on the other side of the pond, under those trees? The two people with baby strollers? Look closer—see the tiny glint of light reflecting in between the strollers? Well, let's just say that's not a pacifier."

Mokolo squinted and realized what he was seeing.

"That's right, *mon*." Jarrah's tone was mocking, angry. "Any time you are with me, beware the sniper. You want us to keep working for you? You think this is a game?" He was speaking faster now. "It's no fucking game, you Jamaican asshole. The price is two million per event. Today before 2 p.m. you'll transfer half the money, as usual."

"Meestah tuff guy, eh?" said Mokolo. "I'll not be playin no games needah. If there's a new price, I got to meet de hiyah-ups. I am not dealin' wit no low-leval peepol like you, mon. You introdoos me to you boss, and we continue our beezness relashunsheep."

Jarrah stayed a quiet minute.

"Half the money first. Then we'll talk about an introduction."

A flock of mallards with wings extended banked left and right, slicing through the air. They extended their feet and skidded down onto the calm water.

59

J ana shook the cobwebs out of her head. She stuck to the back roads and headed southeast but didn't know why. They had to keep moving, and she was afraid the stolen vehicle would be spotted.

"Cade, I think we need to ditch this vehicle. I'm afraid someone's going to spot the license plate."

"What are you talking about?" said Cade. "You switched the license plate before we parked last night with that of another Ford Explorer. The chances that they even noticed is almost impossible."

"Wait, what?" said Jana. "Oh my God. I completely forgot we switched license plates. Man, I need to concentrate. Last night was so . . . everything's blurry in my memory. Okay, you're right. I think we'll be safe for a while. When's the last time you ate something?"

Cade said, "I'm starved. Let's find a place to eat in one of these little towns. You have any cash on you? We can't use credit cards. I've got about thirty bucks on me."

"That's what you had in your pocket for our big date last night? Thirty bucks? Cheapskate."

Cade reached down and turned the volume up on the radio.

". . . speculation swirling at this hour about the events in Buckhead last night, and whether they are connected to the car explosion downtown near the Marriott Marquis on Peachtree Center Avenue. The FBI has not been forthcoming with information about these events. What we can confirm is that eleven FBI agents were killed, along with fourteen other individuals inside a building at 3340 Peachtree Road. That building is global headquarters for a company called Thoughtstorm, an e-mail service provider. The FBI has stated this is an ongoing terrorist investigation and that they do not comment about ongoing investigations. What ties Thoughtstorm, Inc. has to international terrorism are not clear . . ."

Cade and Jana looked at one another. They were right in the middle of it. Eleven agents killed. Cade cringed at the thought that Kyle was now just a statistic. His stomach clenched.

Jana stayed on Old Route 41 and slowed to enter the business district of Forsyth, Georgia. She pulled into the old town square, then drove around behind one of the buildings to park; she still wanted to keep a low profile. They got out and walked into the beautiful town square. It reminded her of the downtown square in Roswell or Marietta. The age of the buildings looked like they predated the Civil War. But, since only buildings belonging to northern sympathizers were spared from General Sherman's fires, the original structures had probably been burned to the ground. The town hall itself was grand to say the least. It was a three-story colonial built in brownstone, its spire reaching up to a baby blue sky.

Cade said, "Hey, how about that place?"

They walked across the square into a tiny restaurant nestled in between the old Ross Theatre and a flower shop. The Grits Café was an unassuming little place that looked to be straight out of an issue of *Southern Living* magazine. A little bell tinkled as they pushed open the old glass door. It had a kind of diner charm that was accentuated with a dreamy aroma of roasted potatoes and banana crème pie.

"Y'all just sit anywhere ya like," said a smiling waitress with blazing red curls that should have been gray. "I'll be right with ya."

They sat down at a two top close to the counter in chairs that were something you'd see in a 1950s movie: gleaming chrome, thick padding on the seat, with sparkly red plastic covers.

"Now how are y'all? My name's Loraine. Y'all ever been here before?" said the waitress, practically speed talking. "Well you're gonna love it, we don't have nothin' your momma wouldn't approve of, and none of it's fattenin', honey, not even that lemon meringue pie, I made that myself, not that a skinny little thing like you couldn't use a few pounds, but listen to me just a carryin' on, can I get ya a nice tall glass of sweet tea? I'll bring 'em right over, y'all just take your time and don't forget to look at the board for the specials, I'll be right back." She was gone almost faster than she talked.

Cade grinned. "So, I guess we're having the sweet tea?"

"Yeah, it's the law in these small towns."

"You know we're going to have two slices of lemon meringue pie that show up whether we want them or not, right?"

"Yeah," said Jana. "And I get the feeling we're not even going to order the food. My money says Loraine just shows up with two plates of something fried."

Jana was thinking more clearly now. Her mind was once again working on the problem of how they were going to get the data into the right hands. It was a challenge that had to be met quickly. She was keyed up and still nervous about someone spotting them. The plan to give the data to Uncle Bill had been brilliant. He was someone that Latent trusted with his life. But now that Bill was dead, they had to come up with something else. Everything was going sideways.

Right on cue, Loraine arrived with plates of food stretched across her arms.

"Now y'all will have to forgive me. I couldn't help myself. I took the liberty of ordering for ya." She placed the plates on the table.

Jana was steeped in concentration and barely noticed. She was staring out the large window and onto the town square. Loraine looked at Jana's gaze and stood, staring at her with a curious little smile on her face. A glorious aroma of homemade fried chicken and dumplings rose delicately up at Jana. It beckoned her senses and pulled heartstrings she'd long forgotten. Memories of being on her grandpa's porch when she was seven years old flooded forward. She would sit on his lap, and the gentle man would reach his arms around her, cut the fried chicken, and put each bite into her tiny little mouth.

Jana glanced down at the plate and stared. It was exactly as she remembered it. When she finally looked up at Loraine, she instead saw her grandma. A little tear welled in her eye; the emotions were still raw.

"Aw, sweetie. Now somethin's wrong. Now don't tell Loraine any lies, I can tell. Somethin's wrong with the food. Oh, I always do this! I get carried away and just order food and look at what happens. Oh now, don't cry, honey, I have a strict rule in the Grits Café. Nobody's allowed to cry alone in my presence."

A tear rolled down Jana's cheek.

"I'm okay, ma'am. I am. I had a tough night last night, that's all. It's not the food, honest. I thought I was back on my grandpa's front porch for a minute." Loraine pulled a handkerchief out of her pocket and touched it to her own eyes.

"Is there anything Miss Loraine can do for ya, honey? Well, I'm here, honey. If you need anything, I'll be right over there." Loraine sniffled and walked back towards the kitchen.

Jana said, "I've got to get a hold of myself. We've got to be much more anonymous than this. People need to see us then forget we even exist. Maybe I'm paranoid."

"Are you okay?" said Cade.

"Look," said Jana, "instead of being paranoid, let's take action. Let's take control of the situation. The situation is dictating us, and we need to dictate it. Let's come up with a plan and let's execute it."

The two talked over lunch, but they weren't coming up with what they believed was a safe way to get the data into the right hands. A few customers who were obvious regulars mingled in and out of the restaurant. Loraine chatted them up and they returned in kind. And the little doorbell swung back and forth, tinkling gently.

60

J ana reached behind her to pull out the stack of papers that she
had taken from Rupert Johnston's office. She'd almost forgotten
she had stuffed them back in her waistline. But just as her hand
gripped the papers, she stopped moving. She wasn't sure why. Perhaps
it was that his shirt looked out of place for someone from a tiny
Georgia town. Or perhaps it was the unkempt hair. Something did not
belong, and Jana was on edge. The stranger came across the road from
the town hall and headed right for the diner. Jana's heart jumped. The
door swung open and he held it in place, the bell ringing gently
overhead. Jana shifted her hand from the stack of papers and onto the
grip of her Sig Sauer. The man stood there, staring at her. No smile,
no friendly nod—nothing reminiscent of small-town-Georgia life. His
eyes carried a look of blankness, and she knew this was trouble. *CIA*,
she thought. The firearms instructor from Quantico's voice piped up
from somewhere in the recesses of her brain, *Double-tap, center mass, then
one to the head.* It felt as if all the air had left the room. He was fifteen
feet away.

The stranger walked forward; the door swung closed behind him.

Thirteen feet away . . .

Ten feet away . . .

Jana thumbed the safety off the holster.

Seven feet away . . .

Jana jumped up, her stainless steel chair flying sideways and
crashing against another, her weapon drawn.

In her deepest voice, Jana yelled, "FBI, FREEEZE! Everybody
down! Show me your hands! Show me your hands!"

People screamed and dove for cover, the sight of Jana's gun
blinding them to anything else.

The stranger stopped and stood there. There was a long pause, and
then from within the blankness, a meek voice peeked out from behind
the thick, grizzled beard.

"Miss Baker?" It was soft and disarming, almost like feathers. It cut
the tension as easily as Loraine had cut into her lemon meringue pie.

218 ▫ THE FOURTEENTH PROTOCOL

Cade looked at Jana. Jana didn't move. Whimpers could be heard from the corners of the restaurant, and somewhere in the kitchen, a plate shattered.

"Miss Baker, I'd really be appreciative if you didn't kill me right here in front of these nice people. I've kinda had a bad day."

"Bad day? Tell me about it. You flinch, and I'll cut you in half. Who are you?"

"I'm William Tarleton." The name meant nothing to Jana. "My mom always called me Billy. But in college, my roommate always called me Uncle Bill."

"More information coming in now in what is being referred to as TerrorGate. Hello, this is Mike Slayden, WBS News. In a statement issued moments ago, US Attorney General Robert Ashton handed down sweeping indictments that include dozens of employees of the Central Intelligence Agency. Also indicted are several executives at Thoughtstorm Inc., an Atlanta-based company, who are believed to have been involved in a terror plot. For more information, let's go now, live, to Buckhead, with correspondent, John Carden."

"That's right, Mike, in a prepared statement, Attorney General Ashton said that during a terrorist investigation of its own, the Central Intelligence Agency crossed the line and committed treason against the United States. An *insidiae*, as he referred to it, which is Latin for conspiracy. The allegations leveled against CIA officials indicate they were taking a page right out of the Drug Enforcement Administration's playbook. The CIA operation, which was known as Operation Ladder, centered around funding a known terror organization that was operating within the borders of the United States. Their goal was to climb further and further up the chain of command of the terror group in a manner similar to the way the DEA breaks up drug rings. When asked for comment, the Attorney General stated, and I quote, 'This is an *insidiae* that reaches the uppermost echelons of the US government. Earlier this morning, a Senate subcommittee met behind closed doors to hear evidence against the president of the United States over his possible knowledge of the CIA's clandestine activities.' Now, as of yet, Mike, the White House has no comment. But it is apparent that this case is far from over. Reporting live from Buckhead, John Carden, WBS News."

"Uncle Bill?" said Jana. "Uncle Bill was killed right in front of me. How do you know that name? Who are you? Pop out some identification before I pop you a new asshole."

"Miss Baker, please . . ."

"Who else is with you!" screamed Jana, looking over the man's shoulder and out onto the street.

"Miss Baker, I am Uncle Bill. Look, I know what this looks like. I know, I'm supposed to be dead, right? That minivan must look like Swiss cheese right now . . ."

"That minivan was shredded! Uncle Bill would have been blown to bits. If you're Uncle Bill, how come you weren't killed? That chopper ripped the minivan apart," said Jana, applying light tension to the trigger.

"I was monitoring the bureau's frequencies the whole time. I heard them. I heard everything that was going on. They knew they had incoming air traffic, and they knew it was hostile. When I saw that chopper round the corner in between the buildings, man, it was like I had a flashback to 'Nam. I was out of that van in a heartbeat. I was knocked unconscious when the missile struck it though. If I hadn't dived down the stairwell to the MARTA train . . . man, I'd be toast."

Jana was taking no chances.

"Bullshit! Credentials. Show me your credentials. I'm not going to ask you again."

The man slowly pulled out a thin, black leather wallet. He held it forward—they were credentials identifying one William Tarleton, National Security Agency.

"Okay, if you're Uncle Bill, tell me something about your college roommate that no one else would know."

The restaurant was silent, all except the muffled sobs of Loraine crouching behind the counter.

The man looked down a long moment then said, "Well, Stevie always told me to never tell anyone how many times I'd held his head over the toilet while we were at Georgetown. He always had this idea that it would sort of curb his career ambitions. You know, FBI director and all that."

Jana thought back to when she and Kyle were in the Atlanta field office, talking to Latent. He had said that exact thing. She lowered her weapon, never taking her eyes off of Uncle Bill. "Loraine, it's okay now," said Jana. "It's over. It's all okay. You all right?"

From behind the counter, Loraine stood up in trepidation and dabbed at heavy mascara pushing its way down her face.

"We should go now," said Bill. "If I can find you, they can find you."

"How did you find us?" said Cade.

Bill simply turned and looked back toward the door. Up above the tinkling little bell was a security camera.

"The police did a felony stop on the Ford Explorer you switched license plates with. Probably scared the hell out of the driver. After that, I started looking for a vehicle with a matching description with the other license plate. It didn't take long. Hopefully, we have a head start over those assholes at CIA."

Jana said, "Loraine, honey? You mind if we use the back door?"

"Oh, of course," said Loraine, wiping mascara out from under her eyes. "But y'all take some of Loraine's nice lemon meringue pie, now."

"Yes, ma'am," said Cade.

The three left out the back, jumped into Bill's car, and were gone. Bill wove into the neighborhoods to avoid any more cameras.

"What's the plan?" said Jana.

"I've got a he-lo waiting on us," said Bill. "There's a soybean field just up the road here. We're going to Maryland, to Fort Meade. On board we'll get to work on that data. But we have one stop to make first."

61

The cargo van was white. It had no windows, less the driver and passenger sides, and those were tinted dark enough to cast a somber glow on the dingy interior. After making a straight fourteen-hour trek from Atlanta, it pulled into the sliver-thin driveway of Old Mrs. Neebody's house in Queens, New York. Only little Jimmy who lived a few houses up noticed. The single garage door rose quietly then engulfed the van. As Jimmy rode by on his Huffy, he thought it looked like a mouth that had just swallowed a great big Tylenol.

As the windowless door swung shut, the garage was almost pitch black.

"We are here, Waseem," said the driver from behind bloodshot eyes.

In the floor of the cargo van, a long, flat metal door popped upwards, revealing a secret compartment beneath. Waseem Jarrah rose from a horizontal position inside the hidden compartment, sat upright, and stretched.

"The time is close, my young friend," said Jarrah. He placed his arm on the young driver's shoulder. "Soon, we will be in the arms of Allah, and we will be hailed."

"Death to the beast," said the young apprentice. But his voice was timid and lacked conviction.

Bill's car bumped across ruts in the recently scraped dirt road.

"How much longer?" said Jana.

"Oh, about ten minutes or so," said Uncle Bill.

Jana pulled out Rupert Johnston's handwritten papers once more.

"What cha got there?" said Bill.

"These were a stack of papers from inside Rupert Johnston's office. I'm almost afraid to ask you. He's dead, isn't he?" said Jana, though she already knew the answer.

Bill just looked at her.

Jana replied, "He was burned up. Completely burned up. I've been trying to read these papers of his. I'm getting the impression he had no idea what he was getting into when this thing started. After that, he just couldn't figure out how to get out of it."

62

The front tire bumped the edge of a washed-out spot and began to rattle as the car's tires thumped across the washboard-like dirt road, its ridges having formed after heavy rains.

"You're going to want to study these, Bill," said Jana. "I think these papers tell the whole story. There's even details about the encryption."

Plumes of dust rose from the dirt road behind them and drifted into the quiet rows of pines on either side.

"Hey, Bill," said Cade. "There was something on the news this morning. I didn't really catch the rest of it. It mentioned a car bomb? At first, I thought they were talking about the minivan you were driving, but they said it was in downtown."

Bill stayed quiet.

"Bill?" said Jana.

"All right." Bill sighed. "I was hoping to avoid this. Yes, there was a car that was blown up in downtown Atlanta last night."

He paused, collecting his words like a kid trading bottle caps, wanting to be sure he got the best ones.

"It was the Apache helicopter. It was a surgical strike. The vehicle didn't have a chance."

Jana said, "What do you mean? What vehicle? Why did the Apache go after it?"

After a moment, Bill simply said, "It was a taxicab."

The sentence hung in space for a moment.

"A taxi?" said Cade. "But why would they take out a tax . . ." Cade gasped as he processed the thought. "No, don't tell me . . . it was my fault, wasn't it? Oh my God, they killed a taxi driver because of me? Because of what I did?"

Bill again said nothing as Jana tried to catch up.

"What do you mean, Cade? What did you do?" she said. But then it hit her all at once. Their cell phones. They had placed their cell phones in the underside of the bumper of a taxicab. The Apache tracked their cell signals and assumed they were in the cab. The nightmare they were in didn't seem to have an end. Jana looked out the window. And the pines passed and the tires rattled and the dust swirled behind them.

The rows and rows of planted pines gave way to fields of soybeans, cotton, and tobacco. Not as flat as Kansas, but close. The farm belt stretched wide. Hundreds of acres of fields were edged by a dividing line of tall pines. As they came up a very low rise, Jana saw a triad of tall grain silos in the distance. And there at the base, a whirlwind of dust circled. The squat-low Huey was waiting with rotors turning.

Adjacent to the grain silos stood an old wooden farmhouse tucked beneath three broad oak trees. The white paint had been flaking away for years. On the porch, an old man in overalls stood next to empty rocking chairs, arms crossed, his straw hat flapping in the wind.

"Man, you weren't kidding," said Cade. "You really do have a helicopter waiting. Hey, Bill, you said before we go to Ft. Meade that we had one other stop first? What was that?"

"We'll get to that," said Bill.

The man on the porch paid the approaching car no attention. He was focused on something high in the sky. When Jana looked up, she could see the faint outline of two military jets banking to the left. A low roar from their engines reverberated through the car.

"Those are for you," said Bill.

"What do you mean?"

"F-18s, out of Dobbins. That Apache is still out there. We aren't taking any chances."

"You mean we've got air cover?" said Cade.

"Yep," said Bill. "And as soon as we get on the chopper, Cade, I'm going to take that thumb drive from you and start working. My equipment is on board."

"Got it."

"Jana," said Bill, "hold on to those papers tightly. I don't want them spread across ten acres of soybeans while we board that Huey. I'll need you to keep reading through them. There may be some clues we need to decrypt the data."

Moments later, buckled into their seats and headsets on, the helicopter blades roared and whumped to life, kicking up more dust. Jana looked at the old man on the porch and saw he was still facing them, bracing against the wind. His face was defiant. It was as if he knew this was something important, something utterly important. Jana waved, and the man stood sturdy and proud, then nodded back. For the second time that morning, she catapulted back in her memory into her grandfather's warm arms. Looking at the old man on the porch was like looking at an angel.

63

The basement was dark and dank. The back room, however, was brilliantly lit. The smell was something of a cross between an epoxy factory and an old high school locker room. Waseem was disgusted. On his first visit, he expected better. Things should have been in order and more cleanly in anticipation of his visit. Two decrepit couches lined either side of the box-shaped space, one man sleeping on each. Waseem glanced at them; his face twinged against the sharp odor.

In the center of the room, lying on a heavy hewn, homemade workbench, was the prize. It was cylindrical in shape, about three feet long, and twenty-five inches in diameter. On the left end was a heavy metal collar with handles surrounding an aluminum valve and threaded nozzle. Had it been smaller, it would have passed as a standard propane canister, the type found underneath every gas grill in America.

One of the men stirred. Waseem expected him to jump up, kneel at his knees, and kiss his hand. But the man's eyes were milky and twitching. The dark face, which was full of heavy razor stubble, brightened at the sight of Waseem. Then the man mouthed a few words that neither Waseem nor his young driver could understand. Jarrah realized the man was deeply ill. He leaned down beside the stained couch and put his hand on the coarse fabric; then placed his mouth next to the man's ear.

"What is it, my friend?"

In a dry whisper, the man said, "It is ready . . . it is ready. Go, go now. It is not safe for you here. We will be with Allah soon—I can almost see him."

"What is wrong with them?" said the frightened apprentice.

Waseem looked over his shoulder but did not acknowledge the question.

"You have done well," said Waseem. "You have struck a blow against the infidel. Allah will reward you for this." Waseem looked at the other couch. The second man was not breathing; radiation poisoning had taken its toll.

"You must leave this place," whispered the man, coughing. "You must leave this place now. Do not stay. It will make you sick. Take the package. Go, go now, and . . ." The man was gone.

Waseem turned to look back at his driver. "Bring the hand truck from the van. We must load the device. Time is short—move now."

The driver hurried up the stairs with fear in his eyes, tripping as he went.

64

"Congressional leaders have called for the president's resignation once again. The president is meeting behind closed doors at this hour, testifying in front of the Senate Oversight Committee on the events leading up to yesterday's chaotic shootout between the FBI's Hostage Rescue Team and security officers of the Central Intelligence Agency. In related news, there are developments in that car bombing at the site of the Marriott Marquis in downtown Atlanta. First reports indicated a car bomb, but now, it seems clear that the vehicle was struck by a missile, possibly fired from—of all things—a military helicopter. Unconfirmed reports out of Dobbins Air Force Base corroborate that story. Those reports indicate that a Marine Corp Apache AH-64 attack helicopter, attached to the Naval Air Station there, was commandeered last night without proper authorization. Commandeered by who is a question that is not known at this time, but when this reporter asked about the current whereabouts of the chopper, neither Air Force nor Navy officials would comment. On top of these developments, we're getting new word . . . hold on, yes we're going live now to a press briefing just taking place at the Pentagon."

"Good day," said General Marcus Mears.

Camera shutters discharged in the background. It sounded like a swarm of locusts were tap dancing.

"As of exactly 12:32 PM Eastern Daylight Time, the US terrorist threat level went from yellow to red. We have verified information that indicates a significant terrorist event may be imminent. All precautions are being taken. We urge citizens to remain indoors, but to stay calm. If you do not need to travel, stay in your homes. The president has put all US troops and US embassies on high alert. At this time, I will be available for a few questions." A cacophony of noise erupted in the room. "Yes?" said the general, nodding to a reporter.

"General Mears," the reporter said, "you said an event might be imminent. Is there an indication as to where the event might take place?"

"We cannot confirm the location. But our best intelligence at this time is that this event will occur within the borders of the continental United States."

Background noise erupted again, and reporters yelled and shouted over each other.

"Yes, Mable," said the General.

"General, can you be more specific as to the type of threat?"

"No, ma'am, at this time we are not sure of the type of event, but we are running all scenarios. The president is urging people to remain calm, and to stay indoors." There was a long pause. The general continued, "I'd like to add one more thing before I go. This country was founded as a Christian nation. But at this time, without regard for religion, I'd like to ask all citizens to . . . pray."

There were more shouts from reporters as the general left the podium.

"John Carden back with you. Well, we've just heard from the Pentagon. Two-star General Marcus R. Mears indicating that the terror threat level has been elevated to red, its highest level. The general also urged people to remain calm, to stay indoors, and to pray. Keep it glued to WBS for the latest news, weather, and traffic. For now, reporting live from downtown Atlanta, this is John Carden, WBS News."

65

Uncle Bill worked an array of decryption equipment while the helicopter was in flight. He looked like an airline pilot, or perhaps an astronaut, working multiple systems at once. He keyed his mic and turned towards the cockpit, "Hey, can we get these two on the comm, please?" The noise from the Huey would have been deafening without the noise cancelling headsets.

A moment later, Jana and Cade's headsets lit up with military radio chatter.

"Cade," said Bill, "what's this?" inviting him to lean over.

While the two of them engaged in a technical conversation about decrypting the data, Jana listened to the radio chatter in her headset. She could hear communication from the F-18s, currently off their starboard side. Strangely, she had never felt this safe. Looking out the port side window, she gauged that the Huey and its military escort were heading west towards Atlanta, the city growing large in her view. When they flew directly over Hartsfield-Jackson International Airport, Jana keyed her mic.

"Pilot, we're right over Hartsfield. Why are we not going around their airspace? Why aren't any of the planes on the ground moving?"

The pilot replied, "Ah, roger that, Agent Baker. Ah, ATL is tango uniform as of zero nine hundred today. Everything is grounded. Nothing in or out, ma'am."

"Grounded? Because of the terror threat? But, Jesus Christ, it's the busiest airport in the world."

"Ah, roger that, yes, ma'am. Ma'am? We'll be touching down on the he-lo pad at Emory Crawford Long hospital in zero-three mics."

Jana said, "Crawford Long? Why are we going there?"

"Apologies, Agent Baker, I'm not at liberty to say. And, ma'am, when we touch down, you're instructed to remain in your seat, please. We don't have much time, ma'am."

Two minutes later they were hovering directly over the roof of Crawford Long, one of Atlanta's central hospitals. Cade leaned towards Jana.

"What's up? Why are we here?"

"I have no idea," she said.

They bumped hard against the landing pad. On the far end of the roof, a doorway opened, and a nurse leaned against it to prop it open.

Bill put his hand on Cade's shoulder. "Son, you need to go inside."

"Me?" said Cade. "Inside? Inside where? What are you talking about?"

"Hurry, son." Bill glanced out at the nurse. "There's not much time."

It wasn't until Cade saw the nurse standing there that it hit him. A hospital, a nurse, not much time. His father. His father.

Cade flung open the heavy sliding door of the Huey, ducked his head, and ran to the open doorway. For as quickly as he moved, he did not want to go inside.

66

"You have memorized your final objective?" said Waseem as the white van barreled down the New Jersey turnpike. The van's driver was stoic, almost mechanical.

"Yes, it is memorized. Routes, times, alternates. I am ready."

"You will be named in the hall of names. You strike against the beast and all that is evil."

Cars passed on their left, and Waseem held the AK-47 rifle low and out of view. If they were tailed by a police cruiser, he would not hesitate.

"Once we're at the dock, you will be alone, with Allah at your back. You understand the detonator? Do everything in your power to reach your final destination, but should you be stopped, detonate the device. Always look to the east, my son," said Waseem. "You are the sharp end of the stick, now."

The nurse took Cade by the arm. The hallway was lined with secret service agents. Cade saw no fewer than ten as he entered, several more on the elevator, and a dozen on the eleventh floor where they stopped. The elevator door swung open. Cade spoke for the first time.

"Nurse, what's happening? Is it my dad?"

"Yes, honey. Hurry, we don't have much time. He's very weak."

They crossed through double doors into the intensive care ward and stopped at room 1117 where the nurse pushed open the hospital room door. Cade stood, staring into the room, he was frozen. He could see the end of the bed and had an irrational thought that if he didn't go in, none of this would be happening. From behind him, a secret service agent put his hand on Cade's shoulder.

"Sir, the second F-18 is almost finished with midair refueling. Once it's done, we have to go." He held his arm up, motioning Cade to enter the room. "Please."

Cade walked into the darkened room where clear plastic formed a large box over his father, protecting his shattered immune system. To enable him to speak to his son, Cal Williams' ventilator had just been removed. His breathing was labored and choppy.

Cal craned his stiff neck to the left. "Cade? Is that you, son?" The voice was raspy like the winds of the Mojave Desert.

Cade went to his side. The nurse silently unzipped the plastic enclosure.

"Yes, Dad, it's me."

"Son, I want to say something to you." His dry cough ended in a distinct wheeze. "Son, I'm proud of you. I'm proud of the man you've become. And . . . I'm proud of the things you are doing right now."

"You know what's going on, Dad?" said Cade.

"I had to twist their arms, but yes. They told me everything. I guess they figure spilling a few national secrets to someone who won't be here in a little while doesn't matter much."

"Dad, don't talk like that." Cade clenched his throat.

"I'm glad I got to see you one last time, son. You need to go now. You need to help those people, son. And, Cade? Remember what I always told you"—and they said in unison—"never do anything you're going to regret for the rest of your life."

Cade felt like he was ten years old again.

"Promise me?"

"Yes, sir."

"You need to go. Don't waste any more time on me. I've said my peace."

"I love you, Dad."

"I love you, too, son."

Cade turned to leave then stopped. But before looking back, he thought better of it. Outside, the secret service agent spoke into the mic tucked into his left shirt cuff, "All posts, all posts. Server is on the move. I repeat, Server is on the move."

Cade rushed out onto the roof then into the Huey, whose rotor blades thumped wildly. As they lifted off, Cade could see the green space at the street level of the hospital below. A grandfather in a white robe pushed a portable IV and played with his grandchildren. And somewhere on the eleventh floor, in the intensive care ward, a heart monitor's alarm sounded in a long, continuous fashion before being switched off.

"All right, we're patched into the decryption center now. Running diagnostics. Roger that, you should have the package," said Bill into his headset. The Huey took only four minutes to touch down on the far end of the tarmac of runway four at Hartsfield-Jackson

International Airport. The trio boarded a heavy Gulfstream Five whose jets were roaring. It took less than sixty seconds to load Bill's equipment.

"Ft. Meade has the decryption algorithm running now. It won't take long to crack it," said Bill.

The jet's engines rumbled, and the plane hurtled down the long, empty runway, then banked northeast.

Cade said, "It won't take long? Really? Isn't that a CIA cipher?"

"Sure it is," said Bill. "But it won't take long to crack. I wrote it."

Jana smiled and shook her head from side to side. "Bill, remind me to kiss you later."

"I don't think the missus would appreciate that," laughed Bill. "Besides, I think Cade here would be jealous."

"Pilot, can you patch me into FBI headquarters?" said Jana. "Into the director's office?"

"Yes, ma'am. One moment, ma'am."

A phone rang in her headset. "Director Latent's office," said a female voice.

"This is Agent Baker, I need to speak to . . ."

"Yes, Agent Baker. The director is expecting your call. One moment please."

Jana was taken aback that anyone would be waiting for her call, much less the director of the FBI.

"Baker? This is Latent. You all right?"

"Yes, sir," said Jana.

"Thank God. Baker? Baker, listen, I'm sorry about what happened to Kyle. There's some things about Kyle . . . some things you don't know, things we should talk about later."

"Yes, sir. Thank you, sir." Jana gritted her teeth in an effort to quell her emotions.

"What's the sitrep?"

"Sir, Uncle Bill has the package. He's working on it here, and it's been sent to Ft. Meade. He thinks we'll be able to crack it quickly, sir," said Jana.

"Well, if anybody can crack it, it's Uncle Bill. Damn, last night I thought that son of a bitch was dead. Baker, once the data is decrypted, I want you in the field. We still have to catch that asshole Waseem Jarrah. He's just graced the ten most wanted list, and you've got operational experience dealing with him."

"Yes, sir."

"Oh, one more thing," said Latent. "Tell Bill he's not off the hook for that twenty bucks he owes me from Super Bowl XVI. Thinking he's dead doesn't count."

67

The dock looked like something out of a movie, only the smell was worse—dead fish, stale beer, and sea gull crap. Jarrah stepped onto the Egyptian cargo ship, *MV Red Glory*. From the top of the gangplank, he turned and saw the white cargo van pulling away.

"Allah be with you," he said, then disappeared into a cargo hold on the port side.

Uncle Bill was viewing three different computer monitors and talking to NSA headquarters, known to insiders as The Box, at the same time. He pulled Cade's thumb drive out of the USB port and looked at it; 8GB was stamped onto the side.

"Cade, where did you get this thumb drive?" said Bill.

"Ah, I don't know. Wal-Mart maybe."

"Yeah, I don't think Wal-Mart sells thumb drives that can hold this much data."

"What do you mean?" said Cade.

"We've got a compressed file here. The Box is telling me they just decompressed it, and the file is huge."

"How huge?" said Cade.

"In its uncompressed state, it's 1.5 terabytes. You'd have to be a government agency to even have compression software that can do anything close to that."

"Holy crap. You can compress a 1.5 terabyte file onto an 8 gig thumb drive? So what does that mean?"

"Well, it looks like we've got two ciphers to crack instead of one. I've got The Box working on the first cipher, decrypting the server calls that were going on during all those e-mail jobs. That's what's in the huge file. From the looks of it, I'd say you were right. Thoughtstorm was definitely calling outside the firewall during e-mail campaigns. If I'm right, the end result is that they were sending encoded messages to specific e-mail addresses. In a little while, The Box will tell us what the text of those messages said. That means we should be able to ascertain where and when they are to carry out their last assignments."

"What's the other cipher?"

"Separately, I should be able to isolate the IP addresses of where the terror cell members were when they last accessed their e-mail accounts. We'll find out their locations, how many . . ."

"Sir," interrupted the lieutenant. "I've got flash traffic from The Box, sir."

"Hold your horses, will you?" said Bill. "Like I was saying . . ."

"Sir, this can't wait," insisted the young officer.

"Ah, shit," said Bill as he picked up the call. "This is Tarleton. What do ya got, Knuckles? Uh huh, uh huh." Bill shut his eyes and concentrated, then turned and looked out the plane's oblong window and stared down at the ground. "Are you sure? You double checked? . . . And the quarterback doesn't know yet? Okay, good work, son. No, no. I'll tell him."

"What was that all about?" said Cade.

"Baker?" said Bill. "Pick up that headset. You're going to want to hear this."

Bill dialed a phone number then waited. "Stevie, Uncle Bill. We've got a problem."

"I haven't slept in three weeks," said Stephen Latent. "I thought you were dead, and the first thing you tell me is we've got a problem?"

"Sorry, Stevie, I know how cranky you get when you don't get your sleep."

"Yeah, yeah, yeah. What do you have, Bill? What's your ETA?"

"We're about forty-five minutes from The Box. My boys just called. They cracked the first cipher. Steve, the countdown started. Their final objectives, the countdown for the terror cell members to begin carrying out their final objectives—the clock is ticking already."

"Oh shit," said Latent. "What can you tell me? How many subjects are we dealing with?"

"The Box says they've found thirty-seven different sets of instructions to terrorists. Each set appears to be addressing a different e-mail recipient."

Latent said, "Thirty-seven bomb chuckers?"

"I'm assuming I'm going to find thirty-seven different e-mail addresses in the other cipher that I'm working on right now. We're going to crack this cipher to try to track these assholes right down to their physical location."

"Bill, this can't happen fast enough. I've got to have those locations. What do the instructions say?"

"It's being sent to you right now, everything we have. It's everything from mass shootings, bombings, aircraft, snipers, poisonings. It's bad, Steve, it's all bad. Worse than we thought," said Bill.

"You said the countdown for them to begin carrying out their final objectives started; but how much time do we have left before the countdown ends? When do they start?" said Latent.

"The countdown culminated twenty-three minutes ago, Steve. They've already started. I'm sorry."

68

"This is Mike Slayden, reporting live in Atlanta from Peachtree DeKalb Airport. As commuter planes continue to trickle in after the FAA's closure of US airspace, fire crews are battling a huge blaze around the airport's fuel depot. You can see the thick plumes of smoke billowing violently behind me. This blaze was threatening to spiral out of control, but seems to be nearly contained now. Now listen to this. One witness tells WBS News that he passed a stopped motorist here on Buford Highway, just adjacent to the fuel tanks. Allegedly, the stopped motorist threw something towards the fuel depot. This all happened moments before an explosion took place. The vehicle then sped off. Local residents have complained for years that the airport's fuel depot, which sits just thirty yards off the road, is too close to the road for safety. We're getting . . . hold on . . . we're hearing something in the distance. It sounds like . . . it sounds like fireworks. It's a good distance away from us, perhaps on the far side of the airport, out by the end of the north-south runway. There it goes again. That sounds more like gunfire. Charlie, can you zoom in over in that area? Can you see anything? A man with a gun! Folks, we're about three hundred yards away from what appears to be a man with a rifle . . . or an automatic weapon of some type. He's firing in the air! It looks like . . . he's firing at an incoming aircraft! It looks to be a smaller corporate jet of some type coming in for a landing. He's firing at the plane. Folks, I don't know . . . FIRE! The jet's on fire! It's twisting sideways now . . ."

69

Little Jimmy was proud of his Huffy. It had been his father's bike when he was a kid. His dad fixed it up and repainted it, and Jimmy was proud of that. It was fire red with bright cobalt blue stripes down the body. Some of the other neighborhood kids thought it looked stupid, but Jimmy would have none of it. He showed them how inferior their bikes were compared to his, the weakness in the construction, and how much heavier and better built his was. And that would shut them up. That and his ability to jump a ramp farther than anybody else in the neighborhood.

Old Mrs. Neebody's house had always appealed to him. Not because he cared anything about the well-kept yard or the dormer windows. Instead, he liked the little knee wall that stretched down the left side of the driveway, separating the grass. Queens was fairly flat, but there was a slight downhill slope that ended at that house. Jimmy had eyeballed the knee wall probably a thousand times and knew it was something he had to jump, and he was going to be the first nine-year-old on the block to do it.

The problem was Old Mrs. Neebody wasn't around anymore. If she had been, this would have been a breeze. The old bat wouldn't even know there were kids playing in her yard, much less do anything about it. As it was now, no one knew the new owners or what they were like. No one ever saw them. In fact, Jimmy was the only one who had ever seen a door open or a curtain drawn or a car come or go from the house. The garage door was always shut. Yet, somehow lights turned on and off inside the house at night. He knew someone lived there. Maybe there was a ghost in there.

He pedaled up 175th Street to Vinny's house and rang the bell.

Vinny was out in a flash. "Yeah, yeah, Ma. I know, geez. Yeah, I got my helmet. I'm nine yea's old already. Hey, Jimmy! Whatdoya wanna do?"

"Let's do some jumps, okay?"

"Yeah, yeah," said Vinny, "but not here. My ma's gettin' stern about it. Hey! Let's take the ramp up the street a bit."

"I gotta better idea," said Jimmy. "Let's take it to Old Mrs. Neebody's yard."

"That old bag? Man, she's dead. Who lives in that place anyway?"

"A ghost. What's a matter? Yous a'scared?"

The two hefted the plywood ramp onto two skateboards and pulled it up the street and stopped at Mrs. Neebody's.

"Hey, the garage door is open. I ain' never seen that," said Vinny. "Man, what if somebody's in there?"

"A little garage door is open? You scared, Vinny? Bok, bok, bok, bok," laughed Jimmy.

"I ain' a'scared a nothin'," said Vinny.

"Okay then, because we're puttin' the ramp right ova there." Jimmy pointed to a spot just to the left of the long brick knee wall, dead center of the front yard. He looked back at Vinny with daring in his eyes.

Vinny was apprehensive, but refused to show it.

"Okay, but if somebody comes out and yells at us and I lose this ramp, my dads'a gonna be mad."

They wrestled the curved bike ramp into place, pointing it over the knee wall in the direction of the driveway. Then they tore off up the street so fast it looked as if they were fleeing an avalanche.

"All right, me first," said Jimmy.

Vinny's eyes were wide. "Hey, man, you gonna jump that brick wall? You'll land on the driveway. If'n you crash . . ."

"Oh shut up, Vinny. Yous sound like my motha." And with that, he pushed off hard and started to peddle; the rocket red Huffy with cobalt blue stripes thrashed back and forth, picking up speed.

Vinny held his breath and craned his neck so he could see Jimmy. The bike sped down the sidewalk and at the last second veered onto the grass, bolting straight for the ramp. It lay waiting for him like a slingshot.

Jimmy hit the ramp and arced high into the air. Vinny knew this would be trouble and broke into an immediate run. Jimmy's bike cleared the knee wall and slammed hard onto the white pavement. Jimmy flipped over the handlebars and sprawled onto the grass just beyond the driveway like a sack of potatoes.

Vinny yelled, "Jimmy!" The boy rolled on the grass, not uttering a sound. "Jimmy! Yous all right?" But Jimmy had the wind knocked out of him and couldn't speak. In a few moments, he grasped a deep breath of air and hunched over, holding his knees to his chest.

Jimmy said, "Aw, man, that hurt so bad."

"Yous all right, Jimmy? Yous all right?"

"Yeah, yeah. Geez, you worry like my old lady."

For the first time Vinny looked up. In the darkened garage there was no car. There was nothing. No shelves or boxes or garbage cans. No ancient freezer or laundry machine. Nothing. It was a little spooky.

"What's that smell?" said Vinny. "Oh gawd." He began to wretch.

"Worse than down by the docks," said Jimmy, starting to cough. "Maybe a rat died or somepin."

As the light breeze stagnated, so did the odor. It was horrific and hung over them like a quilt too heavy to get out from under.

"Man! Let's get outta here," coughed Jimmy as they ran home to tell their mothers.

"WBS Radio, John Carden here at ten minutes before the top of the hour. We've got breaking news to report. At least nineteen people are now reported dead and an unknown number wounded in a mass shooting just outside of the town of Russellville, Arkansas. The victims were all attending a sailing regatta, called The Russellville America's Cup, which takes place each year on Lake Dardanelle. Early reports indicate that a sniper, hidden from sight, began firing, first at sailors on their small boats, then turned the gun onto the crowd of spectators. Apparently the sniper used a silenced weapon, making it difficult to determine his location. The list of dead is feared to rise. For now, stay tuned to . . ."

70

As they cruised past Baltimore, Maryland, the Gulfstream jet leaned into its descent, tilting everything onboard. Jana could see Ft. Meade. It looked like a small city with dozens of buildings, all surrounding one giant building. The Box, as they called it, dwarfed the width of most modern city buildings. The sprawl of parking lots made it look like a major league ballpark on game day.

A roaring noise ripped past the Gulfstream that was only feet off the runway now. It was the F-18 fighter escort that had shadowed them the entire flight. Jana felt the thunderous engines and was exhilarated. As the Gulfstream touched down, four jet-black Chevy Suburbans accelerated down the runway keeping pace. The plane slowed to a stopping point, and two of the vehicles ground to a halt as smoke poured from their wheels. Bill jumped from his seat and was already at the door as it opened.

"Let's move, people!" All three of them jumped off the plane and sprinted straight towards an open vehicle. Ten or so people boarded the plane, secured various pieces of Bill's equipment, and ran for the other open vehicles.

Within four minutes, they entered The Box. Other than its dwarfing size, it looked like any modern building: dark glass and a brightly lit, marble-covered lobby. A huge NSA symbol stretched across the center of the marble floor. About a dozen armed security personnel were present. It looked like an American embassy expecting an imminent assault.

"This way," said Bill, flashing his badge. "They're clear," Bill yelled to the guard. "I said they're clear, goddammit!"

Once inside the large control room, Bill sat down to his equipment as it was reassembled. Jana and Cade stayed out of the way.

"All right. Bring it up on three," he said, pointing at a huge computer monitor. "Okay, people, listen up. This is a national emergency. I want to draw your attention to these two people," pointing at Cade and Jana. "These are the two most important people in the room right now. This is Cade Williams and FBI Special Agent

Jana Baker. They procured the data you're about to analyze. And in case you're wondering, their security clearance is higher than yours," Bill said, lying through his teeth. "I want team three on the cipher. Cade, I want you with that team. Teams four and six, prep the server. We're going to run each scenario one at a time. We've got to move, people. This is NSA priority level fifteen. Any questions?"

Cade whispered to Jana, "Yeah, I've got a question. Where's the head? Loraine's sweet tea is killing me."

"I doubt your security clearance level is high enough for that," said Jana, "sorry."

71

The black and white patrol car rolled up to 217 175th Street and stopped, blocking the driveway. The officer in the driver's seat keyed the mic attached to his left shoulder, "Central, unit 487 awn site. Yeah, the g'rage door is up. We'll be ten-eighteen, ovah."

"Roger that, 487. Ten-eighteen. Proceed with caution, over."

The two officers walked up the driveway, the sun bright against the bleached white cement.

"Hey, Pete, wait down heyah by the garage. I'll try the front door."

But before the officer got up the steps, his younger partner called out.

"Paulie, hold on a minute. Come down here." He squinted hard and pulled out his flashlight, trying to see inside the dark, cavernous garage. "Sweet Jesus, smells like a dead body in there. Holy Mary mother'a God."

"Central, this is 487. Send me two more units," said the younger officer into the radio.

"Roger that, 487."

"Oh my gawd," said the other officer, "they's a bahdy in there for shu'ah. I haven't smelled anything like that since Iraq," covering his mouth.

"Central, 487, go ahead and send Hawmicide while you're at it."

The radio replied, "You found a body, 487?"

"Negative, Central. But from the smell out heyah, it won't take us lawng."

72

The van driver's name in Arabic meant *follower*. He had never dwelled on that fact much, but in these last days of his life, he thought it appropriate. His mother would never understand, but his jihadist father, were he alive today, would be very proud.

He kept his eye on the speedometer and traveled only the back roads to avoid attention. Small town officials were always looking for outsiders to write speeding tickets, and he wanted to take no chances. He also was wary in case anyone had seen the van leave the ghastly smelling house in Queens. If someone had spotted it, staying out of sight now would be critical.

It was strange to be in this country with its rolling hills, sprawling oak trees, and horse farms with their endless white fences. In his experience, the land was nothing but sand, yet in this place, the color green covered everything as if a bucket of paint had been dropped from a low-flying airplane. All of it seemed like another planet.

The driver had only known the crowded, filthy shanties, the hunger, the sandstorms, and the need, no, the requirement, to obey. To obey was a part of his fiber, as if it had been sewn into the cloth of his very soul. The sun rose every morning, and his soul's embroidery stitched itself deeper and deeper into a woven tapestry of Allah.

This was hilly country in a place called Kentucky. And, after so many hours on the roads, his mind wandered back to his childhood. His father had been taken away when he was sixteen. The driver was a young man at that point, but his three little brothers, so much younger, were not so lucky. As children, they would have to survive the slums, the scorpions, and worst of all, the soldiers wearing sunglasses—all without their father.

The Americans came for his father in the night. They were not wearing sunglasses in the dark of night, but the driver knew they were there, tucked into a pocket somewhere. It was a level of fear he had never known. He was barely able to console his mother. It had taken over a week to find that his father had been taken to a prison many miles away, to a place called Abu Ghraib. He knew nothing of such places. The only thing he did know, however, was that people taken there never tended to come home again. He was afraid. Those sunglasses became a thread intermeshed into the fabric of his soul.

And so it was to be. Allah's will. Volunteering his life wasn't something the driver fretted over or considered for very long. It was simply his destiny. As he came down the far side of the mountain pass, he slowed to round a rather sharp curve in the road and then downshifted into a low gear. He glanced in the rearview mirror at the tall, fat canister in the back of the van. *They did a good job camouflaging it,* he thought. *It looks just like a propane cylinder.* Several boxes of un-inflated balloons and rolls of twine provided the perfect cover story. If he were stopped by authorities, they would think he was just a balloon vendor on his way to a carnival or festival. In fact, he was on his way to just such an event. Resting on the gritty floor of the van, a small poster lay. The headline read, "Tammy Lynn's Bluegrass Pickin' Party and Hog Roast—Pineville, Kentucky." *Allah's will be done,* and he rounded the next curve.

73

"O kay, people, come on," yelled Uncle Bill. "What have we got?"

Cade noticed that Uncle Bill's mouth only became exposed from underneath all that facial hair when Bill was yelling.

"Knuckles, how about those e-mail addresses, son? Where are they?"

"Coming on screen five now, sir," said a kid with thick-rimmed glasses and unkempt hair.

Jana whispered to Cade, "Why do they call that guy Knuckles? He doesn't look like a Knuckles. He looks more like an . . . Alice."

Cade whispered back, "Oh come on, when I was nine I looked just like that."

"Okay, run the list. There should be thirty-seven e-mail addresses," Bill yelled, squinting at screen five high against the wall. "That's thirty-five, thirty-six, thirty-seven . . . thirty-eight? What the hell? Knuckles, recount that. We should have thirty-seven e-mail addresses to correspond to the thirty-seven different sets of instructions sent to these bomb chuckers. Come on, son."

"Sir, I count thirty-eight, not thirty-seven," replied the young man.

Jana whispered, "There's an extra e-mail address. What does that mean?" But Cade was lost in thought.

Bill said, "Thirty-eight. Thirty-eight. Hmmm. Either there's a senior member of the terror cell that just gets copied on these messages, or . . ."

Cade stepped forward. "Or there's a thirty-eighth terrorist out there who already knew his final objective."

Bill looked at him. The blankness had returned.

"I don't like the sound of that," said Bill. "All right, people, new priority. Teams one and two, concentrate on those first thirty-seven e-mail addresses. I want to know their IP address, I want to know where they were the last time they accessed their e-mail accounts, I want to know their shoe sizes, I want it all. Listen up! It doesn't get any more important than this. Beg, borrow, steal, hack. I don't give a shit. Just find those locations!" Then he turned to the kid and said with the voice of a father, "Knuckles, I want you on number thirty-eight. Move, son."

Bill picked up a phone next to him. "Get me Stephen Latent." Their phone conversation was brief. When it was over, Bill hung up the phone and rubbed his neck.

His eyes flew back and forth across monitor three, which displayed the last known locations of where each terrorist had accessed their e-mail accounts. To Jana, for the first time, Bill looked like he had come alive. But she could see the worry in his eyes. It was as though his brain was in overdrive yet he'd left his poker face at home.

"That's great work, people. Knuckles, transfer the data on the locations of the thirty-seven bomb chuckers over secure six to the bureau right now."

"But I haven't isolated number thirty-eight yet, sir," replied Knuckles.

"That's all right. Transfer the data we have and keep working on it. They need those locations now."

Bill was on the phone again. "Stevie? Bill, the data is coming your way. We've isolated the last known IP address and physical location each terrorist used to access their e-mail accounts. Most look to be Internet cafés, a few Starbucks, and a public library or two. You'll want to pull surveillance footage from each location to ID your targets."

"That's great work, Bill. Are you listening to this? We've got reports of seven different incidents that have already occurred. It's hard to know that each is one of our bomb chuckers, but confidence is high. They're in full swing."

"Steve, these locations are everywhere. From downtown Chicago to Hahira, Georgia. How are you going to . . ."

"I'm ready. We've got every badge in the country suited up and ready for a raid, local and federal. I'm talking everybody. I've even got six military teams that have gone hot—four Navy SEAL teams and two from Army Delta Force. Those, along with my HRT teams, are airborne right now. If I could recall the rest of the military special ops teams from Af-fucking-ghanistan, I would. Airspace over the US is shut down. I've got fighter jets cruising from Florida to Washington State. We're going to descend on them like flies on shit. I've got to go. Oh, and Bill?"

"Yeah, Stevie."

"No one's going to forget what you did here. You put your life on the line, and nearly lost it. Thank you."

74

"... and that was Press Secretary Erik Childs, live from the White House press room; he's just leaving the podium now. To recap, Mr. Childs indicated the president had temporarily, in his words, stepped down from office. Vice President Palmer has been sworn in and is the acting commander in chief. It's unclear at this point whether the president stepped down of his own accord, or whether he was ordered to surrender his powers under federal indictment by the US Supreme Court. The Supreme Court met in closed session today, wrapping up within the last hour. The contents of that session are sealed, but it appears highly coincidental that the president's announcement comes so soon after the Supreme Court broke session. The president is under enormous pressure in the wake of the latest series of terrorist incidents. Those incidents appear to have been funded with taxpayer dollars—something that was allegedly conducted with the president's knowledge. As his last act of office the president ordered the FAA to clear the skies over the United States, a response designed to protect the country from hijackings. For now, I'm John Carden, reporting live from the White House, WBS News."

Alyssa passed through the little town of Pineville. It was more of a hamlet really—lots of box-style houses, long single-wide trailers, and abandoned shacks hovelled under rusted tin roofs. Still, the views of the approaching hills were pretty, though not quite idyllic. Little stone walls lined some of the yards cut into the hillside. Not the kind of stone walls you might see in the New England states, but flat, gray, lifeless stones stacked on top of one another. Houses on the left side of the road sunk down deep, well below the level of the road, and appeared to lean downhill towards a rambling streambed. There was a distinct absence of horses, but one thing in plentiful supply were pickup trucks that anchored each home or country store.

As the road's elevation lifted, Alyssa felt her own weight press back against the driver's seat. The road bed cut itself into the adjacent hillside, and craggily rocks reached out with tiny fingers towards her.

Curving up the low mountain pass, Alyssa gunned the engine of the little yellow VW Beetle into the twists and turns; a peace flower bobbled on the dashboard. This part of Kentucky was sparsely populated, and today, there was hardly anyone on the roads. She rounded the curves hard and felt alive.

Back home in Atlanta, Alyssa loved the color of autumn. But the springtime here decried colors that were lucid and turbulent. Sunlight shattered into dozens of beams, free-falling through the amber and popsicle-yellow canopy, creating a soft glow that sprinkled across the greens painting the forest floor.

As she climbed Pine Mountain, she noticed that the stone along the roadside was thicker and almost blocky as compared to below. And the trees seemed to creep ever closer toward the road. When she drove under a banner that read "Tammy Lynn's Bluegrass Pickin' Party and Hog Roast," she gawked at the number of cars parked on the shoulder ahead. *No wonder I haven't seen many cars,* she thought. *They're all here.* A deputy stood in the roadway ahead directing traffic. Alyssa pulled closer and leaned out.

"We can park anywhere along in here?" she asked.

The deputy, whose grin was as wide as his waistline, said, "Oh, yes, ma'am. Your first time with us at the festival? Well, you're gonna love it. We're real glad you came. We want ya to have a good time, but don't eat too much, you hear?" he said, slapping his hands on the spare tire around his waist and adjusting his baseball-style deputy cap.

"This place is packed!" said Alyssa. "I had no idea how big it would be. How many people do you think are here?"

"Oh well, let's see. Last year the pickin' had about 12,000. Well, that's what the sheriff said anyway. This year, well, don' know rightly. Looks bigger to me. Must be 15,000 or more. Hey, just listen to that. Kin you hear it? They got Pearly Jenkins and his bluegrass band. Man, they's gonna be a crowd fer him. Hey, my name's Skeeter."

"I'm Alyssa," she said, reaching her hand out the window.

"Proud to meet cha. Well, jes let us know if there's anythin' we kin do for ya, Miss Alyssa. Have a good time, now."

Alyssa drove ahead and parked at the first space she found. As she got out, the soft smell of hickory smoke ushered in on a breeze. The sun was warm on her face, and a light harmony of bluegrass music emanated through the trees. It made her feel . . . something. She couldn't quite place it. The feeling was a bit familiar and settled deep in her chest and lined her heart. She was relaxed. She felt welcomed, like she belonged somehow. It was like having a guardian angel push the last vestiges of stress from her system, in the same way you might pick up a dandelion and blow the seeds out into the wind.

It was then she realized that in her day-to-day life, she carried a small blanket of stress with her everywhere she went. Maybe it was the city life, the traffic, the job, the fear, or the pollution that did it. Or maybe it was the sudden loss of her mother and the feeling of having to face the world without her. The stress laid upon her for so long it felt normal. But now, it was time to blow the dandelion seeds far and wide. Let them settle where they may.

She headed into the trees and towards the sounds of laughter, a picking guitar, a few fiddles, and perhaps a mandolin, and a lot of people stomping their feet to the rhythm and laughing. It sounded like . . . life.

75

"John Carden, WBS News. The video you're watching now was recorded six hours ago as we accompanied federal agents on a raid. We weren't allowed to broadcast the footage until now." The video began to roll.

"'We're on the scene here just outside of Boulder, Colorado, where federal authorities are raiding an apartment complex. We can't see much beyond the first building, but moments ago we could hear muffled gunfire and yelling. Just before the raid, we saw several residents being quietly evacuated from nearby apartment units. This is a scene, according to authorities, that is repeating itself in thirty or more places across the country as arrest warrants are being served in the largest terrorism case in US history.'"

The New York City field office at 26 Federal Plaza sat near the base of Manhattan, not far from Battery Park. Its main working area consisted of a single, wide open office space. It was a cube farm of biblical proportions. On a normal day, the space was bustling with agents working on hundreds of open cases. Today, the cavernous room went quiet. In the center standing high on a desk was FBI Director Stephen Latent, a tiny clip-on microphone attached to the loosened tie around his neck. Double the normal numbers of agents were present, each agent sharing a cubicle built for one.

"All right, people, listen up," began Latent. "You've been working tirelessly, and your country will thank you for it, but not yet. Bear in mind, there is nothing more important to the sovereignty of the United States than this case. Here's the sitrep. Of the thirty-seven known bomb chuckers, we've executed warrants on twenty, all of which are in federal custody. Of the remaining seventeen, sixteen have already executed their final objective. You've seen the news. Most of these have been smaller events with a low body count. There have been multiple mass shootings in New Mexico, Arkansas, a sailing regatta in Delaware, Washington state, and Ohio. Small bombs were used in Rhode Island, Montana, Oklahoma, and at a small airport near

Atlanta. Most of those terrorists are dead. Either killed by authorities or by suicide. The three survivors are in custody.

"Even before this terror cell started carrying out their final objectives, a wave of fear has paralyzed the country. People are afraid. Except in a few rural pockets of the country where people seem determined to go about their daily lives, they don't go to work, they don't go to the grocery, they're not on the roads, they don't go out to eat, nothing. I'm proud of the work you've done so far. But understand one thing. I am sick of this shit. And make no mistake, people, even though these last seventeen events are considered minor, a small loss of life is not acceptable under my watch."

Jana leaned against the side of a cube, about twenty feet from Latent. She was exhausted and wondered if the deep circles under her eyes would become tattooed on her face. Latent looked down at her for just a moment. "And that's the good news," he said. "Now time for the bad news. As most of you know, as a result of the raid on the Thoughtstorm building in Atlanta, eleven of our brothers fell. But during the infiltration we obtained information that led us to the locations of all the thirty-seven terror members. While we all feel an overwhelming sense of loss, we cannot stop to address that loss."

His last words trailed off, like they'd fallen into a deep dark lake.

"I've just finished a conference with the National Security Agency who has been invaluable in decrypting the data we obtained."

The room was frozen as everyone awaited the bad news. No one uttered a sound.

Latent continued. "We have a thirty-eighth terrorist." Those words "thirty-eight" hung in an abyss as chatter erupted across the room. It sounded like a covey of quail had exploded off the forest floor and into flight.

"Quiet down, people, quiet down," he said, holding his hands in the air. "We have a lead." A hush fell over the room once again. "It's not much, but it's all we have, and we're going to milk it for everything it's worth. About ten miles from here, in Queens, the police walked into a house that contained two dead bodies. Both bodies were of Middle Eastern descent and were on terror watch lists. And . . ."— agents began leaning in, hanging for the next words to roll off his lips—"there are strong indications of radioactive material present at the site."

A few seconds of silence separated the time it took for agents to connect the dots between a thirty-eighth terrorist and nuclear material. The room erupted again as agents' hands found homes on their mouths and in their hair. The exhaustion and pressure had taken its toll.

"Now, that's not known to the public," said Latent. "But the presence of radioactivity is so strong, the EPA and Nuclear Regulatory Commission have evacuated a two-block radius. People are being told there were toxic chemicals found in the house. We can't let on that what we've discovered is likely the workshop of a nuclear weapons manufacturing site. If the public gets word of this, we'll have outright bedlam in the streets. People will panic. Our scenarios predict rioting, looting, mayhem, and God knows what else.

"Keep your mouths shut. Am I understood? If I find anyone has leaked this info, I'm going to tear out their Adam's apple and hand it back to them. I've also just been told that the emergency alert system is about to be activated advising people to stay in their homes. But we're predicting people in smaller towns are going to ignore the warnings. I don't know, maybe they're more resolved to live their lives than the rest of us. Before we hand you your immediate assignments, are there questions?"

From the back, a tall agent with long wavy hair that probably served him well during undercover work yelled, "Just tell us what to do, sir! We'll get the son of a bitch." Everyone laughed.

"All right, people, let's settle down. At this time, you are to report to your section chief for your assignments. We've already checked and there have been no thefts or misplacements of any nuclear material in North America. We'll be checking other parts of the world as well. We've got teams to investigate the background of each of the deceased bomb makers, teams to canvas the hell out of that neighborhood in Queens, and teams to pull video surveillance from every camera in the area. Oh, and let me make one thing perfectly clear. We have a nuclear threat to the continental United States. It will not happen on my watch. I am authorizing you to use any means necessary. I don't care if it's legal. I don't care if you have to kick in doors with no warrant. Wiretap, hack, forced entry, whatever. I don't care. Do not wait for permission. These are my direct orders. If I find you pussy'd out to wait for a warrant, I'll kill you myself. You let me deal with the rash of legal crap those maggot lawyers in Washington will throw at me afterwards—after the nuclear threat is contained. All right, people, move. That means right now!"

Jana pushed towards Latent against the throng of people as the room erupted into chaos. "Sir! Director! Sir," she said, bulling her way through.

"Baker. Yes, what is it? Jesus, you look like shit. Sorry, no offense. How are you holding up?"

"Sir, you've got everything up here in Queens covered."

"And?"

"And have we thought about the . . . well, I mean I know we've already checked for any lost or stolen nuclear material, but what if the loss wasn't reported?"

"Baker, they've got to report any known loss or theft of nuclear material immediately," he said.

"Exactly. Any *known* loss or theft. What if they don't know it's missing? The facility wouldn't know to report it."

Latent reflected on that a moment.

"Highly unlikely. But I see where you're heading. What did you have in mind?"

"I know it's a long shot, but I'd like to go up to that facility in Connecticut. The one that was right next to the bridge where the commuter train bridge was bombed, and the train fell into the river. It's a long shot, but it's worth a try."

"I don't know, Baker, sounds like a goose chase to me. And right now, I need every swinging dick in the field . . . oh, sorry. I need every agent in the field working these more direct leads."

"Sir, you've got four hundred agents working every other angle. They're on the house, neighborhood, surveillance cameras, backgrounds, bank accounts, they're checking overseas for missing nuclear material, everything. They're all over this. Sir, I don't need a team. It's just another stone I think we should turn over."

"All right, Baker. All right. Tell your section chief I've assigned you to this and check out a bureau car downstairs."

He started to walk away but stopped.

"Baker? Baker. You've got guts, and guts is enough. Just watch yourself out there. No one is going to forget what you and Kyle have done here, especially me. Be careful."

"Yes, sir. Thank you, sir," Jana said, choking down the lump in her throat.

"This is the emergency alert system. In cooperation with federal authorities, this station is conducting a broadcast of the emergency alert system. This is an actual emergency. People are urged to remain in their homes. A terrorist threat alert has been issued. The threat level is high and terrorist attacks are expected to occur at any time. This alert is for the continental United States excluding Alaska, Hawaii,

Puerto Rico, and all US outlying islands. Please remain in your homes. For more information on this actual emergency, tune to your local news station. This has been a broadcast of the emergency alert system."

76

Alyssa made her way through the trees towards the glorious smell of roasted pork and the sound of pure bluegrass music. A grin as wide as the Kentucky sky molded onto her face and revealed pearly white teeth. There were people everywhere, yet it was not at all like the mob scenes she was familiar with at big events like Music Midtown in Atlanta. There, she'd keep her distance from the mosh pits and throngs of people glued together and banging into each other like stalks of wheat in a wind storm. Looking into a sea of people like that was frightening. It was too confining, and you never knew what might happen. Here, people were more spaced apart. Lots of them held hands and many ate at picnic tables. People smiled and said hello everywhere she turned. She had that feeling inside that was like greeting an old friend you hadn't seen in years, then sitting down together and telling stories.

Alyssa wandered past the craft fair booths and over towards the amphitheatre where most people were gathered. The amphitheatre was carved into the edge of the mountain and was dotted with row after row of people seated on wooden boards, each supported on either end by rock quarried from the mountain. The whole space formed a sort of bowl that pushed its way right up to the stage. There wasn't a bad seat in the place. Deputy Skeeter was right, the people loved their bluegrass. Couples danced in front of the stage under a sky that was as blue as it was radiant.

And surely, Alyssa thought, *mom is watching, and she's proud of me for going on this odyssey, and for finding my soul.*

77

Jana shook Cade by the shoulder. He stirred, then startled awake and jumped to his feet. "What! What is it . . . ?"

"Easy, easy, tiger. It's just me."

Cade rubbed his eyes and tried to clear the cobwebs, barely remembering he was in the lobby of the FBI's New York field office.

"Man, I fell asleep. I was dreaming," he said, his voice shaking a little.

"About Kyle?" said Jana.

"Yeah."

"Listen, we've got to go."

"Where to?" Cade said as they walked towards the elevator. "They're going to let me come with you?"

"I didn't bother to ask, so yes," Jana said. "Come on, let's run across the street first. There's a little deli over there, and they've got a great pastrami on rye. We've got a short road trip. Oh, and leave on that FBI Visitor tag, the deli gives us a discount."

Ten minutes later they left the basement garage and drove out paralleling the East River on the FDR. Maybe it wasn't clean enough to swim in, but the river was pretty this time of year. Sunlight glittered across the water between Manhattan and Roosevelt Island, a ridiculously thin strip of land that seemed to always find room for more buildings. They crossed the JFK and headed straight for the Bronx. When they finally cut onto I-95, Cade interrupted the silence.

"So you never said where we were going."

"We're going up to Stratford," said Jana.

"Connecticut? The train derailment?" said Cade. "Why? What's up there?"

"A nuclear facility. It's just a hunch, but it's worth a shot."

"So, you going to tell me? Or am I going to have to beat it out of you?" said Cade.

Jana looked at him, then flipped the dashboard blue strobe light on and accelerated.

"You know," she said, "I could whip you in a fight."

"Yeah, I know," said Cade.

"It's just a hunch. We're looking for the source of nuclear material."

"Wait, what nuclear material?"

She explained the situation and her theory to him. Then he said, "Man, we're really in this deep, aren't we? I mean, this is really happening, isn't it?"

"There are a lot of things that go on, Cade. A lot of things we don't tell people. The stuff I've seen already. We don't tell people half of this shit because they'd react just like this. They'd stay in their homes. America would stop being America. Which is exactly what these bomb chuckers want. It takes a lot to protect a nation."

Sixty miles later they crossed over Stratford and passed a highway sign for the Housatonic River.

"That's it," said Jana. "That's the bridge. It happened right here." As they crossed the six-lane bridge, silence befell the car. Several cranes leered over the heavily damaged train trestle that once sistered the highway bridge. Twisted metal at either end of the trestle bent like the fingers of a person with acute arthritis.

"Down below. That looks like the nuclear plant," said Cade.

They exited, turned left in the direction of the plant, and headed down a winding neighborhood street.

"Listen," Jana said, "we're going into that nuclear plant. Whatever happens, just follow my lead. Whatever I say, whatever I do, just act like it's totally expected. Don't act surprised. Play right into it. Let people assume you're an agent too, but don't say that you are—that would be a crime. Hell, don't say anything."

"You're kind of freaking me out."

Jana pulled the car off in between two yards in the neighborhood and jumped out. Cade followed her to the trunk where Jana slipped on a navy FBI windbreaker and put her badge on a chain around her neck. She pulled back the windbreaker, exposing the firearm on her waist.

"Wait," said Cade, "you don't think we're going to get trouble from them, do you?"

"No, absolutely not." She smiled. "Why do you ask?"

78

The neighborhood had been evacuated. There were no cars on the road and no boys on bicycles terrorizing the sidewalk. The mail truck did not come down 175th Street or the surrounding blocks. Electric and heating oil service had been shut off in the area. Whether through leaks or outright observation, the media now knew the contamination was from nuclear material, not chemicals. In order to keep the media's low-flying helicopters away, the Nuclear Regulatory Commission pressured the FAA to clear the airspace above. The media were told there was a danger in spreading the nuclear material that had been found at the house.

From the air, it looked like a scene out of the movie *E.T.* Old Mrs. Neebody's house was shrouded in a dome of thick, milky plastic. Decontamination trucks lined the street both in front and behind the house. Long plastic tunnels that looked like habitrails led from the house to the decontamination stations. The overcast sky created a diffuse gloom across the area as FBI agents dressed in space suits ambled through the habitrails, looking like the Michelin man.

The media had coined it The Hiroshima Hilton. Radioactive contamination was far worse than originally estimated. Neighbors who lived on either side of the house had been hospitalized, showing early signs of radiation poisoning. And the two police officers who initially responded to complaints of a foul odor at the house had spent the night in isolation in the critical care unit of Mount Sinai Hospital and were now being transported to Bethesda Medical Center's acute care unit.

Both deceased bodies discovered in the dwelling had not been moved. It was deemed too dangerous to move them yet. A specialized vehicle was being brought in from Ft. Carson, Colorado, to handle the removal of bodies and later removal of the house itself, which would have to be totally demolished.

"Hey, Jones, get over here," yelled an agent through his facemask and helmet while walking within one of the habitrails.

"Yeah, what cha got?" said the other agent.

"Get on the horn to Federal Plaza. Tell Director Latent that I said it's worse than I thought. Tell him this stuff is weapons grade. This radiation emanates from high core uranium-235."

"Roger that."

A pair of crime scene specialists worked the basement for hours, documenting everything. The crime scene was the most complex thing they had ever encountered. The element of radioactive contamination made every bit of their job ten times harder. All samples, fibers, and other evidence had to be handled in such a way as to not contaminate the FBI crime lab. Photographs were made on site and uploaded wirelessly for evaluation. The cameras would later be left on site and destroyed with the house. They were working as fast as possible, but the enormous space suits they wore slowed them down.

Two other Michelin men wobbled left and right down the groaning basement staircase. Agent Larry Fry, who was one of only a dozen or so agents dual-trained in crime scene investigation and hazardous materials threats, stopped at the bottom of the stairs and surveyed the boxy basement space. To Fry, it looked like a cinder-block coffin. He hoped it wouldn't be his own.

"You guys notice anything strange about this space?" he said.

"You mean, besides the four of us assholes dumb enough to put on these suits and walk willingly into the Hiroshima Hilton?"

"No, besides that. I mean, look at the shape of the basement."

"Yeah? It's a square, so what?"

"It's a perfect square," said Fry.

"So what? You don't like squares?"

"The upstairs isn't a perfect square. Where's the rest of this basement?"

"Well, maybe they were just cutting corners when she was built," said the other agent.

Fry shuffled his feet across the gritty cement floor and rotated a tripod holding bright lighting equipment, pointing it against a wall.

"Yeah? Well look at this," Fry said. "When you point the lights towards the cinder block wall, you can see the mortar on this wall is much whiter than the rest. The cinder blocks themselves look old, but the mortar looks brand-new. In fact, this is the side of the house where we should be seeing more basement."

"What are you saying? That this is a fake wall?"

"Damn right that's what I'm saying. Call outside, get us some sledgehammers. Hurry."

79

Stephen Latent stayed in New York instead of returning to headquarters in Washington. He wanted to be on the ground with his men and moved between the field office and the command post near the site of the contamination in Queens.

"Are those the images from the basement?" he said, looking at a computer screen. "Anything that stands out? Anything we can use to track down this bomb?"

"Yes, sir, this is coming live from the dwelling's basement. Nothing solid yet, sir. But we now have a list of all the nuclear facilities in the country that use the high core type of uranium-235, which is what has been identified here. Unfortunately, the list of facilities is huge. And again, not a single one has reported any misplaced or stolen nuclear material. The lab is further isolating the exact isotope so we'll be able to match the uranium against any possible suspects."

"What do you mean?" said Latent.

"Each nuclear facility uses a specific and unique tag, almost like a signature, to identify their uranium. It's kind of like the way we tag ricin and other types of poisons that the CDC or other labs produce. It's a way of being able to identify exactly where the radioactive material was produced, so we can narrow down the source in the event of a breach. Once we isolate it, we'll know exactly where it came from."

"How long will that take?" said Latent.

"About twelve hours, sir. We've got the best people on it right now."

Latent started to walk away, but the agent called back to him.

"Oh, sir? One more thing."

"What is it?" said Latent.

"The agents in the basement are asking for sledgehammers."

"Sledgehammers?"

"Yes, sir. Larry, ah, I mean, Agent Fry thinks there's a false wall down there."

80

"Here, hold this in your hand," Jana said, handing Cade a handheld radio. "And remember, don't say a word."

"Yes, ma'am," but as Cade took it, he was taken aback by the gaze in her eyes. It was like looking at case-hardened steel. "Are you okay?" he said.

"You might see a side of me you don't like."

The parking lot was straight ahead. Jana flipped on the car's blue lights and sped through the sea of parked cars towards the entrance, jerked the car up onto the walkway, and screeched to a halt. They both jumped out and ran towards the door. The security guards at their post just inside the lobby stood up in alarm. Jana pounded the locked glass door.

"Federal Agent, open the door! Federal Agent. Open the door right now!"

One of the guards scrambled to the door in bewilderment. He opened the door and leaned out but couldn't peel his eyes off of Jana's blue windbreaker.

"Ah, yes, ah, ma'am, ah, Agent-ma'am? Can I help you?"

Jana bolted through him like he was made of marshmallows. Her hand wrapped around the ID tag clipped to his cheap button-down shirt. The guard backpedaled as fast as he could, trying not to trip. The other guard stepped up, "Hey! What are you . . ." but Jana stiff-armed him back down in his seat.

"You. Shut up." She turned her attention back on the first guard. "You, where's the control center?"

"Control? Ma'am, you can't just barge in here like that. You've got to have a warrant or appointment or somethin' . . ."

The seated guard said, "Yeah, what authority do you have to barge in here?"

"Authority!" Jana yelled, "how about the United States fucking government!" She ripped the name badge off the guard's shirt in one violent motion, then read it out loud.

"Jonathan Tipton. Well Jonathan, you've got about two seconds to show me to the control room before I arrest you and charge you with obstructing a federal investigation."

"Yes, ma'am, ah, Agent ma'am."

"And you," Jana said, "I don't like your mouth. You want to play ball with me? Then sit there and shut up. If not, I'll introduce you to a new set of steel bracelets. All right, let's go."

Jonathan looked like a kid who'd just been caught graffitiing the school by the principal, with a can of spray paint stuck to his hands. He shuffled down the hallway to the elevator bank, nearly tripping over his own feet, and stood at the elevators.

"Ah, ma'am? I need to hold that. My ID? It's to get us into the elevator." He reached out a trembling hand as if he was afraid it might not come back to him.

As they got off the elevator several floors below, Jonathan swiped his ID badge again, and they were in the control room, the central nervous system of the nuclear plant.

". . . we bring you breaking news as it happens. The face of the man you're seeing now is listed as number two on the FBI's most wanted list. Baer Wayland has just been apprehended by federal authorities on the isle of North Caicos in the western Antilles, under a false passport. Wayland, a twenty-three-year veteran of the Central Intelligence Agency, has been sought in connection with the TerrorGate cover-up. He is believed to have masterminded the CIA's funding of a terror group in order to eventually penetrate and disrupt the organization. Those funds ended up being traced to direct attacks on American citizens that stretched from coast to coast. We'll bring you more as the story develops. For news, weather, and traffic, stay tuned, to WBS News."

81

Swinging a sledgehammer while dressed in what amounted to a space suit was awkward to say the least. Agent Fry hoisted the twelve pounds of steel over his head in a large arc, then blasted it downwards into the cinder blocks. Cement fragments exploded off the block and sprayed against the face-shield with ferocity. It was more of a backlash than he expected.

"Hey, Dan, you think there's any chance we could puncture one of these suits doing this?"

"No, not really," said Agent Dan Keller. "The outer core is Kevlar fiber. We just need to be careful and keep our distance from one another. Do me a favor—don't crush my helmet with your sledge."

The two pounded against the cinder blocks. It was slow work, but the block began to relent under the force of their blows.

Fry stopped. "Hey, you hear something?"

"Huh? No, I don't hear anything," said Keller.

"Must be my imagination." The two continued the pounding, but this time, Fry's hammer penetrated through and exposed a gaping hole about one-and-a-half feet in diameter. Darkness, thick and pure, oozed from the hole as if to consume their light and scoop them up along with it.

"I told you," said Fry. "If this wasn't a false wall, we'd have hit dirt. There's hollow space behind here."

"I'm going to hear about this for years. I hate it when you're right," said Keller.

The sledges pounded faster. They could hear large chunks of cement block fall to the floor and then crack apart in the echoing cavern.

"Hey, wait. Did you hear that? I know I'm not imagining that," said Fry.

"I heard it too. Where the hell is that coming from? Sounds like . . . like . . . moaning."

Fry picked up a tripod supporting one of the sets of lighting equipment and placed it close to the wall, then angled the lights into the dark oblivion. He wasn't quite tall enough, so he climbed a stepladder and peered through the hole and into the unknown.

"Can you see anything?" said Keller.

"Just an open space. I guess there's about another five feet of floor space in there. Lots of crap laying around. Looks like trash . . . oh my God! That's a body in there! Holy shit, a body!"

The moaning sound came again.

"Holy shit!" said Fry. "It's moving! We've got a person in here. He's alive! We gotta get this wall down!"

Fry leapt from the stepladder onto the ground and yelled into the radio, "This is Fry! We've got a victim down here! He's alive! Send me some more manpower! We need two more sledgehammers and maybe a battering ram. Get me a medic. Expedite that. Over."

82

The control room was wide and circular with at least a thirty-foot ceiling. Twenty people sat at control consoles or studied large monitors hanging in the center of the room. The guard, Jonathan, stood with his ID badge trembling in his hands. He looked like a man on a first date that had wet his trousers.

Without waiting for an introduction, Jana blurted out, "Everyone listen up! I need your attention! F—B—I. This is a federal investigation. I need your full attention and cooperation right now. Who's in charge here?"

"Ah, that would be me." Allen Mize was senior operations chief and was responsible for monitoring and controlling the operation of the reactor. "Ah, what, who are you?"

"Special Agent Jana Baker, FBI. This is a federal investigation and there is precious little time. What type of nuclear material does this facility use?"

"I'm not authorized to disclose that information. Now if you'll . . ."

Jana crunched his shirt collar in her hand and yanked him to the wall near a large digital control panel.

"Listen up, dipshit. We can do this the easy way or we can do this the hard way." Mize started to speak, but she cut him off. "The easy way is where you cooperate, and I mean, right-the-fuck-right-now. The hard way is where I toss your ass on the ground, and when you get up, you're wearing handcuffs. Got it? I'll ask you one more time—what type of nuclear material does this facility use?"

"Yes, ma'am. If you can be more specific in what you're looking for, I can tell you what we use."

Mize's skin flushed. All the heat in his body wanted to jump ship.

"If you were a terrorist, what material from this facility would you be interested in?"

"Uranium-235. We use uranium-235. It's the high-core type. It can be weaponized. If, if it got into the wrong hands, it would be . . . well, it's highly enriched. It would be really bad."

Jana said, "Has any, and I mean *ANY*, gone missing? Can you account for every tiny bit of the shit?"

"Well, sure. I mean, no, none of it is missing. How on earth would it go missing? This place is like Fort Knox."

"How do you know? How do you determine the amount of uranium-235 that you have on hand?" pressed Jana.

"Agent Baker, I assure you, none is missing."

Jana rapped the back of her hand onto his nose causing his head to recoil backwards.

"Ouch!"

"You didn't answer my question. I don't have time for this. Turn around, put your hands on your head, and interlace your fingers . . ."

She grabbed Mize by the shoulder and spun him into the wall.

"No, no! Wait, I'm not trying to be evasive. I . . . I . . . ouch! Damn, that hurts. No! Listen, okay. Listen. I'll do, I'll do whatever it takes. What do you need? There's no need for this, please. Honest. I swear to God."

Jana let him turn around. "I'll ask you again. How do you know that none is missing?"

"We do an inventory. I don't know how often—it's not my department. Probably every week or so, I suppose. We could find that info in our system though."

Jana returned her handcuffs to her belt and tucked them into their holster against the small of her back. Mize walked over to the center of the room to a large computerized console.

"Charlie," Mize said in a scattered voice, "pull up the inventory control records. We need to see the logs."

"Inventory control? Jeez, I don't know if I even have access to that system. Hey, you got a warrant or something?"

But before Jana could even pounce, Mize said, "Charlie. Look at me. Just do it."

"All right, all right. So let me see," said Charlie. "I think I know where to access it from. Mind telling me what we're looking for in the logs?"

After several clicks and log-ins, the three leaned in closer to the monitor.

"No, I don't see any irregularities here," said Mize. "Certainly nothing reported missing, anyway. Hmmm, right here . . . the sixteenth of the month. See how the inventory level shifts? Seems like on this date they must have done the swap out."

"What's the swap out?" said Cade, leaning over them.

"It's where the fission material in the reactor is removed and replaced with new material. That must be what we're seeing here. See how the inventory went from sixty-four units down to twelve, all on the same day? That's what happened—the swap out."

Jana stood straight up. "The sixteenth?"

"Yeah," Mize replied. "What's the big deal?"

Jana looked at Cade. "The sixteenth was the day of the train bombing and derailment."

83

"What do you mean, *a body*?" yelled Latent.

"Not a body, sir. A victim! They've got a live victim down there!"

Latent burst through the door of the command post and sprinted towards the habitrail enclosures.

"What's happening?" he yelled deep into the decontamination chamber.

"It's coming on the video monitors now. They've got a live one down there, sir. He's barely alive, but he's talking," said an agent through his double-walled helmet. "Over there," he said, pointing towards a bank of computer monitors.

Latent was glued to the video feed. "Give me that headset," he said. The younger agent yanked them off his head like they were on fire. Down in the basement, Agent Fry and Keller were kneeling over a man stretched out on the ground. His breathing was shallow. He appeared to be of Middle Eastern descent.

Agent Fry said to the man, "What's your name?" The man seemed to drift in and out of consciousness, and even when he was conscious, he was barely lucid. "Hey, can you hear me? What's your name?"

The man mumbled something that sounded like "Thu-su-me . . ."

"I think he's speaking in Arabic," said Agent Keller, struggling to hear the low mumbling.

Fry yelled, "Can you speak English? What's your name?"

The man lost consciousness but then snapped back, his black eyes fluttering.

"Shakey. They all call me Shakey." His accent was heavy but his enunciation clear. He was punch-drunk—a cross between semiconscious and buzzed.

"Shakey? Okay, what's your last name, Shakey? Your surname."

"They all call me Shakey. Shakey Coon-deeeee . . ." The "d" sound rolled off of his tongue and seemed to reverberate against the cement walls.

Keller whispered to Fry, "Did you get that? I can barely hear him."

Fry said, "Shakey?" He was yelling again. "Shakey? Stay with me, okay? What is your final objective? Hey, man, wake up. What-is-your-fi-nal-ob-jec-tive?"

Shakey grinned, and his head bobbed from side to side like he was listening to music. His eyes shut against the bright light as though he thought it might scorch his retinas.

"It is too late, my friends. Yes, too late . . . too late . . ." said the man.

While Fry distracted him, Keller knelt down and pressed the man's right pointer finger and thumb against a small digital pad, about the size of a cell phone. The screen blinked to life and scanned the fingerprints. Keller clicked the upload button. The prints would be instantly run through the National Crime Information Center's database.

"What are we too late for?" said Fry. "Shakey? Shakey?" But his eyes, still slightly open, froze then the pupils rolled upwards. And where the whites of his eyes should have been, only a bloodshot shock of red and umber remained. He was gone. "Shit, where's my goddamn medic? Quick, grab his feet, let's get him out of here. Maybe they can revive him." But both agents knew it was too late.

84

"All right, now, roll the video back to the sixteenth, the date of the train derailment. Right, good," said Jana, peering over Charlie's shoulder and looking at the surveillance video. "Scroll up to about the time of explosion. I want to see what happened inside this plant when the bridge blew up."

"Okay, well, that's going to take a while," said Charlie. "We have sixty-four cameras inside the facility. Where do we start?"

"It's easy," said Jana. "Start with the cameras that monitor where the nuclear material is stored. Not the material that's inside the reactor, but where the excess uranium is stored prior to use."

"Okay, inside the storage facility. Here you go. This camera angle shows the entrance to the room where the material is normally stored."

The view on the video screen revealed a room deep inside the recesses of the building. The room was triple-walled in glass or some type of thick Lucite. While some workers were entering the room, a few stood on opposite sides of a sealed, translucent box that ran most of the length of the room. Their arms reached deep inside the box through small circular openings that were lined with thick, arm-length rubber gloves. At the bottom of the screen, a digital readout displayed the time of day down to the millisecond. The numbers rattled by.

Cade said, "Can you fast forward this? Good, good. Okay, we have people working inside the room . . . what are they doing in there? What's inside that giant aquarium thing?"

"See, I told you," said Mize. "It was a swap day. They're collecting the canisters of enriched uranium to move them to the reactor."

"This is ridiculous," Jana said. "You can't even tell who's who. All of them are covered head to toe in those damn space suits. If you put them all in a police lineup, you'd be staring at twelve guys dressed as the Stay Puft Marshmallow Man."

"They're all removing canisters from the box and placing them on that sealed cart," said Cade. "What about this guy? The guy on the end. He looks a little . . . I don't know . . . twitchy?"

Jana focused on the man. It was hard to distinguish any features, but he appeared to be of average height and build. There was no way to see his hair color, much less his face.

"So wait," said Jana. "Check the time of day. 8:38 a.m. Jesus, that's about five minutes prior to the train derailment. Can you zoom in on that subject?"

"Ah, sure. But I don't think it will help. His mask will obscure everything." They watched closely as the man ambled back and forth.

Cade said, "It's almost as if he's appearing to be busy without actually doing anything."

"Yeah, but look at that," said Jana. "He just checked the time on that wall clock. He's checking the time. What does this asshole think he's waiting for?"

The view from the surveillance camera rattled sharply, causing the video to shake and distort.

"That's it," blurted Jana. "That's it! Freeze the video. Look at the time stamp! 8:43 a.m. That was the exact moment the bombs detonated on the bridge." Red strobe lights in the room erupted into a frenzied pulse due to the shockwave from the nearby bomb blast. Most workers froze in their tracks and looked at each other as tremendous vibrations rippled under their feet and shook the facility. One of them, likely a supervisor, waved his hands wildly, motioning everyone out of the room. As other workers evacuated, the lone subject rushed to the far end of the huge incubator-looking box containing the uranium tubes. He pushed his arms into a set of the arm-length rubber gloves built into the sidewalls of the box and grabbed one of the thick, cylindrical tubes. He placed it into a sliding metal drawer, yanked the drawer open, then removed the cylinder. In the chaos, no one noticed the cylinder at his side as he shuffled out of the room and disappeared from camera range.

"My God, my God," said Mize as he collapsed into a swivel chair. "I just, I just . . . I can't believe it. Right from under our noses. Oh my God." Mize looked like a man who had just jumped off a high dive only to realize there was no water in the pool below. "Everything went haywire when that train was derailed. You don't know what it was like. We thought it was an earthquake. Part of the train fell onto the roof of the loading facility. The entire facility went into full alert. We scrammed the reactor because we were afraid of radiation leakage. There was chaos. Just chaos."

Jana's hand pounded down on Charlie's shoulder. "I want you to follow this motherfucker on camera wherever he moves. You got that? Pull up every recorded camera angle you have. If he moved anywhere in this facility, I want to know it."

Jana stepped aside and pulled out her cell phone. "I need Bill Tarleton please. This is Special Agent Jana Baker . . . no, I can't hold . . . I don't care where he is! You listen and listen closely—you tell him this is a bright boy alert! I say again, this is a bright boy alert! This is not a drill. Do you understand that?"

Within moments Uncle Bill picked up the call, "Jana? Bright boy? Jesus Christ, where are you?"

"Bill, no-time-to-explain." The words rolled off her tongue so fast it sounded like an auctioneer in high gear. "I'm going to be sending you a bunch of video streams from surveillance cameras inside of the Millstone Nuclear Power Station. We've got to identify someone in the video, and it's not going to be easy."

"Roger that. We're on it. Just hand the phone to whoever's there. I can give them instructions on how to send us the files."

Three minutes later, on the video monitor, they watched the subject weave his way through hallway after hallway and out a side exit towards the employee parking area. At every view from the recorded video cameras, red strobe lights pulsed. People ran in all directions. The facility had gone into an emergency state as percussion from the blasts tripped an earthquake sensor. The reactor was shut down. Mize was right, it was chaos.

The camera that peered out onto the parking lot was obscured by a bright spot in the morning sun. The subject had shed the bulky white protective suit and was now visible as a male with a dark complexion and black hair. He wove across the parking lot, holding what looked like a particularly heavy small sack in his right hand. His face was obscured in the grainy images, but it appeared as though he stopped at a car that was just out of view on the far side of the lot. After a few moments, he returned to the facility—the bag was not in his hands. Even though he was walking into the camera angle, his face was still obscured.

Jana said, "Dammit, we can't even see his vehicle. Okay, he's walking back. He's entering the building. We've got to have a face shot of him when he gets inside that doorway."

"Hold on, hold on," said Charlie, working the controls as best he could to find the proper camera angle. "Okay, this one is the north entrance. It's pointing right at that door. Let me pull up the image."

But as the image came on the screen, the sea of people darting in all directions made it impossible to tell which one was the subject.

"Shit," said Jana. "All right, box it up. Get all those video streams to NSA."

"Yes, ma'am," said Charlie.

Senior Operations Chief Mize stared off into space. "I, I don't understand. How did you know? How did you know we were missing some nuclear material?"

Jana said nothing.

"It was a hunch, wasn't it?" said Mize. "You didn't have a shred of evidence, did you? What brought you here in the first place?"

Jana looked at him. "The train derailment. It was too much of a coincidence that it occurred almost on top of a nuclear facility. We had to find where they got the nuclear material. And now we know. I'm sorry."

85

Two hours later, Jana and Cade stood on the edge of the radiation containment zone in Queens. All residents had been evacuated and were waiting in queues to be interviewed. Dozens of agents were taking statements about anything and everything that might be related to the Hiroshima Hilton. All of the information from the Millstone Nuclear Power Station had been relayed to Latent, who was thrilled to get a break in the case.

Latent barged out of the command center tent and spun back around, yelling into the entryway. "Goddammit! Where are my fucking fingerprints? We should have had an ID on this dead asshole already! I want some prints, and I want them yesterday."

A muffled set of "yessirs" ushered out.

"Baker! Damn good work. Unbelievable work." He leaned towards her and said, "Before we sent you into the Thoughtstorm building, I took a look at your personnel file. You were raised by your grandfather? Let me tell you something, Jana. He would be very proud of you right now." The sentiment, sincerity, and thought of just how right he was reminded Jana of the emptiness of her past. Her throat tightened.

"Thank you, sir," was all she could muster. "Sir, about Uncle Bill, I'm betting he's going to have an ID for us on the subject at Millstone. He's got everyone working on it."

"I know he does, Baker," said Latent. "Bill and I just talked. Listen, Mr. Williams has been invaluable up to this point."

"But?"

"But I'm afraid it's going to get a little dangerous from here on out. Besides, Bill wants Cade working with him directly. He's still poring over Rupert Johnston's papers, and Cade might be instrumental in spotting anything in those writings that would tip us to the last bomb chucker. There's an NSA jet inbound to pick him up."

"Yes, sir," said Jana.

"We've got more agents than we need on these civilian interviews," said Latent. "So far we haven't turned up shit. I tell you what, that jet won't be here for a little while. Why don't you two report over there to Agent Hill. He'll give you a few houses that are just outside the containment zone to canvas. I know it doesn't sound like exciting work, but if there's a thirty-eighth terrorist with a nuclear device out there, we can't catch him if we don't know what he looks like, what he's driving, or where he's going."

"Yes, sir."

"And, Baker, keep your eyes open for anything, anything at all. It could be the littlest thing that catches him right now."

Forty-five minutes later, Jana and Cade knocked on their seventh door. The previous six interviews of civilians produced exactly the result that Jana anticipated, nothing. Latent was right, this was boring work.

"Well, this has been a colossal waste of time," said Jana.

"Hey remember, Agent Baker, he said the littlest thing could be important right now."

"Damn, you might as well be an agent yourself," she said.

"Who is it?" called a female voice from behind the home's front door.

"Federal agents, ma'am." Cade looked at her; Jana just shrugged. "We have some questions, please open the door."

The woman was in her late twenties and carried the burden of a little black-haired boy, whose legs swung wildly against her sides. The grin on his face was as wide as a banana.

"LOONS, Mama, loons. Loons, Mama, loons," said the boy, his eyes darting up to the ceiling each time.

"Hush, honey, hush," said the mother. "Let's talk to these nice people. I'm sorry, he gets a little excited. How can I help you?"

"FBI, ma'am," said Jana holding out her credentials. "As you know, there's been an incident a few blocks over. We're asking residents if they've seen anything unusual in recent days or weeks."

"LOONS, LOONS, LOOOOOOOONS, Mama, loons!"

"Now hush, honey. I'm real sorry about that. Yes, I saw all the commotion. And you evacuated four square blocks? Wow. That must be some incident."

"Nothing to be sorry about, ma'am. He's just fine. Have you seen anything unusual that you can think of? Anything at all?"

"Mama-loons, mama-loons, mama-loons!" The words rolled off the boy's tongue with the rhythm of a freight train clicking across the tracks. The boy laughed hysterically and buried his face in his mother's hair.

"Now, honey! Here, you go play." She put him down, and he ran off, dragging a white security blanket along with him, giggling the whole way. "Loonloons, loonloons, mamaloons . . ."

Jana smiled at the boy. "What's he saying, by the way? What are loons?"

"Oh! Loons, yes. That's his word for bal-loons. He's obsessed with balloons. A four-year-old. Can't clean up his room but he can darn sure blow up a balloon all by himself. I don't know what made him start spouting off about balloons just then. Anyway, ah, no, I can't say I've seen anything unusual. Was there anything specific?"

"We're trying to locate anyone who may have seen people going or coming from the house. Here's a card with a number you can call. If you think of anything, even a small detail, please let us know. We appreciate your cooperation."

As the door closed, Jana and Cade walked to the next house.

"That just about cracks the case, huh?" said Cade.

"Well, sometimes you get to knock on a few doors asking inane questions, and other times you get to go to a nuclear plant and tell the supervisor you're going to crack his skull if he doesn't cooperate. You take the good with the bad, I guess."

86

"Sir? We've got an ID on that body in the basement. NCIC flagged his fingerprints, not to mention the driver's license in his wallet. His name is Shakhar Masmal Kundi, a Saudi national. He entered the country several years ago on a student visa. Now he's on a work visa."

"Who sponsored the visa?" said Latent.

"Apparently the Nuclear Regulatory Commission did, sir. IRS has his last known employer listed as the Millstone Nuclear Power Station."

"That's our man. Well, we've traced our source of who stole the uranium we've been finding all over that house." Latent shook his head, and his scowl tightened.

"Isn't that good, sir? We've identified another piece in the puzzle."

"Good? . . . What? Oh, yeah. Well, hell no it's not good. Right now, what I need is an identity of someone who's still alive. Somebody drove that uranium out of here, presumably in the form of a bomb. We've got to have a face, a vehicle, something to go on."

"Yes, sir. Sir, I've got a team headed back to Millstone right now. We'll dig up anything we can about him."

Latent replied, "We've got one team on the ground in Oman and one in Jordan. Get them both on a plane to Saudi Arabia ASAP. I want them doing a thorough background on this guy. And call the Saudi consulate in DC. I want their cooperation on this."

The younger agent scrambled off with a look of justified entitlement on his face.

Latent dialed Uncle Bill's number. "Bill? What cha got for me?"

"Stevie. Man, was just about to call you."

"Tell me."

"I've got the identity of your uranium thief," said Bill.

"Hold on," said Latent, "let me guess. Is his name Shakhar Masmal Kundi?"

"You were always an asshole," said Uncle Bill.

Latent laughed. "Seriously, what have you got on him?"

"He worked at the plant for about a year and a half. And by a not-so-miraculous coincidence, his last day of employment was the same day as the train derailment—the day he stole the uranium."

"Funny how that works out," said Latent.

"Steve, this is serious stuff. This was a coordinated effort. And not just an effort to quit your job on the same day that you steal forty pounds of enriched uranium either," said Bill.

"How do you mean?"

"The timing of the theft was perfect. I mean fucking perfect. It was no coincidence that the guy was in the uranium storage room at the exact moment that the train was derailed. This took serious, coordinated timing. Think about it. They had to set up the bridge to detonate. They had to know they'd have a train coming by at that exact time. They had to plan how to set the charges so the train would derail off the right side of the bridge, catapulting most of it into the water, but with the last few cars smashing into the shore, right on top of part of the nuclear facility. The result was that the safety systems inside the facility sensed what it thought was an earthquake. The facility went into lockdown. The reactor was scrammed. You should see these surveillance tapes. That place went into chaos. They looked like little ants down there."

Latent said, "So, let me follow this. The terrorists timed the explosion to coincide with the exact arrival of the train, during a window they knew their inside man would be able to be in the storage room . . . they knew the percussion from the blast and impact from the train hitting the roof would cause the safety systems to trip . . . what then? He just grabs the stuff and walks out?"

"That's exactly what he did. Nobody noticed. It was pure chaos. Utter chaos. Oh, Shakhar Kundi? He goes by the name Shakey."

"Shakey. Great. It will be all over the news. A guy named Shakey steals nuclear material. Those media assholes will love that one. Listen, I know they sent you all the surveillance tapes. But how do you know it was his last day of employment? How did you know he went by the name Shakey?"

Bill laughed. "Personnel records, internal memoranda, e-mail chains . . . and don't ask how I got those."

"Okay, okay. Don't worry, I won't. Hey, by the way. He's dead, you know."

"Who?" said Bill.

"Shakhar Kundi, Shakey. I've got his body right here in front of me at the Hiroshima Hilton. We pulled it out of the basement. He died a couple of hours ago."

The line went as silent as if the call had dropped. Latent waited a moment and said, "Bill?"

"He's not dead, Steve." Uncle Bill's voice dropped an octave. "He's alive and well. I've got Shakey Kundi on a surveillance camera at a gas station on Route 119 just outside of Charleston, Kentucky. This was forty-five minutes ago."

87

Cade and Jana returned after canvassing their thirteenth house. They were tired, hungry, and their feet were sore.

"Come on," said Jana. "Let's head over to the command center. I've got to get something to eat and find out what else is going on. And it's probably time you get to the airport."

Cade grabbed Jana by the arm.

"Is that what I think it is?" he said, pointing to the right.

Jana looked over. Inside one of the plastic habitrail enclosure tunnels leading away from the Hiroshima Hilton was what looked like a body.

"I bet you're right," said Jana. "Come on."

The body was laying just inside the translucent sidewall of the enclosure. The man wasn't resting. He wasn't sleeping. He wasn't acting. The man was dead. His eyes were still one quarter cracked open, but there was no life in them. Aside from the bloodshot red and purplish hues, the eyes were coated with a stale, milky quality. Cade shuddered. Neither of them spoke.

Cade said, "He looks . . . bloated. I guess the radiation exposure did that. God, look at his skin. It looks like it would peel off. I mean, look at his hands; the underside of his fingers are peeling."

The two stared and shook their heads.

Stephen Latent was on a dead run towards the command center tent when he burst in through the opening. The agent walking out the door never had a chance. Latent, in a flashback to his football days at Georgetown, reflexively leaned his left shoulder in and knocked the blue windbreaker to the ground. Without so much as skipping a beat, Latent began yelling.

"Everyone, listen up! Put out an APB to every law enforcement agency within three states of Kentucky! We're looking for one Shakhar Kundi. Get our field office in Louisville on full alert. We need every man we've got headed in that direction. We need air transport. Get on the horn to the National Guard. They've got a detachment on Staten

Island, and I think there's a Naval Air station attached to it. We need every damn plane or chopper they have. Move!"

"But, sir!" said an agent with a buzz cut and black glasses. "Shakhar Kundi is dead. I don't understand. His body's right over there . . ."

"Trust me, he's not dead. We're looking for a white van. Unmarked, at least on the left side."

Jana heard all the yelling and came running in. She noticed the blue windbreaker'd agent lying on his back, his moans barely audible.

"We don't have a license plate on that yet. NSA is working on it. Give me a map of Kentucky!" yelled Latent. "And someone start searching on everything about Kentucky. I want to know stadiums, parades, events . . . anything that is big. Any event that's going to happen, starting right now." He stared around the wide tent at agents still frozen in place. "Give me a map of Kentucky!"

The chatter level escalated as agents scrambled onto phones, shouted orders, and banged on laptop keyboards.

An agent with a buzz cut so tight that it looked like it would prick your finger if touched said to another much taller agent, "I still don't get it. You were the one to pull the prints off that body. Those fingerprints came back as Shakhar Kundi. I mean, he's lying on the ground in that plastic tube over there. Why are we looking for a dead guy who's supposedly driving a white van in Kentucky?"

"I know, I know," said the tall agent. "Those prints were perfect. NCIC doesn't lie."

Cade interrupted them. "You say you took fingerprints from that dead guy?"

"Yes," said the taller agent. "We were in the basement. We were the ones that found him. We scanned his prints with one of these," he said, holding up the handheld scanner. "Ran it through NCIC. The prints were clean. A perfect match."

"Well, how could you be sure the prints were good?" said Cade. "What with the skin on his fingers peeling off and everything."

The two agents looked at each other.

"Skin peeling off?"

"Yeah. Come on," said Cade, "take a look for yourself."

They walked over to the edge of the habitrail enclosure and knelt down.

Cade pointed. "Look. See how the skin on the ends of his fingers is peeling. God, that's disgusting. It looks like cellophane. Like he's shedding or something."

Agent Fry looked over at Dan Keller and said, "Holy shit. Look at that. Did you see that before? When you were printing him? I was trying to get him to talk. Did you notice it?"

"Hell no," said Keller. "I know that wasn't there before. Well, I don't think it was anyway."

"We better have a closer look."

Keller looked at him. "The Michelin man suits again? Ah, shit."

88

The tarmac on the Staten Island Naval Air Station bustled with activity. The noise from small jets and helicopters made it hard to communicate. Agents boarded several corporate jets, and others jumped into Hueys for the ride out to LaGuardia to take a larger plane to Kentucky.

"So I guess this is good-bye," yelled Cade as he braced against the jet wash that buffeted the two of them.

"Just for now," yelled Jana. "Look, I'm sorry. It's the best thing. Uncle Bill wants your help deciphering Rupert Johnston's papers. You knew him best, and we're desperate to see if there are any hidden clues in those writings that might point us to a time or location. And," she said, looking back at the plane, "the director thinks we're headed into harm's way. It's a nuclear device we're after. God help us if the damn thing goes off. He doesn't want to risk a civilian getting hurt where we're going."

"I understand. It's just that I thought we'd be able to finish this thing together. It's not like I have a job to go back to or anything."

"I guess not," said Jana. "Look, they're calling for me. And that's your jet over there. Call me if you learn anything, and I mean anything."

"Hey, don't get yourself killed, okay?" Cade said, smiling. "It's been a long time since I kissed a girl."

Jana blushed. "That's not what it seemed like to me."

There were fourteen agents crammed into a Gulfstream Four that was designed to seat twelve. As the jet taxied towards the runway, Latent grabbed the headset hanging from the fuselage interior.

"Pilot. Get a move on. We're not on a pleasure cruise. What? I don't give a shit about your procedures. You get this thing in the air, and I mean right the hell right now. And no, don't bother waiting for clearance from the tower. As far as you're concerned, I am the tower."

The jet rocketed down the runway, banked hard left, and picked up a straight course for Lexington, Kentucky.

"Pilot, what airport are we headed for? What? Bluegrass Airport? You're making that up, aren't you? All right, never mind. Get on the comm, make sure there are two choppers waiting there for us. That's right, heated and ready."

Latent spun his swivel chair to face the other agents, and all eyes locked on him.

"We've got three HRT groups in-air. They might be on the ground before we are. Also, Navy SEAL and Army Delta Force teams are airborne and en route as well. We're headed for Lexington, but we still don't know our final destination. NSA has eyes on every damn camera they can find and hack into. The problem is that since this asshole was spotted on a rural route—where's that map again—okay, Route 119. It's a rural highway. He's likely staying off the larger roads where we'd be more likely to find cameras. Yes, Agent Baker, what is it?"

"What's the plan, sir? I mean, once we're on the ground. If we don't know where he's headed, where do we go?"

"I know, I know, we don't have his agenda. We're going to cover every event we can. Everyone should pray NSA can tip us either by spotting the vehicle on a camera or finding out some other way. Who's got that list of Kentucky events?"

"Sir?" said another agent. "With the emergency alert system active, telling people to remain in their homes, wouldn't all these events be cancelled?"

"One would think," said Latent. "But no, these events are not cancelled. Remember, this isn't the big city. Everybody anywhere in small-town America is determined to not let their lives be upended by a bunch of bomb chuckers. You've got to give them credit. They've got guts. Okay, here's the list. This is a list of every large-scale event we could find that's happening in the state. Keep in mind that we aren't even sure Kentucky is his target. In fact, I'd be surprised if he's not heading for a major city. Chicago would have come to mind. Anyway, here's the Kentucky list. This is the best we can do at the moment. We've listed each event in the state. He could be anywhere. There are about a dozen large universities with big sporting events. University of Kentucky, Western Kentucky, Eastern Kentucky, Murray State, Morehead State. Jesus Christ, anyway, three of those have football games today or tomorrow. We're talking about large stadiums here. Also, our people say that based on the amount of uranium stolen, the largest device they could construct would be nominal, say half a kiloton. That's not enough to take out a small town, but it could damn sure take out a stadium and probably a lot larger. We're thinking a target like a stadium would be ideal. The blast radius isn't that large, but you put a half kiloton into a bowl shape, like a football stadium, and you'd have devastation. Let's see, other events—we have a town parade in Evansville; there's the state fair in Bowling Green. A state fair would be huge. That one scares the shit out of me. I've got one HRT team touching down there in about fifteen minutes. There's a bluegrass festival, whatever the hell that is, up in the mountains somewhere. A national Boy Scouts conference in Paducah; God help us."

"The list doesn't narrow it down much," said Jana. "I mean, they've been targeting things that are so . . . American. You know, American to the core. A Little League baseball game in Phoenix, a town barbeque in Montana. All the final objective targets were places like shopping malls, community picnics, craft beer festivals . . . things that you'd identify as American. And all things you'd like to destroy if you were a terrorist. Your list, it just doesn't narrow it down much. Nothing jumps off the list as the obvious target."

"All right, Baker, think like a terrorist for a minute. Use your intuition. If you had to choose just one, which would it be?" said Latent.

"I would have said the Kentucky State Fair," said Jana. "But you've got that covered with the Hostage Rescue Team. If I'm choosing where we go, I'd say either the town parade in Evansville or the bluegrass festival in . . . wherever the hell that was."

Latent said, "Perfect. You're on Agent Jones's team. I'll be there as well. That's right, people, don't look at me like I'm an old man. I'm going into the field with you. That team will be heading to the bluegrass festival. Is *bluegrass* one word or two? Anyway, gather all the info you can right now: maps, routes, how many people will be there, when does it start, when does it end, all that shit. And, people! As you study your assignments, don't forget to consider evacuation routes. If we have any reason to believe we have our target, we'll use the emergency broadcast system, loudspeakers, or whatever we can to get people out of harm's way."

Jana shimmied back to the tail section of the plane and sat down with Agent Jones and two others to discuss their options.

"More news coming in at this hour regarding the so-called Hiroshima Hilton in Queens, New York. Authorities are neither confirming nor denying reports that three bodies have been found inside the radiation-filled structure. At this time, a four-block radius has been cordoned off in the area, and residents evacuated. Federal authorities are considering widening the radius of the containment zone and are conducting tests in the area to determine if there is further risk to public health and safety. In other news, Acting President John Palmer has lifted the ban on commercial aviation, which originally went into effect two days ago. The move had rocked Wall Street, as stocks tumbled to their lowest levels in seven years. Further complicating airline industry woes, a person's ability to fly commercially may not be of much benefit to the airlines. Recent polls indicate most Americans are too afraid to travel, citing fears of more terrorist incidents. The US retail sales report was released earlier today, indicating a grim outlook as shoppers are simply not showing up at retail stores. Fears are escalating that the US economy is headed into catastrophe."

89

Winding his way through the hill country on Rural Route 160, the van's driver, Shakey Kundi, passed a tiny hamlet named Kingdom Come, Kentucky. It was an appropriate name for what was on his mind. He tried listening to radio news broadcasts that might alert him if authorities had a description of his van, but there was nothing.

Shakey was confident his identity and vehicle description were unknown. Although, it wouldn't take a rocket scientist to figure out there was a false wall in the basement in Queens and locate the third body hidden behind it. At any rate, the likelihood that anyone would dispute that body's identity as being that of one Shakhar "Shakey" Kundi was highly unlikely. The corpse actually belonged to the van's original driver, the young apprentice that brought Waseem Jarrah to the house. The man was roughly the same size and build as Shakey, only now his face was so swollen from exposure to radiation that not even facial recognition software would be able to accurately identify the body.

The location of the body, the fact that Shakey's driver's license and wallet would be found on him, and the fingerprints—those brilliant false fingerprints—would certainly seal the identity. Authorities would believe they had positively identified Shakey Kundi.

No, his anonymity was safe. They wouldn't even know who they were looking for. The van itself was also unlikely to be identified. It was plain white and nondescript, with no markings or obvious damage. It was the kind of thing you'd see driving every road in America. The one thing he had wanted to do, switch license plates, had been done at a gas station just outside of Lexington. So, even if the van's license plates had been spotted leaving Queens, they were now different.

All he wanted to do was get to his final destination. If he could just get there—even if he was discovered—he'd be able to detonate and strike a blow against the beast. If authorities looking for him set up a roadblock out here on these mountain roads, and he became trapped, detonating the device would result in little loss of life. Since he was getting so close to his objective, he decided now was the time to affix the large, magnetic signage to the outside of the van. His disguise as a balloon vendor would have to be convincing in order for him to position the device in the most opportune—and most lethal—location.

He rounded the bend and crossed a small babbling stream. There weren't many places to pull off on winding roads like these, but he found a turnoff into a small elementary school. There were no vehicles in the parking lot of the little red brick building that read "Kingdom Come Settlement School." It looked a little like a small factory building with a loading dock but was used as an elementary school nonetheless. With the backdrop of tree-covered hills and no one around, he jumped out of the van and stretched his legs. There was a tiny outbuilding with a faded sign that read, "Pine Mountain Search and Rescue." Well, he was on the right mountain, anyway.

Shakey decorated the backside of the building with urine and then walked back to the van, still shaking the cobwebs free. It was then he noticed something that stopped him in his tracks. The van—the right side of the van. It had a large magnetic sign on it that read "Marvin's Balloons." The van was supposed to be clean and free of markings. The signage had already been applied to that side of the van, and he simply hadn't noticed. This was an unbelievable oversight on his part. The magnetic signs weren't supposed to be placed on the outside of the van until closer to the final objective. *How could I have been so stupid?* he thought. *What if someone spotted that damned sign with the huge bushel of balloons on it?* It could be just the thing that might give him away. His heart pounded. What if he had been seen leaving the house? What if they were out looking for the dumbass Middle Easterner driving the balloon truck right now? He was furious. This was his fault and no one else's.

After careful consideration, he decided it was too late now. He was so close to the final objective. And besides, he had to attach the magnetic signs prior to entering the site anyway; they were his ticket in. Without any hesitation, he popped open the back doors, grabbed the other sign, and stuck it in place. There was no turning back. When he departed, a light cloud of dust sputtered up from underneath the accelerating tires.

The little stream babbled on, quietly basking in the comfort of its ignorance.

90

Listening to the siren from the backseat of the black Ford Excursion took its toll on Jana's head. They'd been barreling down Kentucky Interstate 81 for over an hour, weaving in and out of cars. The headache started low in the back and was accentuated by ever-tightening neck muscles. And now, it crept its way forward. The intensity of the past few days was manifesting itself physically. Her neck and shoulders were in knots, but in the boy's club of the Federal Bureau of Investigation, this was no time to show weakness.

She'd spent so much time with Cade that to separate now seemed so abrupt. For the past several days he had acted as a sounding board for her, but now she felt more on her own, more alone. To ease her pounding head, Jana needed a distraction. Staring off into the Kentucky countryside would have normally been soothing, but barreling down the interstate at ninety to one hundred miles per hour had its downside. She pulled out a snug-fitting pair of earbuds, closed her eyes, and listened to music.

Before long, she drifted into that space between sleeping and waking, where your ears pick up sounds that are then incorporated into your semi-dreams as they unfold around you. In this dream, softly flowing light cascaded across a single framed photograph. It was an image that was held in her memory since she was just a child. It was a picture of her grandfather who had raised her from the age of four. Back then, he had become her life, her everything.

As she held the photograph, the image went into motion. Her grandfather slowly stepped out of the frame and stood beside her. He was radiant—his smile, glorious. He held out his hand and touched it to Jana's face as a tear formed in his eye. It was not a tear of sadness but more an expression of solemn pride only a parent can know. Jana's heartbeat increased as real tears of her own formed. Her grandfather whispered one word. It was the word "soon."

The vehicle hurtled down the highway, rocking back and forth as the music in her earbuds picked up tempo.

Can you take me with you
To the place where lame men walk
Can you take me with you
To the place with gold-lined streets

The driver hit the brakes, jarring the vehicle and startling Jana awake; her seatbelt barked into her chest.

"Whoa! Goddamn, guy. I swear, if we weren't in such a hurry, I'd pull his ass over," said the driver.

"Calm down there, Little Hoss," said Latent. "Don't want to get sidetracked." He was probably the only FBI director in the agency's history that would participate in an active field investigation. This was one of the reasons the agents loved him—he was one of them.

While all the other agents were distracted with the traffic, Jana dabbed her eyes against her shirt. The tears in her dream were real, and the song playing in her earbuds continued.

Up here I feel like I'm alive
I feel like I'm alive for the very first time
Up here, I'll take these dreams
And make them mine
I'm strong enough, strong enough to take these dreams
And make them mine

Can you take me with you
To the place where lame men walk
Can you take me with you
To the place with gold-lined streets

Jana pulled off the earbuds and rubbed her eyes. The powernap was just what she needed. The headache was still there, but she felt much better. By this time, law enforcement agencies all over the tristate area were in full swing. They had set up roadblocks to inspect cars, check trunks, and look for anything out of the ordinary. FBI teams were arriving at destinations all over the state, hoping to be the ones to stop a terrorist in his tracks. The wooded hill country grew larger in the windshield. They were getting close.

91

The white van idled as Shakey checked his watch. *Right on time*, he thought. There were at least twenty cars and pickups in line waiting to enter a parking area where they would catch a bus and go up the hill to the bluegrass festival.

Eighteen cars to go.

Shakey's nerves were starting to fray. The deputy at the top of the hill seemed to be checking cars before they were allowed to proceed, and it scared him.

Thirteen cars to go.

The bomb sat ten feet behind and mocked him through the rearview mirror. If the deputy became suspicious, Shakey wouldn't have enough time to arm and detonate it. As he edged farther up the hill, he closed the distance to the deputy, and his heart raced.

Seven cars to go.

Up ahead, another deputy inspected the undersides of vehicles with a mirror on a long pole, waving it underneath each car, scanning for explosives. Shakey's heart pounded harder, and a small bead of sweat pushed its way onto his forehead.

Four cars to go.

He sat on the very precipice of an event that would make his name known the world over. Brothers in arms would be filled with pride once he unleashed the fury of a nuclear weapon inside the heart of the beast.

Three cars to go.

Never before had any of his brothers been able to bring this type of fury and retribution.

Two cars to go.

Shakey pushed his right hand down between the seat and console. *Where is it? Wait, ah, there.* The hardened plastic handle of the Glock 17 nine millimeter snugged into his hand.

One car to go.

His throat tightened, and his breathing went erratic. The sense of panic was unbearable. *Kill the deputy? Gun the engine, run him down? Race up the hillside toward the festival? I can do it, I know I can do it, I have to do it, otherwise the deputy might get the drop on me, even shoot me, I wouldn't have time to detonate . . . wouldn't have time to detonate, everything I've worked for, everything is riding on this . . .*

"Afternoon, partner," said Deputy Skeeter McAfee. "Glad you could come up and visit with us." His giant grin produced a calming effect. "Hope you don' mind, but we need to check yer ve-hicle right quick."

Shakey's grip tightened on the Glock.

"Oh, no. H-h-h-e-help yourself. Why the need to check?"

"Oh, you know, jes makin' sure there ain' no dynamite nor TNT nor bazookas or nothin'!" Skeeter laughed to himself. "Ya mind openin' the back fer me? Sure would 'preciate it."

"Oh, no, not at all." Shakey loosened his grip on the handgun and jumped out of his seat, pasting on a fake smile.

"So, what cha got back here?" smiled Skeeter. "Looks like balloons and stuff. Hey! You mind blowin' me up one? Oh wait, gosh, I shouldn't ask ya that. It's jes that I think it'd be fun for folks to see a deputy with a balloon tied to his wrist. Might make the kids laugh."

"Of course, oh no, don't worry about it."

Shakey reached into a box, pulled out a red balloon, and hoped the deputy wouldn't notice the shaking of his hands. The top portion of the device's canister was filled with a small amount of compressed helium. It was the perfect cover.

"Oh, pardner, that's jes so nice of ya. Now, I tell you what. Since yer a vender, you jes pull right on around the bend up there. You keep a-goin' till you see that first right. You can't miss it 'cause Old Man Lipton's oak tree? You know, it fell over last spring. Anyway, you'll see it there. You jes turn in there, and that'll lead ya right to the vender parkin' area. Have fun now! We're glad ya came."

Tension vacated Shakey's spine like water poured from a glass. *"We're glad ya came." You won't be glad in a little while, you fat pig. You and sixteen thousand others. I'm going to light you up like the fires of hell.*

92

irector Latent spent most of the car ride on the satellite phone coordinating other teams. Across the country, the terror cell's wave of final objectives abated. All the members of the terror cell were now either captured or dead. People quickly tired of staying in their homes, and many went out. There was a clear level of anger that reverberated through the very fiber of the land. Citizens targeted anyone that looked like they deserved it. Riots erupted in Los Angeles and Detroit. In Dayton, a mosque in the midst of services had its exits blocked and was firebombed. Police attempted to battle their way through the rioting crowds to rescue those trapped inside. The last word Latent received was that the worshipers were still trapped.

There were hate crimes happening in many other areas as well, and all of them were directed at people of Middle Eastern descent. A mosque was on fire in New York City about six blocks from the FBI field office. The streets filled with people fleeing the area, and agents on the seventeenth floor said the thick billowing smoke reminded them of 9/11.

A huge mosque in downtown Atlanta, still under construction, was desecrated. In Philadelphia, a woman wearing a traditional veil was the victim of a hit-and-run. Hate crimes popped up everywhere. Anyone with a dark complexion and black hair feared for their safety, no matter what their background or where they grew up. It wasn't safe to go outside their homes, and sometimes, it wasn't safe to stay inside either.

Local law enforcement personnel were to blame for some of the hate as well. They descended on towns all across America, throwing up roadblocks, conducting random searches, and raiding mosques. Not since the days of the civil rights movement had one group been so targeted; only this time, it wasn't simply for the color of their skin, it was also for their religious beliefs.

Latent turned around in his seat. "All right, folks, listen up. I know we're all distracted by what's going on all around the country. Some of you are even concerned for your family members back home. I know,

I know. The president activated the National Guard in seventeen communities. There will be hell to pay in the end, but they will restore order. As for us, we've got to maintain focus. Let's stay on point. I realize that us showing up at some festival might seem like a needle in a haystack kind of operation, but we've got to be boots on the ground. This won't be the last stop we make. If one of the other teams doesn't stop this asshole, we'll bounce from place to place until we do.

"Now, let's talk about this specific spot. This is a local bluegrass festival. Looks like it's been going on for decades. There are an estimated sixteen thousand people in attendance. They come from small towns all over the surrounding areas. And remember, it's not just the eight of us—there are dozens of local cops there as well. At the moment, they're looking for anything. Stopping all the vehicles, searching trunks, the whole nine yards. When we get there, leave the blue windbreakers in the vehicle. Am I clear? I don't want to give away our position. I want all of us as inconspicuous as possible. We'll break up into four groups of two. I expect everyone to be listening in to your earpiece. Stay in communication. Here's a map of the event site. Looks like a wide-open plateau kind of area, surrounded by all these hills. One thing scares the shit out of me—this place is fed by nothing but two-lane mountain roads. If we had to, it would take several hours to evacuate. There's no quick way out. If the bomber is able to set a timer or set the detonation in motion in any way . . . God help us all."

An agent in the back row said, "Sir, one thing that makes me nervous here."

"Just one thing? What is it?"

"Well, if I'm reading this topo map correctly, and the elevations are correct, this site forms kind of a bowl."

"A bowl. And?" said Latent.

"Well, the device we're after is nominal, less than half a kiloton, right? That means it wouldn't have much of a blast radius. An area as wide as this festival would only be about 30 percent covered by the blast. The bomb chucker would obviously know this, and thus he wouldn't choose this as a target."

"So you're saying we're wasting our time?"

The agent continued as if he hadn't heard the question. "But, you put half a kiloton into a bowl-shaped space, like this one, with mountain walls on all sides . . . the effects would be . . . let's just say, the effects would be magnified."

"Like how magnified?" said Latent.

"A half a kiloton would vaporize every living thing."

"Mike Slayden, WBS News. We're live just outside of Dayton, Ohio, where a pitched gun battle is raging in the streets just a few blocks ahead of us here. Police have restricted media access to the area, but all reports say that a local mosque in the midst of services was firebombed. Worshipers were trapped inside, and the building was surrounded by an angry mob that prevented people from escaping and prevented police and emergency personnel from entering to aid in the rescue. Moments ago, those trapped inside did receive aid when about sixty men, all allegedly of Islamic descent, crashed vehicles into the blockade and created a perimeter of defense with their cars. They evacuated the trapped worshipers out the back of the mosque and exchanged gunfire with the mostly Caucasian rioters. Here's an interview we recorded earlier with resident Charles Denny, a native of Dayton, who witnessed the atrocity. 'We can see the smoke from here . . . it's just unimaginable that here in the United States, in the land of Dr. Martin Luther King, that people could resort to something like this, to hatred like this. There's blood everywhere. Blood in the streets. I saw a mother carrying a baby that was so black it looked to be charred. It makes me sick, just sick to be an American right now. This is not the land my father fought for.' For now, Mike Slayden, WBS News, Dayton."

93

The struts squeaked in pain underneath the van as it ambled up the grass and over the roots of a sprawling oak tree. Shakey drove in between the long line of about two hundred vendor tents that sliced through the middle of the festival. Off in the distance in each direction, Shakey could see four stages with bands playing on each; throngs of people crowded around. He eased to a stop in what appeared to be the dead center of the festival, cut the engine, and looked at his watch. He was ahead of schedule. To his left, there was a food vendor selling typical American hot dogs, hamburgers, and fries. *What a land of pigs*, he thought.

To his right, a vendor stood behind tables that displayed some very unusual art objects. They were completely unidentifiable, and Shakey squinted to read the sign. It read "Cast Aluminum Anthill Statues" that were apparently made by taking molten aluminum and pouring it down the mouth of an anthill. Once cooled, the metal was dug from the ground and cleaned up. After being inverted and placed on a stand, the result might be described as something that looked like a small tree, with branches poking up in several directions. A young woman had one in her hand and was obviously admiring it.

"They're really quite beautiful," said Alyssa McTee. "They're just so . . . different." Alyssa put the object down and picked up another that had a red tint embedded.

"Thank ya kindly, ma'am. I enjoy makin' em. I enjoy seein' people enjoy em."

"What made you first think to make one?" said Alyssa.

"Well, ma'am, I had this here pile of ants. Red 'ens. My baby girl, well, she was little back then. She stepped on 'em and got all stung up. Well, I was so mad, see. And I fig'rd I'd make sure they was gone. Don't know why I thought to pour aluminum into 'em. But then, the next day, I thought 'bout the aluminum and how it would'a hardened. So, I dug her up."

"Well, they're fabulous," she said, grinning as the low afternoon sun cast an angelic glow through her hair. "If there's anything I remember about Kentucky, it's going to be this. Thank you."

"Any time, ma'am."

Shakey turned back to his work, and his anger stewed. *This country—full of so much potential, yet so much waste. While our great ones die, these beasts sleep like the lazy sloths they are. Retribution. What a beautiful thing,* he thought. *Retribution.*

"Pull on around this traffic," said Latent. "Get up there to that officer."

As the SUV pushed its way uphill, Deputy Skeeter cocked his head sideways at it. *What in hell's that guy doing drivin' up around everybody else, on the wrong side of the road no less,* he thought. But he'd have a word or two for them. "Now y'alls hold up, now," he said. "What do you think yer . . ."

Latent jumped out from the passenger side, holding his credentials.

"Oh, yessir," said Skeeter. "What can I do for ya, sir?"

"FBI. Tell me about the number of units you have onsite. What's the sitrep?"

"The sit . . . what? Oh, wellsir, number of units. Let's see. There's Lester an me, an Billy. And a course Sheriff Tatum, and then there's . . ."

"Where is the sheriff now?"

"Yessir, he's jest up at the command post. He give us strict instructions on a'counta that APB y'all put out? We been searchin' every livin' car that come up here. But y'all go right 'roun' this bend here to the command post, and you'll see the road b'cause Old Man Lipton's oak tree? Well, it fell . . . an anyways, ah, it's a mess. But y'all jes turn up there. You can't miss it."

Latent jumped back in the SUV. "All right, let's get up there and find the sheriff. I want to talk to someone that reminds me of a human life form."

Skeeter's words trailed off. "Glad y'all came. Ya come back agin real soon . . ." His signature grin peeled back across his face as he greeted the next car in line.

94

While Latent talked to the sheriff, the other agents piled out of the vehicle and stretched their legs, but they quickly split up into groups of two and headed toward opposite sides of the festival. The bluegrass music was lively, and people were everywhere. There was an even number of agents, but with Latent busy coordinating other teams on the satellite phone, that left Jana as a single. While the others walked to the far corners of the park, Jana headed up the middle. Her headache and growling stomach were not aided by the intoxicating smell of pork roasting nearby.

Walking around out here alone was nothing unusual to her. She'd spent a great deal of her short career doing solo surveillance work and was accustomed to it. She adjusted the earpiece. *These damn things must have been built to fit a man,* she thought. One glance at the absence of signal bars on her replacement cell phone told her there wasn't a cell tower within miles of this mountainous place. The other agents started checking in on the radio. "Sector two, all quiet. Sector six, all quiet. Sector one, all quiet . . ."

She searched the vendors moving from booth to booth, but these seemed hardly the people to be hiding a lethal package of enriched uranium wrapped in a nuclear trigger. It was easy to tell they were all locals. Something about their gait and the way they held their shoulders. They looked relaxed, at ease.

Walking around out here was like searching for a needle in a stack of needles. To Jana, this was about the friendliest place she'd been in a long time. If you had to be on a duty like this, it didn't seem there would be a nicer place to do it. Walking up a little farther, she noticed yet another in a series of white vans. This one had some kind of signage on it and was parked in the center between the rows of tents. At the back of the van, she rapped her hand against the windowless door. The crowd around a music stage off to her right began to cheer loudly. The music poured in from all directions, but none was completely distinguishable at this distance, particularly with music being played on all four stages at once.

Rapping again on the dirty steel, she stood and listened. There were no sounds inside the van. She knocked once more—this time, harder—and checked the door handle. Locked. Jana peered into the driver's window through a thin layer of grime. A curtain hung across the interior behind the driver's seat, and both front doors were locked as well.

"Excuse me, ma'am," said Jana to a nearby vendor. "Is this your van?"

"Oh hey! I didn't see you a standin' there, Miss. You startled me. The van? No, not ours. Kin I intrest ya in some pork rinds? Fresh fried?"

"No, thank you, ma'am." Jana glanced back at the van with its colorful balloon sign on the side and trudged up the hill to the next set of booths. Her neck muscles tightened and her headache intensified. The search continued.

95

Cade and Knuckles spread Rupert's papers across a large table at NSA headquarters and grouped them by age. Of prime interest was the stack dated within the last six months. Rupert's writings had become more fragmented at that time, and it seemed his belief in the project was shifting. The two were mostly quiet and paced back and forth, reading one paper after another. After six hours, Cade finally broke the silence.

"I'm exhausted. I've got to take a break. Hey, Knuckles, let me ask you a question. There's something that's been bothering me. Why do they call you *Knuckles?*"

"Huh? Oh, it's because of my threatening persona. Are you saying my peach fuzz and hundred and twenty-two pounds of manliness doesn't scare you?"

"Well, now that you mention it . . ."

"Hey, Cade," said Knuckles. "Listen to what Johnston says in this one:

> '*I keep interrupting muffled conversations. These assholes are keeping something from me. It's as if the mood has changed. They're scared, really scared. I pressed them this morning about it, and I got nothing but blank stares. I don't know how they talked me into this shit. I keep thinking back to that first meeting. It was the CIA, I mean, I thought we were doing something important for the country. But after all that garbage the government spouted to us in 'Nam, I just can't believe I trusted them. They assured me no one was going to get hurt, that they'd be watching the terrorists. I can't believe my life has come to this.*'"

"Sounds like he's seeing the media reports and knows the bombings are related to his project."

"Yeah," said Knuckles.

"Okay, so listen to this one. It looks like it's dated about three weeks ago:

304 ◦ THE FOURTEENTH PROTOCOL

*'I again questioned that son of a bitch Baer Wayland about the obvious
fear that has permeated all CIA discussions. The pasty little bastard had
the balls to tell me to shut up and just be thankful I don't wake up with
my throat cut. Whatever they are scared about must be big. I can't be a
part of this anymore. I'm going to try something crazy, and I'm getting to
a point that I just don't care if I get caught anymore.'"*

"Wait, who is Baer Wayland again?" said Knuckles.

"That's him," said Cade. "The one we used to call William Macy."

"Right."

Cade flopped into a chair and rubbed his eyes. "So you're done
with your stack too?"

"This is the last one," said Knuckles. "Well, except for all those
older papers he wrote back in Vietnam."

Uncle Bill walked in, his hands in his pockets. "So how's it going?
Do we have anything we can use?"

Knuckles said, "No. It's apparent he was becoming aware there
was a big problem, but it's not as if he says anything that would show
us something we didn't already know."

"Dammit," said Bill. "We're hitting a brick wall out here as well.
We thought we had something a little while ago that would help us
narrow down the final objective of terrorist number thirty-eight, but it
was a dead end."

Cade said, "What did you find?"

"The files you downloaded from Johnston's laptop included a file
of browser search history that showed every website search he
conducted," said Bill. "Virtually all the searches are for events. All
kinds of events—football games, county fairs, art festivals, music
events, Girl Scout camp sites, everything. When I saw events, I
thought we'd find out which event they were targeting. But then we
ran into a problem."

"Which was?" said Knuckles.

"There were over fifteen hundred separate Internet searches for
events. It doesn't narrow down the list much, does it? Unless we can
find some other piece of evidence that clues us in to which one of
these events they are targeting, we're dead in the water."

"Wait, what?" said Cade. "Hold on a second. I didn't export
Johnston's browser cache from his laptop. If there's a browser cache
file, it isn't a list of searches that Johnston conducted."

"You didn't?" said Bill.

"No. That means the file you're looking at is just like any other file sitting in some directory on his computer. I downloaded all the files, but didn't export anything. Those aren't Rupert Johnston's Internet searches."

"Then whose Internet searches are they?"

The three men looked at one another for answers. It was Knuckles that lofted the first idea.

"What if the browser cache file is the search history from another computer?"

"Tell me what you mean by that, son," said Bill.

"Well, in these papers, it's apparent Johnston was at a breaking point. He says in this one that he's going to try something crazy and doesn't care if he gets caught or not. What if he hacked into William Macy's—I mean, Baer Wayland's—computer? Maybe that was *his* browser cache."

"Or," said Cade, thumbing through the oldest stack of Rupert Johnston's papers, "maybe those aren't William Macy's searches either. Maybe the file was just sitting on Macy's computer when Rupert hacked it."

"Goddammit. Twenty years in the NSA . . . I'm getting too old for this shit," said Bill, shaking his head. "So whose Internet searches are they?"

96

Five hundred yards from the mobile command center, Shakey shifted to the back of the van and sat on his knees, his prayer mat on the rusted floor beneath him. In these final minutes, he knelt toward the east, bowed his head, and prayed, *Allah give me strength. This is the moment I've been waiting for. This is what I am prepared for. Your retribution is near.*

Something pounded against the van door. Shakey froze, not wanting to move. The rear door handle clicked and squeaked as it was pulled from the outside. His heart leapt in his chest, and he scanned for the handgun. The rear door did not budge. Just underneath muted tones of music, he heard footsteps walk up the side of the van towards the driver's door. His heart thumped again, and his eyes followed the footsteps. He looked at the curtain straining in the low light to make sure nothing could be seen by prying eyes. *Someone is checking the van. The pigs. I will not be captured. I will not fail.* His hand gripped the Glock now pointed in the direction of the intruder, the beast. The driver's door handle strained and was let down. His chest heaved. *I am so close, so close. Not now. Allah, not now. Don't let the beast discover me now.* He held his breath, and finally, the footsteps trailed off. He let out a long exhale. His watch read 1:58 p.m. Eighteen minutes to go. He crept over to the device and began unscrewing the false top of the canister. He would be ready, ready to meet Allah.

97

Cade put down the stack of Rupert's oldest writings and fanned them out across the table. The yellowed, faded papers were dated starting in 1965 during Johnston's tour of duty in Vietnam. Cade's eye locked on one particular sheet.

"What the hell is this?"

"What cha got?" said Knuckles.

"Look at this piece of paper. It's not old and yellowed like the rest. Hell, it's dated a couple of days ago. Holy shit, that's the same day he died. But it's all gobbledygook. I can't read any of it."

"Let me see that," said Knuckles.

Knuckles took the paper and studied it. Then his eyes lit up like a kid tearing the wrapping paper off a new train set on Christmas morning.

"It's encoded! He's using some kind of manual encoding to prevent prying eyes."

"Can you crack it?" said Cade.

"Does the pope shit in the woods?"

"I'm not sure I should justify that with an answer," said Cade.

"Yes, yes, I can decode it. Christ, it's probably a cipher he got off of a decoder ring from a box of Cheerios."

Knuckles rushed out into the main room, scanned the handwritten paper, then pulled it up on one of the large screens.

"What do you have, son?" said Bill from across the room.

"This was one of Johnston's papers. It's dated a few days ago, but it was buried in the stack of letters he wrote in 1965. Not sure how it got stuffed in there. Must have gotten shuffled somehow."

"Or he put it in there on purpose so no one at the office would find it," said Cade. "He was scary as hell. I doubt anyone would snoop through his personal war letters."

Bill said, "Hidden in plain sight, eh?"

"Exactly," said Cade.

Knuckles worked for a moment and looked up. "Okay, I was wrong; it wasn't a decoder ring in a box of Cheerios, it was a decoder ring in a box of Wheaties, the breakfast of champions. The decoded version is coming on the screen now."

> *If anyone finds this note, maybe you'll understand the actions I've taken. I hacked into their server and downloaded as much as I could onto my hard drive. I just don't give a shit anymore. I've been studying these files, and now I think I know why they're so scared. The server is bloated with files the CIA has stolen from the laptop of someone who works at a nuclear facility. Maybe he's the subject of their investigation, I don't know. They exported all of the Internet searches from his computer, and it looks like a laundry list of events going on all over the country. I'm sick to my stomach. These are the same type of events where Americans have been dying in terror attacks. Since the CIA is onto someone at a nuke facility, I can only assume they're afraid the terrorists will detonate a device at one of these events. They were supposed to catch the terrorists, not finance them. This whole thing has to be exposed. I love my country. I want people to know that. I'm a patriot, and I can't let this continue.*

Uncle Bill started yelling again, "All right, people, listen up. The CIA was investigating a terror cell, right? It looks like that file of Internet searches is probably one they hacked from the computer of one of the terrorists. Did anyone cross-check each one of the events on the Internet search list against all the targets already hit by a terror attack?"

"Yeah, we did," said a woman from across the room. "There was no overlap. This list is completely separate from the events that were hit in earlier attacks."

"That means we might be looking at the list of Internet searches for events that terrorist number thirty-eight will select from," said Cade. "That's the list of possible targets for his final objective."

"But that leaves us at square one," said Knuckles. "We still don't know which of the fifteen hundred events he's going to hit, or when."

"All right, people, new priority," yelled Bill. "We've been concentrating on what was contained in the encoded data that Mr. Williams brought us. That's everything encrypted or hidden. Let's start looking at all the files in plain sight. Team three and six, I want you looking at every file that's sitting on that computer. Look in all the usual folders, My Documents, My Pictures, My Videos, all that crap. Now move!"

98

Agents along the perimeter of the bluegrass festival were again checking in with each other on the secure radio frequency and updating their status.

"Sector eight, all quiet. 100 percent coverage."

"Sector five, all quiet. 95 percent coverage."

Every large truck that had been used to bring in equipment for the various bluegrass bands had been searched. Other trucks that were used to bring in equipment for stages, lighting, and sound were equally empty. All of the stages themselves had been searched, including underneath. One agent even got into a tussle with a roadie when the agent insisted on opening a set of huge amplifiers to see what was inside. The only area that hadn't been fully covered at this point was vendor row, and even that didn't seem like much of a possibility.

There were a lot of vendors, but most of them had pop-up awnings stretched over folding tables. Many of their vehicles were open pickup trucks, hardly good places to hide a nuclear device, even a small one. Not to mention that virtually no one at this event looked even remotely Middle Eastern. The crowd was at least 99 percent Caucasian—pure southern Kentucky.

Jana radioed back to the other agents, "Sector four, all quiet. I'm at 50 percent coverage here."

Her head pounded. She must have covered a hundred vehicles, tables, and tents, and there were still many more to go.

At the top of the hill, Jana turned in a full circle; the view spanned the entire venue. In spite of her headache, she drank in how beautiful this place was. The headache itself felt like a water pot at a low simmer—strong enough to put out steam, but not strong enough to boil over. She rubbed her neck, trying to loosen the tightening ropes.

An old man's voice called out to her. "Little miss? Miss? Ya don' look so well," said the man from a mouth that had once held more teeth. "Kin I git cha somethin' fer that head a your'n?"

His blue-jean overalls were faded, and he reminded her of her grandpa standing on his wide-open farmhouse porch.

"Now, don' be polite and go off'n say no," he said. "I'll jes make ya take them aspirin anyway. I seen that look in my own mirror more'n a time or two in my day. Ain't pleasant, but it'll pass."

He stood behind a table full of the most colorful display of antique glass bottles Jana had ever seen.

"Thank you," said Jana. "Yes, thank you. I'd love some aspirin. Your antique bottles are wonderful, by the way. Just wonderful."

She squinted into the colors kaleidoscoped against the sun's rays, which pierced a lime green bottle, bounced sideways through a pinkish red, and finally into deep, azure blue.

"Yer not from 'roun' here, is ya? Well, don' worry 'bout that none," said the old man. "We don' hold it agin ya. And we won' bite none, neither."

He pulled out a small box labeled "Goody's," removed one of the folded wax paper packets, and walked to her.

"Here, pour this'n powdered aspirin on yer tongue and drink 'er down with some of this here water."

Jana accepted his hospitality and felt her own grandfather's gaze in the soft crinkly eyes. She could almost smell her grandpa's Aqua Velva aftershave.

The man looked across the sea of people and smiled through his remaining crooked teeth.

"It's a sight, ain' it? Festival's been goin' on since I was jes a youngin. My grandpappy used to take me here." Holding out his hands, he inhaled deeply. "Breathe it all in, missy. This is what the Bible means when it say thy kingdom come. This is heaven come to earth, right cheer in front of us. These days though, I don' know; seems they's lots a youngins jes wanderin' 'round like they's lookin' fer sumpin. Reminds me of the d'pression; folks wanderin' to and fro, always lookin' fer sumpin. Ain' no d'pression no more," he said, tilting his straw hat. "Like them youngins in the sixties; they's lookin' fer America or sumpin. Well, if they's still lookin' fer America, you ain' got to go no farther. America's here. She's right here."

A single thought crossed Jana's mind. The terrorists were attacking things uniquely American. *America, it was right here.* She became uneasy, and a cold shiver rode the length of her spine.

99

A man on team three yelled across the room, "There's only one file in the My Videos folder. I'm watching the video now, but I don't know what it is. It's some kind of military special ops raid or something."

Bill ran over to the monitor and peered down. The dark greens in the video vibrated almost to a point of complete distortion, and a digital time stamp in the bottom right corner counted off the seconds.

"Night vision goggles," said Bill. "This is being recorded through night vision goggles. It's definitely a special ops raid; you're right about that. But where the hell is this? It's inside a house or something. I don't get it. What's the significance?"

They watched the video as the military unit breached doors and scaled flights of stairs inside a building.

"Oh shit, they just shot that guy," said Bill. "Jesus, yeah, this isn't some clip from a movie, this is real."

"So why is this the only video in the whole folder?" said Cade. "What's the file name of the video?"

"Ah, the file name is '2011-05-01-BL.wmv.'"

Bill stood up straight, and his mouth dropped open. "That's a date. Five-one, two thousand eleven? May first, 2011?" Bill glanced at a clock high on the wall. The clock read 2:10 p.m. "Oh my God."

100

Bill bolted towards team six who was analyzing images found on the laptop. "Anything?" His eyes screamed desperation, like he might vomit.

"There's a bunch of images, sir. But it's all like, family stuff," said a balding man with glasses and at least three chins. "Pictures of a dad and some kids."

"Yeah," said Bill, "but that's an image of Shakhar Kundi! Flip through these as fast as you can."

Bill wheeled around, tripping on the edge of a desk, then yelled, "Anybody else got anything!"

"Well, sir," said the same man, "here's one that's out of place. I don't know what it is. There are a thousand family photos in here, then all of a sudden there's this."

Uncle Bill spun back around. The photo was taken from inside a business office, high above a metal desk and office chair. Manila folders and files were scattered across the desk.

"The photo's just stuck in the middle of all these pictures of him and his kids."

"Ah, all right," said Bill, "put it on screen six. Look sharp, everyone. See anything? Shit, there's not much to see. Why is this picture in here?"

"What's that on the bottom of the screen?" said Knuckles. "Looks like some kind of brochure or poster or something. Let's zoom in on that."

"I'm sorry, sir," said the man. "It's all obscured by the folder sitting on top of it."

In the image, the small, tan poster sat underneath a manila file folder. Only a small section of the poster was visible. It read:

arty and Hog Roast
ille, Kentucky
aturday, May 1

"No, no, no, no! Gimme the phone!" screamed Bill.

101

At the mobile command center, Latent looked over his shoulder.

"Hey, is that the satphone I hear ringing?" he said to the sheriff. "Hey, Deputy? Can you grab that call for me? Probably another one of the teams checking in. Should be on the front seat. Yeah, just hit the red button." Then Latent continued his conversation with the sheriff.

The deputy answered the phone but yanked it away from his ear, wincing in pain against the volume. He ran to Latent.

"Sir! Call for you." He clutched the phone tightly as if he was holding his mother's antique china and was terrified he'd drop it.

"Tell them I'll be there in just a sec," Latent said to the deputy.

"Sir," implored the deputy. "He, he says it's urgent! Something about a bright boy? He says his name is Uncle Bill."

Latent's eyes rocketed wide, and he grabbed the phone.

"Holy shit. Bill? Bright boy? What do you have?"

"Stevethere'snotimetoexplain!" yelled Bill. "Get out of there! Get everybody out of there. You've got to evacuate! You've got to evacuate RIGHT THE FUCK RIGHT NOW!"

Latent spun around and stared into the vast sea of people sprawled out in front of him.

"Jesus Christ, Bill . . . we . . . we can't! There's no way to get these people out of here quickly on these mountain roads. What? What is it? What do you know?"

"He's there! He's there! We've got files from his old work laptop. There are searches, Steve! Internet searches. My God. It's right in front of me. He searched the term festivals. Then he spent a lot of time on a website that was all about a festival called 'Tammy Lynn's Bluegrass Pickin' Party and Hog Roast,' Pineville, Kentucky. That's you! He's going to detonate!"

Latent's worst fears flooded over him, and his knees went weak.

"God help us . . . Bill, there are sixteen thousand people here. How am I going to get them out? These mountain roads . . . how much time do we have?"

"Steve, listen closely. This terrorist group is all about timing. This is a timed event. It's all about Bin Laden. This is retribution for Bin Laden . . . they're going to detonate on the anniversary of his assassination, at the precise time of day he was killed in Pakistan. It's today! May 1. Don't ask me the details, it's today!"

"But what time today?"

"Adjusted for your local time, the Bin Laden assassination was at 2:16 p.m. Eastern." Bill's voice settled into a low, defeated tone. "You've got four minutes."

102

Shakey looked at his watch. 2:12 p.m. Four minutes to go. He reached inside the mouth of the thick, steel-walled canister, its faded pea-green paint flaking off in spots around the rim. His hands shook as he reached in to remove the smaller canister of helium nestled at the top. As he pulled it out, the pressure hose thudded against the thick steel and caused him to freeze. He laid the helium canister on the prayer rug to prevent any sounds coming from the van's ridged metal floor. Beads of sweat matted against his hair. His breathing was choppy.

Inside and halfway down the length of the canister hovered a perfect sphere four inches across—the uranium core. It was suspended in midair by a series of powerful magnets on all sides. His instructions were simple. To initiate the nuclear reaction, push the core downwards out of the first magnetic field. It would enter a second magnetic field and would be propelled downwards into an industrial-strength magnet at the base and smash into the detonator. From there, the nuclear reaction would ensue, and within seconds, every living thing at the festival would attain an internal temperature of 1500 degrees Fahrenheit. A small-scale Hiroshima.

He looked at his watch. 2:13 p.m. Three minutes to go. Staring at the sphere, Shakey's breathing slowed. There was no point in fretting the inevitable.

103

The deputy stood motionless and watched as the satellite phone dropped from Director Latent's hand. He didn't know what a bright boy alert was, but the look of terror in the FBI man's face was paralyzing, and it infected all around him. The satellite phone seemed to hang in space for just a moment and then dropped towards earth, bouncing hard on the rock-like dirt. The deputy jerked backwards as Latent yelled into his radio, "ALL TEAMS, ALL TEAMS. BRIGHT BOY, I REPEAT, BRIGHT BOY. The bomb is here! We're out of time! Report in! Any sector not 100 percent contained?"

Jana spun in her tracks and looked back in the direction of the mobile command center, accidentally knocking the old man into his table of glass bottles. Several bottles rattled and knocked into one another.

"Good Lordy, missy," said the old man.

Jana yelled, "Sector four! Sector four. I'm only at 50 percent coverage! This is the only unsecured sector."

"All teams, converge on sector four," yelled Latent. "The center of the park, the vendor booths. This is a timed event! We've got two minutes! Two minutes before detonation! Move, people! Run!"

"Start on the north end," yelled Jana into the radio. "The north end!" From all directions, agents dropped anything they were doing and sprinted towards the center of the park. People yelled as agents crashed through the crowd, knocking several down in the process.

The old man grabbed Jana's arm to steady her and noticed the radio earpiece. It was as if he knew something terrible was about to happen.

"I've got to think! I've got to think," she said aloud, looking in his soft eyes. "There's no way we can search all the rest of those booths." Her body shuddered.

"Okay, okay," said the old man. "Now calm down, missy. Jes calm down. Ya kin always think better when yer calm!"

The pain in her head was almost dizzying as she thought about everything she had searched down the hill in the direction she had come.

"Close yer eyes, youngin. You kin concentrate better," he said as he temporarily placed a soft, arthritic hand across his own eyes as an encouragement.

"What was out of place?" She was almost whispering. "Was anything out of place?"

"Stay calm now, stay calm! It'll come to ya."

The old man was shifting back and forth like a five-year-old schoolboy.

She had searched everything up the hill. There must have been over a hundred booths down there. There was nothing, not a thing out of place. Then she thought about the van.

"Ya got sumpin? What is it, missy?" he said.

"Well, there was that van," she said, shaking her head. "That van down the hill. It was locked. I couldn't see inside, but . . ."

"What else? Think! What else 'bout the van?" In his excitement, he bounced up and down. "Think, missy, think."

Jana's eyes landed on the table of bottles whose colors swirled together almost like a bouquet of balloons.

"Balloons," she said. "Balloons. The van was a balloon vendor with a great big painted bouquet of balloons on the side." Then, a thought crossed her mind that made her throat tighten. *Mama loons.* "Oh my God, Mama loons. Loons! Loons! Bal-loons," Jana yelled. "That little boy at the house in Queens . . . he, he kept saying those words. Loons, Mama! Loons! Mamaloons! Maybe he saw a balloon truck drive by his house?"

She snapped her head back to the old man, "Do you see any balloons around here?"

"Heh?"

"Balloons! Do you see anyone holding balloons?"

They both spun around, looking in all directions and scanning for any hint of color.

"I ain' seen no balloons, missy!" bouncing in his boots and laughing. "Not a dang'd one!"

Jana tore off down the hill. Behind her, the old man jumped up and down and knocked into his own table. Bottles rocked into one another and fell, bouncing and breaking as they hit the ground.

"Go git 'em, missy!" he yelled, jumping up and down. "Go git 'em! This is America, gosh dangit!"

Jana bolted down the hill, darting in between people, vehicles, and booths, and yelling into the radio, "Abort! Abort! It's a white van! A white van. A huge painting of balloons on the side. South half of sector six! Converge on the south half of sector six!"

Latent yelled back into the radio, "All units, all units. Move! Sixty seconds! I say again, we've got sixty seconds before detonation! Converge on the south half of sector six!" Latent himself broke into a sprint up the hill. The sheriff's deputy watched in horror, having no idea what was about to happen, but knowing, whatever it was, it was bad.

Latent had another flashback to the football field at Georgetown. He shouldered into two people, never slowing.

Jana was at a dead run, weapon in hand, and screaming at people to get out of the way. Just the sight of her elicited screams as she smashed into one person after another. She leapt over a large cooler, gasping for breath as she reached the van. She slid just past, skidding to a stop at the back doors. Without a thought or an instant's hesitation, she raised the gun and fired three rounds in rapid succession into the door lock, then ripped the door open. People screamed and ran in all directions as she was greeted with a hail of gunfire coming at her from point-blank range. The man was firing with his right hand while his left hand reached deep inside a large metal cylinder. The first few rounds sizzled by her face and shoulder as she fired back, squeezing the trigger in rapid succession and unleashing a spitfire torrent of flame and bullets from her Sig Sauer. Jana felt loud, crashing thumps smash into her torso as everything in her vision went hazy. The next instant, her head slammed into the ground, and everything flashed an electric black. The acrid smell of gunpowder hung thick against her nostrils.

The firefight had lasted less than two seconds. Everything was buzzing in her head, and she could no longer hear the screams as people scrambled in all directions. As quickly as the cacophonous gunfire had ruptured the relative calm of the festival, everything in her hearing went suddenly silent.

Moments passed, and people from all sides began to stand up. Latent charged forward, panting to catch his breath, and saw a small circle of people gathered around the back side of a van. Another group formed about fifty feet away as apparently a bystander had been hit in the crossfire.

As the blackness faded, Jana's eyes focused onto the gloriousness of the blue sky above. And there, silhouetted amongst the clouds, was a picture from her oldest memory as a little girl. She was sitting in her grandpa's lap, rocking back and forth on the porch of his farmhouse. Rocking. Just rocking, ever so slowly . . .

"We interrupt this broadcast to bring you a special report. Reports are coming in now that a large-scale terrorist attack may have just been thwarted by federal authorities. Details of the type of attack are unknown at this time, but AP News is reporting a full-scale evacuation is under way at this hour, for all people in a fifty-square-mile radius of Pineville, Kentucky. Speculation is swirling that this may have been a nuclear threat, requiring the massive evacuation; however, federal authorities will neither confirm nor deny this allegation. There are fifteen known casualties at this time—two are confirmed fatalities. An FBI agent is one of the casualties and is listed in critical condition with injuries that are described as grave. The agent's identity is being withheld. WBS News has learned of the two fatalities—one, the alleged terrorist, the other, a woman identified only as Atlanta resident, Alyssa Josephine McTee, twenty-three, who lived in Atlanta's Little Five Points area. More on this breaking story . . ."

104

The low pulse of a digital monitor beeped with each heartbeat. Jana felt like she was in a dream. Yet, an unbelievable feeling of calm ushered into her core. There was no pain. It felt simply like all the worry in the world had vanished. At first, she didn't want to open her eyes, but after a few minutes, she realized she couldn't open them. She couldn't move either, for that matter. Yet the feeling of calm so permeated her, she saw no need for worry. Instead, she lay listening to the faint sound of music playing somewhere in the distance.

Little visions appeared to her. Beautiful light shimmering off old glass bottles, soft crinkly skin on a smiling face so reminiscent of her grandfather, running through a crowd of people, and lastly, she saw her head slamming into the ground as everything went black. Then, she heard faint voices that seemed to be in the room with her, muffled as though they were speaking into a thick paper bag.

". . . she's got a fighting chance. That's what you need to hold onto, son," said the voice.

"Doctor, come on," said another person. "I've been in love with this girl from the moment I laid eyes on her. We've just been through the most terrifying events of our lives. I owe my life to her. Level with me. Look me in the eye and tell me the truth."

The doctor removed the hospital-green surgeon's cap but couldn't loosen his gaze off his shoes.

"Her chances are not good," said the doctor. "We've done everything we can for her. It's not in my hands any longer. All we can do is wait. Stay with her, son. Stay with her and pray. She may be in a coma, but sometimes patients respond to the presence of loved ones."

The doctor put his hand on Cade's shoulder.

"Pray for her, son. I'm just a doctor. I don't make the big decisions. Pray to the man upstairs. He's deciding if he needs her more here, or up there. Pray to him."

Jana drifted in and out of what she thought of as consciousness. But as some of the haze lifted, she came to understand she was in a hospital. She couldn't move anything. The word *coma* hung in the forefront of her mind. Things came to her in clips and bits—muffled conversations, the occasional nurse taking vital signs, and voices, familiar, yet hard to place.

Director Latent stood in the doorway and could just overhear Cade's conversation with the physician. As the physician left, Latent eased into the room and put his hand on Cade's shoulder.

"How's our patient?" he said to Cade.

Cade looked despondent. "Not good," he said, "not good."

"When's the last time you ate something?"

Cade's gaze drifted out the window. "I knew her, you know."

Latent looked at Jana. "Jana? You knew Jana? I know the two of you were close . . ."

"No, not Jana. I knew her, the other victim, the other victim at the shooting. Alyssa"—Cade let out a long exhale—"her name was Alyssa McTee." Latent stared at him until the name registered in his mind. "We met at a restaurant just outside of Quantico right before Kyle's graduation. It was a fluke thing, I guess."

Latent shook his head in disbelief. "Cade, I know this has been an emotional rollercoaster for you. It's been that way for all of us." Latent drew in a deep breath of his own and held it.

"You look like you've got something to tell me," said Cade.

"I do." The director crossed his arms, then he too looked out the hospital room's window to the tree line in the distance, searching for the right words.

"Mr. Director," said Cade, but then he was cut off.

"Steve, please. Call me Steve."

"Okay," said Cade. "Steve, look, whatever it is, you may as well just say it. I'm not sure things can get much worse." Cade looked over at Jana.

"You'll have to understand, there's been a lot of security concerns. We didn't want anyone to know. It's about . . . it's about Kyle. There's more you should know about Kyle. But now's not the time. There are more important things at the moment," he said, looking down at Jana.

"What about Kyle?" said Cade. "What, you mean like something about the way he died?"

Latent exhaled, lost in thought. After a few moments, he said, "Yeah, something like that."

The director put his hand to his mouth.

"That night. The night Kyle died, there was another team . . ."

"Director?" said an agent in the doorway with a thick voice. "I'm sorry to interrupt. There's someone here to see Agent Baker. This is Mr. Herbert Deere. He says he was with Agent Baker just before the shooting. He'd like to visit with her, if it's all right. I've confirmed his identity and that he made an earlier statement to our team."

Latent looked genuinely glad for the interruption. Cade, however, wanted to hear more.

"Mr. Deere. Yes, sir. Yes, thank you, Agent McDaniel, I'll take it from here. I'm very glad you're here, sir," said Latent.

The old man looked uncomfortable, as if he had dropped his Bible during church services and everyone turned to stare. The man's eyes darted back and forth between Cade and Latent while his lower lip quivered, a straw hat rotating in his hands.

"How's young missy a'doin? She don' look so good," he said, choking back his emotions. "She don' look so good a'tall." He nodded in respect to Cade.

"Yes, sir. Mr. Deere, I'll level with you. In this past week, I've read all statements taken from the scene. I read your statement . . . as well as the details of the background check we ran on you."

Herbert looked at Latent from the corner of his eye.

"Yes, sir, I'm sorry about that," said Latent. "We do that kind of thing. We had to be thorough."

"Yessir. I s'pose you do."

"Your background said you served during the battle of Iwo Jima? I want to thank you for your service to the United States. I mention that because if you've been there, and stood on that ground, you've seen some of the worst things imaginable. I think you deserve to know the truth. Agent Baker is not doing well." He glanced at Cade. "She's not expected to survive, Mr. Deere. It's all we can do to just sit here with her and pray."

Herbert's head nodded up and down, but he didn't say a word; the hat being crushed in his rotating hands spoke volumes.

"Like to sit with her a spell, if'n you don' mind none."

"She'd like that, sir," said Latent. "She'd like that very much. Cade? Would you mind if Mr. Deere came in for a bit?"

Beep.   Beep.   Beep.

Cade wiped his eye on his shirt sleeve and said, "No, not at all. I'll just step out. It's an honor to meet you, sir."

"Thank ye, son."

The two men left, and the only sounds in the room were that of the heart monitor and Herbert's breathing. As the door swung closed, the old man looked at all the machines and tubes attached to Jana. He shuffled forward, afraid to make any noise, then looked back over his shoulder. He took Jana's soft hand in his and stood, rocking back and forth. A teardrop landed on the back of his hand and he whispered, "You jes hang in there, little missy. You jes hang in there. I tol' cha. This is America, and it's a place would'n' be the same without you in it. Jes, jes hang in there, little missy."

Herbert looked up at the heart monitor. Its beeping had slowed and changed in tone. A red light on the device started flashing. Moments later, a nurse burst through door.

"Step back please, sir," said the nurse, rushing to check Jana's vitals. The beeping slowed further, and then, the heart monitor's piercing alarm sounded in one, long, continuous shrieking cry.

The old man shuffled back against the wall.

"Oh Lordy, oh Lordy," was all Herbert could muster from underneath his breath.

The nurse ripped a phone receiver from the wall.

"Code blue, 2117. Crash cart, 2117. Code blue." She was calm, but her tone urgent.

The heart monitor painted a flat green line. Herbert averted his eyes and pulled open the door, holding it for the approaching medical team running down the pristine white hallway. A physician and four nurses bolted in with a medical cart, and the yelling began.

In the hallway, Stephen Latent held Cade by the shoulders.

"Let them work, son. Let them work."

Jana couldn't tell if she was hearing people around her or if she was dreaming again, but the distant sound of music, coming from somewhere, increased; it was familiar and intoxicating. She sat straight up and looked around. A hazy fog clouded her vision; everything glowed around the edges. But as things came into focus, she could see she was back on her grandpa's farm.

The smell of scrambled eggs, just fried in the morning's bacon grease, wafted through the screen door and was strong enough to almost touch. The sun was huge and low on the horizon, yet didn't hurt to stare at. In fact, it was the most comfortable, beautiful light she had ever seen. Thick dew glistened on hundreds of rows of baby corn. A burnt umber hue emanated from the horizon, which seemed to stretch on forever across the farm's rolling flatlands. Her grandfather sat on the porch in his old rocking chair. As Jana traversed the three creaking porch steps, he set aside the tall glass of iced tea and rose. His smile was as big as the morning sun was wide. The two embraced.

"I've been sittin' here a spell, just waitin' to see if you'd come," he said. "I got your music on. Got breakfast inside."

Jana looked in through the screen door, past the sitting room, and into the kitchen beyond. It was exactly as she remembered it.

"Grandpa? Is this heaven?"

His smile was approving and warm.

"I'm so proud of you, sweet pea. So proud."

Jana stared into the house; the music was coming from somewhere inside.

Can you take me with you? said the song's lyrics.

She looked back into his eyes and saw something that looked like an outline around the baby blue. It was like a gateway to the edges of his soul. The outline represented purity; it was clean, it was white, and it was unending. She glanced back at the sun.

"I tried so hard, Grandpa. Tried so hard. I just wanted you to be proud of me, that's all. Proud of my life."

The music continued, and Jana struggled against its pull.

To the place where lame men walk.

"I never wanted you to feel like you had ta live up to somethin'," he said. "But you did. There's never been a grampa more proud, ever."

Can you take me with you?

"I think I understand the words to the song now, Grandpa. It's about heaven, isn't it? They're singing about heaven."

To the place with gold-lined streets.

"Yes, sweet pea. It is."

"Is it my time now, Grandpa?" Jana turned and faced the sun, and this time, could not avert her eyes. "Is it my time? Do I get to choose?"

"Everybody out of the way! Set three hundred," yelled the doctor, shock paddles in hand.

"Three hundred," returned a nurse.

The doctor applied the paddles to Jana's chest.

"CLEAR!"

Jana's body rocketed upward. Everyone held their breath and looked over at the heart monitor.

~~~~~~~~~~~

Note from the author:

What you just read was the end of this story. When I wrote the original manuscript, this is how it ended, with Jana clinging to life. I wanted you, the reader, to decide for yourself if she lived or died.

But, after so many readers asked me what I think would have happened, I decided to write a free novella to answer those questions.

You can download the post-quel novella, free, for a limited time. Just visit NathanAGoodman.com/postquel

Read the sequel, *Protocol 15*:

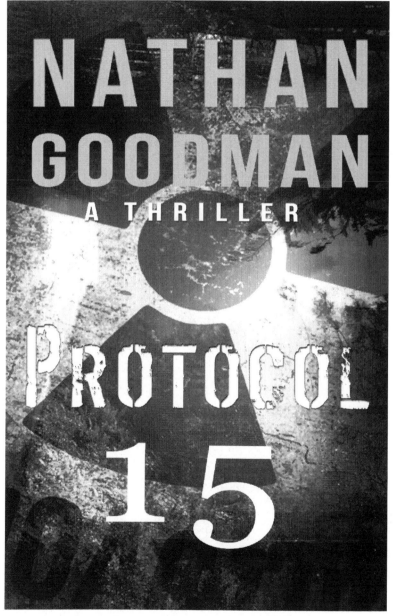

An excerpt from *Protocol 15*

1

I AM BECOME DEATH

Somewhere in Pakistan. June 3.

The coal-black of Waseem Jarrah's hair was distinguishable only by a chiseled patch of white that tore through one side. Jarrah, the most wanted terrorist in the world, put his hands on the trembling nineteen-year-old's shoulders.

"Khalid Kunde, your time is near," he said. "You are a soldier of Allah, and Allah's rewards will be grand. Remember, what you go to do now is but the first step."

A tear welled in the young man's eye, yet did not fall.

"I will not fail you," the apprentice replied.

"You are the younger brother of Shakey Kunde. His name is legend. His efforts to detonate a nuclear device on American soil were valiant, his sacrifice noble. But he failed in his ultimate mission. Nevertheless, he sits at the right hand of Allah, as will you. Do you know the words?"

The young man knew Jarrah wanted him to quote the words of Robert Oppenheimer, the original inventor of the atomic bomb.

Khaild nodded his head in affirmation, stared at the floor, then choked out, "The words are, *I am become death.*"

Jarrah's eyes widened as he basked in the glow of his new apprentice. He replied, *"The destroyer of worlds."*

2

A SLEEPING ISLAND

NATO Listening Post, Kosrae Island, Micronesia. The Solomon Sea, 1379 nautical miles north-northeast of Papau New Guinea. June 19, 11:33 p.m. local time (8:33 a.m. EST)

"You hear the chatter last night about the spy plane, that Air Force RC-135?"

"The Cobra Ball? Yeah. I think they were just flying around monitoring a Russki thing though."

"Which Russian thing?"

"Same old thing. Naval maneuvers. A pretty boring night, as usual."

"The Cobra Ball flying that same figure-eight pattern they normally do?"

"From what we could tell by watching on radar, yeah. But, they were way the hell out there, on the edge of our radar cup. We were only able to . . ." His attention diverted to a computer monitor in front of him. "Wait, did you see that? What the hell?"

A radar alarm blared on speakers mounted overhead and the two men scrambled to place headphones over their ears.

"Holy shit, that's a missile launch!" one said.

The other keyed his headset then spoke into the mic. "NATO COMSAT, NATO COMSAT, this is Listening Post Kosrae one niner two. We've just detected a missile launch. Currently tracking an inbound hostile from North Korean airspace. Can you confirm?"

A crackle from his headset replied. "LP Kosrae one

330 □ THE FOURTEENTH PROTOCOL

niner two, this is COMSAT. Roger that, Kosrae. We see the launch, but we've got no track. You are our eyes."

"Understood, COMSAT. We see the inbound from central North Korean airspace, pushing through six thousand feet. Banking, banking now, turning due west. The heat signature of the missile registers as a Taepodong or Taepodong-2 class ICBM. This is the real thing. Repeat, this is not a drill. Given attitude, altitude, and direction, this could be a North Korean attack on Japan, sir. The hostile is headed right for them."

"Roger that, Kosrae. All stations have just been issued the alert command."

"The bird is increasing in altitude. The computer is recalculating the flight path. Hold on . . . I don't think its target is Japan, sir. At that altitude, the hostile will fly right over."

"What else is directly along that trajectory?" the other man said. "I don't care how far away it is. We've got to know what they're shooting at."

The operator traced his finger across the map on the computer monitor. "Let's see, there's the Midway Islands, but there's nothing there. After that . . . oh shit." The two operators looked at each other. "Hawaii."

The computer recalculated and spit out new coordinates for the projected trajectory of the hostile missile, and its most likely destination:

Latitude: 22-01′10″ N -- Longitude: 160-06′02″ W
Lehua, Kauai, HI

"Oh my God, you're right. The computer confirms. It's Hawaii. Find out what's on the island of Lehua. Not that it'll matter if that ICBM showers the entire island chain with multiple independent warheads. The entire

Hawaiian population will be incinerated." He keyed his headset again. "COMSAT, this is LP Kosrae. We've got confirmation." He read off the coordinates. "It's Hawaii, sir. Lehua, Kauai, Hawaii."

There was no reply from the other side. Only static.

"Sir?"

"Ah, roger that, Kosrae. Estimated time till impact?"

"Based on the calculated distance of 4,485 miles from the original source to target, and the fact that the hostile is now suborbital, traveling at an estimated 13,200 miles per hour, the computer says the estimated time till impact is three and one half minutes. That would make it exactly 3:32 a.m. Hawaii local time."

3

TO NEW BEGINNINGS

Headquarters of the National Security Agency, aka, 'The Box.' Ft. Meade, Maryland. June 19.

In the NSA command center, the months had passed. First one, then another, and Cade wondered where they went. The passage of time knows no enemies. It has no friends. It holds no grudges. It's only solace is that it never changes, except when there is a hole in your life that you cannot fill.

Cade stared across the room at Knuckles. Ever since he had met the kid, he wondered how old he was. For all Knuckle's intelligence experience as an analyst at the National Security Agency, the chin on the kid's face could barely produce peach fuzz. He looked sixteen, maybe younger. Regardless, Cade knew the kid had brainpower that rivaled even "Uncle" Bill Tarleton, the NSA section chief, and the most brilliant code breaker in NSA's history.

Knuckles looked at Cade, who was still staring at him. "You look like you're trying to conjure the next winning numbers in the Pennsylvania state lottery," Knuckles laughed. "I know you're dying to find out how old I am. I'm twelve years old," he said.

"No you're not," Cade said. "You're older than that. Come on, how old are you?"

"Not in this lifetime, pal."

"Oh come on. We work at the NSA. We're supposed to be able to find out anything about anyone. You know I can find out."

"Personnel records are sealed, bright guy," Knuckles said. "Although . . ."

"Although what?"

"We could work a trade."

"What kind of a trade?"

"You teach me how to talk to girls, I'll tell you my real age."

Cade stared back, grinned, and then started to laugh until people turned to see what was going on.

"You want *me* to teach you how to talk to girls? I couldn't talk my way out of a paper bag where girls are concerned. Now, my friend, Kyle, he's who you want. He could convince a girl . . ."

"Well," Knuckles said, "from what Uncle Bill tells me, you and that hot FBI agent seemed pretty tight."

The prior year, during what was known as *the Thoughtstorm case*, Cade had become the FBI's only insider in the sweeping terrorism investigation. At the time, he worked as a hardware systems administrator for Thoughtstorm, Inc. When it turned out Thoughtstorm was involved with terrorists, he found himself in the middle of the biggest terrorism investigation since 9/11. It had been the beautiful female federal agent that had convinced him to be a material witness in the first place, and now he was in love with her.

Cade looked down. "Yeah, I know. She's the most beautiful girl I've ever been around. We worked so closely during the Thoughtstorm case. Things were so intense. I don't know, I guess we just spent so much time together that we kind of became a couple there for a while."

As the case ended, Uncle Bill offered Cade an analyst role. Working at NSA had never occurred to Cade. But, with his old job as a systems administrator at Thoughtstorm gone, the idea of being more involved in espionage work appealed to him.

"But what about now? You're not together?"

"Doesn't seem that way, no. I wonder about it all the time. Whether coming to work here was worth it. Sometimes I feel like I stepped into a really cool new career for myself, but I lost Jana in the process. She spent so much time at Bethesda Medical Center recovering from the shooting. I spent a long time watching over her first in the intensive care unit, then all that time in physical therapy. To tell you the truth, she shouldn't have survived it. But, the good thing is, she's been back at Quantico for a few weeks trying to get in shape to requalify for active duty."

The hardest part in Cade's decision to work at the NSA had been separating from Jana. He may have been in love with her, but he never knew if she felt the same way. And, he always knew she was way out of his league to begin with. Both Jana and Agent Kyle MacKerron were now back at the FBI Academy at Quantico regaining their strength, healing from physical injuries, and requalifying as federal agents. For Cade, who now lived in Maryland near the headquarters of the NSA, having the two of them nearby at Quantico was both heavenly and torturous at the same time. They were close, but he rarely saw them.

"I go over there whenever she lets me," Cade said. "We're both just so busy, you know? I get the feeling she's pulling away from me, almost as if she knows she's only going to be at the academy for a short time, then she'll get assigned to a duty station far away from here."

"Where's she going to be stationed?"

"From what FBI Director Latent tells me, due to her heroism during the Thoughtstorm case, she can choose to be stationed wherever the hell she wants."

4

WEAPONS GRADE POSTURING

Outside the United Nations Headquarters building, New York. June 19.

"Okay, Mike," the cameraman said, "they're cutting to us live in three, two . . ."

"This is Mike Slayden, WBS News, reporting live from UN headquarters in New York. More info coming in on yesterday's statements made by supreme leader of the Democratic People's Republic of North Korea, Jeong Suk-to. As you know, the country of North Korea has become a thorn in the side of the United States, as well as other world nations. Supreme leader Jeong Suk-to's consistent rhetoric and threats have alarmed world leaders. This morning, United Nations Secretary-General Ashanti Birungi made a statement in front of the UN General Assembly. Mr. Birungi stated, and I quote, 'The North Korean government has made past claims as having achieved the manufacture of fissile nuclear material.

Although these claims are as yet unsubstantiated, the United Nations has issued an edict to Supreme Leader Jeong Suk-to urging him to immediately withdraw his quest to obtain a nuclear weapon. North Korea now also claims to be nearing launch capability. If weapons-grade fissile material is combined with a long-range missile, the threat to human life is great. The time is near and the United Nations must act.'

"Tension between North Korea and western allies has grown considerably in past months as the North Korean leader continues in a tirade of posturing.

"To further complicate an already escalating situation, in an unrelated issue, the Russian delegation to the UN is pressing the North Korean government as to the whereabouts of one of their delegates who went missing one month ago on a diplomatic mission to the North Korean capital of Pyongyang. North Korean leaders in Pyongyang are refusing comment, fueling further speculation and distrust between Russia and North Korea. We'll keep you abreast of developments as they unfold. For now, I'm Mike Slayden. Watch your twenty-four-hour news leader, WBS, for news, weather, and traffic on the fives."

5

THE OVAL OFFICE

The White House, Washington, DC. June 19, 9:35 a.m. EST

"Mr. President."

"Goddammit, General, what is it? I'm in the middle of a call with François Hollande!"

"Sir, we're tracking an *inbound*. Taepodong-class ICBM

336 ▫ THE FOURTEENTH PROTOCOL

from North Korean airspace. Launched just minutes ago."

The president stared at the man, then blurted into the phone, "Président Hollande, mes excuses. Une situation plus urgente. A most pressing situation. Urgent matters of state."

He hung up the phone then looked at the General whose face looked like the blood had drained from it.

"Where is it headed?" the president said. "Can we intercept?"

"Hawaii, and no."

"Hawaii? But there's over a million people in Hawaii! We can't . . . we can't shoot down the missile?"

"Population 1.4 million. No sir, we tried. Patriot anti-missile defense systems out at Pearl missed, twice. She slipped through, sir. I'm sorry."

The president buried his face in his hands.

"Time till impact?"

"Any moment."

"You can't mean that!"

"A SATCOM device is being moved in here now, sir. We've got two communication uplinks. One to Navy Hawaii Command and the other to a NATO listening post at Kosrae, Micronesia. The listening post is tracking the missile."

Two young Air Force officers burst into the Oval Office, flanked by the national security advisor and two members of the Joint Chiefs of Staff.

The captain spoke into the SATCOM's mic. "Go ahead, Kosrae. The president is listening. Repeat what you just said."

"Roger that, captain. This is NATO listening post Kosrae, Micronesia. The hostile missile is in full descent. Time till impact on the island of Lehua, Kauai, Hawaii, sixty-five seconds."

"What's the population of that particular island?" the president said.

"Zero, sir," the major replied. "Lehua is an uninhabited outlying island of the Hawaiian chain, about twenty miles off Kauai. But I don't think that matters. If the North Korean government has finally combined long range missile launch capabilities with a nuclear tip, we could be looking at a total loss of the Hawaiian Islands."

"Forty seconds."

The volume of the president's voice exploded. "But we've had security briefings for months on the topic of whether or not the North Koreans had the technology to combine a long-range rocket with a nuclear tip, dammit! CIA was so sure that they hadn't achieved it yet," the president said as he slammed his fist into the desk. "Why did I listen to them? Shit, we knew they had launch capability, but not the damn nuclear tip. My God, if I'd only known. If I'd only known. I could have done something . . . but I had no idea that that lunatic leader would actually take a first strike at us. A madman. A madman."

"Thirty seconds to impact."

The president paced the room. "How come we're not hearing from Hawaii Command right now?" he screamed. "Where are they?"

"It's three thirty in the morning there, sir," said the major.

"General, bring our military to DEFCON 2," the president said.

"Fifteen seconds to impact."

"Ah, sir?" cracked a young voice across the SATCOM radio device. "Ah, this is Seaman Jimmy Timms, Hawaii Command. Third watch, post number four, sir."

"Seaman Timms, this is Major Walter R. Robbins, United States Air Force. Son, just stay on the line with us."

"Yes, sir," the young seaman mumbled.

"Ten seconds to impact. Nine, eight, seven . . ."

"Ah, sir, what impact?" Seaman Timms said with all the timidity of a mouse.

"Three, two, one," the operator at LP Kosrae said. "Hostile missile is down. Hostile is down."

The president's hands dug into his hairline and he leapt towards the SATCOM device. "Seaman Timms, are you still with us? Son? Are you there? Dear God, where is he?"

"Yes, sir. I'm here, sir. I just, I don't understand what's happening. What was that countdown? I don't know who I'm on the line with, sir."

The men in the Oval Office looked at one another. The general whispered, "I don't know. Maybe it didn't detonate?"

"Don't you worry about it right now." the Major said. "You just talk to us, son. Tell us where you are stationed and what your duties are," He released the mic and said, "General, this seaman would be stationed on Kauai, correct? Kauai is just twenty miles due east of the missile impact zone. If a nuclear blast just occurred, he'd be able to see it. Hell, he should be dead right now."

"That's correct, Major."

Seaman Timms droned on in the background about his duty station, what his duties were, where he was raised, his mother's favorite recipe for chocolate chip cookies, which he was currently enjoying. The major interrupted him. "Seaman Timms, can you pinpoint which direction is west of you right now?"

"West? Well sure, sir. The sun sets just out past the flag pole right out the window over there . . ."

"Son, stand up and look to the west. Tell us what you see."

"Yes, sir. Ah, sir, I don't see anything really. Just darkness. It's the middle of the night here. I mean, I can see the flagpole, of course, but after that, the hillside slopes off and drops down to the beach. But off in the distance, if that's what you mean, I can't see anything. No lights or anything like that, sir."

"All right, Timms, just keep looking out in that direction and report anything unusual. Someone will stay on the line with you. Thank you, son."

"Listening post, Kosrae," the Major said into the SATCOM. "Can you confirm a detonation?"

"Negative, sir. We see no detonation signature."

The president was the first to speak. "What the hell happened? The missile didn't detonate? Was it a dud?"

The general answered. "That's what we'll want to discuss with the joint chiefs. But if you ask me, it was no dud. My bet is that the psychotic leader of North Korea is playing with us. He wants us to know he can get us whenever he wants. He's crazy enough to do it, and he's this close to putting a nuclear tip on one."

"A madman. An absolute madman," the president said as he straightened his hair. He cast a gaze on National Security Advisor James Foreman.

Foreman registered the president's piercing gaze and a cold shiver rode his spine.

"General," continued the president, "cancel that order to take us to DEFCON 2. Let's find out if the public knows about this missile launch. If not, keep it quiet, very quiet. I don't want a panic on our hands."

The president stared out the twelve-foot window in the Oval Office. "Something is going to have to be done about North Korea."

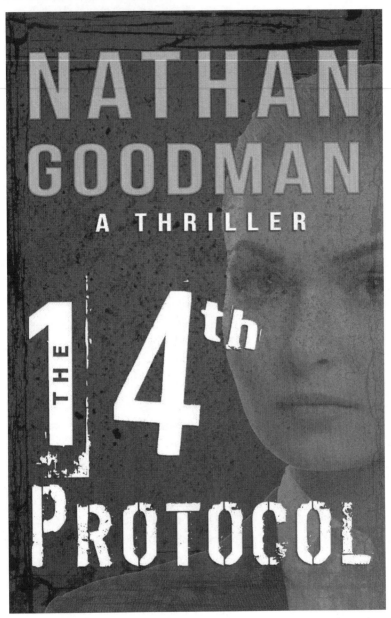

Nathan A. Goodman is a husband and father of two daughters and lives in the Atlanta, Georgia, area. The novel *The Fourteenth Protocol* was written with one very specific goal—the author wanted to show his daughters a strong female character. He wanted them to see a woman in difficult circumstances with the strength to prevail. And he wanted them to know that if they have the guts, they can succeed even in places that are perceived to be "a man's world."

Receive email updates from the author:
NathanAGoodman.com/email

Heartfelt thanks to these supporters for their contributions to this project. This list is not inclusive of all supporters, but instead represents those whose support met the threshold for being included in the finished work. Your generosity will always be remembered.

John Assad, Steve Gordon, Shawn Collins, Hope Hawkins, Leigh and Greg Kershner, Gay and Ken Buxton, Barbara and Bill Coats, Frances and Marc Overcash, Jennifer and Dan Gastley, and Jana Pierce, whose first name inspired that of the heroine.